Torste

The Brazen City

The 13th Paladin

Volume III

Translated into English by Tim Casey

English Proof-reader: Neil McCourt

I dedicate this book to you, my readers.

If it weren't for you, I'd just be just some fellow randomly throwing words together.

And remember

a story finds nothing more enjoyable than being experienced for the first time...

www.tweitze.de

www.facebook.com/t.weitze

Instagram: torsten_weitze

© *Torsten Weitze, Krefeld, 2017*
Picture: Petra Rudolf /
www.dracoliche.de
Editor/Proofreader: Janina Klinck /
www.lectoreena.jimdo.com

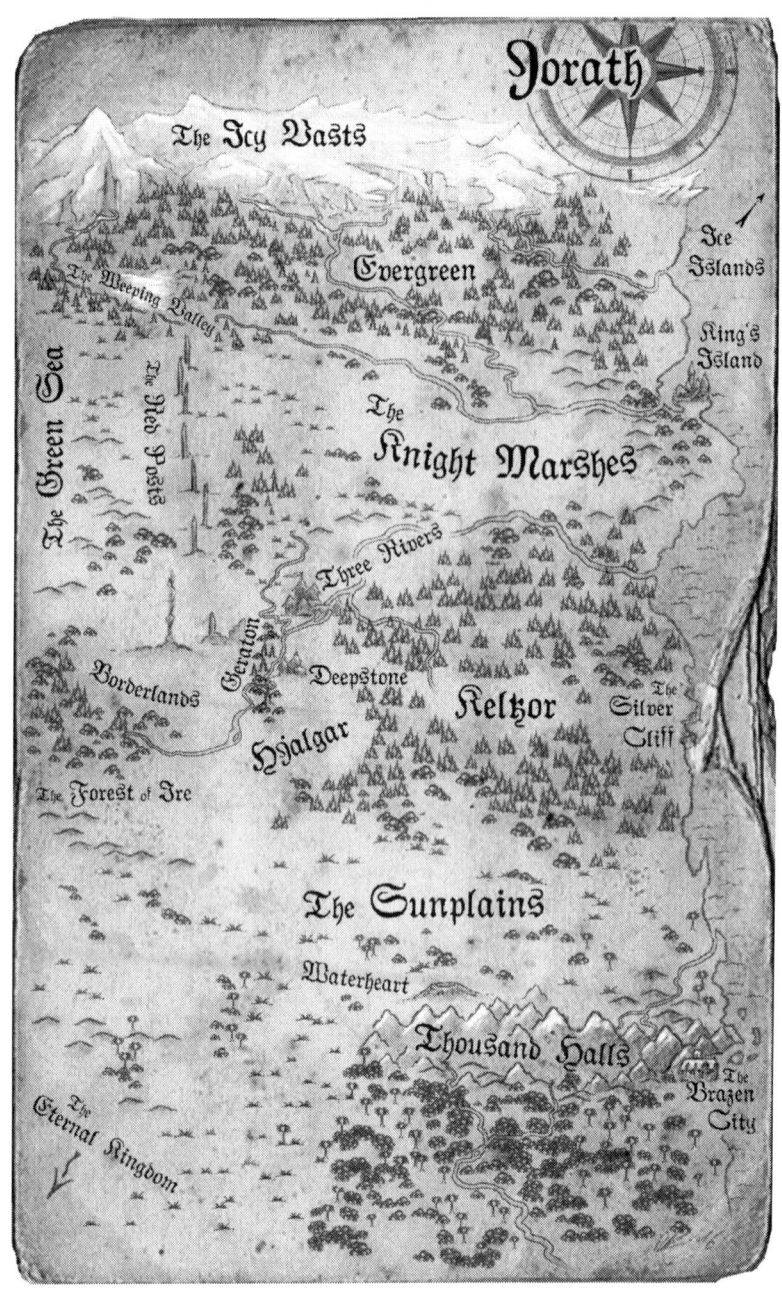

Chapter 1

Like a butterfly flitting past, Ahren felt something tickling his consciousness. He and his disparate companions had spent the days following his Naming frantically fleeing the Borderlands, and during this time Jelninolan and Uldini had been forced into casting one disguise spell after another.

They had just entered the first group of trees that, according to Falk, belonged to Hjalgar. A light snowfall prevented them from seeing more than a dozen paces in front of them, and Ahren wasn't sure what it was he had felt. Suddenly, Culhen shot out from among the trees like a ghost, his white fur making him almost invisible in the snow.

'Ahren? Ahren!' he heard in his head and the apprentice dropped down on one knee with a smile, wrapping the wolf in his arms, while bravely enduring the wolf's slobbering tongue. Selsena too approached them from the trees and emitted waves of welcome. The two animals had raced on ahead of the others during their flight as a security measure so that the two Ancients could conserve their strength. Then they had awaited their companions in the security of the forest.

Culhen kept on babbling his name, the only thing that their spiritual connection would allow yet, and Ahren stroked the animal's fur until the wolf finally calmed down.

Happy that that they were all reunited safely, the troop travelled onwards, and Ahrens heart leaped with joy when Falk announced: 'Only a few more days and we'll be in Deepstone.'

Ahren's master was right in his prediction. Six days later they crossed the Eastern Forest and the warm feeling of home increased in Ahren's breast with every familiar pine tree and fondly remembered stream they passed.

He found himself nattering on to Jelninolan, telling her stories of his training, which had mainly taken place in this forest. The elf priestess responded to his talk with an indulgent smile. A heavy covering of snow lay over the countryside, and so Deepstone appeared tiny and sleepy as they at last walked along its solitary street one clear winter's day. They were nearing the village square, and the simple wooden structures, standing in a row within the protection of the forest edge – no house further than an arrow's flight from the trees – seemed to Ahren to be both strange and familiar. He recognised each of the houses of course, but they all seemed smaller and less impressive than in his memory.

He was musing over this change in his perceptions when Trogadon poked him in the side with his elbow.

'Why did you people make your village so long? Seems a bit impractical. Getting from A to B must take forever,' he said in surprise. It was true that the warrior was anything but your typical dwarf, but he still possessed the pragmatic instincts that were typical of the little folk.

'Our houses are too draughty. The East Wind brings the Blue Death to many, so we build close to the trees, and they give us the necessary protection,' said Ahren curtly. His mother too had died in this way, shortly after his birth, and the apprentice didn't like talking about the illness.

Trogadon rubbed his beard thoughtfully. 'Hmm...I understand,' he murmured as he looked at the surrounding houses with a critical eye.

Ahren was just about to ask the dwarf what he was thinking when a loud scream caused him to spin around. They had managed to remain unnoticed up to this point in the cold winter morning, but now the baker had spotted them through his shutters, and he was shouting the village down.

They managed to make it to the village square with its mighty oak, its brick forge (which had been built since Ahren's departure), and the little chapel of the THREE, where Ahren's journey had begun. But now the villagers of Deepstone were hurriedly flocking together and they were soon surrounded by a crowd that was both fearful and exuberant. Falk had deliberately left Selsena back in the Eastern Forest as her appearance might have been too much for the villagers. Even so, the sight of an elf and a dwarf was a sensation in the sleepy little village. The familiar faces of Falk and Ahren, however, ensured a hearty welcome.

The mayor, Gordo Pramsbildt, was just stepping out of his house with his mayoral chain hanging crooked and his clothes in disarray when Uldini floated upwards into the air to the amazement of the onlookers, and thundered in a resonant voice: 'I am Uldini Getobo, chief of the Ancients and Beloved of the gods. With whom do I speak regarding accommodation?'

The crowd immediately parted in front of the unhappy mayor, who wanted nothing more than to retreat within the safety of his own four walls.

Uldini floated over to the trembling man and began speaking to him in lofty tones, but Ahren heard very little before he was pulled around and found himself in a violent embrace which caused him to gasp for breath. It was Holken, one of his friends from his youth, now dressed in the colours of a fully fledged bailiff, who was squeezing him tightly and smiling broadly. 'Wow, Ahren, it's great to see you again! We were really worried about you, ever since you disappeared the night of the Fog Cats attack,' he called out heartily.

Ahren was about to answer when he felt a hand come down on his shoulder and he was spun exuberantly around. A heartbeat later and the apprentice was in the considerably weaker but just as friendly embrace of Likis, his loyal best friend from his childhood days.

'Ahren!' screamed the slender merchant euphorically into his ear. 'Where have you been hiding? Is that your sword?'

'Did you bring the dwarf with you?'

'Are you a Forest Guardian now?'

'Did you see any dragons?'

His friends' questions were raining in on top of him and laughing, Ahren raised his hands protectively. 'Slow down,' he gasped, tears of affection and joy rolling down his cheeks.

'Why don't we look for a cosy warm place and I'll tell you everything.'

Hungry

The word penetrated violently into Ahrens dreams and destroyed the wonderful image of a comforting clearing in the wood, which his subconscious had just created.

Hungry, the word sounded again in Ahren's head.

He opened his eyes with a groan and stared accusingly into Culhen's loyal eyes. A slobbery, stinking welcoming lick of the wolf's tongue and Ahren was wide awake.

Hungry, resonated through Ahren again as Culhen gave vent to his seemingly endless desire for food.

The apprentice rolled his eyes in annoyance and got up quickly so as to avoid another lick from the wolf. He questioned, and not for the first time, the benefit of the miracle that connected his mind to Culhen's. The wolf was now his companion animal, chosen by HER, WHO FEELS, created to help Ahren in his dangerous war against HIM, WHO FORCES. But all he had heard from the animal up until this point had been insistent demands for more food, more cuddles, and then still more food. If the dark god wasn't ready to be cuddled to death or wasn't in a food bowl waiting to be gulped down, then Culhen wouldn't be much use.

The wolf gave a short howl before sitting back on his hind legs and staring at Ahren with an offended look.

Unfair. The thought sounded in the fresh-faced Paladin's mind.

The apprentice sighed bitterly while he rubbed his head in frustration. Culhen could read his mind just as much as the young man could read the wolf's. Which meant that he was never alone, and every one of his thoughts could be read by his four-legged friend without any filter whatsoever.

He called to mind a memory that he had of Culhen, how he had escaped from the Weeping Valley with the Silent Lute in his mouth. The memory of this moment of glory placated the young wolf every time and usually gave Ahren a moment of respite while the conceited animal sat there in the warm glow of his famed exploits.

The light in the hut darkened as Falk's broad silhouette appeared in the doorway.

'Well, are you getting used to each other?' rumbled his voice through the small room. A deep warmth and considerable mirth resonated in the old man's question.

Ahren threw his hands in the air and with a look of frustration pointed at Culhen, who was still sitting there dreamily, captivated by his past heroic deed. 'It just won't get any better. He doesn't say anything more than individual words and basic feelings – and they're almost always about food,' the young man exclaimed.

Falk's amusement was plain to see. 'I've told you plenty of times. It takes time for the connection to grow. Practise with him. Use full sentences when you're talking to him. And above all, have patience. Up until now he's only been a very clever wolf, but his mind has undergone a greater change than yours. Help him come to terms with this and you will get used to your connection too. Then you'll never want to do without his presence in your spirit.' A wistful tone had crept into the Forest Guardian's last few words.

Ahren gave his master a compassionate look. The old man had had a falling out with his animal companion, the Titejunanwa, Selsena, which had lasted for decades. And during that time, they had lived apart from one another. The thought of not seeing his conceited and greedy wolf for even a week gave Ahren a lump in his throat, and he quickly cuddled the animal, who pushed in beside him, panting happily. Their affection for each other fused into a harmonious feeling of togetherness, and Ahren smiled happily.

'There you go!' grunted Falk contentedly. 'Come into the village as soon as you're ready. Uldini has news for us.'

Ahren pricked up his ears and was about to enquire further, but his master had already turned on his heels and left the hut. Ahren dressed excitedly, putting on the elf ribbon armour that Jelninolan had given him over half a year earlier. For one thing, Ahren wanted to continue practising how to put on the complicated network of leather strips and ribbons more quickly and without assistance. And for another, he found the admiring looks of the village youth very encouraging when he sauntered in his armour through his home village of Deepstone. Ahren was burning to know what had happened in Deepstone over the previous moons, but he still took the necessary time to concentrate fully on his task. He knew what could happen if he got tangled up in the ribbon armour and he suddenly had a vision of Jelninolan the time that she was lying on the floor of her room, helplessly entangled in her own armour, and he had to laugh out loud.

Culhen gave an amused yelp and Ahren tousled his fur. *You understood that then, did you?* he thought, communicating silently with the wolf.

Culhen tilted his head and Ahren felt a confused sensation. 'It'll all work out,' he said aloud, and tousled his friend's head again.

He finished putting on his armour, then hung his quiver and Wind Blade on his back, not forgetting his bow. The thought crossed his mind that he was overdoing it a bit, but he assuaged his conscience with the excuse that he was planning on training later anyway, and he would have his weapons close to hand.

Culhen gave him an admiring look, and as he walked out through the door Ahren asked himself if the wolf's vanity was rubbing off on him now through their thought connection. Maybe that was why he had decked himself out so impressively. Winter was coming to an end; the cold air filled his lungs, and he smiled again when he heard and smelled the familiar sounds and scents of the Eastern Forest. He slowly turned around on his own axis and enjoyed the warm familiar feelings that the trees and Falk's hut released in him. The mighty firs all around seemed to provide a protective roof over the little wooden hut, and the bright rays of winter sun made the snow on its roof sparkle hypnotically.

He had taken his first steps as an apprentice to a Forest Guardian here, and it was from here he had left the previous year on a dangerous journey to be appointed a Paladin of the gods. There had been times over the last few moons when he had been certain he would never see the Forest Guardian's hut again. He had barely escaped death on more than one occasion and his quest for the three *Einhans* had led him farther and farther away from Deepstone. Finally though, he had found the advocates for his Naming, and they had completed the ritual whereby he had been named Paladin and been granted the gifts of the THREE.

Two of them, at any rate, because he still hadn't received the armour and weaponry of HIM, WHO IS. The first gift had certainly put him at his ease: HE, WHO MOULDS had protected Ahren's spirit and body from any outside influence. Gone was the danger that the Adversary or anyone else could force his way into his head and tinker about with his thoughts and emotions.

Well, apart from Culhen, he thought wearily while his thoughts were being abused by an insistent hunger, which was clearly coming from a wolf source.

You'll get something soon, he assured the animal, and Culhen licked his chops in anticipation.

The second gift he had received was the magnificent wolf as his companion animal, a gift from HER, WHO FEELS – although Ahren thought a little bit of cheating had been involved there. After all, it was he himself who had saved the Blood Wolf single-handedly from the control of the dark god when the wolf was a whelp. And now he was getting it as a gift from the goddess?

Culhen whimpered at the thought and Ahren quickly stroked the animal's head. If he were honest with himself, he wouldn't swap the wolf for any companion animal in the world, not even for a dragon or a griffin.

Reassured, Culhen scurried off into the undergrowth, and Ahren sensed through their spiritual connection that he was chasing a rabbit who had foolishly ventured too near the forest path. While Culhen was catching his light breakfast, which would be followed no doubt by a little well-deserved nap, Ahren continued on his way toward his home village. A few things had happened since their arrival in Deepstone.

Uldini had taken full advantage of his status of course, and within half a day the mayor, who'd been caught on the hop, had offered the Arch Wizard, along with Trogadon and Jelninolan, accommodation in his own house, while he suddenly found himself retiring to the little hut for visitors to the village – his own home suddenly bursting with celebrities.

The tavern bustled every day now with curious villagers listening in as Trogadon endlessly and unashamedly told of his adventures. He spoke of his days as a mercenary, and he wasn't afraid to exaggerate as he imbibed vast amounts of beer, laughing and singing dwarf drinking songs. His fellow travellers were eternally grateful to the warrior for drawing all the villagers' attention to himself. This meant that they hardly had to answer any questions and could recover their energy in peace. The dwarf, on the other hand, was so full of joie-de-vivre that he thoroughly enjoyed his unofficial role, and his consequent success with the ladies of Deepstone. More than one jealous admirer of the now distracted ladies had wanted to give the dwarf warrior a thrashing, only to end up with a bloody nose, which was then stanched by the winter snow. The dwarf's standing rose further among the villagers when he shared his knowledge of dwarf architecture. He taught them how to make up a new mortar mixture which enabled them to insulate the walls to such an extent that at last the threat of the Blue Death was consigned to history.

The excitement over the new arrivals gradually died down during the following weeks, and although the tavern was still full every night and the dwarf's arms never empty, the sheen surrounding the travellers had mostly faded away.

Ahren had really enjoyed the winter. The weeks had flown by and he had spent his time either sitting with his old friends or keeping up with his training.

The wizards may have had to have their rest, but Falk had quickly made it clear to his protégé that the same did not apply to him. 'You didn't perform any magic, so you don't get a break,' was the only thing he said on the topic before shooing Ahren off hither and yon through the snowy Eastern Forest. The old man had created an obstacle course and painted targets on tree trunks all around the forest. Then he had used an hourglass to check the time that Ahren needed to run the course and at the same time hit all the targets with his arrows. These training sessions were interspersed with swordplay practice where Khara constantly gave him a sound hiding, much to the wonder of the village boys.

Now that spring was almost upon them, everything fell into a certain routine. Uldini and Jelninolan had almost completely recovered, Trogadon was still living it up, and Ahren spent his time either with his friends or training. The only annoying thing was that Holken and Likis both insisted that he bring Khara to their meetups, and they were constantly trying to outdo each other in impressing the girl. Much to Ahren's displeasure, Khara seemed to enjoy their attention and in one afternoon she smiled more often at his friends than she had in the previous half a year.

Ahren blinked in surprise when he reached the edge of Deepstone. His thoughts had preoccupied him all the way to the village, and now he saw the liveliness of the little hamlet as it slowly awoke from its winter slumber. A lead-grey sky hung over the Eastern Forest, warning of a heavy snowfall, but it hadn't struck yet and everyone in the village was hopeful that the cloud would move on without incident. And so, inventories were checked, the first deals were made for jobs to be done early on in the year, and here and there busy hammering could be heard. Friendly faces greeted him wherever he walked, and the apprentice noticed that some shyly averted their eyes when he gave them a friendly hello. He still hadn't got used to his new-found status as Paladin, and it was clear that some of the villagers were finding it even harder to come to terms with his new position. Ahren had received over a dozen apologies from embarrassed-looking fellows who had made his life hell when he was younger. The young Paladin found the first few apologies refreshing, but with the later ones he simply interrupted the repentant youths, assured them that further speaking was unnecessary and forgave them.

There was, however, one person who didn't apologise, the one who most needed to. Sven, the miller's son, didn't exchange a single word with him, but Ahren felt the resentful young man's hate-filled eyes bore through him on more than one occasion.

The apprentice reached the main square and spotted Trogadon, sitting contentedly on a bench in front of the tavern, a beer tankard in one hand and Hilda in his other arm. The maiden had indicated her interest in the warrior in no uncertain terms and was now spending almost every free moment in the cheerful dwarf's company. The woman was asleep and was snuggled against the dwarf's barrel-shaped chest. Trogadon gave Ahren a cheerful wink.

Ahren didn't want to wake Hilda and so he gave a silent greeting in return and carried on towards the mayor's house, where he expected to find Uldini and the others. The municipal leader of Deepstone was standing awkwardly in front of his own home, clearly uncertain if he should knock or not. When the chubby man with his impressive moustache and thinning red hair spotted Ahren, he breathed a sigh of relief and quickly strode towards the young man.

'Good morning, Master Paladin, I hope you've slept well,' he said with a little bow. 'If you could perhaps do me a little favour?' Ever since the man had learned of Ahren's being named a Paladin, he treated Ahren with tremendous respect and formality, and the young man repeatedly found himself checking that this politeness was aimed at him and not at somebody who happened to be standing behind him.

'Good morning, mayor. What can I do for you?' he asked with similar formality if a little shyly.

'If you could ask the esteemed company, how long they intend to continue living here? Spring is approaching and I would need to be getting back to my businesses at some point...' The man's voice petered away, and Ahren had to suppress a grin. Uldini had already dislodged this man for the whole of the winter, and it must have taken all poor Pramsbildt's courage to present his request to Ahren.

'I will ask him, but I can assure you that it won't be long now until we journey on.' Ahren hoped he hadn't promised too much, but he couldn't imagine they would be spending much more time in Deepstone. There were still eleven Paladins yet to be found, and they had only a few years before the dark god would rise again. Uldini had apparently received some important news, which strengthened the young man's suspicion that their peaceful break in his home village was coming to an end. Ahren felt a sharp pang of regret at the thought. The mayor gave him a thankful, almost enthusiastic nod before parting with another low bow.

Ahren suppressed his sorrow at the impending farewell and opened the door of the two-storied building. By Deepstone standards the house was opulently furnished. The living room was covered in carpet that was hardly faded, there were some well preserved wall hangings, items of simply decorated furniture and an enormous solid, brick fireplace, with a fire radiating a comforting warmth. The middle of the spacious room was dominated by an expansive table with eight chairs, on some of which his companions were sitting. They looked at him expectantly.

'Well fancy that. Our high-born Paladin has come to honour the plebs with his presence at last.' It was good to see that the Arch Wizard was back to his old self, and Ahren scrutinized him closely. The voice of the ostensibly ten-year-old boy dripped with sarcasm as he sat there at the head of the table in his black robe. Uldini had discovered the secret of immortality in his young years, and now he was trapped in this boyish body and sometimes tried to compensate for this with a caustic tone. Ahren knew that the Ancient could behave differently, for example when he was in the company of courtiers, but here and now he was giving his jovial manner free rein. 'If you've nothing against it, we wouldn't mind setting about saving the world from an insane god – that is, as long as you have nothing better to be doing.'

'That's enough - he understands,' interrupted Jelninolan in a soft but determined voice. The elf priestess was wearing her green costume made from Elven material under a heavy fur cloak, a present from Jorek, the tanner. The elf, to everyone's surprise, had taken the quiet little man to her heart and had spent more nights at his house than in her own bed. Ahren had felt pangs of jealousy in the beginning as he hadn't fully overcome his feelings of infatuation towards the elf, but eventually he had acknowledged to himself that he preferred to see the priestess as a mother figure rather than anything else.

Falk grinned at his apprentice and pushed a chair towards him with his foot. The broad-shouldered, grey-haired figure was wearing his normal leather gear, which showed that he saw himself as Forest Guardian this day rather than as a Paladin. Depending on the situation, he presented himself either as Baron Dorian Falkenstein, defender of the gods, or as Falk, the Forest Guardian. Ahren wished that his master would finally find a way of unifying his two ways of life, but he himself had found out how difficult that could be. For the first thirteen years of his life, here in this town, Ahren had simply been the pitiably shy son of the village drunk. Then the cantankerous man in front of him had taken him on as an apprentice, and Ahren's life had been transformed. His long and dangerous journey, and his Naming as a Paladin had left their mark on him too. When he looked at his reflection in the iced-up pond behind the hut, Ahren sometimes didn't recognise himself. What could it be like then for a man who had spent centuries playing one role only to play a completely different one for decades after that?

'Are you going to go on gawping at me in wonder or are you going to sit down today?' asked Falk humorously. The young Paladin blushed in embarrassment and took his seat quickly.

Khara giggled at the apprentice's misfortune and threw him an amused look from under her long black eyelashes. The girl with the dark, almond-shaped eyes and small nose would often let her hair fall in front of her face in the last while and then look out at the world from behind a black veil. Ahren was sure she did that just to seem exotic, but Holken and Likis had really fallen for this annoying habit of hers. He gave Khara an angry look, then turned around to Uldini in a deliberately relaxed manner.

'Falk said there was news?' he said as casually as possible.

Jelninolan chuckled behind her hand at his attempt to hide his rising curiosity, and Uldini came straight to the point. 'I spent all of yesterday communicating with the other Ancients to get as thorough an overview as I could regarding what's going on in Jorath at the moment.'

'Are you still not a bit weak for that?' interrupted Falk with concern in his voice.

Uldini gave a dismissive wave of his hand and continued. 'We need information and we need it quickly. We won't be able to plan our next moves unless we know what's going on out there.'

'Aren't we travelling to the Brazen City?' asked Ahren in surprise. During the night of his Naming, Khara had been visited by a strange old woman, who had revealed to her that there was a Paladin in danger, who was under siege and that a furious Emperor wanted his head.

Uldini rolled his eyes. 'And I thought I'd already made it clear that we don't direct our plans according to strange old grannies who are able to move easily through pitch-black terrain full of Dark Ones. She's hardly the most reliable source now, is she?' The Arch Wizard's last words were accompanied by a tone he normally reserved for particularly stupid people, and Ahren had to bite his tongue to stop himself from responding with a smart answer.

'And? What did the Ancients have to report?' asked Jelninolan, cutting in and impatiently rapping her fingers on the table.

Uldini leaned back, closed his eyes and fell into a pontificating speech pattern.

'Eathinian is arming for war. Your folk are taking the danger very seriously with fighting bows and hardened arrows being manufactured as fast as your sorcerers can manage. The Animal Whisperers are scouring Evergreen for willing predators and are taking the most promising under their wings in order to train them and fit them with armour. The Titejunanwas are patrolling the edges of the forest, and apart from the trade paths you can't take ten paces in Evergreen without being checked.' He opened his eyes and looked at Falk. 'The Knight Marshes are in an uproar, but King Blueground has managed to gather together almost all the barons around him. The border towers facing the elves are empty again, but large knights' festivals are being held all over the place. Elgin advised him to organise them so that the knights and vassals would be battle-ready, without heightening tensions through the threat of war. It gives the peasants something to gawk at, keeps them happy and also prepares them for any eventuality. It's true that it's costing the crown a heap of gold in prize money that has to be handed out, but Senius was clever enough to realise that the state coffers are being well invested. You'll be delighted to hear that Erik Greycloth has proven himself to be a very competent steward, and he's slowly but surely knocking your estates into shape.'

Falk nodded gratefully, and Ahren was delighted for his master. The Falkenstein barony had been in corrupt and incompetent hands for a long time, and when they had visited King's Island, Falk had ensured that his property would be managed from then on by a simple captain. Apparently, this had been the right decision. It was also incredibly important for the future of Jorath that the Knight Marshes had been pulled back from the point of civil war to normality. They were going to desperately need the help of the kingdom's knights in the forthcoming battles with the Dark Ones. Ahren placed an affectionate hand on the old man's shoulder, and Falk smiled, relieved at the turn of events.

'What I have to say now though, is less rosy. The Green Sea clans are incommunicado. All attempts to make contact with them have failed. There's something going on, and I'd like to investigate it, but the clans are peculiar. If we were to burst in on some religious ritual, then we could forget about any cooperation with them for the next ten years, so we'll hold off for now. Thousand Halls and the Silver Cliff are still trading away energetically, but I'd never expect anything else from the dwarves. The little folk will make no preparations for war until we talk to the King of the Halls ourselves and present the situation to him. On the other hand, they've been almost continuously battle-ready for a thousand years, so I really don't see any need for rash action.'

'As we're on the subject of dwarves, where is Trogadon?' interrupted Falk. Uldini rolled his eyes in annoyance at having been interrupted again.

'He's made himself comfortable with Hilda in front of the tavern,' said Ahren drily.

'Isn't he asking for trouble by flirting with every unattached lady in the village?' asked Falk and making a suggestive gesture over his stomach.

Uldini shook his head. 'Dwarves can't procreate with humans. That's why they behave so...freely.'

'I'll get him,' said Khara quietly and stood up in a single flowing movement. As he watched her move away Ahren asked himself for the umpteenth time how she managed it. Every movement of the ex-slave seemed to happen seamlessly and without effort. Whenever she moved into action, she did so without hesitating or wasting energy, and always at a perfectly measured pace.

Khara left the room, and the Arch Wizard took a deep breath before continuing his monologue. 'This is where it gets really interesting. The wretched war between the Sunplains and the Eternal Empire has escalated now that both armies have dared to come out of their entrenched positions, which they'd been cowering in for years. It seems that Justinian has had to suffer some embarrassing defeats in the southwest, and domestic political pressure is growing on him. Many senators are already sharpening their knives and hoping that our beloved Sun Emperor will fall out of favour among the common folk. If that happens, then every one of them will imagine themselves to be only a knife stroke away from the Emperor's throne because Justinian has no children. Quin-Wa on the other hand is still ruling with an iron fist and sees herself as the leader of all of Middle-Jorath.'

An awkward silence ensued, and Ahren took the opportunity to ask a question. 'Could we not just end the war somehow? I mean, now that the Dark Days are coming back, the different peoples should really stick together, shouldn't they?'

Uldini gave a derogatory snort, and it was Falk who answered. 'In theory yes, but the conflict between the two human empires has been going on for over forty years and had been planned by Quin-Wa over a very long period. She is one of us, a Paladin. Nobody knows what her goals are and getting to her palace unscathed is nigh impossible. It's true that she's both an enchantress and a Paladin, but she lets no other magicians or Paladins into her empire.'

Uldini fixed his eyes on Ahren. 'The best we can do is to persuade Justinian to ensure that it's static warfare, and to hunker down until we're personally standing in front of Quin-Wa and we can persuade her to abandon her plans. But that could be difficult because I've no idea of how we can smuggle ourselves through an enormous empire where everyone hates or fears us, or wants to put us in the stocks. But you're right, the two greatest armies in the world have been laying into each other for decades – and every time somebody dies, HE, WHO FORCES is laughing up his sleeve.'

'So, what's your plan?' asked Jelninolan impatiently.

The little figure had just sat up bolt-upright and was about to answer when Trogadon and Khara entered the room. The dwarf nodded silently to the others and winked conspiratorially at Ahren. The young man couldn't help smiling, and while Khara and Trogadon were sitting down, Uldini cleared his throat to get the attention of the group.

'The Forest of Ire elves report that the Borderlands have been barely passable since our flight. It's crawling with Dark Ones and the Ire Elves are stretched to the limit. And there are also stories of nomad raids in the Southern Icefields. But that's by the by. The most important thing for us is that Khara's night visitor was right. For some reason the 17th Legion is laying siege to the Brazen City, and there's a bounty on the head of the captain of the Blue Cohorts – dead or alive. I couldn't find out what's going on in the middle of the city, but we need to get there before it falls.'

'How long do we have?' asked Falk curtly.

Uldini thoughtfully rocked his head from side to side. Then he spoke. 'If neither side behaves particularly stupidly, then maybe until next winter. But only if nobody comes up with the idea of turning over the Blue Cohorts to win the favour of the Emperor. For the moment the mercenaries are being treated as heroes for standing up against Justinian, but there's nothing like an empty stomach to make most people reconsider their priorities.'

'Who exactly are the Blue Cohorts?' asked Ahren curiously. He had picked up a few snatches of information over the previous weeks and knew that they were a legendary group of mercenaries held in high esteem by all the rulers.

Jelninolan looked at him and her face seemed lost in reverie, as if she were half dreaming of a time long passed. 'Their leader is Bergen Olgitram, the fifth Paladin. He was always a ruffian and had little time for authority of any kind. After the Adversary was chained under the Pall Pillar he vanished without a trace, and a century later the Blue Cohorts were first heard of. Two dozen warriors – never more, never fewer – blessed with incredible tenacity, who take on the toughest of assignments and almost always emerge victorious from a conflict.'

Trogadon's eyes lit up with joy when he heard the elf's description. 'They sound just up my street. There's nothing I'd like more than to meet this Bergen Olgitram and his troop. But why is the Sun Emperor after the captain when he and his men have such a good reputation?'

'Because both Bergen and Justinian are stubborn blockheads,' snarled Uldini furiously. Little flashes sparked from the figure of the Arch Wizard as he spoke on, waving his arms around in an agitated manner.

'The Brazen City is controlled by three families who steer the fate of its citizens. The city is right beside Thousand Halls which makes it by the far the greatest trading location for dwarf steel, and its blacksmiths are second to none. Over half of all weapons supplied to the legions of the Sunplains are forged or traded there. The population is a mixture of Northmen, dwarves and the people from the Plains, and they all place great value on their independence. The best that every Sun Emperor could achieve up to now has been sole trading rights. All of the Brazen City weapons are sold in the Sunplains, and the Emperor pays through the nose to acquire them.' Uldini had gradually calmed down during his monologue, but then his anger flared up again. 'Justinian, in a moment of absolute madness, decided to capture the city in an effort to push down the prices for the weapons. His plan was to employ the Blue Cohorts, who were at that time contracted as a garrison for ten summers there. Justinian was not permitted to shelter any legion soldiers in the city, and so he paid Bergen's mercenaries to keep an eye out and make sure that the agreement between the Triumvirate and the Plains was being adhered to. But then he changed the order from one of watching to one of attack. He wanted to capture the city in a surprise move. Twenty-four elite mercenaries in the heart of an unsuspecting city – capitulation would have been inevitable, but when the soldiers of Justinian's 17th Legion were about to storm the city, they realised that the Blue Cohorts were not going to open the gates to them and had also warned the Triumvirate. Since time immemorial Bergen has lived according to a very strict code of honour, and so he had decided not to participate in the treachery towards the Brazen City.' Uldini gave a deep sigh and covered his eyes. 'Justinian can't retreat now without losing face. He has to capture the city and have all members of the Blue Cohorts executed for insubordination. If the arms shipments from the Brazen City fail to materialise for more than two summers, then the Sunplains will in turn lose the war against the Eternal Empire. Justinian will have to negotiate sooner or later and as a consequence, tighten the cordon around the city – in a city where no food is cultivated it's only a matter of time before its citizens will be up in arms, and heads will roll. Because we need Bergen, we'll have to get him out of there before he falls victim to the starving citizens or the vengeful Emperor.'

Ahren looked at Uldini in shock. 'The Sun Emperor wants to kill a Paladin because he didn't help him perform an act of treachery on an allied city? Now of all times? Nobody can be that stupid!' Before he knew it, the apprentice had slammed his fist down on the table in an explosion of anger and frustration.

Nobody reprimanded him, and when the young man looked around, he realised that the others shared his feelings.

'Justinian doesn't know that the Thirteenth Paladin is back,' explained Falk in a grim voice. 'It makes no difference to him whether one or two Paladins are missing. Over the centuries, some have even come to believe the misconception that HE, WHO FORCES won't come back as long as there is no Thirteenth Paladin. Which is why there have been several misguided attacks on us. Another reason why many of us have preferred anonymity and seclusion in the last few centuries.'

Ahren had to digest that information first. Of course, it was difficult to comprehend that the magic of the Pall Pillar was tied to the return of the Thirteenth Paladin. But the idea that you hunted down the other Paladins in an effort to always keep the number under thirteen was incomprehensible to him, and a shiver ran down his spine.

Uldini spoke again. 'Luckily, this misconception isn't widespread. If we talk to Justinian, hopefully he'll see that Bergen will be needed in the coming war. My Emperor is stubborn but he's not stupid.' The Arch

Wizard shook his head. 'I'm absent from the court for one summer and everything immediately goes wrong.'

Ahren vaguely remembered that Uldini was actually the Sun Emperor's Court Wizard. The Ancient, however, had dropped everything the previous spring once Ahren's prospective entitlement to the title of Paladin had been revealed, and had hurried to the completely unaware young man and saved him from an attack by Dark Ones. So now, the lord and master of the Sunplains was without magical advice and without the assistance of one of the Ancients, who could tell him what had happened in the intervening time.

'Did you not send him any news?' asked Ahren, surprised. He couldn't imagine that an immortal wizard could have been so careless.

Uldini glared at him but suppressed a rejoinder. 'Quin-Wa is a talented manipulator. She's been plying the Sunplains with false information, bogus messengers and fabricated omens. Any news of consequence that reaches the Sun Emperor must be confirmed from several sources or examined by me before it can be considered genuine. And as I'm not there...' Uldini let his sentence trail away, and Ahren understood the full consequences of the Arch Wizard's hasty departure.

'So, what's the plan?' he asked numbly. He hoped he wasn't in for any more bad news. With all the complications he'd just been informed of, his Naming was sounding more and more like a walk in the park.

Uldini shrugged his shoulders with feigned serenity. 'We're going to travel to the Sun Emperor, we'll present you as the Thirteenth Paladin and talk him out of his idiotic plan to execute Bergen. Then we'll find a way of saving the relationships with the Brazen City in such a manner that Justinian doesn't lose face. As soon as Justinian is able to procure new weapons, we can prevent Quin-Wa from being victorious and ensure that the Sunplains remain stable.'

Trogadon whistled through his teeth approvingly. 'Well, we certainly have a mountain of work ahead of us.'

Falk shook his head morosely. 'That was just the version where everything runs smoothly. This whole mess could get considerably more complicated for us.'

The old Forest Guardian's warning hung like a cloud of foreboding in the room and nobody felt like adding anything as they stared into the open fire and considered what trouble the spring might have in store.

They sat there for most of the morning and discussed the imponderables and risks of their undertaking and how they could be counteracted, but soon the little group realised they were going around in circles. Many things simply couldn't be planned for and in the end, they were certain of only one thing – that they would travel south into the Sunplains.

All the talking had worn Ahren out, and he stood up wearily. He longed for the forest and a round on the northern course - something that would take his mind off things and occupy the whole of the afternoon. 'Will we be setting off in the next few days, then?' he asked his companions while he mentally ticked off all the things he needed to do before they left Deepstone. He didn't want to upset his friends a second time with a hasty departure.

Much to his surprise Falk shook his head. 'Not before the Spring Ceremony in six weeks.'

Stunned, Ahren stopped in his tracks. Was he hearing things? 'I thought the situation was critical and we had to act as quickly as possible?'

Jelninolan responded. 'Uldini and I are still far from having regained our strength.' And she pointed to the Arch Wizard and herself. Ahren could still see signs of exhaustion on their faces. Deep lines creased their cheeks, and their eyes had the pallid look of tiredness, common to those who push themselves beyond their limits for an extended period. He had clearly underestimated the high price the Ancients had had to pay for the Naming ritual and their subsequent flight.

'Just because we're a bit livelier again around here, doesn't mean that we're ready to perform powerful magic,' she continued. 'When we do leave, we need to be prepared to react to any eventuality we encounter.'

Uldini pointed his index finger dramatically at Ahren. 'It won't do you any harm if we stay here longer. HE, WHO FORCES feasted a lot on your blessing before Tlik put a stop to him. During the Spring Ceremony the connection with the sleep of the THREE is extremely strong. Jelninolan and I will be able to regain our own strength in that one day, and your Blessing can similarly be re-nourished.'

Ahren still wasn't convinced. Much as he wanted to stay on a little longer, the frantic race against time before his Naming had had too much of an effect on him. 'We can take part in the ceremony somewhere along the way. There are bound to be temples of the THREE in the Sunplains,' he insisted.

Falk chuckled at his apprentice's stubbornness before he answered. 'It was in Deepstone that you were recognised as a future Paladin. Therefore, the gods' Stone contains a mighty power, here in this temple. If we were to participate in a Spring Ceremony somewhere else, then its effect on our strength would be far weaker.'

Ahren's face clearly betrayed his discontent, so Jelninolan gave him an encouraging look while spreading out her arms in a calming gesture. 'Please trust us in this matter. The rest will do Uldini and me good, and you will learn that sometimes you need to tarry if you want to reach your destination sooner.'

The apprentice was about to protest again when Falk's bushy eyebrows lowered, and the young man bit his tongue. It was being made clear to him that he would only be arguing for the sake of it if he continued, and so he nodded reluctantly.

'If it's of any comfort,' Uldini interjected, 'This is the last such ceremony you will have to participate in. Then your Blessing of the gods will be as fresh and as strong as that of any other Paladin. Plus, this time we won't have to worry about a Glower Bear.'

The others were familiar with the Arch Wizard's black humour, but they still exchanged nervous glances as they remembered the enormous monster that had almost overpowered them during Ahren's Naming Ritual. It had only been thanks to the goblin Tlik's self-sacrifice that the spiritual connection between the dark god and his beast-servant had briefly been broken, and they had escaped with their lives. Ahren still didn't quite understand why the spiteful creature had given up his own life, but he was determined to honour the goblin's death by putting an end to the Adversary's terror once and for all.

'Are we finished now?' asked Trogadon impatiently. 'I'm needed outside, don't you know.' He smiled suggestively, and Uldini scowled, giving a dismissive wave of the hand.

'Yes, we don't want to hold you up while your beer goes stale or your girlfriend starts to miss you.' The Arch Wizard's tone was dripping with disapproval, but the dwarf ignored the implicit criticism, jumped energetically to his feet, punched one hand into the other enthusiastically and quickly walked towards the door.

'Ah, the heavy weight of responsibility,' he called out laughing, and was filled with the thrill of anticipation. Then he swept out through the front door, which closed with a crash behind him.

'You were right, old man,' said Uldini grudgingly. 'You can't but like him all the same, even if he does behave crudely at times.'

Falk looked affectionately towards the doorway, where the broad figure of the dwarf had just been seen. 'What you think of as crude is open honesty and pure unbridled love of life. Am I glad he's decided to continue accompanying us.'

A chill ran down Ahren's spine. He'd never considered the possibility of any of his travelling companions leaving their little group. Uldini, Jelninolan and Trogadon were all Einhans, worthy representatives of their tribes, essential to the Naming ritual when he had been confirmed a Paladin. However, their official duties had, in fact, ended there. If they wanted, they could go on their merry ways unchecked. Only Falk and he were Paladins, and as such the only ones in the group whose power could be dangerous to the dark god. He looked wildly at the others, but Jelninolan pre-empted him.

'Calm down. None of us will leave you or the other Paladins in the lurch. We're going to stay by your side. Until the end,' she said softly.

'Whether you want us to or not,' added Uldini drily.

Ahren nodded. He was touched, but Falk shooed him towards the doorway with an impatient hand movement. 'Get out of here before everybody starts getting sentimental. Why don't you show Khara the new circuit I've laid out in the north-east? It's designed for nimbleness and speed, and all the targets are hung in such a way that they can also be reached by sword.'

The apprentice scowled in surprise, but Khara was already up on her feet. She gave a thankful bow towards Falk and then threw the apprentice an impatient look. It took him a moment to recover himself. This was the first time that Falk had altered a training workout in such a manner that Khara too could profit from it. Of course, he had involved the swordsgirl to improve Ahren's ability with the blade, but he had customised it only for her. Ahren suppressed a wave of jealousy and nodded curtly. Then he stormed out without saying a word, with an eager Khara close on his heels.

Jelninolan looked after the pair with an amused smile and then placed a sympathetic hand on Falk's forearm. 'I don't think your apprentice understands that you wanted to do him a favour.'

Falk shrugged his shoulders impassively. 'If he doesn't appreciate an afternoon alone with a smashing girl in the forest, then he's an idiot.'

Uldini laughed grumpily, and the three continued with their conversation regarding the preparations for their upcoming journey.

Chapter 2

The snow front had moved away much to everyone's relief and had been replaced by a mild late winter sky, casting a soft, almost dreamy light that the surrounding snow reflected in a warm tone. Ahren and Khara were about to leave the village so that they could try out the new training course when they bumped into Likis, who had just come out of the merchant's shop and was heading home.

'Where are you two off to?' he asked curiously. He looked critically at their martial outfits and continued: 'Is there trouble?'

Ahren shook his head. 'No, we just want to go training. Falk constructed a new obstacle course that we want to try out.'

'Wow, that sounds exciting. Can I come too? There's not much happening today, and a little exercise wouldn't do me any harm.' He was looking mainly at Khara when he spoke, and she gave him an encouraging smile.

'Sure, if you trust yourself,' said Ahren in a warning voice. 'Falk's training runs are getting testier, just like himself.'

'I'll tell him you said that,' teased Likis, and the friends laughed and headed towards the forest.

Ahren trudged sulkily through the Eastern Forest snow, searching for the starting point of Falk's newest obstacle course. He kept ahead of his two chattering companions, who generally ignored him anyway. The old Forest Guardian usually tied a scrap of yellow material around the top of the highest tree near the starting point. After marching for an hour in a north-westerly direction he climbed up a tree to look around at the snow-covered canopy surrounding him. He spotted the yellow cloth atop a tall blue spruce to his right, clambered down again and gave a satisfied sigh. It wouldn't be long now before he'd spot the marking from ground level too and he could finally begin his training. He tried ignoring the merry chatter behind him, but when Likis gave a loud laugh, Ahren turned around to face his best friend.

The feisty little figure with his blue eyes and black hair was convulsed with laughter by some comment that Khara had just made. Ahren hadn't been listening but he was convinced that nothing she had said could have justified Likis's reaction. Khara smiled at the flattery, and Ahren suppressed an urge to roll his eyes in disgust.

He had intended to have a talk with the merchant's son about their imminent journey, but he had been unable to get a word in edgeways during their walk. Khara now spoke the Northern tongue fluently, albeit with an unusual singsong in her voice, which gave her words a melodious tone without disturbing her clarity. Quite the contrary in fact, as both Ahren and Likis found it undeniably attractive.

Khara was savouring her newly acquired language skills, and Ahren was relegated to the position of listener as she and Likis had a lively discussion over, of all things, Ahren's most embarrassing blunder from his childhood days.

The Forest Guardian stared in silent disapproval at his friend, but Likis was completely oblivious to it. The young merchant's over-the-top fit of laughter had finally died down and he threw Khara a mischievous look.

'Did I ever tell you about the time when Ahren lost his fishing rod, his catch, his bait and his basket all in the one day? And all that, when he was fast asleep?' he whispered conspiratorially.

Khara shook her head and hung onto every one of the lanky youth's words as he told the story of one of his friend's greatest misfortunes, embellishing it wildly.

Ahren considered briefly whether to correct his friend, as he hadn't in fact lost his fishing rod that time but decided to leave things be. Trying to get the better of Likis with words was as hard as trying to catch the wind with a net. Besides, he found it impossible to be angry with the feisty young man. What really surprised him more was how charming Khara could be. This was not the heartless girl that he had got to know, who would regularly slap him in the face, wear him out with physical exercises and criticise his every move. He could see clearly that this exotic visitor to Deepstone had left a lasting impression on Likis. When Ahren remembered how he had made a complete idiot of himself at the Autumn Festival only a few years previously when in the company of Sven's sister, he decided to give his friend some leeway. He would have plenty of opportunity in the years to come to tease him regarding his present behaviour towards Khara. Ahren turned away with a smile and walked onwards, leaving the dallying lovebirds in his wake.

At last he found what he was looking for and pointed up a tall tree at a tiny yellow dot on top. 'We've arrived. Are you sure you want to do this as well? Maybe you'd prefer to stay here and keep gossiping.' As soon as he'd spoken, he cursed silently to himself for making the sarcastic comment, but it hadn't seemed to bother the others.

'Of course, we'll run with you,' said Likis with determination. 'I'll leave out the targets because I can't handle a weapon, but I'm sure I'll be able for the obstacles.'

Ahren remembered that his friend had always been as nimble as a fox, and gave him a challenging look. Then he looked over at Khara as he walked to the trunk of the tree. Falk had carved a small sign, just deep enough to be recognisable, but shallow enough so as not to damage the tree.

'Here is the start. We have to keep following the signs and always in a straight line. Running around the obstacles is not permitted. Khara, wherever you see red dots on the trees, they're the targets we have to hit.' He pointed to a tree roughly fifty paces ahead which had a red marking on one of its lowest branches.

The girl's eyes followed the direction of Ahren's hand, and the merriment disappeared from her face. It was replaced by the look of serene concentration she always exhibited whenever she drew Wind Blade. The swordsgirl had hung the scabbard around her neck and the weapon slid out with a scraping sound. Then she nodded gravely in Ahren's direction.

He took his bow from his shoulder and indicated again into the forest.

'Can you see the next marking?' he asked in a concentrated voice. Khara's almost ceremonial behaviour spurred his ambition on, and he was eager to test himself against her.

'I think so,' responded Likis nervously. The sudden change in mood and the drawn weapons clearly made him anxious, but he pointed at the broad oak with its red dot, the tree weighed down by the heavy snow.

'You have good eyes,' said Ahren encouragingly and winked at Likis. 'Just try to keep pace and don't end up between Khara's sword and her target.'

The merchant's son laughed loudly but broke off nervously when he saw the intent eyes of the girl and realised that Ahren's warning had been serious. Likis nodded uncertainly, but the other two were already running. He immediately gave chase with a curse.

Although it would have been more sensible for Ahren to ration his breathing, he couldn't help whooping with joy. Falk had surpassed himself with his choice of course. The route led them over fallen trees and under snow-covered branches which threatened to punish them at the slightest contact with their freezing loads. The old Forest Guardian's signs led them through thorny bushes and even over a frozen pond, testing their steeplechase skills to the utmost. That in itself was challenging enough, but with every manoeuvre Ahren had the bow in his hand and an arrow at the ready, preparing for the next target that had to be hit. In this respect too, his master had shown an unerring instinct. There were targets that truly tested Khara to the limit when she had to pull herself upwards or leap off branches to hit them. Ahren was able to hit those ones as quickly as he spotted them, and so he would pull ahead of the agile girl. But then there were the targets that were hidden at ground level or concealed behind an obstacle. Here Ahren would be forced to spend more time, slowing down, and swinging his bow around at the last moment while Khara swung her blade over her head and downward in a flowing movement, leaving a tiny score on the target as she raced past. And so, the two were forced into constantly varying their speed, and Falk had masterfully ensured that they wouldn't hit each other in their enthusiasm, as they were always focussing on different targets.

All in all, it was simply wonderful to be running through the winter forest, spurred on by the swordsgirl who was sometimes a step ahead of him, sometimes a step behind, but always forcing him to stretch himself to the limit.

Ahren heard a loud howling in his head as Culhen awoke from his digestive nap, sensed his master's joie-de-vivre and reciprocated in his own manner. It wasn't long before the wolf was running beside him, open-mouthed and with his tongue lolling. Ahren's heart was ready to burst with joy. The clear forest air in his lungs, his loyal friend beside him and in his head, the sound of the leaves as he ducked between them, all these combined into a magnificent feeling, everything melting together into a perfect experience as man and wolf raced as one through the snow-covered Eastern Forest.

Five marked trees later and they had completed the course, with the feeling of elation being replaced by mild exhaustion. The apprentice collapsed on the ground and embraced his wolf, who wagged his tail, licked his master's face repeatedly and called out in Ahren's mind again and again: *Hunt? Play!*

Khara joined them after only a few paces, leaned her body over, placed her hands on her knees for support and gasped for air. 'Your...endurance...is good,' she panted.

Ahren tried to grin broadly at her but only succeeded in grimacing terribly as he continued to gasp. 'But on the other hand, ...you're faster...than me,' he managed to say before he ran out of breath.

Khara nodded in agreement, but then frowned and looked around. 'Where's Likis?'

They found the unfortunate merchant's son two hours later. He had overlooked a marking and then got hopelessly lost. He was perched sullenly on a stump of a tree and was singing a song about villainous friends in the forest. Doubtless he had composed it while he was waiting.

Ahren felt a wave of guilt for a brief moment. They had abandoned Likis and left him to get hopelessly lost while they had battled it out between themselves. It didn't take him long to realise though, that his guileful friend was really milking the situation. He had linked arms with Khara after explaining to her how exhausted he was, following his solitary search in the forest.

Ahren scowled and led the little group back to Deepstone, while Likis held on tightly to Khara, who was laughing.

Culhen could feel his master's annoyance and looked at Likis while licking his chops. *Bite?* he asked Ahren in his head.

Khara gave another peal of laughter, and Ahren considered for a brief moment how he should answer the wolf.

They were freezing by the time they arrived at Falk's hut. The wind had freshened, and Ahren predicted that there would be a heavy snowfall later that evening.

'Come in with me for a moment. You'll catch your death of cold if you go the rest of the way without a break,' said the apprentice.

Khara and Likis stepped inside gratefully, and Ahren quickly followed, closing the door behind him to prevent the warmth from the hearth escaping. He hadn't extinguished the embers when he had left the hut that morning but had made sure it would stay alight as Falk had taught him, so that the heat was retained throughout the day. It wasn't particularly warm in the Forest Guardian's dwelling, but in comparison to the temperatures in the forest it was quite cosy.

It wasn't long before Ahren had the fire blazing again and gestured to the others that they should gather around it. Likis had sweated profusely earlier and then rapidly cooled down on their return journey. Ahren did not want to be responsible for his friend becoming ill.

Of course, Likis would get Khara to nurse him back to health! The thought flashed through Ahren's mind. He forced himself to think of something else and turned his attention to Culhen. The wolf was still cavorting in the forest snow, and if Ahren couldn't really see through his eyes, he was slowly getting better at reading the impressions that the animal was sending him. He smiled when he perceived that Culhen was chasing snowflakes but gave a start when Likis suddenly addressed him.

'What's it like, being able to sense him?' asked his friend curiously. Ahren heard an air of wistfulness in the young man's voice, and for a moment he wondered if his friend was envious of his new ability.

'It's hard to explain,' began the apprentice haltingly. He hardly understood how it worked himself, and now he was supposed to explain it to others? Likis and Khara looked at him curiously as he struggled for the right words. 'It's as if Culhen is in my head and I'm in his. If I concentrate, I can read his thoughts – well, at least what the little whippersnapper considers to be thoughts.' An offended howl resounded in the forest and Ahren winced guiltily. 'The same applies to him of course, as you can hear. His new understanding is still very young, the magical connection still has to grow, but Falk says he's clever enough that sometime I'll be able to communicate with him normally.'

'So, you can send information to each other?' asked Likis doubtfully. Ahren realised that his friend couldn't really follow him. The apprentice felt a stabbing pain in his chest as he began to understand his world was different to his friend's in that one respect. They might well remain friends forever, but Ahren saw a distance in the eyes of the merchant that hadn't been there before.

'It's more than that. We can always sense what the other is feeling. We really have to make the effort to suppress that sensation, and it's exhausting at the moment and not particularly successful. Falk says we have to keep practising, but sometimes I'd really like to have my head to myself.'

Ahren sensed Culhen's immediate offended snort but was too concerned with responding to Likis's reaction. Ahren could clearly see in his facial gestures how his understanding was trying to make sense of the rules governing Ahren's new life.

'So, it's like the two of us devising some prank or other? One of us always knew what the other was thinking,' he finally said with his famous half-smile, which only reached one corner of his mouth.

Ahren laughed out loud with relief. Likis's nimble spirit translated the apprentice's words into a picture he could comprehend, and the young Forest Guardian gratefully jumped on the idea.

Soon they were relating to Khara the pranks they had got up to in Deepstone, and before long it seemed as if the moment of alienation had never occurred.

Falk arrived back in the hut late that evening only to find three figures sitting at his hearth and so engrossed in conversation that they hardly noticed him. Likis and Ahren had persuaded Khara to tell them of one of her fights in the arena, and the girl, who now trusted them enough to accede to their request, was basking in the amazed looks of the young men.

Falk smiled, but then his eyes fell on the almost empty pot of venison stew which he had prepared for the week, and whose miserable remnants barely covered the bottom.

'Boy,' he growled, 'have you eaten up all the stew?'

Ahren spun around as if he'd been bitten by a Needle Spider and looked into the pot with horror. 'Ehm...to be honest I didn't really notice. It tasted so good and... we were...so hungry...' The apprentice's voice faded away to nothing as the old man's face darkened.

'So, you decided that you would reward *my* hard work in setting up the obstacle course by gobbling up all my provisions for the week?' His master's voice had become so deep and ominous that Ahren believed he could feel it reverberate in his bones.

The three young people looked at each other in embarrassment, but Falk only threw his arms in the air and stomped out into the night.

'I'd better go out and shoot a stag so I can prepare another stew. That will calm him down again,' said Ahren hastily.

'Now? In the middle of the night?' asked Likis in disbelief.

Ahren nodded. 'The best way of apologising to Falk is by owning up to your mistake and then making up for it.' He turned to Khara. 'Can you make sure Likis gets home safely?'

She nodded, but Likis sat up angrily. 'If anything, it'll be *me* bringing *Khara* safely home. That's how it goes.'

Ahren suppressed a grin as Khara buckled on Wind Blade with deliberate slowness and murmured, 'If you say so.'

Likis sensibly left it at that, and they said their goodbyes. Ahren trotted out into the dark forest while Khara and Likis headed back to Deepstone.

That left Falk, grumpy and growly and venting his spleen at greedy young people in general, and thankless apprentices in particular. He stamped back into the hut and proceeded to scrape out the remaining stew from the bottom of the pot.

Chapter 3

The night was deep, and the moon only a faint memory behind the rolling clouds, whose icy load had covered the landscape that evening in a thick blanket of shimmering new snow. Visibility was severely hampered, and Ahren could barely make out the outlines of things ahead of him. If it weren't for the powdery snow crunching under his steps, which reflected the faint moonlight, the young man would have no chance at all of a successful hunt.

Hunt? Culhen had absorbed his thoughts, and Ahren couldn't help smiling when he identified the wolf's joy and excitement as the animal eagerly awaited the young Forest Guardian's response.

Yes, we're going hunting, answered Ahren solemnly. This would be their first hunt together since they had become connected, and somehow this still and snow-filled night seemed ideal to the fledgling Paladin.

Culhen's nose immediately turned upwind. After a few sniffs he sent Ahren an image of a hare and sank his nose in the direction of the scent.

Joyfully surprised, the young man tickled the wolf's fur.

Well done, big lad. But we need something more impressive to satisfy Falk, he thought regretfully.

Culhen whimpered quietly and cocked his head as if he didn't fully understand what Ahren wanted to tell him.

The apprentice thought for a moment and then sent the animal the image of a stag. The wolf understood immediately. His nose in the air, he ran ahead of Ahren, and the two of them went further into the heart of the Eastern Forest.

It was around midnight when the wolf suddenly stopped and cocked his head.

Do you smell a stag? asked Ahren hopefully. He was frozen and tired, and the romance of their first hunt together had diminished considerably. He just wanted to get it over with quickly so he could return home to a warm fire.

All thoughts of a comfortable hunt faded when the wolf responded. *No stag...rotten. Dead.* And the young animal perceived a fear and confusion that gave Ahren the feeling that the scent was new to his friend and didn't fit into any system of hunting that the wolf understood.

He knew of only one thing that might smell like that to the predator. Dark Ones.

Ahren hesitated and considered the situation. Should they follow the scent on their own or would it be better to get help? The dark Eastern Forest suddenly seemed much less familiar and much more dangerous to him, and Ahren wished he had the calm self-confidence that Falk always radiated when he was out in the wilderness. The memory of his master's mood settled it. If Ahren asked for help without knowing what Culhen had discovered, his master would certainly be far from impressed. But if he were to return with a detailed report concerning how many and what kinds of Dark Ones there were, and where their stomping ground was, well then, the old man would simply have to forgive him his transgression regarding the venison stew.

He squared his shoulders and took his bow from his back. It was a done deal: he and Culhen would hunt down the Dark One. The wolf reacted with cautious enthusiasm, took up the strange scent again and purposefully led Ahren northwards through the snow-covered trees.

The night was almost half over when Culhen reported that the smell of death and putrefaction was becoming ever stronger. By now Ahren's nose had smelled the rotten stench too, and he had tied a cloth over his nose so that he wouldn't retch. Culhen kept looking up at him pleadingly, and finally the young Forest Guardian understood and told the animal to stop. Culhen pressed in against him thankfully and then rolled up into a ball, his nose in the fur of his tail, so that he could have a little relief from the appalling stench. *Me ensure drawback*, he said slyly, and Ahren hesitated for a moment. Had his wolf just cracked a joke?

He suppressed the question and concentrated on their prey. The wolf had led him out of the Eastern Forest and to the little lake north of Deepstone, where it lay in a low valley, surrounded by wheat fields, now dormant in their well-deserved winter sleep.

The Dark One had to be somewhere nearby, and the way in which its aroma penetrated over a wide area gave Ahren an idea of what he might be following. The stench became so intense that Ahren's eyes streamed and he felt as if he were standing in front of a mountain of bloated cadavers on a humid summer's day, and so he dropped down onto the cool carpet of snow and crawled slowly towards the edge of the depression and the smell of fermenting death. The black of the night was normally a problem for hunters, but Ahren was using it to his advantage now. At least, if he was on the right track. If he was mistaken, then he would probably be in trouble. A Fog Cat could use his present conduct to its advantage and, as Ahren was in a vulnerable position, slice open his veins within a couple of heartbeats. Ahren pushed the unpleasant images out of his head. No Fog Cat would tolerate such a stench, and just as he was calming himself down with this thought, he caught sight of what he had hoped to see. Barely two hundred paces north was a solitary baleful point of light, which was undoubtedly being emitted from a glimmering red eye. Ahren was overwhelmed by feelings of both relief and fear. He was certain he had found a Pallid Frog, one of the three sub-species of Grave Frogs. They all shared the same horrendous smell, and their skin secreted a highly poisonous substance whose fumes could be dangerous even at a distance of some paces. The Pallid Frog was the least harmful of the three. At least in close combat, thought Ahren, correcting himself. Pallid Frogs were usually precursors to the appearance of many Dark Ones in a swathe of land. The frog-like creature, one pace in diameter and with a pallid white body containing a single large eye on its back, liked to borrow into muddy banks where it would gradually befoul the waters and the surrounding ground with its secretions. Other Dark Ones from miles around could smell the contamination and were drawn towards it. Then healthy fields, meadows and forests would be quickly transformed into nothing less than death zones through the influence of several Pallid Frogs. Ahren swallowed hard when he considered what disaster would befall Deepstone if the creature was left alive to carry out its baleful work undisturbed. A failure of the following year's crop would be the very least of the evils that might occur.

Ahren quickly took his bow from his shoulder and raised it upward just far enough to be able to shoot an arrow. Pallid Frogs buried themselves deep into the water-bed at the first sign of danger, and this one could only be up on the bank out of necessity. The creatures absorbed moonlight once a night, which they needed in the production of their vile secretions. This one clearly felt safe enough in the middle of the night and in the depths of winter. For this reason, it had broken through the thin layer of ice on the bank of the lake, and now it was perched, with its snow-white body half on land and its worm-like legs still floating in the water.

Ahren placed an arrow on the bowstring, which he tautened into the shooting position. He sought out the Void but only found Culhen, whose hunting instincts were distracting the apprentice and urging him on at the same time. The wood of the bow creaked in his hand as he increased the tension further with his arms. His muscles were burning as he quietly aimed at the red point and brought the tip of the arrow into the correct trajectory. He released the bowstring, and the projectile flew in a precise arc towards the red eye. At the last moment, however, the Pallid Frog sensed the danger it was in, and Ahren saw the red point of light jerk to the side before his arrow slammed with a satisfied squishing sound into the flesh of the froglike creature. Ahren cursed and swiftly pulled another arrow out of his quiver while the creature let forth a hissing wheeze. There was no time for finesse now – the Pallid Frog would dive down in a second and bury itself somewhere deep in the slime. Without hesitation, Ahren shot off a hail of arrows towards where he could barely make out the almost closed eye, and only when his hand grasped thin air and he realised all his arrows had been used up, did he pause for a moment.

Panting from his efforts, Ahren listened for any other sounds in the night air. The eye was no more to be seen, and Ahren couldn't be sure if the unholy light of the Dark One had been extinguished forever, or if the animal had found refuge in the lake. A cloud had covered the moon, leaving the apprentice to listen anxiously.

While he was waiting for the moon to re-appear, Culhen nudged him with a thought in his head.

Air better, the wolf informed him gratefully, but that wasn't much help to the young Paladin. Was the Pallid Frog dead now, or did the wolf not smell anything because the creature had burrowed into the mud?

There was nothing for it. He would have to go down and be absolutely certain. He had used up all his arrows, so he drew out Wind Blade and slithered down to the lake, before carefully treading silently forward along its curved edge, all the while keeping his eyes fixed on where his arrows had fallen.

The confounded cloud simply did not want to move away, and so the young man, sweat dripping down his back with fear, was only a few paces from the Pallid Frog before he finally knew what fate had befallen it.

The creature, almost round in shape and with colourless eyes and a wide toothy mouth, was lying motionless on the bank, a hand's width from the safety of the water, which came forth from the jagged hole in the ice and was lapping the stubby extremities of the Dark One.

Ahren's first arrow, which he had shot with all the power of his bow, had stuck deep into the back of the creature, nailing it to the riverbank, so that it never had a chance of escaping the succeeding volley of arrows.

Over a dozen of them had driven all life out of the Pallid Frog, and the young Paladin lowered his weapon with relief. The smell was still almost unbearable, but what Culhen's sensitive nose had picked up was nothing more than the dwindling secretion of the dead frog.

'We can't leave you here like that,' murmured Ahren to his defeated adversary. He stuck Wind Blade into the pallid flesh and pulled the frog away from the lake so that it would sully its waters no more. Even though its activities were over forever, the young man didn't want the Dark One to decompose in the lake, causing further damage in the process.

He pulled the blade out of the corpse and cleaned it thoroughly in the snow. 'We'll take care of everything else tomorrow,' he murmured, and made his way back to the wolf, who was lying curled up, protecting his nose from the remaining stench that was hanging in the air.

'Well now, you were a great help,' scolded Ahren in jest, but Culhen sat upright and looked proudly into Ahren's eyes.

Ahren killed. But Culhen found, thought the wolf emphatically, and the apprentice burst out laughing.

'You've hit the nail on head there,' he said, agreeing with his friend and ruffling the wolf's head. Then they turned for home, and the moon finally won its battle with the cloud.

Ahren's moment of glory was as splendid as he had hoped – and that despite the fact that he had returned from the hunt without a stag. As soon as he had related the night's events, Falk had set off with him and Culhen again so that they could show him the Pallid Frog's cadaver. Much to Ahren's surprise, the old man incinerated its remains on the spot with lamp oil.

'Not a word to anybody. We don't want to create a panic,' he explained curtly, and Ahren nodded fearfully.

They passed the return journey in silent contemplation, and Ahren couldn't get it out of his head that Deepstone would remain unprotected once they headed off again. 'What will happen if another one comes here?' he asked finally with a tremor in his voice.

Falk gave him a serious look. 'We can only hope that it won't happen.'

Once Ahren had heard this sobering response, his head became filled with horrible visions of Deepstone, contaminated or destroyed. Later, even his master's praise of his heroism that night failed to lift his mood.

Falk had graciously allowed him to sleep for the rest of the morning, at least until Khara turned up for her daily sword-training in front of the hut.

Ahren, overtired and unmotivated, was black and blue by the time he had finished crossing swords with the one-time fighting slave. He had hoped that Khara would exercise some leniency after their training run the previous day, but nothing could have been farther from her mind.

'Can't you indulge me just a little bit?' he finally asked in a whining voice as he massaged an aching rib.

Khara just shook her head. 'This is a good lesson. You need to be able to fight when you're tired too. I'm going to talk to Falk about night training.'

Ahren looked at her dumbstruck as he tried to digest her latest idea only to be hit three times most painfully before being thrown to the ground.

Another two weeks passed by, during which time Ahren enjoyed Deepstone as intensively as he possibly could, and his fears concerning what lay ahead for the villagers abated somewhat. Any spare time he had, he would spend with his friends, and however ruthlessly Khara behaved towards him during their sword-training, she was now treating him in an almost friendly manner, albeit he was reading her body language in the most charitable light. Holken and Likis found it easy to make her laugh, whereas he was overjoyed when she didn't frown at him, so he would hardly have described it as significant progress.

Following the incident in Falk's hut, they changed to meeting in the tavern, where they would huddle together in a corner. Holken would always join them too, and so the four of them would listen to Trogadon's tales of derring-do as he entertained the whole tavern, or they would wallow in reminiscences of their childhood days.

At least, the three offspring of Deepstone would. Any revelations Khara gave about her past were indeed exciting to hear about, but also dark and bloody. Ahren had to admit that he admired the fact that despite her experiences, she still possessed a modicum of humanity. No more than a modicum though, he thought as he rubbed his aching bruises. Every now and then he would hint at the impending dangers the Dark Ones might present, but his tentative suggestions always led to questions regarding his own adventures in tackling Low Fangs or Swarm Claws.

It was early afternoon of a dreary winter's day and the four of them were once again sitting together. Half of the village had retreated from the bitter cold into their shuttered ice-bedecked houses. The tap room was filled with those looking for company on this most inhospitable of days. Old Cossith was there in his regular corner, playing at dice with Holken's father and the mistress cobbler. Edrik, Ahren's father, was thankfully nowhere to be seen. Ahren had heard that his father limited his tavern visits to the evenings, when the young Paladin was gone. They had reached a silent agreement to stay out of each other's way, and that suited Ahren perfectly.

Evening was still a long way off, but because of the weak light from outside, the innkeeper had already lit candles on the tables. Likis and Holken were vying for Khara's attention as usual, and Ahren's mind was wandering when he became aware of Culhen in his head.

Ahren? Paws numb, he heard the wolf say. Ahren frowned and stood up, ignoring the others' questioning looks, and went out the front door of the tavern. There was Culhen, sitting in the snow, looking up at him and whimpering quietly.

'If your paws are cold, then come in out of the snow,' said the young man playfully and held the door open for the wolf. The animal had already been popular among the villagers before Ahren's departure, and everyone was always happy to see him, which meant he was welcome into the tavern. Culhen however, stayed sitting and began carefully nibbling his forepaws.

Not cold. Numb. Paws numb, Culhen responded.

Worried now, Ahren went over to his friend. He knelt down beside the big wolf and put an arm over his shoulders.

Are you telling me you can't feel your paws? he asked mentally.

Yes, came the answer, and it was accompanied by uncertainty and fear. Gingerly, Culhen began nibbling at his forepaws again.

Ahren bit his lip uncertainly and then reached a decision. 'Let's go look for Falk. Maybe your paws have got a chill from too much larking around in the snow, but we're better safe than sorry.'

Ahren stood up and walked towards the mayor's house, only to stop after a few paces. Culhen had tried to totter after him, placing one paw down after the other in a comical manner. The sight would have been amusing were it not for the wave of fear that now flowed from one to the other. 'Stay there. I'll come back with Falk,' said Ahren quickly and trotted over to the large house where he thought his master would be.

Falk would meet up with the Ancients once a day to consider further details of their upcoming journey, and the apprentice hoped his master was still there.

He pushed open the front door and found the three long-living comrades-in-arms gathered around the large table where they were poring over a map.

'Boy, why did you barge in like...' said Falk, only to stop when he saw Ahren's concerned look.

'There's something wrong with Culhen!' cried out the young man and immediately turned to leave again. Falk was up in an instant, Jelninolan followed suit, and Uldini flew up into the air and floated over the table.

Ahren waved his arm urgently and ran out, calling over his shoulder: 'He says his paws are numb, and he's moving in a very strange way.' His concern for his friend was mixed up with the animal's uncertainty which he was sensing in his head, and he sobbed: 'I think he's sick.'

Falk and Jelninolan exchanged worried looks before sprinting past Ahren, whose pulse began to race when he saw how alarmed they had become. His worst fears seemed to have been realised! He caught up with them, and two heartbeats later they were at Culhen's side. He was still sitting in the market square, whimpering quietly.

Ahren's friends had arrived in the meantime, and Khara was stroking the wolf's white fur, speaking to him soothingly all the while.

Falk swiftly approached the animal, immediately cupped Culhen's head in his hands and stared deep into his yellow eyes before releasing his hold. 'Wolf Ice' was all he said.

The elf opened her eyes wide and immediately cast a charm over Culhen. As soon as she placed her hands on his body, his fur was covered in a blue fog. The wolf yelped in surprise but did not resist.

'Ahren, he must remain as still as possible,' uttered Jelninolan sharply. 'He's been given Wolf Ice, and the more he moves, the more the poison will spread throughout his body!'

Ahren stood there frozen for a heartbeat.

Poisoned? Culhen's been poisoned? The unbelievable thought raced through his head.

He quickly gathered himself together so that he could communicate mentally with Culhen. *Listen to me now, big boy. We're going to play a game, alright? You have to lie on the ground and you're not to move a muscle.*

Play? responded the wolf uncertainly.

Ahren quickly shook his head as he tried to control his rising panic. *No, not play*, he corrected himself. He hesitated for a moment. *Disguise. Hide.* He gave the hand command that would always prompt the wolf to lie flat on the ground. Hand gestures had hardly been necessary ever since they had begun speaking to each other, but at this moment the gesture helped to make it perfectly clear to the frightened wolf what Ahren wanted him to do. Whimpering quietly, he lay down and looked up at Ahren with confused eyes.

Legs cold. Paws gone, he said fearfully, and Ahren flinched pityingly.

'His paws are still numb, and his legs are cold,' he said. 'Is the magic not working?' he shouted anxiously to the priestess.

Jelninolan ignored him and turned instead to Uldini. 'The poison is extremely strong. I'm going to need you to slow down its process.'

The Ancient nodded and placed his hands on her shoulders. The blue fog which was radiating from Jelninolan's hands and swirling around Culhen's body immediately strengthened, and Ahren could feel a faint warmth emanating from the magic. While this was happening, all the guests from the tavern had spilled out onto the village square and were curiously watching the drama unfold. Trogadon was standing there too, looking more earnest than Ahren had ever seen him before. 'What can we do?' he asked. That was exactly what Ahren was asking himself as he fought to control his own emotions as well as those of the wolf.

Jelninolan glanced around her before issuing a list of commands. 'Trogadon and Khara, you make sure that nobody comes too near Culhen. I don't want the charm being interrupted. Not that anybody here would be superstitious of the magic and try to incite the people of Deepstone – our last encounter with an angry mob was not long ago. Falk, I'm going to need Fire Weed, and quickly. That's the only way I can burn the poison out of his veins. Please tell me that it grows here in the Eastern Forest.' Her voice had taken on a pleading undertone, and Ahren was now frightened out of his skin.

While the others carried out Jelninolan's orders, Falk wavered and shook his head. 'I really don't know. Fire Weed is a poison and so I never really kept an eye out on where it might grow. Vera won't have any either, she doesn't allow poisons into her house.' The old man feverishly rattled his brains, and Ahren was on the point of exploding with rage, and giving vent to his fear, uncertainty and helplessness.

'All those lessons and we can't even save Culhen?' he said through gritted teeth. He stared at his master and clenched his fists so hard they hurt. It was only the compassion in his master's eyes that prevented him from lashing out at him.

'I'll ask Selsena. The old lady knows the Eastern Forest as well as Evergreen by now, and she has an amazing memory for all sorts of plants. If there's any Fire Weed growing around here, then she'll know about it.'

Ahren clung to this hope and used it to control the emotions that were threatening to overwhelm him. He fixed his eyes on the face of his master, who had closed his eyes and was communicating with Selsena. He heard Culhen's heartbreaking whimpering in his ears and in his head and tried hard to communicate a feeling of security to the wolf, but kept failing miserably. He almost burst with rage at his own inadequacies, and when Falk opened his eyes again, Ahren leaped forward, grabbed his master's shoulders and shook him vigorously. 'And? What did she say?' he screamed into his face.

'She knows of two places where Fire Weed might be growing. But it's winter and everything is covered in snow. She can't burrow into it with her hooves without trampling the Weed to bits. We have to go there and find it ourselves,' he said forcefully, grasping Ahren's upper arms, and physically controlling him.

'I'm going to look in the south and you look in the north. You know the place where the enormous tree was uprooted. Where we cornered Culhen's mother.'

Ahren turned on his heels without uttering a word and ran northwards, out of Deepstone and into the icy forest, which harboured the last remaining hope for his dying friend.

The blood was pounding in Ahren's ears and he was seeing spots in front of his eyes. He had already been running through the forest for three hours, heedless of the injuries he was doing to his own body. His face had cuts from branches whipping against it, his shins were flecked with bruises from stumbling through the undergrowth. It had taken them a full day to reach the Blood Wolf that time, admittedly at walking pace, but Ahren was convinced that Culhen had little time left. He was still only a little distance away from the wolf, but already the connection with him was becoming weaker, and with every elapsing moment Ahren's fear increased. Again and again he heard the poisoned wolf pleading with him for comfort and questioning him in his head.

Ahren? Ahren?

The apprentice, tears in his eyes, kept sending calming messages to his companion animal. He knew that Culhen really needed him now and was depending on his strength, and this thought gave him the energy to urge his tired body onwards. And once that was no longer enough, he cut himself a chunk of Moon Fungus, which was growing rampant on a rotten tree trunk, and shoved the slippery fungus into his mouth. The bitter, disgusting taste made him want to throw up as his body warned the young man of what he was about to digest, but Ahren swallowed the poisonous mushroom and ran onwards. It was normal only to take small amounts after having boiled out the worst poisons, and then only in emergencies. But the Moon Fungus had an immediate and brutal effect, and Ahren's exhaustion and pain vanished. His heart began pounding wildly in his chest as if it wanted to break free, and Ahren increased his tempo in order to expend the renewed energy that was streaming through his body.

At last he came to the natural hollow which had once been the Blood Wolf's lair and he stopped in his tracks. The bones of the enormous animal were lying in the snow like a baleful omen of Culhen's imminent death.

The effects of the mushroom were playing with Ahren's mind, and he stumbled into the hollow, which had been created when the enormous tree had been wrenched out of the ground. Its withered roots were still jutting into the sky.

His whole body was bathed in a slimy sweat which smelled putridly sweet, but Ahren was hardly aware of the stench. Instead, he was drawn magnetically down to the pale wolf skull, which was lying chest-high in front of him, staring at him accusingly out of hollow eye sockets. Caught in the poisonous delirium, Ahren laid his hand on the skull and mumbled in a whispering voice: 'I'll take care of him well. I'll save him. I promise.'

Then he stumbled back up onto his feet and began looking around feverishly.

Everything was covered in snow, and no plant was to be seen protruding through the thick white blanket. Ahren furiously began digging and then suddenly realised he had no idea what he was actually looking out for! In his hurry he had forgotten to ask Falk what Fire Weed looked like!

Crying with rage and frustration he pounded his fists on the snow before clearing the forest floor with his claw-like fingers, all the while ignoring the painful iciness.

Tears streamed down his face, and for a moment he was tempted to simply roll himself up into a ball and surrender to the forest cold because the pain he was feeling inside was threatening to overwhelm him. But he could still hear Culhen's pleading voice in his head and giving up was simply not an option. He systematically cleared more and more of the hollow from snow, concentrating on the sensations emanating from Culhen, which kept him focussed on the goal of his endeavour. The wolf seemed to be lying on his side, his legs were numb, his lungs felt as if they were filled with ice and he was struggling with his breathing. There were hands on his back, and their warmth was fighting against the cold within him. That had to be Jelninolan. The wolf's head was lying on somebody's lap, and Ahren could just about smell, as if through a veil, Khara's scent, and that it was she who was stroking Culhen's fur. It was clear that Jelninolan had given her permission to comfort the wolf by touching him, and that he really needed her by his side. The apprentice bit his lips until they were bleeding, in an attempt to overpower another wave of frustration, and continued his search. He found two different herbs that he threw into his mouth and chewed in an effort to stabilise himself. The mushroom poison was still raging inside him and Ahren was dimly aware of the fact that he wouldn't be able to help Culhen if he collapsed himself.

At last his fingers uncovered a small, inconspicuous plant, whose thin green leaves ended in a weak dark red colour. That had to be it!

With a cry of triumph, more animal than human, Ahren dug the plant out of the hard winter ground, taking no heed of the injuries he was doing to his hands. His fingers bloodied, he pushed the plant into the herb bag attached to his belt, turned to head back and glanced one last time at the wolf skeleton while silently repeating his promise.

He would save Culhen!

It was night now and the Eastern Forest lay in darkness as Ahren stumbled from tree to tree. He had been forced into slowing down his tempo in order not to crash into branches and tree trunks although he could see more than should have been possible. The Moon Fungus clearly had a positive effect on night vision, and although the effect of the poison was wearing off, it helped him to move forwards at a faster pace.

He arrived back at the tree trunk with the Pallid Mushroom and paused briefly. His strength was waning, and he wasn't sure if he could risk eating some more. His body had barely coped with the first portion, and he really had no idea what effect a second portion would have. He was about to move on without taking more of the stimulant when he heard a sound in his head. Culhen had become suspiciously quiet, but now he was sending a soft, sad howl to Ahren, which portended grief and farewell.

Ahren tore the rest of the mushroom from the tree and stuffed it into his mouth along with some splinters of wood while he raced with frustration through the night. The effect of the mushroom ensured that Culhen's howling increased in an ever more powerful crescendo, driving Ahren into a madness.

Light.

Voices.

Ahren, guided by only the tiniest thread of reason and a large portion of instinct, tumbled out of the forest and into the strange flickering cloud of brightness, created by the torches that lit up Deepstone. Ahren spotted unfamiliar, grotesque faces, none of whom he recognised, but whoever they were, they quickly gave way to him. There was one person standing in front of him, smaller and broader than the others and with a funny dancing grey beard, and the person was saying something that he didn't understand. The person grabbed his arm, and he weakly defended himself, but the iron grip moved him along. There were silhouettes kneeling around an animal that was lying there, breathing weakly and looking up at him out of tired yellow eyes. There was something wrong with the animal, and Ahren sensed instinctively that it was serious. It had something to do with the bag on his belt, but what? Dazed, he tinkered with the laces and finally opened the leather wide enough and pulled something out. There were screams and cries all around him, and the apprentice was sure he had done something wrong. But then the broad figure took the plant he was holding in his hands. How did *they* get there? While he was trying to figure that out, his tortured body collapsed under the thundering onslaught of the poison – and then there was nothing.

Chapter 4

It was the scent of honey dissolved in milk that awoke Ahren, and he slowly opened his eyes. He was lying on his bed in Falk's hut and when he tried sitting up, his body refused to co-operate. Falk's tired face came into view and broke into a smile.

'Stay lying down for another while. That was a hellish run through the forest you managed,' he said, and there was pride in his voice.

Ahren tried turning his head but his neck muscles too were letting him down. 'Culhen?' he whispered weakly.

'The greedy guts is fine. Can you believe that the minute he was healed he started eating again? You would have thought that after his poisoning he would have been more careful, but he gulped down everything the villagers brought him – and that was some amount.' He looked down at Ahren and gave him another good-natured smile. 'There seems to be no lasting damage done, either to him or to you although you seem to have been through the wars. What was it you took?'

'Moon Fungus,' answered Ahren in a faint voice. He was finding speaking difficult, and he was surprised at Falk's calmness. The last time that Ahren had almost died, Falk had been devastated.

The man put the milk and honey drink to Ahren's mouth and carefully poured some in. 'This will help you with speaking. And I've also added plenty of healing herbs which your body needs to counteract the paralysis. Jelninolan performed some magic which prevented your heart and lungs from packing in, but she had no energy for anything else. She and Uldini are absolutely shattered. It's good that they can regenerate themselves during the Spring Ceremony.'

The old man was rabbiting on, and his demeanour was making Ahren nervous.

Falk noticed his apprentice's concerned look and he smiled again. 'Don't you worry. You're not getting a lecture from me today. If Selsena had been at death's door, I'd have done exactly the same as you, and even more. Our companion animals are a part of us. Every Paladin who has seen theirs die has been shaken to the core and many of them have been mentally broken by the experience. There's no doubt you took an enormous risk, but it was worth it. Jelninolan says that Culhen wouldn't have lasted another hour, and unfortunately, I didn't find any Fire Weed in the place in the forest that Selsena had described to me. If you hadn't done the necessary, he would have died.'

Relief and a deep sense of happiness flowed through the apprentice's battered body, and he gave a barely perceptible nod. He concentrated on his connection to Culhen and sensed that the wolf was lying in a languorous food coma. His companion's tiredness came rolling over him and he was swept away into a deep, peaceful sleep.

'When you see them like that, you see that they're two of a kind.' Uldini's voice was full of its biting humour again, and yet there was also sympathy in his voice.

Ahren glanced up from his food towards the Arch Wizard, who was keenly watching both apprentice and wolf gulping down everything as soon as it was placed in front of them.

The apprentice had been ravenous when he had woken up and the same had been true of his friend. Now they were sitting in the dining area of the tavern, bolting down the enormous portions at lightning speed under the approving eyes of their travelling companions, not to mention half the villagers.

Falk had shooed the pair of them out of his hut and steered them in the clear winter sunshine towards the tavern where, much to the surprise of the innkeeper, he had laid a gold coin on the counter. 'I'm not a canteen kitchen for starving whelps. You'll both get your fill in here', he'd growled. The food had been served and Ahren had become lost to the world.

Now the Arch Wizard's waspish humour had torn him from his feeding frenzy, and he had to admit that his table manners had seen better days. There were leftovers lying around his plate, his fingers were greasy from having ripped apart sides of roast meat, which he had stuffed into his mouth with large chunks of dark bread. He could feel the remains of the gravy from ear to ear and all over his face.

Culhen was still transmitting waves of hunger, but Ahren's stomach objected and finally surrendered in its own heavy weight, so that the apprentice quickly dropped the remaining food he had been holding in his hands.

Scarlet with embarrassment, he looked around and saw benevolent and amused faces looking at him and his wolf. He sighed when he noticed both Likis and Khara smirking, who were clearly highly entertained by his gluttonous episode. His lanky friend deliberately took a tiny morsel of breakfast, which he raised to his mouth in an exaggeratedly polite manner before chewing it slowly, all the while looking at Ahren and wiggling his eyebrows in a meaningful manner.

Ahren snorted and exploded with laughter, thereby ensuring that the contents of his mouth were scattered across the table.

The rest of the tavern joined in the laughter, and Ahren felt the general goodwill and relief at the fact that the two had fully recovered. He felt a lump in his throat as he wiped his face to get rid of the remaining gravy and to hide the tears welling up in his eyes.

Falk strolled over to him, a pail filled with water, and a brush in his hands.

'When you've regained your self-control, you can tidy up the place and wipe away the mess you've created.' He ignored the protests of the innkeeper, who stammered that you couldn't order a Paladin of the gods to clean up. 'He caused this chaos and he has a healthy pair of hands. So, it's up to him to get rid of the dirt.' And with that, the Forest Guardian folded his arms, and there was enough steel in his voice to dissuade anyone from contradicting him, least of all Ahren.

He grabbed the pail and began cleaning the table. Falk continued speaking in a low voice. 'You have to learn to control Culhen's impulses. He's a predatory animal, and his urge to feed is powerful, especially now that Jelninolan has healed him. Her magic has dramatically replenished his reserves - you know the effects of her healing charms. If you and Culhen amplify each other's manners, that can really backfire.'

Ahren nodded and tried to ignore the protests from his over-full stomach while he scrubbed the tabletop. He was clearly more approachable now, and the area around him no longer resembled a battlefield, and so all his friends gradually came closer to reassure themselves that he had recovered.

He fiercely embraced Jelninolan and Uldini, and the Arch Wizard rolled his eyes in response. 'Are you serious? Hugging again?' he groaned loudly, but he embraced Ahren firmly, nonetheless.

'Thank you for saving Culhen,' said Ahren before his voice cracked.

The wolf pulled himself away from his nearly empty bowl, leaped up to the two Ancients and slobbered them with wolf kisses, his gooey tongue plastering their faces with the remains of his meal.

'If I'd know this would happen, I'd never have helped Jelninolan,' sighed Uldini as he tried in vain to keep the wolf from his face.

Ahren took the opportunity to turn around to Khara, who was clearly enjoying the grumpy Arch Wizard's discomfort. 'Thank you for comforting Culhen. You really helped him.' Suddenly he got her scent in his nose, and Culhen's memory of being helped by her came forcefully back into the apprentice's mind. Before he knew it, he was embracing Khara in a bear hug. A heartbeat later and he suddenly let go and took a step backward. The girl was a budding champion in unarmed close combat, and up until that moment any sudden body contact had ended very painfully for Ahren. This time, however, the ex-slave bowed towards him in the manner of the Eternal Empire. 'We all really love Culhen,' she murmured simply, and left it at that.

The wolf had finished his slobbery display of affection, and Likis placed his arm around Ahren's shoulder in an expression of friendship before asking quietly, 'Have you any idea yet where Culhen ate the poison?' He looked with concern at Ahren, who instantly became anxious.

He hadn't even considered the question. The poison must have come from somewhere! He turned to his master, who began to answer Likis's question.

'Trogadon and I have been asking around, but nobody knows anything', he said. 'Wolf Ice is rare and expensive. The plant is mainly used by shepherds who are at their wits' ends, because a pack of wolves has been worrying their flock. That happens rarely enough, and even then, it's difficult to acquire the substance.' The old man made a sweeping gesture. 'I asked everyone in Deepstone who might have used it. None of the farmers, shepherds or big landowners had any trouble with wolves, and so they don't possess any Wolf Ice.'

Ahren considered what he had heard, and suddenly a terrible thought struck him. 'Somebody deliberately poisoned Culhen,' he whispered aghast.

Falk nodded, a stony look on his face. 'That's what we suspect too. You should ask your wolf, where was the last place he ate something before he was poisoned. Your friend had an incredible amount of toxicity in his body. If he hadn't been able to speak to you, and if he hadn't told you immediately, we would have noticed the symptoms far too late...' Falk trailed off, but Ahren understood the implication. If Culhen had been the normal, faithful wolf he had been before the Naming, he would now be dead.

Culhen, where did you eat before your paws became numb? Ahren asked gingerly.

The wolf sat back on his hind legs, tilted his head and looked at Ahren with his faithful yellow eyes. Finally, he answered. *House with wings.*

Part of Ahren was overjoyed that Culhen's messages were slowly becoming more comprehensible, but the other part was frantically trying to ascertain what his friend meant. What sort of a house had wings?

He looked out onto the village square, which lay peacefully in the late-winter sunshine, and gazed at the houses which were visible to him. Did the wolf mean a drawing or decoration? Could he even correctly interpret such an image? Ahren wasn't sure how far the animal's growing understanding had developed – but then the penny dropped, and he knew what the wolf had meant.

Ahren moved stiffly towards the tavern door. 'What did Culhen say?' asked Falk insistently, his voice sounding increasingly concerned.

'He said it was at a house with wings,' answered Ahren in an ominously quiet voice.

'A house with wings? I wonder does he mean the windmill?' mused Uldini with a quizzical look.

Falk's face froze as he put two and two together. 'Sven.'

Ahren stormed up the hill towards the wooden door of the mill, which rose up a stone's throw from the village. There was not much work for a miller at this time of year apart from doing repairs, and so the mill was standing idle.

Ahren kicked open the door and was propelled in by his own force. Sven and two of his cronies were drinking beer at the enormous millstone in the middle of the room. The air was sticky with the sweat of the three drinking buddies, who must have been celebrating for quite a while, and the young Forest Guardian suspected he knew why. The chubby miller's son with his small, devious eyes had hardly changed since Ahren's departure from Deepstone, and the same held true for his two friends. They had jumped up clumsily when Ahren literally appeared from nowhere, and now he was standing there stock still, a pace inside the entrance as the door, now split, crashed to the ground.

'What do you think you're...' protested Sven, but Ahren cut him off.

'Why?' he asked in a low tone, still standing motionless.

'I don't know what you're talking about,' mumbled Sven, but with an oily smile, and he gestured to his two friends that they should sandwich Ahren between them.

The young Forest Guardian simply ignored the pair and fixed the miller's son with his stare.

'Why did you poison Culhen?' Ahren blurted. Saying the words had stirred up his emotions again, and the makeshift Void into which he had fled shattered.

He had only rarely attained that meditative state devoid of emotion since he and Culhen had become connected, and when Sven again smiled slimily at him, he had neither the strength nor the desire to put the shattered pieces together again.

'The brute should never have come here. This hill is *our* land, and we have the right to protect it from roaming predators,' said Sven with a false sorrow in his drunken voice and a hateful glint in his eyes.

Even if his life depended on it, Ahren would not have been able to explain what happened next. A red mist descended on him and a cry of rage overcame his reason. When he at least partially came back to his senses, he was standing, bending over and holding onto Sven, who was painfully touching his clearly broken right arm. His cronies were lying unconscious at the blood-spattered millstone, which also had a few knocked-out teeth lying on it. The budding miller's face was beaten black and blue, both eyes were swollen shut, and his right cheek was strangely dented. Ahren's fists were cut and bloody from the ferocity of his blows, and he was gasping and breathing heavily.

The apprentice stepped back in shock and dropped the bloody bundle to the ground, which was now a sobbing mess at his feet. Culhen's wild howling was beginning to ebb away in his head while Ahren looked down at his companion's tormentors.

Ahren could feel the wolf's triumph and had to pull himself together so as not to emit a similar animal howl, torn as he was between his disgust at his own rage and the joyful emotions of the animal.

He was about to pull Sven onto his feet when suddenly it seemed like the end of the world. Through the damaged doorway he could see a snarling windstorm whipping up the snow from the ground, and within a few heartbeats the whirling mass of snow had reduced visibility on the slope to fewer than five paces. The cosy winter's morning had been transformed into a raging inferno of wind and ice, which raged through Deepstone with elemental force. A silhouette approached through the sudden storm, and with a commanding gesture it burst the walls left and right of the doorway outwards, creating a gaping hole, five paces across, where the remains of the door had previously been hanging.

Ahren was stunned to see that the figure entering the mill was Jelninolan. Her feet left prints that were smooth as glass and of pure blue ice, and the air around her skin seemed to vibrate. Ahren instinctively retreated a step as she examined Sven with piercing eyes.

'Is this the malefactor who has poisoned a messenger of the goddess?' she asked in a resonant voice. At that moment there was no evidence of the maternal elf. Here was Jelninolan, the Ancient, the priestess of HER, WHO FEELS, in all her power. The snow seemed to be paying homage to the majestic sorceress, and was forming mysterious, magical symbols, while the glittering crystals of ice slowly transformed themselves into a mist.

'Yes, this is he,' gasped Ahren in amazement. 'But he's endured enough...' and he got no further.

'Enough? I think not!' said Jelninolan in a voice burning with rage. At which point the mist sprang forward and wrapped itself around Sven's toes. The gossamer began to spin around his feet, and Ahren heard in horror the bones snapping as the magic bent the miller's son's limbs into impossible shapes.

Sven let out an ear-shattering scream of pain, and Ahren watched dumbstruck as the mist began moving ever higher.

The priestess wanted to kill Sven; the apprentice was in no doubt about that.

Ahren was fully aware of the irony of the situation as he made himself as large as could in front of Jelninolan, spurred on by the courage of despair. He then pleaded for Sven's life.

'This isn't you, Jelninolan. You can't kill him in cold blood,' he began. He could hear another bone breaking behind him and he quickly continued. 'He can be convicted! We can bring him before the village council! But what's happening here is wrong! What I've done is wrong!'

He went up close to the elf, he could feel the coldness she was radiating, and he forced himself to smile at her. 'You're good-natured. And friendly. You have a sympathetic word for everyone, and you hate causing pain.'

He cupped the elf's face in his hands, her eyes seemed to be looking through him. 'You're like a mother to me,' he blurted out in a pleading voice, and at last his words seemed to get through to her.

In an instant the windstorm died down, the snow fluttered to the ground, warmth and compassion appearing once again in the elf's countenance.

She looked down at the maltreated miller's son, and her face flickered between satisfaction and horror. Then she turned around and without a word disappeared into the forest, the trees closing protectively behind her.

Ahren considered for a moment if he should follow her, then decided to stay. He needed to get help for the miller's son. Sighing, he trotted over to the main house to tell Sven's family so they could look after him. He tried in vain to ignore the bitter taste in his mouth caused by his own deeds.

A heavy calm lay over the area during the next few days. Deepstone was in a state of shock following the chain of events that had afflicted the sleepy village. The deliberate poisoning of Culhen had of course been terrible, but Jelninolan's mystical outburst of emotion had truly shocked the inhabitants. Her magical storm had berefted three houses of their roofs, severely damaged the mill, and almost killed one person. That seemed to be a case of really overdoing things in a normally peaceful community, and so the little village seemed to have huddled down behind closed doors so that it could lick its wounds.

With stubborn determination Ahren would do his training alone while the wounds he had received during his march through the forest gradually healed. He spoke rarely and always made sure Culhen was close by his side. Falk gave him the necessary breathing space and concentrated instead on helping Trogadon repair the damage Jelninolan had meted out in her rage. The elf had returned that same evening from the forest and retired to the mayor's house where she had remained since. Khara stayed by her mistress's side and so out of Ahren's sight.

Uldini, meanwhile, patched up any political damage and explained to the village council exactly what had happened. Ahren was grimly satisfied when he found out later that Sven had been banished from Deepstone. His exile would come into effect as soon as his injuries had healed sufficiently.

Ahren was returning from yet another gruelling trek through the forest, Culhen close by his side. The apprentice had planned to complete all of the obstacle courses in the one day, and had, in fact, done so successfully, if only just about. It was dark already and Falk was awaiting him at the door of his hut. His master's silhouette was lit up by the flickering light of the tempting open fire coming from within the cabin, and suddenly Ahren couldn't wait to be home again.

'Didn't think you'd make it home at all,' the old man grumbled as he obligingly made room for him.

Ahren could only nod with exhaustion and collapsed on one of the stools at the table.

Falk slowly closed the door and sat down beside the young man, placing a steaming bowl of stew on the table in front of him. Gratefully, Ahren began to devour it, and Culhen, who had placed his nuzzle on Falk's lap and was giving him begging looks with his wide eyes, started whimpering impatiently.

Falk frowned as he looked at the wolf sternly. 'He's learning too, is he?'

Ahren nodded mutely, enjoying his food and the warmth that was slowly filling his tired limbs. Then he spoke. 'He's figured out what behaviour works for different people. Yesterday he sat up and begged in front of the butcher, who promptly gave him a fat piece of ham. He might still speak like a baby, but he can trick you like a master thief.'

Culhen stared at him, the picture of innocence, before finally responding with *thanks* uttered in such a dry tone that Ahren laughed out loud. 'Oh, and he's developing a sense of humour. Unfortunately, he's imitating Uldini's style.'

Falk grinned and ruffled Culhen's thick fur energetically. 'The THREE save us,' he said jokingly. Then he became serious and looked searchingly at Ahren. 'Are you ready to talk about it?' he asked softly.

Ahren closed his eyes in exhaustion. 'What's there to talk about? Jelninolan and I both blew our tops, it's as simple as that. Would I turn the clock back if I could? I really don't know. I'm only glad I was so hungry that morning that in the rush I left all my weapons lying in the hut. Otherwise Sven would be dead now.' His voice had been becoming quieter until it was no more than a whisper.

Falk scratched his beard and poked the embers in the fire in order to bring it back to life, and for a moment the flames threw dancing shadows onto the walls. Then he turned back to his apprentice.

'It's not quite that simple. You understand that Culhen influenced you, don't you?' he began to explain. Ahren barely shook his head but Falk nodded, confirming what he'd said. 'I've already told you that Culhen is a predatory animal. A self-centred, greedy, cuddly predator. It's not only his greed that he'll convey to you. But also, his hunting instinct. Or his fighting frenzy.'

Falk left his words hanging in the air, and Ahren gulped in surprise. He hadn't thought of Culhen as a normal wolf in such a long time that he never considered what impulses might be slumbering in the animal.

'Culhen has better control of these instincts than you do because he was born with them. But they are new to you. Which is why it's vital for you to learn how to invoke the Void again and to maintain it so that the next time, you can control your emotions and those of your wolf,' Falk continued. 'I have it easy with Selsena in that respect. Titejunanwas are as intelligent as humans in their own way – and they aren't hunting animals. You, on the other hand, have to deal with all the usual problems that come with a companion animal.' His master was smiling again, and he stroked Culhen, who groaned contentedly in response.

Ahren was secretly pleased that he wasn't solely responsible for his actions. Ever since the incident in the mill he had been at a loss to explain how he had lost control so completely and had found the experience deeply shocking.

Pondering all this, he put the remains of his stew on the floor, where Culhen gobbled it down at lightning speed. 'But what about Jelninolan? How come she almost became a murderer?' he asked. Now that he had an explanation for his own behaviour, he wanted to understand what had happened to the compassionate priestess.

Falk exhaled and closed his eyes for a moment. 'You know how magic has an effect on its creators? Fighting magic makes them aggressive, healing magic makes them passive, and so on?' he asked.

Ahren nodded and the old man continued. 'If the sorcerer is exhausted, just as Jelninolan and Uldini were in the last few weeks and especially after saving Culhen, then they are in a particularly vulnerable state. If they then take on too much, or something throws them traumatically off course, then you have an Unleashing. That's what you saw.'

'An Unleashing?' repeated Ahren, confused.

'When creators of magic deliver magic directly from their emotions. That almost always occurs involuntarily and is a sign of complete exhaustion or extreme aggression, which is why it often manifests itself in an excessive deployment of destructive magic. Occasionally an Unleashing is deliberately created, mostly as a last resort. It hasn't happened with Jelninolan since the Dark Days. Unleashings are far too unpredictable' said Falk darkly. 'When she heard that a villager had poisoned Culhen – a gift from her goddess – well, that led to this Unleashing, mild and all as it was. You were finally able to bring her back to her senses with your words.'

A cold shiver ran down Ahren's spine. If that was a mild Unleashing, he really didn't want to experience a fully-fledged one. 'How else can you deal with one, apart from using words,' he asked curiously.

'The normal practice' said Falk in a serious tone 'is to run away.'

Ahren had a restless sleep that night. He dreamed of lightning flashes, of mists and of an all-swallowing abyss. In the middle of this bubbling chaos sat Jelninolan, and she was smiling at him good-naturedly.

The sounds of busy hammering and sawing filled the air, drawing Ahren irresistibly towards them. Thaw had begun to set in a few days earlier, and by the previous afternoon the remaining snow had disappeared from the meadows, with only a few stubborn remnants of snow remaining in the spots that the sun hadn't reached. The retreating winter led to an explosion of activity in Deepstone, and as soon as the first delicate signs of spring were in the air, the first repairs, which had been agreed upon between the various families during the winter months, were put into effect. Almost everybody was roped in and helped as much as they could – even Uldini could be seen slowly floating a heavy beam down onto the butcher's house, whose roof had been a victim of Jelninolan's Unleashing. Hardly had the beam been set on the ridge when half a dozen villagers were hammering away, ensuring that the beam would be firmly fixed in place as the butcher cheerfully called out his gratitude to Uldini, who responded politely before moving on.

Ahren was so surprised by Uldini's behaviour that he approached the Arch Wizard and examined him curiously. 'You're in a very magnanimous mood today,' said the apprentice delightedly.

'Stop gawping at me as if I were a five-legged calf. I'm just undoing the damage that Jelninolan caused. In more than one respect,' he snorted in a low voice and scowled grumpily.

Then they arrived at the next house and the smile reappeared as if by magic on the childlike face of the Arch Wizard as he used all his charms and asked how he could help.

Ahren dropped back and shook his head in bemusement at the Ancient. Uldini would undoubtedly never change. He alone in their group had the ability to smooth the waves in a politic manner.

The young man ran past the busy activities of scurrying villagers and was approaching the mill, only to be astounded by what he saw in front of him. Trogadon was standing there, stripped to his waist and was just shoving an enormous stone into the newly constructed wall of the large building. Eight villagers were lending him a hand and were trowelling mortar into the gaps. There was little sign of the jagged hole that the elf had ripped out of the mill in her rage. In its place a stone porch stood proudly, built of a wonderfully intricate arrangement of newly mortared stones.

As Ahren approached he could hear Trogadon's booming voice, which echoed a merry song in the Dwarfish tongue down the hill. Ahren couldn't prevent himself from smiling and he was filled with deep affection. A day never passed without Trogadon's joie de vivre infecting him. He walked swiftly up to the thickset figure and swallowed hard when he saw the massive bundle of muscles which were constantly rippling along his broad Dwarfish back as he worked away. The proportions of the Little Folk generally appeared alien to humans, and the strained broad torso on the warrior's thickset legs gave him an almost square shape as he shoved a heavy stone into the appropriate gap in the wall. The fact that he still had enough breath to sing was the icing on the cake.

'A nice song,' said Ahren, by way of greeting. 'Can you sing it in the Northern language as well?'

Trogadon gave the stone one last shove and it slid into place with a grating sound. Then the dwarf turned around to face Ahren and gave him a broad grin. Sweat was dripping from his long beard, whose normally carefully braided plaits were hanging down to his belly button in a dishevelled manner. The dwarf would usually tie the plaits behind his back with his other hair, and this unexpected sight made Ahren grin.

'I'm not sure how appropriate that would be,' he answered with a side glance at the villagers who were standing around listening to them. 'It's about three young damsels, a merchant and his cart.'

Ahren shrugged his shoulders. 'Sounds very pleasant.'

'The four don't use the cart for travelling,' said the dwarf and gave the apprentice a mischievous grin.

The young man knew the warrior well enough by now to understand what he was suggesting. 'I think you might be right regarding the appropriateness, sir.'

Trogadon gave a loud guffaw and slapped Ahren on the back with his powerful hand, causing the young man to gasp out loud. 'Enough of this formal address, boy. You are a Paladin of the gods, and I am a simple dwarf. No need to "sir" me!'

The apprentice wanted to protest; after all, the person he was speaking to was at least two hundred years his senior and also bore an Ancestry Name – one of the names of the revered heroes of Dwarfish history. Only one living dwarf could lay claim to such a name at any given time, and although every member of the Little Folk strove to get the proverbial name for themselves, only very few managed it, and so Trogadon's accomplishment was remarkable, to put it mildly. But when Ahren looked at the friendly face with all its laughter lines, his resistance cracked. 'Whatever you think, friend,' he said, trying out his new privilege immediately, and when the dwarf nodded in recognition, Ahren's chest swelled with pride. This was the first time that any of the others had treated him as an equal, even if it was in the small matter of a form of address.

Distracting himself from his emotions, Ahren pointed at the porch. 'A fine piece of craftsmanship. What gave you the idea?'

Trogadon shrugged his shoulders. 'Dwarf pragmatism. We always made necessity into a virtue. I asked the miller family if I could improve anything now that I was repairing the damage. They had an old stone shed that wasn't up to much, and after a lot of humming and hawing, they asked me if I could build a storeroom onto the mill out of it.'

Then he lowered his voice. 'Uldini told me to make myself as useful as possible so I used a few tricks of the trade that you don't find outside the Dwarfish caves.' He tapped on the stone approvingly and added: 'Worked out well, didn't it?'

Ahren was about to respond when he caught sight of a plump figure who was conscientiously pushing mortar into a wide gap. Asla, the miller's wife, was kneeling five paces away at the new wall, trying to make herself as inconspicuous as possible.

With a lump in his throat and his hands dripping with sweat Ahren went over to her and struggled to find the words he needed to apologise for the worry and damage he had caused to her home and family.

Yet before he uttered a single word, the blond-haired woman burst into tears and began to speak in a broken voice. 'There's no need, Ahren. I know who is really to blame,' she sobbed. My Sven should never have harmed poor Culhen, even his father says the same. The wolf was always such a good animal and now he's even a Messenger of the goddess, and to do it in such a cowardly underhand way, with poison...' she broke off, convulsed in sobs of shame. Ahren tried to calm her down.

'Culhen is well again. And I'm sorry that I lost control of myself.' He faltered in dreadful fear of the answer to his next question. 'How is Sven? Did I injure him very badly?'

The memory of the boy's battered face had haunted him ever since, and up until this point he hadn't found the courage to ask about the young man's condition.

'The priestess visited us last night. She too wanted to ask for forgiveness for her deeds, and she healed my boy while he was sleeping. His right arm will continue to be stiff and his feet will be largely useless, but at least she was able to reconstruct his face and legs half-way decently.'

Ahren gasped in shock. He couldn't imagine how much damage he and Jelninolan had inflicted if the elf's powerful healing magic had proven so ineffective. Then he remembered that the priestess was in a severely weakened state and would have at her command very little power until she fully recovered herself. That meant that Sven would just have to live with his injuries for the moment. Without even noticing, Ahren began to feel pity for the young man. Not even the memory of Culhen's suffering could stop him from speaking his next words. 'Perhaps Keeper Jegral can help?' he suggested hopefully. The priest of the human god, HE, WHO MOULDS, had treated Ahren's broken hand that time and had healed it through magical powers. Without that kind deed, the young man would never have succeeded in becoming Falk's apprentice.

Asla shook her head and began crying again. 'He's refusing. Culhen is a sacred animal, sent by the THREE to help you fight against HIM, WHO FORCES. He said he wouldn't use the magic of the gods to help a malefactor.'

Ahren stood there thunderstruck. The other workers had retreated a respectful distance and Trogadon had retired inside the porch to continue his work there. Only he was standing there with Sven's mother, broken by grief and shame.

It was only then that Ahren fully understood the extent of the disgrace that Sven with his cowardly deed had wrought on his family. The apprentice still looked on Culhen as his loyal wolf, albeit one who could speak to him now thanks to the Blessing of the goddess. As for the rest of the world, the animal was a symbol, a sign that the Thirteenth Paladin had returned and a walking wonder. The miller's son could hardly expect help, and somehow that seemed right, thought Ahren sadly.

'I could ask the village council to let him stay,' he tried again, but again Sven's mother shook her head. 'His father never wants to see him again. The fact that he's still under our roof is only down to his injuries. I do have one request of you though.'

Ahren nodded quickly. 'Of course. Anything,' he said quickly.

'If I could apologise to Culhen? He should know that we regret our son's deed,' she said meekly.

Ahren stopped himself from sighing and from contradicting her. He wanted to tell her that an apology was unnecessary, but he realised that Asla need to make the gesture for her own peace of mind. 'Of course, I'll call him,' was his answer, and he carefully got into his friend's mind. Culhen was in the middle of his morning nap, which he always took after an opulent breakfast, and Ahren had learned to make good use of that time, when he was alone with his own thoughts. But this time he didn't waste a heartbeat and sent out a soft call.

His spirit was immediately filled with joyous excitement as the young wolf leaped up and bounded off enthusiastically. The apprentice could hear the animal barking with his ears, and he couldn't resist a grin. Culhen had been practising the sound – rarely used by wolves – over the previous few weeks after he had noticed that humans in the vicinity reacted by stroking and feeding him. It wouldn't have surprised Ahren if Culhen were to imitate a cat's purring if it increased his chances of getting food.

The wolf came storming up the hill, his tail wagging furiously, and he leaped joyfully up at Ahren. Because the animal on his hind-legs was even taller than the apprentice, he had learned to avoid his wolf's giant paws before he had a chance to throw him backwards to the ground and pin him down.

Calm down boy, was the message Ahren sent to him, and at the same time gestured to him to stop with his hand. The apprentice had found the combination to be very effective and had decided to use words and gesture as a temporary solution until Culhen's understanding had sufficiently developed.

The wolf sat down on his hind-legs and gave Ahren a questioning look while tilting his head. Meanwhile Asla, who had sunk down onto her knees and was sobbing uncontrollably, cautiously stretched out her hand towards the animal.

Comfort her, please, said Ahren softly in the head of his friend. Then he sent an image of a she-wolf, mourning for her cub.

To Ahrens relief, the wolf understood immediately and began whimpering and licking the woman's hand, all the while gently rubbing his head against her.

Out of the corner of his eye Ahren could see the villagers standing around, observing the scene with great interest. Erring on the side of caution he spoke loudly and clearly. 'Culhen forgives you and your family for the deeds of your son. Neither the wolf nor I can find any fault in your behaviour.' Then he lifted the miller's wife to her feet, and she looked at him gratefully before he spoke again. 'You are true servants of the THREE and should be treated as such.'

Asla collapsed into his arms, sobbing gratefully, and the apprentice was glad to see compassion for the miller's wife in the faces of the villagers who were observing the scene. Ahren might not be able to save Sven, but at least he had spared his family from being ostracised within the community.

'That was a big-hearted gesture,' said Trogadon as Ahren entered the porch. Lina, Sven's sister and an old flame of Ahren's, had led her mother into the house, whispering her gratitude to the apprentice in the process. Then the young Paladin had fled into the mill to escape the looks of the other villagers, leaving Culhen to bask unashamedly in their admiration.

Ahren shrugged his shoulders in embarrassment. 'It was only a few words.'

'Yes, but they were important and soothing,' said the warrior insistently. 'I patched up stone and wood, but you healed the hearts of the poor people. Word of this will spread like wildfire and do Deepstone a lot of good.'

Ahren looked doubtfully and asked himself if the dwarf might not be exaggerating things a little.

'Think about it,' said the broad figure with unusual seriousness. 'Small communities such as this can be very resentful, and smaller transgressions than Sven's have led to terrible feuds.'

Ahren had to admit that there was something to what the dwarf had said. Now he was doubly pleased he had helped the miller's family. Then his face darkened. 'I can't help Sven though,' he said grimly.

Trogadon's eyebrows flew upwards. 'Do you want that at all? After everything he's done. Falk says this wasn't the first time he's harmed you.'

Ahren chewed his lips and looked deep into his own heart for a moment. 'I think I do. He's been punished enough. Jelninolan and I punished him severely, and now the village has sentenced him to banishment. Nobody should have to pay three times for his deed.'

Trogadon looked at Ahren with pride and appeared at that moment like an undersized grandfather. 'Never forget this lesson. Ideally you two would have dragged Sven before the village council, you and Jelninolan would have accused him there, and he would have been sentenced according to the rules of the village. One sentence, one punishment.'

Ahren vowed never to forget the dwarf's words and gave a determined nod.

'Cheer up,' grunted the dwarf. 'When it comes down to it, you protected him from Jelninolan. If I'd laid my hands on the lad, he'd be dead now.'

Chapter 5

Ahren walked in a daze towards the threshold of the mayor's house. His mind was taken up with what he had just experienced, and he was pondering Trogadon's words when he pushed open the heavy door before realising what he was doing.

The room was quiet and empty, and the abandoned table around which they had so often sat looked strangely different.

The apprentice stood in the main room, hesitated and looked at the stairs that were situated at the other end and led up to the elf's bedroom. It had been his earnest desire to talk to the priestess about what had happened in the mill, but as it had been a subconscious decision, his courage now failed him.

He was on the point of turning back to leave when he heard a sound on the steps and Khara came swiftly but lightly bounding down the stairs. She had Wind Blade in one hand, and she stopped suddenly when she recognised him.

'I was asking myself who would slip in here without saying a word, but I should have known it was you,' she said crossly and loosened her grip on her weapon.

'I don't even know why I'm here myself,' said Ahren, attempting to explain himself with a rather lame excuse. But Khara simply shook her head, tossing her long hair.

'Stuff and nonsense!' she barked. 'Of course, you know why you're here, and so do I. I think my mistress has been waiting ages for your visit.'

Ahren shifted uncomfortably from one foot to the other and only the swordsgirl's piercing look stopped him from hotfooting it out of the room.

His resistance finally cracked, and he nodded acquiescently. 'It might help both of us,' he said, more in an attempt to persuade himself.

Khara gave him an encouraging look, as if to a little child who was just taking his first steps, and the gesture put him into a rage that eclipsed the uneasy feeling that had been weighing so heavily on him. The stairs seemed to stretch endlessly upwards as he clambered up one step after the other until he finally reached the darkened first floor. The curtains were drawn across the windows and the short corridor was only dimly lit through an open door on the left, the three closed doors being on the right.

Ahren was trying to figure out where Jelninolan had retired to when he recognised a familiar sound in his head. A sad, melancholy melody seemed to be unfolding within his very mind, and the apprentice realised that the elf was playing on Tanentan, the soundless lute. This elfish artefact was powerful, and the priestess used it, among other things, to influence the mood of people within hearing distance. She had a healthy respect for the power of the magical instrument, and the fact that she was using it to help herself didn't bode well regarding her emotional well-being.

The young Paladin sensed that the lute song was coming through the open doorway, and so he walked through it, cautiously knocking on the door frame to announce his presence.

Jelninolan was sitting in a crouched position on the floor of the darkened chamber, which must have served as the sleeping quarters for the mayor's late wife. The colour shades of the modest furnishings were elegant, yet also warm and friendly as if reflecting the deceased mayor's wife herself, who Ahren vaguely remembered, and who always had a friendly word for everyone.

Jelninolan didn't look up - her eyes with a faraway look in them, were focused on the lute strings. 'Sit down, Ahren,' was all she said, but her voice had an undertone of urgency, and so the young man did as he was told. He sat facing her on the floor, and finally the priestess looked up.

Her pupils appeared pitch-black in the diffuse light of the darkened room. A strong feeling of unreality came over Ahren's perception and he felt himself being sucked in by the elf's gaze.

'You want to understand,' she whispered, and Ahren nodded uneasily. He could hear the suppressed emotions of rage, self-reproach and doubt in the elf's voice, and he couldn't help asking himself how close she was to another Unleashing. He was shocked to realise that at that very moment he was terrified of the kindly priestess.

'I think we can help each other, but it will cost us,' said Jelninolan conspiratorially, and the young Paladin immediately became nervous. What was she planning?

'I can show you a memory, even share it with you completely. Tanentan will carry us back to the time of the Dark Days, and you will understand what it means to experience a true Unleashing.' She raised her hand as he was about to respond. 'It won't be an enjoyable experience, but it will help you to understand, and sharing it with somebody will help me to break the power it still has over me after all this time.'

She sounded terribly fragile, and at that moment he felt a deep compassion for the gentle, warm-hearted woman who had helped him time and again over the previous moons. He would have done anything for her, and so he nodded firmly and without hesitation. 'Show it to me,' he whispered, and the elf strummed the strings of Tanentan. Ahren's world collapsed like a house of cards.

The first thing that struck him was the pungent smell of smoke in his nostrils - it was all pervasive and engulfed his senses, which seemed blurred and unclear. He was under the control of Tanentan's magic to a degree he had never experienced before. When the priestess had called forth the memories concerning the rescue of the Voice of the Forest that time during the festivities in Eathinian, the effects had been as light and unobtrusive as a feather. Whereas now, the images were a raging maelstrom, blinding out everything else. Ahren felt the heat of smouldering fire, and all he could see were billowing clouds of smoke until his sight slowly grew accustomed to what was around him, and he was able to find his bearings.

He seemed to be looking down directly on the scene that the lute wished to show him, and the new perspective made him dizzy for a moment. Jelninolan was standing there with half a dozen soldiers in the middle of a ravaged battlefield, which had to have been a village at some point. The details of the memory were concentrated on the area immediately surrounding the elf, whereas the happenings further away were nothing more than blurred images. In the distance Ahren could make out undulating hills which reminded him of the Borderlands, and it seemed to be a hot summer's afternoon. Not only did he smell the acrid smoke, but also the sweat of the soldiers, and everywhere he could see bodies lying in various degrees of mutilation, the sight of which made him nauseous. Many hundreds of dead humans and several lifeless elves were to be seen amongst the slaughtered Blood Wolves, incinerated Fog Cats and a strangely bloated Glower Bear. Ahren understood that a fierce battle had taken place between warring parties who had been equally matched in ruthlessness.

Jelninolan was staring with a glassy look at the dead bodies and the burning buildings. In each hand she was holding a chain wrapped around her wrists and stretching out at least eight paces. Most of the heavy metal links were lying on the ground engulfed in white-hot flames, and the ends of the two chains seemed to be squirming like blind worms. The brutally destructive force emanating from the two chains seemed so alien to the elf who was holding them that he had to look twice to convince himself that it was she who was manipulating those murderous implements.

'Mistress, we are the only ones left, and the Keketuktur is coming inexorably closer!' pleaded one of her companions to Jelninolan. Ahren couldn't make out the details of the heavily armed person under the visored helmet, but he heard the frightened and exhausted voice of a young woman. 'We must stop it or it will attack the king's cavalry from behind, and the entire west flank will collapse,' she persisted as she pleaded with the priestess.

Jelninolan could only nod wearily. Ahren saw that some of her ribbon armour was missing where the leather bands had been torn through by sharp claws or raw violence, and blood was seeping from several wounds and into her clothing.

'The chains have become heavy,' she said finally. 'I don't know how much longer I can control them.'

'You have to!' cried the soldier, horrified, and the helmets of the other soldiers nodded frantically.

Before the elf could respond, a house literally burst at the edge of the memory, and a creature, the like of which Ahren could never have imagined even in his worst nightmare, stormed directly through the ruins. It seemed as large as a house, with two massive heads closely aligned, each having enormous floppy ears and a wormlike trunk ending in sickle-like bone spurs. The six-legged creature was completely covered in dull-grey scales, and Ahren calculated that the monster weighed as much as a good twenty full-grown oxen. Without hesitating, it trampled through the burning remains of another house before proceeding to charge at Jelninolan and the little group of soldiers.

Whatever it was the elves wanted Jelninolan to do, she still hesitated, and so two of them fearlessly threw themselves forward and stabbed their spears into the flanks of the on-charging Dark One.

The trunks swayed almost playfully left and right, sweeping the thick wooden weapons aside and boring its bone spurs into the unfortunate soldiers. Without slowing down, the Keketuktur raised the skewered warriors up into the air and slung them right and left into the burning building.

Once again, a nauseous feeling overcame Ahren, but he was so much within the grip of the memory that he could not look away.

Jelninolan uttered a cry of despair, which brought the chains to life in a most peculiar manner. The thick iron limbs rose up from the ground and whipped their way forwards like metal snakes and wrapped themselves around the necks of the enormous creature with their white flames and they slowly burned their way through the scales, the metal links tightening evermore with a scraping sound, strangulating the monster and cutting off its air supply.

Worse yet than the fire and the overwhelming power of the grinding metal were the waves of dread that suddenly seemed to emanate from the two weapons. The Dark One had clearly sensed them too, for instead of trampling Jelninolan to death, it was trying desperately to free itself from her and the two unholy weapons that had so suddenly embraced it. Its legs as thick as trees planted themselves in the ground, twisting the body of the Keketuktur around so that Jelninolan made a leap through the air as she was pulled forward. To Ahren's amazement, the elf landed with both feet so firmly in the ground that she created deep furrows in the earth as she braced herself and her magic against the massive weight of the monster.

'The chains are getting too heavy!' she repeated. 'I have to charm them!'

'You can't do that! Too many lives are on the line!' implored the soldier.

Jelninolan looked from the woman fighting beside her to the Dark One, which was still trying to free itself from the chains, and in a fit of madness had ground three further ruins to dust as it grappled with the magic shackles.

The chains were becoming blindingly white and Ahren could hardly make out the surrounding details in the blazing light.

'Run!' screamed Jelninolan in an agonised voice. 'Run for your lives!'

The remaining soldiers reacted immediately, throwing their weapons to the ground in an attempt to flee more quickly, but within a few heartbeats, he saw in horror how their attempts to reach safety had come to nought.

Jelninolan sank down on her knees, and with her head bowed she started murmuring words in Elfish which quickly reached a screeching crescendo. Then she threw back her head, and her eyes were ablaze with the same white fire that surrounded the chains. One last outcry came from the mouth of the priestess before the whole area was ablaze in a searing forest of flames. Ahren heard the stifled screams of the soldiers also caught up in the wall of heat and light, just as was everything else within a two-hundred-pace radius of the elf, who was now slumped over. People, corpses, houses, the Keketuktur itself simply ceased to exist as the invocation incinerated all around it.

Only a blazing white was to be seen for several heartbeats and then the magic was over. Jelninolan was squatting in the middle of an enormous circle of fine ash which covered the area, and within which there was no sign that a village had once stood there. The chains had vanished, and when Jelninolan stood up sobbing and stumbled away towards the east, her footprints in the ash were the only clues that at one time people had been there, who had lived, loved and fought.

Ahren gasped for air when the memory came to an end. It was as if he had come to the surface after an eternity under water. He breathed deeply and sought to come to terms with what he had just seen. Jelninolan had stood up and drawn open the curtains, enabling the sun to do its work and bring warmth back into the room. Ahren closed his eyes in gratitude and basked in the invigorating rays as they reflected off his skin, their golden hue so different to the destructive white of the Unleashing magic. He opened his eyes and looked into Jelninolan's gentle, smiling face.

'Thank you so much, Ahren, for allowing me to share this burden with you,' she said in a warm voice. 'We elves always share our pain and our emotions with one another in order to modify their force, and I had buried this one here deep inside myself for far too long.' She stretched out like a cat in the sun. 'If you have any questions, don't be afraid to ask them,' she said in an easy manner.

The transformation in the elf was a little too much for Ahren, but he knew from experience that her folk dealt with emotions in a different way to humans and so he tried to pull himself together.

'Did you know what was going to happen before the Unleashing?' he finally blurted out.

Jelninolan shook her head. 'The results of an Unleashing are completely unpredictable. Even with ones that are intended, like the one you saw. It doesn't matter which magic you are performing under their influence, whether it's battle or healing magic, the side-effects are chaotic and always extremely dangerous. With a bit of luck, the soldiers could have escaped. But the magic could have just as easily swept through the country, destroying other villages. I had to protect the army whose flank we were guarding. Otherwise I would never have taken the risk,' she explained.

'What sort of chains were they?' asked Ahren fearfully.

'War Chains.' Jelninolan's features darkened. 'A charm of steel, fire and fear. Luckily, we elves don't use them anymore.' An undertone of disgust had crept into her voice.

Ahren compared what he had just seen with what had happened in the mill. 'We were all lucky then, weren't we?' he asked quietly, and the elf seemed to understand what he was referring to.

'Yes, we were. Even Sven,' she said sombrely.

'Have you often experienced Unleashings?' he asked.

'Four times,' said Jelninolan quietly. 'But this winter was my first unintended one. The other three occurred during the Dark Days and two of them were in battle. Every time it was the last option, every time the price was high, and every time it was others who had to pay.' Her voice was raw. 'This Sven fellow can count his blessings that you intervened when you did.'

Ahren shuddered. 'At least I protected you from the guilt of having killed him,' he said comfortingly.

The elf looked at him in astonishment. 'You've misunderstood me. I would have killed him even if I *weren't* unleashed. Culhen is a companion animal, a gift from my goddess. Causing him deliberate harm is, according to Elfish standards, justification for an immediate execution.' She looked out through the window towards the sun. 'My regret concerns my failure to use an Unleashing immediately in order to free Culhen from the poison. I was afraid of the consequences it might have for the whole village. I put you into danger in order to avoid an Unleashing, only to then lose control when I reacted to a worm like that.' She looked pleadingly into Ahren's eyes. 'Please forgive me...it's only that so much could have gone wrong. I might have burned the life out of Culhen's veins if I were in the Unleashed Condition. Or the ferocity of the magic might have damaged his spirit. I just didn't want to risk that.'

The apprentice realised in astonishment that Jelninolan was looking for forgiveness. 'You did everything correctly,' he said hastily. 'Culhen and I are very grateful to you.'

Relieved, she nodded, and again looked out the window at the merry comings and goings of the busy villagers as they went about their work, calling out to each other and laughing.

Realising that those were the words the elf had been waiting to hear, Ahren stood up, embraced her once again heartily and was delighted to see how much life had returned to her eyes. Then he left the room without a word, passed Khara, who looked at him in puzzlement, and went out into the bright sunshine with its hint of springtime. Jelninolan had wanted to impart an important pearl of wisdom to him and had unwittingly revealed to him something else as well. Now he not only understood the dangers of an Unleashing, but also how vulnerable unprepared villages were, once they came under sustained attack from Dark Ones.

Likis beamed when Ahren and Holken entered the little trading shop in which the young man and his merchant father supplied the whole village with all the coveted everyday necessities that had been brought in by the pedlars as they passed through Deepstone. Fine cloths lay neatly stacked on wooden shelves, and here and there were items of clothing. There were also the exotic metal goods which the local blacksmith hadn't manufactured, and some pieces of jewellery glittered through the glass doors of a wooden cabinet. Ahren was convinced that the ruby ring on its top shelf had been lying there ever since he could remember.

Likis was wearing his merchant status symbol with pride, and Ahren had to admit that were it not for the quiet confidence his friend exhibited when wearing it, the sight of the yellow felt hat with its hanging point would be nothing short of ridiculous.

Likis came around from the back of the counter, gave Ahren a quick hug and clapped Holken playfully on the shoulder. 'What brings the two of you here? Can you not wait until I close up shop?' he asked and smiled.

'I asked Holken to come along,' said Ahren firmly. He had seen the bailiff among the villagers at one of the building sites and had waved him over. It said something for their friendship, and for Ahren's growing authority, that the bailiff had followed him without question. 'You both know that the Dark Days are going to come back,' he began and looked at his friends expectantly.

Likis nodded and Holken frowned. 'Now that you've been named the Thirteenth Paladin, it's staring us in the face. Why are we talking about it?' he asked uneasily.

'Because Deepstone is only five days away from the Borderlands. And because you have no town wall. You have to build one,' said Ahren quietly and simply, as if he were talking about the weather. The image of the eradicated village in Jelninolan's memory had shaken him to the core and he was firmly convinced that the same fate awaited his home village if preparations weren't made. 'Otherwise Deepstone won't survive the oncoming Darkness.'

Ahren's intensity and the emotional impact underlying his quietly spoken words knocked his friends for six. They both held onto the counter for support, and Ahren saw how the dreadful truth was gradually sinking in. 'We'll be completely overrun if a horde of Dark Ones swarms through here, won't we?' said Likis and looked towards Holken.

The bailiff swallowed hard and nodded. 'We're only two bailiffs with short swords. What can we do?' he said darkly.

'Without effective defences Deepstone will fall with the first attack,' announced Ahren bluntly. He found it hard, jolting his friends out of their comfortable existence in such a manner.

'Why are you giving us this information?' asked Likis in an accusing tone. 'How are we supposed to rectify the situation?'

'Pramsbildt is blocking every attempt by Uldini to discuss the upcoming war. It seems that the thought of renewed hostilities against HIM, WHO FORCES is too much for him and he prefers not to think about it. Uldini says he's come across that sort of behaviour more than once, sometimes even with kings,' said Ahren in a low voice. After his encounter with the Pallid Frog he had spoken to the Arch Wizard and made him promise to make the mayor discharge his duties to the village concerning defensive measures. But to no avail. 'An attitude like that has never ended well. I've come to you because I trust you. Holken is already a bailiff and you, Likis, have always had the best ideas. Maybe the two of you can think of something that will make Pramsbildt change his mind in the coming years. You still have a little time.'

A heavy silence lay over the room. Likis alternated between staring up at the ceiling and glancing at Ahren accusingly, while Holken tapped the ground with his foot as he ruminated. The apprentice saw with regret how he had burdened his friends with the task he had given them, and looked at them searchingly as they struggled to come to terms with what he had said. He said nothing of the elf's memories. They were too private to share, and his promise to Falk prevented him from telling them of the Pallid Frog. Ahren hoped the young men would be sensible enough to follow his advice and not bury their heads in the sand the way Pramsbildt was doing.

At last Likis's face came to life. 'I suppose I could apply myself a little and help the mayor in some of his less pleasant duties,' he pondered. 'He'll begin to trust me more and more, and when the time comes, I can make an appropriate suggestion to him or the village council. If Holken, as one of the bailiffs, can support my ideas, then our word should carry enough weight to persuade the village.' The merchant's voice had taken on a thoughtful, calculating tone, and Ahren remembered again what the old women had said in those days about the rascal Likis – that his cheek would either earn him banishment or the mayoralty. Ahren smiled in relief and thought to himself that his friend was concentrating now on earning the latter.

Likis and Holken were now in a lively discussion concerning tactics, and the young Paladin recognised that their ideas were good and could ensure Deepstone's survival in the long term. He was amazed to see how well they harmonised with each other, and it pained him to realise that he had nothing more to contribute, so he hugged them both and stepped out onto the street, leaving his friends to continue making their plans.

The first spring rains swept over the land and enveloped Deepstone in a blanket of rain which remained for two days. It was late afternoon and Ahren was sitting with his future travelling companions, while the crackling fire kept the damp cold at bay outside. The Spring Ceremony was only a fortnight away and it was time to make their travel arrangements as they intended departing the day after the festival.

Ahren hadn't seen Jelninolan since their meeting in her room, and but for a slight tiredness, the elf was in better condition than he had anticipated. Khara too was sitting at the table, and Ahren was surprised to recognise that he had missed the presence of the unyielding swordfighter. He gave her a smile and indeed she actually smiled in return.

What Likis achieves in one afternoon, you succeed in doing after more than half a year, he thought self-ironically and he was rewarded with a yawning laugh in his head as Culhen reacted to his mind. Their communication was still limited, but the wolf was beginning to grasp Ahren's more complex thoughts, and he had at least a better understanding of their intentions, if not necessarily their contents.

A further indication of Culhen's continuing development was that he sent Ahren a memory in response of Culhen sitting surrounded by half the villagers of Deepstone, who were looking at him in admiration. *Everybody likes me* was the thought from the animal that he picked up.

Show off! thought Ahren crankily in the direction of the wolf, who was lying at his feet under the table and gave a derogatory grunt before curling up further into a ball.

'Luckily for us Justinian has gone for an honest-to-goodness siege of the Brazen City' Uldini was just saying, which brought Ahren back to the here and now. 'Apparently, he wants to keep the damage and losses to a minimum – after all, ideally he needs the forges to be intact. He's clearly hoping that a few moons of starvation will bring the citizens to their senses, and they'll open their gates.'

Falk looked up at the ceiling and considered for a moment. 'We should be there in three moons to stop this madness. The city should have enough provisions until then,' he said with relief.

Uldini nodded in agreement. 'And not only that, I've let the Sun Emperor know through several reliable sources that I am returning to the

Sunplains. He didn't believe the messengers when it came to Ahren's Naming but at least there will be an official escort waiting for me at Waterheart that will bring us directly to the Sun Emperor.'

Trogadon whistled through his teeth in appreciation. 'That sounds really good for starters.'

Uldini grinned triumphantly. 'I agree. With a bit of luck, we'll already be a Paladin richer this summer.'

Ahren and Jelninolan exchanged doubtful glances and the elf shook her head almost unnoticeably. She didn't, it seemed, share the little Arch Wizard's enthusiasm, but didn't want to destroy the rare moment of optimism that Uldini was experiencing.

'Incidentally, after your midnight excursion, I informed the Wrath Elves, who are patrolling the Borderlands about the pool, and told them to keep an eye out for Pallid Frogs. Since then they've found and killed another five of the beasts, all on the eastern edge of the Borderlands. It seems that the Adversary had ordered the frogs to enter Hjalgar and to spread out so that he could bring the western part of the kingdom under his control. The Wrath Elves know how to prevent this. Hjalgar's king cares little about the security of his border. Otherwise Ahren's discovery would have earned at the very least a medal. It saved a third of his kingdom.'

Trogadon and Falk slapped Ahren on the back and Jelninolan looked at him with maternal pride. Even Khara seemed impressed, and the apprentice almost believed she was going to congratulate him when she opened her mouth to speak. 'We should tell Likis what we are going to need for our journey. Anything that he can't rustle up here in Deepstone, he can get them from the surrounding villages if possible, or from Three Rivers.' The girl had successfully changed the subject and Ahren felt he had been robbed of his moment of glory.

'Good idea,' said Falk. 'I'll look into that as soon as I'm back from the March of Exile.'

As soon as Ahren had heard his master's words, ice water seemed to flow through his veins and the Pallid Frogs were forgotten. 'Is it already time?' he asked, aghast.

Falk nodded earnestly. 'The village council wants Sven out of their sight as quickly as possible, so that everybody can have done with the business, and the Spring Festival can take place as harmoniously as possible. And Jegral is refusing to carry out the ceremony as long as a malefactor is living within the community. As Forest Guardian, I will lead him to the eastern edge of the forest, and he can start his exile from there.'

Ahren remembered that Falk had been obliged to carry out that task once before several winters previously. The idea that his master would accompany Sven on his final march from Deepstone did not seem right to the young man.

'I'll do it,' he said suddenly. 'I'll accompany Sven into his exile.'

There was a stunned silence as the others stared at him. Finally, his master spoke in a hoarse voice. 'Boy, are you sure you want to do this? It's a difficult task and Sven hates you to the core.'

Ahren nodded firmly. 'It's a problem between him and me which has only caused heartache. Maybe I can get through to him on the march, or at least understand why he did what he did.' The apprentice still couldn't put into words what had been done to Culhen, not since he had confronted Sven with his deed. 'At the very least it should be me who brings him through the forest,' he concluded darkly.

'Tradition only states that the Forest Guardian undertakes this task. It shouldn't bother the council whether it's the master or his apprentice. Particularly since you and Culhen are the injured parties in the matter.'

Culhen had by then understood what they were talking about and threw in a harsh 'woof.'

'He wants to come too,' said Ahren, translating his companion's somewhat muddy thoughts.

'I'll inform the village council,' said Falk and stood up. As he went past Ahren he placed a hand on his shoulder. 'Prepare well. You need to head off very early.'

Ahren nodded haltingly as it slowly dawned on him what he had let himself in for. He would accompany a young man that he had severely injured out of the homeland he would never see again. The apprentice reminded himself that it was Sven's attempted poisoning of Culhen that was responsible for his fate, but it made the weight of his upcoming task no less heavy.

It was only the looks of the others at the table, a mixture of pity and pride, that prevented him from leaping up and saying to Falk that he had changed his mind.

The rest of the conversation passed Ahren by. He was caught up in his own thoughts which concerned themselves completely with the following day.

The rain was relentless. Ahren was already soaked through by the time he got to the village square, and the murky morning's dark clouds promised no better. Culhen trotted beside him, his tail hanging, and sneezed grumpily from time to time. An accusatory tone emanated from his thoughts.

Wet. Hungry, resonated in Ahren's head.

He ignored the wolf and the rain as much as possible and concentrated instead on the five figures approaching slowly from the other side of the square.

Mayor Pramsbildt seemed as little pleased at having to be out as Culhen, and his wet moustache hung wilting from his wet face. Likis was walking beside him. The merchant's son had clearly used the opportunity to take the first steps in becoming Pramsbildt's right-hand man by volunteering to help out in this unpleasant task. Every so often the village head would throw him a grateful look. It seemed that Ahren's friend was wasting no time in implementing his plan of making a name for himself in the village, and the thought gave the apprentice courage in the miserable morning rain.

The third person was leaning heavily on two crutches, the bandaged feet were positioned in helpful leather gaiters that were cut open at the sides to make room for the bandages. A heavy woollen cloak hid the rest of the figure, but it was clear to Ahren that it could only be Sven. He swallowed hard and forced himself to look at the other two people who were to the right of the condemned young man. Asla and Lina were walking with slumped shoulders beside Sven, and Ahren couldn't say if their cheeks were laced with raindrops or tears. Every so often Sven's mother would look at her son sorrowfully, but Lina just stared ahead in a strangely emotionless manner. Ahren was surprised to see that she was wearing a short wrap made of mica silk which covered her shoulders. This robe was worn by the Novices who would later become Keepers, the priests and priestesses of HIM, WHO MOULDS.

The five finally arrived at the waiting apprentice and Lina answered his unspoken question. 'I've decided on the life of a Keeper, and Jegral was kind enough to take me on as a Novice.'

Ahren could only nod in surprise but understood the unspoken message behind her words. It wasn't unusual for a family member to enter the Church if a malefactor had resided within the family's four walls. Rumour had it that Keeper Jegral himself had taken office for just such a reason. The god of people seemed to find favour in the fact that his servants might manifest themselves out of a supposedly bad turn of events and mould a better future for themselves and others.

Sven clearly saw things differently. He spat out the word 'traitor!' in her direction in a low voice.

Lina's face froze, but Ahren gave the young woman credit for not flinching at her brother's utterance.

Mayor Pramsbildt cleared his throat. 'We hereby hand over Sven, the miller's son, into your custody. Accompany him to the border of the Eastern Forest and take care that he makes no attempt to return. He is banished from Deepstone for life. Should he, however, set foot in his homeland again no word shall be spoken to him, no door shall be opened to him, and no help shall be given him.' Then he looked at Ahren expectantly. The village leader clearly wanted the leaving ceremony to be as short as possible and kept the traditional address to a bare minimum.

Ahren glanced at Likis, who gave him an encouraging smile. 'As the village council wishes,' said the young Forest Guardian simply, and took a step back, indicating to Sven that he should start moving. Culhen gave a low growl, and Ahren telepathically ordered him to be quiet. The wolf clearly understood who was standing in front of him, and the animal's rage helped the apprentice to remain steadfast and to defy Sven, who looked at him unsteadily with eyes full of hate.

A memory flashed through Ahren's mind – of Culhen, who had been just as unsteady as he staggered on the very same spot in the village square, gripped in the poison that was raging through his veins. The young Paladin used the memory to steel himself against the oncoming hours when he would be going on a slow march beside this man who had afflicted Ahren and Culhen so grievously.

Sven limped painfully away from the village square with Ahren escorting him, neither saying a word. The apprentice looked back and saw Pramsbildt heading straight for the tavern and trying to persuade Likis to join him. The merchant's son was looking keenly at the mayor while Lina was holding her sobbing mother in her arms. The miller's daughter glanced quickly at Ahren and her look was inscrutable.

'Are you happy now?'

Those were the first words Sven had uttered since they had left Deepstone that morning. They resonated with so much bitterness and accusation that Ahren stopped dumbfounded for a moment. The rain was still falling on them and it eclipsed all the other forest sounds. The young Paladin looked at the exiled youth in puzzlement. 'Why should I be happy?' he asked, confused.

'Look what you've done to me,' cried the one-time miller's son in a voice that suggested he had lost his reason. He yanked the hood off his head. Ahren could now see that Sven's face was peculiarly misshapen. His eyes were no longer on the same level...they seemed somehow crooked. Jelninolan really had to have been at the end of her healing powers. It was true that she had performed a fundamental charm that had saved his life, but apart from that, it was clear she had been unable to do anything else for the exile.

Ahren gasped when he understood the consequences of his outburst of fury and heard the self-righteous complaint in the voice of his fellow traveller.

He struggled to keep his cool. He was boiling with rage inside, and this emotion was strengthened by Culhen's disgust. The wolf saw Sven as the enemy who was to be fought.

'Sven, I really didn't care about you at all until one month ago,' began the apprentice in a cold voice. 'If you hadn't poisoned Culhen, none of this would have happened. Maybe you should think about what you've done to everyone else. Your petty and malicious attempt to do me harm almost cost Culhen and me our lives. Instead it's made you an exile and a cripple and caused your family endless grief.' His first words may have been spoken quietly but now Ahren was screaming his complaint out into the forest. He had to give vent to his rage and frustration in order not to attack Sven again. Standing in front of him was the physical result of his loss of control. Sven's physical appearance was testament to his failure that time to find a peaceful solution to the conflict, initially so insignificant, between himself and the miller's son. If he couldn't even manage to prevent a rival from his younger days doing him damage, but instead allowed things to go out of control, then how could he possibly save Jorath?

How was he supposed to live up to his self-imposed aspiration to save as many as possible from the looming Darkness?

'They should all have supported me! He's only a wolf, dammit!' Sven was almost screeching as his voice cracked. 'He was a Blood Wolf! A Dark One! And now everyone is treating him like a lap dog! And the drunkard's son is a Paladin all of a sudden? Don't make me laugh!' he gave a throaty, horrendous cackle, the sound was unnatural and had nothing to do with human merriment.

Ahren was shaking from head to toe and grimly held on to Culhen's fur to stop himself from leaping forward and ploughing into the hate-filled exile. At the same time his firm grip was preventing Culhen from doing the same. Somehow, he could not find his way into the young man's inner world, a world in which the exile blamed everyone else but himself for his failings, and who despised everything he didn't know or understand.

Ahren retreated mentally from his opponent, his anger dissipated and was replaced by a deep calmness. He didn't need to understand him. All he had to do was not hate him anymore. His task was to protect him and all other members of the free peoples, no matter how he felt.

He had to be a Paladin.

Sven recoiled when he saw the change in Ahren's facial expression. His own face betrayed confusion, and for a moment the young Forest Guardian was tempted to explain the situation to the outcast.

But Sven had already made it clear that he didn't believe in Ahren's role, and anyway, it wasn't necessary. Ahren himself would protect him from the dark god, even if the exile hated him.

The night had been long, wet and cold. They had made painfully slow progress the previous day on account of Sven's crippled feet, and Ahren calculated that they wouldn't reach the edge of the forest before late afternoon. They were sitting under the dense foliage of a royal oak, eating their cold breakfast, and Sven's breath was making a worrying rattling sound in his chest. Ahren had offered him a tea to counteract the oncoming cough, but the condemned young man had thrown the brew onto the ground with a scornful look.

Now Ahren was gazing out into the forest, enjoying the first signs of the aromas of spring which suggested the beginning of blossoms coming to life. He listened contentedly to the melodic sound of raindrops as they dripped down from leaf to leaf, each one singing its own song to anyone who wanted to listen.

Ever since he had reached the decision not to hate Sven, his view of the rainy forest had altered completely. His deep love of nature, which he had internalised under Falk's steady guidance, enabled him to recognise the beauty all around him, and also to tolerate the constant revulsion exhibited by his captive, who continually threw him murderous looks and quiet threats which he managed to wheeze out between his coughing fits.

Culhen too had been moved by his master's transformation and was now sniffing the ground as he wandered through the forest instead of constantly growling at Sven. Any discontent the wolf felt now was caused by the animal's hunger. How could it be otherwise?

'We need to get moving,' announced Ahren finally. Sven had tried testing him a few times and had cursed him violently, but the Forest Guardian had remained calm. It was clear to him that the exile was trying to cover up the truth concerning his own deeds with the loudest possible histrionics.

When they had been attacked by an angry mob the previous year that had wanted to lynch Jelninolan because they had irrationally blamed her for the burning down of a granary, Ahren had asked himself afterwards how the farmers had been able to scream and shout in such a rage. The elf's answer had been short and to the point. 'Those who shout loudly enough will not hear the voice inside themselves.'

That summed up Sven at that moment. The more he blamed Ahren for his situation, the more pity the young man felt for the poisoner.

Sven was hoarse when the eastern edge of the forest came into view. His tirades and the worsening cough had affected his voice, and now he could hardly speak.

The limping figure was moving ever more slowly and Ahren walked patiently by his side, not saying a word. Sven had to stop repeatedly as they neared their destination and it was almost dark when they passed the final trees.

'Herewith begins your banishment. Return no more to Deepstone,' said Ahren quietly, intoning the ritual words. At that point he was not permitted to speak to Sven anymore and had to leave him to his own devices, but the apprentice couldn't square that with his own calling as a Paladin. And so he did what he could to help the convict begin his new life in exile. He looked fixedly ahead and pointed into the dusk. 'A few hundred more paces to the east and you reach a trading path. One or two traders pass by every day.' He reached into his rucksack and pulled out a small bundle. 'Here are some provisions, an oil cloth to protect against the rain and some tea against the cough. There are also fifty gold coins sewn into the bottom of the bag, and with that you can start a small business if you're clever.' He still didn't look at Sven as he threw the bag a few paces in front of him. 'Hjalgar laws forbid me from helping you. But if someone picks up a bag that they find on their journey, there's nothing I can do about it.'

Sven stared at him malevolently, and Ahren decided that he'd had enough of his counterpart's hatred. He looked at the bitter young man one last time, then he turned his back on the unrepentant youth and trotted back into the depths of the forest. Culhen gave one last defiant howl, and the outcast was left alone with his hatred.

Sven stood there stock still and perched on his crutches until the night had fully enveloped the forest. A fit of coughing overcame him and he cursed as he grasped the bag in front of him. Then he stumbled out of the forest, grateful to the darkness that was hiding his broken body.

'I thought you might need company,' a voice intoned from behind a tree.

Ahren smiled thankfully as his master appeared into view and leaned against a tree trunk with a questioning look on his face. The young Forest Guardian had marched through the night, lost in his own thoughts. Culhen had stayed close by his side and had tried to interpret what Ahren had been thinking. Now it was noon, and Deepstone could only be another half a league away, but still the young man was grateful that his mentor would accompany him the rest of the way, and he gave his master a friendly nod.

Falk walked beside him and said nothing at first. Instead, he ruffled the wolf's fur and eyed his apprentice keenly. 'Something happened, didn't it? Did he cause trouble?' asked the old man uneasily.

Ahren hesitated, then shook his head. He ducked under a low-lying branch and wiped the rain, which was still falling continuously, from his face. By this time Ahren was freezing cold and soaked through, for the tricks of the trade that belonged to being a Forest Guardian could only keep the rain out for so long, and now he was looking forward to nothing more than a blazing fire and a cosy blanket. He tried to find the words that would explain the truths he had discovered but he found it hard to formulate them out loud.

'I wanted to help Sven for the wrong reasons,' he began in a halting voice. 'Somehow, I wanted to undo what I had done, to fix his arm, to make his face go back to normal. I wanted to make everything good again, but not to make him feel better. I just didn't want to feel guilty anymore.' Those thoughts had enabled him to walk right through the night and now it felt good that he was sharing them with his master. 'But I am a Paladin. It's my duty to help, no matter what I feel or what the other person thinks of me,' Ahren said, explaining his new insight. Then he peered over at the old Paladin walking silently beside him and stroking his beard.

'It's important that you've learned this, Ahren,' said Falk. 'But you've set the bar very high, and of course you might fail. Helping somebody for helping's sake is good and right. And it's just as important to recognise that sometimes you can't undo your mistakes. The best you can do there is to learn from them, so you don't repeat them.' Then the big man laid an arm on his student's shoulder as they continued walking. 'But you must take care that you don't get caught up in the web of your own responsibilities. You made a great effort to help a man who almost had you and your wolf on his conscience, and all Deepstone has seen what you have done, good and bad. But even here, there are over a hundred friendly souls residing. What do you think they would have thought if you had expended all your energy helping a troublemaker while ignoring their cares and troubles?'

Ahren stopped, dumbfounded, and stared at Falk with wide eyes as his master continued.

'You do have a responsibility towards creation, that's true, but if you're going to straighten every blade of grass that you've stepped on, you'll end up trampling down a whole field.'

Ahren was about to protest, but Falk raised a placatory hand. 'It's good that you tried, but Sven didn't want to be helped. You have to husband your strengths. Otherwise, good people will suffer. Weighing up when and where to help is the hardest part of our job.'

The old Forest Guardian walked on, and Ahren followed him pondering.

'By the way, Likis told me about his idea of giving Pramsbildt a hand,' said Falk in a casual voice. 'You inspired him there. If what he and Holken are planning works, then you will have saved a whole village thanks to one conversation. That's something worth thinking about.'

They walked the rest of the way in silence. Ahren's head was spinning as he tried to digest all that had happened over the previous weeks and days. It seemed as if with every lesson he learned, he was always presented with two new ones.

Chapter 6

The Spring Festival lived up to its name. The weather had brightened up considerably the previous week, and little fleecy clouds were floating across the blue sky, while the first rays of sunshine were warming the land below. The whole of Deepstone had been splendidly decked out once word had spread that the village's guests of honour, as well as two real-life Paladins, would be participating. Keeper Jegral had mingled with the villagers in a state of excitement, recruiting dozens of volunteers, so that the Spring Ceremony which launched the festival would be something really special. In all likelihood he wouldn't have managed everything without the assistance of his new initiate Lina, but it seemed that the young woman was flourishing in her new vocation. None of the villagers could refuse the pretty face that peeked out from under the wrap with its mica silk as she asked in a soft and friendly voice for little favours – a cake here and a helping hand there – which, when all gathered together, turned into quite an amount.

The village square was bedecked with garlands and ribbons. Poles as tall as a man were put in place, each one carved and exhibiting inspiring spring motifs.

Every villager wore the best clothing they could find in their chests at home, and there was a boisterous festive mood in the air. All the destruction of winter, including the damage done to the village through the storm invoked by Jelninolan, had been remedied, and thanks to Trogadon's mortar, nobody had fallen victim to the Blue Death.

Ahren looked around at all the happy faces, and his eyes were drawn to Lina with her calm smile as she invited the villagers to visit the chapel.

'She's very pretty, isn't she?' said Khara beside him. She had just arrived and was wearing a dark green, elegantly flowing dress that Jelninolan had made for her.

'You're right, that's true,' said Ahren absently. All in all, her stay in Deepstone had done her more good than bad, he thought, blissfully unaware of the sharp tone in the swordfighter's voice.

'She's certainly the prettiest girl in the village, isn't she?' she asked icily.

'By far,' said Ahren, still lost in thought.

Culhen was sending him waves of unease, and this distracted him further. *Danger*, cried the wolf, and Ahren looked around the square, not understanding what the wolf meant.

'Likis told me that you kissed each other once. Was it nice?' chattered Khara in a voice that contained enough ice to bring on the winter again.

'Wonderful,' replied Ahren abruptly as he continued to look around. Culhen was relentlessly abusing him with warning signals, but with the best will in the world Ahren couldn't see any danger.

'Well, that's great. I'm looking forward to our next training session,' said Khara curtly and hurried away.

Culhen yelped and covered his eyes with one of his paws. Ahren looked down at him in confusion and then at the departing Khara. What on earth had happened?

Ahren heard a guffaw behind him before Trogadon came up to him and slapped him on the back. 'Boy,' he said and there were tears in his eyes. 'If you carry on like that, the dark god will have no chance of killing you because your own mouth will have been the death of you long before then.'

The dwarf walked away, still laughing uproariously, leaving the baffled Paladin standing there with his giddy wolf, who was rolling around on his back and barking up at his master joyfully.

The beginning of the Spring Ceremony was very harmonious. It seemed as if all the villagers were eager to leave the wounds of winter with all its consequences behind them, and when Jegral officially announced that everyone had survived the winter, the congregation burst into a round of applause, and there were many shouts of thanks aimed at Trogadon. The dwarf even blushed for the first time since Ahren had known him, and it was a delightful sight to behold. The young man would have enjoyed everything that was happening were it not for the fact that Khara was ignoring him for some reason. Also, Likis, who was sitting between them, kept glancing at Ahren with looks that veered between pitying and smirking.

He would ask his friend what the matter was after the ceremony, but the main part of the devotions was about to begin and the young Forest Guardian concentrated on the upcoming ritual. The next part was why they had remained for so long in the village.

Jegral called forward those who had completed their fifteenth winter and requested them to lay their hand on the triangular stone in the middle of the altar while they pronounced the oath of the THREE, through which they became fully fledged members of the Deepstone community. This part of the tradition was still apparently important enough to be retained this year even though no Paladin was to be chosen. Today there were three girls and one boy, and as they stood at the front, they kept glancing over at the guests of honour.

One after the other they placed their hand on the gods' Stone and spoke the ritual words, and then they sat down again. Ahren couldn't help holding his breath although it was clear to him that nothing would happen. When he had touched the stone the previous year, there had been an almighty flash of light – the long-forgotten sign that identified the future Thirteenth Paladin. Ahren shook off the sense of unreality that gripped him. So much has happened since then and yet it's been only a year, he thought to himself in amazement.

Then Jegral summoned the guests of honour up to the front and bowed low before them. Uldini and Jelninolan to the left and right of the gods' Stone and placed their fingertips on it so that they could replenish their energy on this day of the gods. The elf in her bright green garment, which also today had the addition of white lace and an equally bright scarf, looked like the slim, hauntingly beautiful and graceful counterpart to the bald, black-robed and almost bored looking Arch Wizard, who floated in an almost careless manner beside the altar and was pulling a disinterested grimace.

Keeper Jegral came to the end of his long litany concerning the gods, and Uldini's face came to life. He and Jelninolan closed their eyes and quietly moved their lips while the stone under their hands began to pulse a deep green, which caused an astonished murmur among the congregation. Every time the stone lit up, the two Ancients seemed to blossom further, to become stronger and more upright. The gods' Stone pulsed a warm green more than a dozen times before the light disappeared and the two conjurers opened their eyes. The green light appeared again in their eyes and once again a murmur went through the crowd. Then the effect vanished, and the chapel was still again when Uldini and Jelninolan each stretched out a hand and gestured Ahren to come forward.

The apprentice was unusually nervous although his experience had been considerably worse the previous year. Yet somehow this strange reliving of the last Spring Festival really got under his skin. The previous year he had had no idea of what lay in front of him, but this time it felt as if his participation meant accepting any tasks that would be required of him in the future. These thoughts were flashing through his mind as he approached the gods' Stone and looked down at the unadorned artefact lying there innocently and harmless, and yet which had turned Ahren's world on its head. He stretched out his right hand, and Uldini muttered in a low voice. Ahren gave him a questioning look.

'Better use both hands. Let's err on the side of caution so we won't have to come back next year.' And he wiggled his ears to such an extent that Ahren had to giggle in a most unceremonious manner.

Then he drew a deep breath and placed both his hands on the stone.

There was light everywhere.

Ahren could hear and see nothing other than a penetrating whiteness that seemed to be burning into the very centre of his existence. For a brief moment Ahren thought he saw three enormous sleeping silhouettes, which were radiating an incredible power. Ahren thought he recognised a human, an elf and a dwarf, but then the light was gone and Ahren was blinking in the warm light of the spring sunshine which was blazing through the chapel windows. Disorientated, Ahren looked around and could see that everyone else had also been as blinded by the light as he. Yet he couldn't recognise the deep reverence that filled him at that moment in their faces, and he was sure that he had been the only one who had seen the three figures in the light.

Uldini gave him a knowing smile, and Jelninolan embraced him quickly. Then the three returned to their places and Keeper Jegral, who had been visibly moved, solemnly brought the ceremony to an end. Likis and Falk embraced the apprentice heartily and everything was perfect –

apart from Khara's murderously offended look, which still puzzled Ahren.

'Did I really see the gods earlier?' whispered Ahren to Falk in disbelief as they sat down at one of the long tables that had been set up outside on the village square.

Falk nodded thoughtfully and murmured: 'In fact, that should have happened during your Naming. We think it was blocked by your other visitor that night.' Falk was referring to the attack by HIM, WHO FORCES, who had mentally attacked Ahren in the middle of the Naming Ceremony. It was only thanks to Tlik's self-sacrifice that Ahren had been able to escape from the sorcerous grip of the dark god. He alone had enabled them to flee once the ritual had been completed.

'So, you also saw them at your Naming?' asked Ahren enthusiastically. It had been an overpowering experience, and the fact that his master had also been privy to the vision of the gods connected him even closer to the old man, who had been his mentor for three years by now.

'The one and only time,' responded Falk in a rapt voice. 'All Paladins experience this. It's something that connects us all and gives us strength in the darkness.'

Then he raised his voice to its normal volume. 'Congratulations on achieving your sixteenth winter, Ahren' he said in a formal voice and shook his hand vigorously. In no time at all the young man was surrounded by well-wishers, and Ahren recognised the self-satisfied look on Falk's face. His tactic for escaping the situation had worked. Falk hated emotional moments, and now he was chuckling, relieved that he had got out of this particular one.

Likis pushed his way in front of Ahren and they both congratulated each other. The slight young man had been standing beside him when the stone had chosen Ahren, and the apprentice was glad he could share this day with his friends once again. Holken, Likis, Khara and himself quickly sought out a table in a secluded corner and huddled together although Khara still refused to look at him. Ahren decided to ignore the girl for the time being. Today was his last chance to be with his friends, whereas he would have plenty of time on the journey to calm down Khara. She gave him a chilly look and at that moment Ahren reckoned that the following few weeks would be far from easy.

Something must have retired into his mouth to die, and it seemed to him as if Trogadon was using his head as target practice for his mighty hammer blows. There was no other explanation for the sensations that were engulfing him as he woke up with a groan. He remembered that Holken had somehow managed to lay his hands on several bottles of mead during the course of the feast day and they had got stuck into them over the following few hours. At some point Khara, on whom the mead had no effect, suggested a fiendishly complicated drinking game, and Ahren had only a hazy memory of anything that happened afterwards. There was something about having to hit one thing with another thing, and if you missed, you had to drink. Something like that. The more he thought about it, the more his head hurt. He opened his eyes in an effort to distract himself, regretted his mistake immediately and closed them quickly when the pounding headache inside his skull multiplied itself many times at the sight of daylight.

He heard whining beside him and he reached out a hand. He could feel the familiar fur under his fingers. So, Culhen was lying right beside him. The wolf reacted by sending powerful waves of annoyance and grief back to Ahren. *Bold Ahren*, he said in the young man's head, and the tone of voice was exactly the same as what the young man used in the forest when he was scolding the wolf.

Ahren curled up into a ball as he began to feel nauseous, and he made every effort to hold onto the contents of his stomach. If he were to throw up now, his head would explode completely.

Sorry, big lad, was the message he laboriously sent back, and he tried to sense his friend's condition. Culhen was clearly suffering his master's pain too, although to a lesser degree. The apprentice felt guilty that he was putting the animal through this, but once he realised that he felt better when he concentrated on Culhen's imagination, he stayed for a while in the wolf's head and enjoyed the alleviation of his own pain. Culhen was calming down too, now that he, for his part, wasn't receiving so much suffering from Ahren.

Ahren was just considering the possibilities that this discovery presented, when directly beside his ear a marching band began to play.

At least that's what it sounded like when Falk called out: 'So this is where you've been hiding. Why don't you come out of there so that people can get their furniture back? A Paladin of the gods who makes a child's fort out of the feast day tables isn't exactly an impressive sight if you get my drift.'

Despite his pounding head, Ahren opened his eyes and forced himself to keep them open. The pain was a little more bearable thanks to his concentrating on Culhen's thoughts, but logical thinking had become more difficult. All around him he saw upturned tables and benches that had been formed into a makeshift circle with him in the middle. Some of the longer tables had been stacked in such a way that they formed half a roof. The upper half of Falk could be seen through an opening in the structure. Behind his master, Ahren could see the old oak tree which dominated the village square and had formed the fulcrum around which the festivities had taken place. Ahren gathered himself together for a moment and was about to answer Falk when he spotted, much to his irritation, Wind Blade ensnared in the top of the tree. How did that get up there?

He blinked owlishly and hauled himself slowly up onto his feet.

Falk seemed genuinely surprised and gave an approving nod. 'Didn't think you'd be capable of standing yet.'

Ahren scowled and staggered a little as he pursed his lips. Speaking was going to be difficult, but he tried it anyway. 'In Culhen's head. Better,' he responded glibly. Then he scrambled over the wall of benches in front of him and stood up as straight as he could in front of his master.

The old man stroked his beard and looked amused. 'So, you've discovered that you can help each other out, if one of you is in trouble. It's actually designed so that you can ignore the pain coming from an *injury*, but of course this gift of the gods also comes in useful if you have an ordinary *hangover*.'

Falk's satirical comment was wasted on Ahren. Instead, the young man nodded and gave a silly smile as his dulled understanding had only picked up that his master had praised him.

The broad-shouldered Forest Guardian rolled his eyes and grabbed Ahren by the neck in order to push him forward. 'We'd better knock you into shape. There's no point in chiding you when you're like this. You don't understand what I'm saying.'

Ahren let himself be pushed along until they arrived at the next water trough. Within a heartbeat he was lying in the cold water, his head being firmly kept under the surface by Falk's powerful hands so that the fog in his understanding was driven out by the shock. The old man's method was as ruthless as it was efficient. Every so often he would allow his apprentice a brief moment to breathe before pushing him down into the freezing liquid again. Finally, he let go of the young man who sat up gasping and looked accusingly up at his master, his head still splitting. Falk looked down at the hung-over young man unmoved and handed him a waterskin. 'Drink it all. The herbal stock will ameliorate the remaining effects of the alcohol. But you'll just have to put up with the headache. That will disappear on its own.'

Ahren forced himself to put the waterskin to his lips. If there was anything he really didn't want to do at that moment, it was to drink. But the threat in Falk's voice suggested that if he didn't do as he was told, he would spend half the morning in the trough, so he swallowed the contents as quickly as possible.

His stomach threatened to rebel, but Ahren ignored it as much as possible. Then he gave the waterskin back to Falk and stood up slowly. To his dismay he could see over half a dozen villagers watching him in amusement, and he went scarlet with embarrassment.

'Good, at least you haven't forgotten to be ashamed,' said Falk in a satisfied voice. 'So tidying up should be no trouble to you. The good citizens of Deepstone will be delighted to have your assistance, don't you think?'

The old Forest Guardian's tone of voice was perfectly normal, but Ahren knew his master well enough to understand when any protest whatsoever would lead to terrible consequences. And so, he nodded acquiescently and repaired to the village square again.

Ahren and more than two dozen villagers spent the rest of the morning clearing up after the Spring Festival. He gave a hand wherever it was needed. He carried tables and benches, swept the ground, and brought down his weapon from the top of the oak, quickly strapping it on and enduring the amused looks of those around him.

'It was a bet,' he heard behind him and the voice suggested that the speaker was in agony.

Ahren turned around and saw Likis, standing there in his crumpled robe, sweeping a particularly filthy spot with a birch broom. The slight young man's felt cap was placed inside out on his head, yet nobody, it seemed, had taken the trouble to inform him of this. Even Ahren couldn't help smiling at Likis but stopped when he imagined what he himself might look like. He went over to his friend, righted his headgear without saying a word before asking quietly, 'a bet?'

Likis nodded thoughtfully. 'Who'd be the quickest going up and down the tree. The loser had to drink something.' The young merchant grimaced. 'That was your idea by the way. After we'd finished Khara's game. And you lost anyway. Your blade got snarled and you just left it in the tree.' His friend shivered. 'I'm never touching another drop of mead again.'

Ahren could only agree with him when suddenly hunger pains came over him. 'Culhen's woken up,' he said with a sigh. 'I'd better look after him. The poor thing had to suffer some of my pounding head.'

Likis grimaced again. 'Oh no, hopefully he won't bite you. I know I would if I were him.'

They smiled at each other with tired faces, and Ahren went over to the white wolf, who was just having a good stretch. The animal had used Ahren's work for another nap and now he was raining down demanding thoughts interspersed with accusations of having missed breakfast on account of Ahren.

The apprentice emitted apology after apology before setting out to organise the biggest portion of meat in the village he could find.

It was already late afternoon when they were finally ready to leave. The whole village had gathered to bid farewell to the travel party, and Ahren had just given Likis, who was halfway back to normal again, a big hug.

'Don't forget what we talked about,' he whispered to his slight friend, and looked knowingly towards Pramsbildt who was wishing Uldini a safe journey in a most self-important manner.

Likis gave a conspiratorial nod. 'You can rely on me. Holken has been keeping an ear out among the village youth to see who might like to become a bailiff next year. He wants to enlist a few apprentices who he can form a militia with before the trouble in the Borderlands hits us.'

Reassured, Ahren nodded and mounted his horse, a good-natured mare with several years under the saddle. Much to the disappointment of Falk, who was a skilled knight and therefore an accomplished rider, his apprentice had no talent whatsoever for the art of horsemanship.

Everyone was still talking, so Ahren took the opportunity to place his hand on Selsena's soft white coat. The Titejunanwa was standing beside him, shimmering silver in the sunshine, and she looked at him with her good-natured gentle eyes.

'I missed you, my dear,' said Ahren quietly. 'Thank you for telling us where we could find the Fire Weed.'

He would have liked to have said more, but he was on the point of tears because of saying goodbye to his friends, and he didn't want to be completely overwhelmed by the emotions he was feeling.

Selsena transmitted her affection empathically and Culhen gave a bark before nudging up against the Elfish charger. The unicorn's enjoyment of Culhen's youthful exuberance was mixed together with the wolf's gratitude and joy in Ahren's head, and the young man rubbed his temples in an effort to concentrate.

'Still got the hangover?', asked Falk in a low voice as he mounted the unicorn and settled into the saddle.

Ahren shook his head. 'When Selsena sends me emotions, and Culhen wants to communicate something at the same time, then it gets pretty full in here,' he said in a pained voice and pointed meaningfully at his head.

His master frowned and looked down thoughtfully at the wolf, who was jumping around with excitement. 'It's time that you learned to isolate yourself. In that way you can minimise your connection if necessary. You can practise that while we're riding along. It's the opposite of what you were doing this morning. Instead of trying to anchor yourself as much as possible in Culhen's spirit, you try to gather your thoughts within yourself, as if you wanted to lock yourself away in your own head. Try it a few times, then you'll understand what I mean. It's as if you're changing your own perspective. You'll only know how it works once you've done it.'

Ahren nodded hesitantly and decided not to try out the experiment until they were on their way.

'Do you want to call into Edrik before we travel?' his master asked carefully.

Ahren looked at him darkly before giving a determined nod. 'I paid my debt to him when I found him in a drunken stupor in the snow and carried him into the house. I gave the innkeeper gold yesterday to cover food expenses, but a talk with him would do neither of us any good.' The young man still hadn't forgotten the horrific vision the Grief Wind had presented him with - that of a possible future under the thumb of his alcoholic father. The memory made him tremble. 'As far as I'm concerned, my proper father nearly drowned me in a water through this morning.'

Falk laughed at Ahren's wording. He was moved by what his apprentice had said and looked at him for a moment before fleeing from his emotions into a conversation with the mayor. There were some things about the old man that would never change.

Ahren looked around and saw Trogadon, who was extricating himself from a throng of single women, all of whom seemed agitated at the fact that he was leaving. The warrior's broad arms were overflowing with presents, and with booming laughter he retreated to the stocky horse that Likis had organised for him.

'He always did that in the old days,' grumbled Falk, who had finished his conversation with the mayor. The apprentice asked himself if his master was jealous of the man from the little folk, who made friends so effortlessly. The old man caught Ahren's searching look, and the apprentice quickly focussed his eyes elsewhere.

Khara was just bidding farewell to Likis and Holken by kissing them both on the cheek, which didn't exactly improve the young man's mood, considering she was still ignoring him.

He quickly looked away and noticed Uldini floating over his horse's back in a most striking manner. The little figure glanced around. 'Are we all ready then? Where's Jelninolan?'

Heads turned in search of the elf, and Ahren realised that he hadn't seen her at all that day.

He had hardly spoken to her since her Unleashing, and he'd had an uneasy feeling concerning her well-being for weeks. Both Uldini and Falk had reassured him that she had fully recuperated, but now her absence made him feel uneasy again.

'I'm here!' called a voice from within the mayor's house. Jelninolan appeared at the door, wrapped up in her travelling clothes and her Elfish ribbon armour. She was holding an engraved circular object in her hand,

and she walked towards the group with it. 'It all took a little longer than I'd expected,' she said by way of excuse. Ahren could now see that the circle was some sort of collar, formed like a delicate snake. The clasp was the head, so that when it was closed, the snake was biting its tail.

Jelninolan knelt down. 'Culhen, my dear, come over to me,' she called to the excited animal. Ahren's own curiosity was mixed with that of the wolf, who trotted over to the priestess, sniffing the air. She placed the collar around him and uttered a single Elfish word, which caused the clasp to glow red for a moment. Then she smiled at the wolf affectionately and stood up. Culhen sat back on his hind legs and tilted his head and Ahren listened carefully to him.

The collar fitted perfectly and was so light that Culhen hardly felt it. Ahren was convinced that the piece of jewellery was magical, and he wondered how long Jelninolan had been working at it.

It feels good, he heard the wolf communicate. The animal looked up gratefully at the elf, and she ruffled the top of his head while Uldini addressed her.

'That's an Elfish Animal Blessing, isn't it?' he asked in disbelief. 'Did you not take on a little too much there? How did you get it done so quickly?'

The elf laughed. 'I cheated a little,' she said mischievously. 'I carried the collar under my clothing during the ceremony yesterday. When we touched the godstone, I used our connection to the THREE to fill it with magic. I just had to finish it early this morning and then adjust it so that it would fit Culhen.'

Uldini was flabbergasted, and Jelninolan looked down at Culhen with a look of satisfaction. Then she mounted her horse and glanced around her. A look of sadness came over her face for a moment when it seemed as though she hadn't found what she had looked for.

Ahren could imagine who she had been hoping to see. The tanner Jorek had been avoiding Jelninolan ever since her Unleashing and hadn't turned up to say goodbye.

Finally, the elf shrugged her shoulders and jutted out her chin. 'Shall we leave?'

Her travelling companions nodded, and they set off on their mission to free the Paladin Bergen from the besieged Brazen City, waved off by the good citizens of Deepstone.

They rode along the Eastern Forest in a southerly direction. Ahren would have liked to have given his surroundings more attention on account of the fact that he didn't know when next he would be returning. But the rest of the day was pure torture for him, and his attention was otherwise engaged. Culhen was so proud of his collar that he kept circling Ahren's horse or standing in front of it, blocking the way until Ahren would assure him how wonderful he looked. Unfortunately, the wolf was constantly seeking out new ways that the praise could be expressed, and whenever the apprentice wasn't putting in enough effort, the wolf would bombard him with feelings of deep grievance.

'What's the point of that collar at all?!' Ahren cried out in a moment of frustration. 'Does it just force wolves to exhibit conceited behaviour or does it serve any other purpose?'

Uldini chuckled and turned his head towards the young man. 'Don't underestimate Jelninolan's gift. The Elfish Animal Whisperers use these collars to honour the best of their animal allies, and also to reinforce their strengths. Culhen will become a little faster, stronger and larger. Also, smarter if I'm not mistaken.'

'And above all else, his body will become more immune to poisons and illnesses,' said Jelninolan without elaborating, but everyone knew what she was referring to.

Ahren had understood the priestess only too well. The collar was undoubtedly a safeguard against Culhen falling victim again to the perfidy of any other malicious person.

Suddenly the apprentice was confronted with a terrible thought. 'Does that mean...,' and he swallowed hard before managing to finish his question, '...he's going to be hungrier?'

'Oh dear,' responded Jelninolan with embarrassment, 'I never thought of that.'

Culhen licked his chops as the first waves of hunger rolled over the young man and the wolf began whining for food.

More than four weeks passed by in delightful harmony and the omens were good for a wonderfully mild onset of spring. They continued to ride south through sleepy Hjalgar, whose luxurious woodlands and rich meadows offered a beautifully peaceful view, and they would settle down for the night in tiny hostelries, or in the barns of wide-eyed farmers who would give their exotic guests as wide a berth as possible. The familiar routines of travelling, training, and sleeping helped Ahren to come to terms with the changes that were taking place within his head. He taught his reason to turn its attention towards, or away from Culhen, and so he could strengthen their connection or weaken it if necessary, so that he could only perceive the wolf within his head as a weak impulse. To his amazement the wolf learned to do exactly the same. A few times in fits of pique they cut each other mentally off, and it didn't take them long to realise that loud calling would always penetrate through to the other. They became familiar with the fact that their connection had its own dynamic, which varied according to the moods of both wolf and apprentice. Ahren was pleased to realise his subconscious seemed to be taking control over the intensity of their connection to an ever-greater degree, so that Ahren could direct it as naturally as he could the movement of his arm.

Falk was delighted with their progress, and one evening when they were sitting around the campfire, having found neither hostel nor farmhouse to sleep in, he took his apprentice aside. 'I'll let you practise for a little longer, and then we'll begin training your bond for battle. If you have Culhen's impressions at the back of your mind and can prepare without being distracted by them, then you'll have a distinct advantage in every skirmish. This is how Selsena and I are always able to work in harmony when we ride into battle. Culhen can cover your back or reconnoitre for you, whatever the situation requires.'

Ahren's eyes lit up, but his master immediately brought him back down to earth. 'It will take some time to get to that point. First you have to learn not to be distracted by him. And then you have to learn to reclaim the Void. After that we'll see.'

Falk retired to sleep, leaving his apprentice staring into the fire and pondering over what he had just been told.

Chapter 7

The ambush was quick and efficient. No sooner had Selsena warned Falk that people with perfidious intent were in the vicinity, than the first armed figures stormed out of the undergrowth left and right of the trading path and towards them. The travelling companions had only just broken camp, and the sun was still low in the cloudy spring heavens so that only occasional rays were striking the undulating landscape here and there. They were riding through the depths of the forest in whose canopy they had rested the previous night, but now twenty fierce-looking men and women were pointing their weapons at them.

Ahren had been ambushed by bandits once before, but these ones seemed different. He followed Uldini's and Falk's example by raising his arms chest-high and making no effort to reach for a weapon, at the same time studying the aggressors intently.

They were all wearing more or less matching leather armour with studs situated for protective purposes. All of them were bearing crossbows that were aimed at the group, and the apprentice could also make out shields on their backs and swords on their belts. Each bandit also carried some kind of red-and-white material on their clothing. Some of them had made head coverings out of it, while others had a scrap of material tied to their arms or legs.

The young Paladin glanced at Falk in an effort to find out what to do, but the old man simply shook his head. 'Too many crossbows,' he murmured. 'We'll be bloodstained pin-cushions long before the wizards have a chance to create a shield.' The grey-haired Forest Guardian turned to Uldini. 'All they want is gold. If they had wanted to kill us, Selsena would have sensed their intentions a lot earlier and warned us.'

'Mercenaries,' said the Arch Wizard dismissively. 'We might be able to buy ourselves out of this one.'

Jelninolan placed a hand on Khara's forearm. The ex-slave had instinctively clutched Wind Blade. It went against the girl's nature to give up without a fight, and Ahren understood where she was coming from.

Trogadon, on the other hand, was sitting at ease on his saddle and nodding approvingly. 'First-rate ambush. Clean and professional execution.'

Ahren stared at the dwarf in astonishment.

'What's up?' asked the dwarf when he saw Ahren's face. 'We dwarves appreciate good workmanship when we see it.'

Once it had become clear that there wasn't going to be any fighting, a woman dressed completely in white and red came out from behind a tree. She was holding two remarkably curved short daggers in her hands. The woman was extraordinarily scrawny, and her blond hair was shaved on either side.

'You've been caught in the deadly web of the Red and White Loom,' she called out in a threatening voice. 'Give us all your gold if you value your lives!'

Ahren was amazed at the mercenary's pompous way of speaking, and he leaned over to Falk. 'I'd say more like a red and white loon,' he whispered in disgust.

Falk frowned and gave a warning look. 'Be quiet. These people are very easy to antagonise. The most important thing in an ambush is to intimidate your victims. A suitable name can work wonders in this respect.'

The old man sounded as though he were speaking from experience, and Ahren remembered once again that his master had gone through a dark period in his life and had mixed up more than once with mercenaries at that time. That was how he had got to know Trogadon over a dozen decades previously.

'Falk, would you be so kind?', murmured Uldini. It was clear that the Ancient didn't want to reveal himself, and anyway, no mercenary would negotiate with what he believed to be a ten-year-old.

'Ah, the burdens of being old,' said Falk in a low voice, and gave a quick grin at the Arch Wizard, who pressed his lips together in fury.

The Forest Guardian instructed Selsena to trot forward a few paces, and then he spoke in a loud voice. 'We all seem to be reasonable people here, and we know how things should proceed.' If Falk was afraid of a myriad of crossbow bolts aimed at him, he was hiding it well. Then, the Forest Guardian and Selsena approached until they were five paces in front of the ringleader and looked proudly down at her.

'One hundred gold pieces and you let us go. Then we'll have a few coins left so that we don't starve on our journey.'

The woman immediately nodded, much to Ahren's surprise. He had expected some hard bargaining or even a flat rejection. Instead, the scrawny woman pointed at the stump of a tree. 'Leave the gold there, and we'll let you go unhindered.'

Falk reached into his saddlebag and pulled out a bag from which he pulled eleven gold coins, which he showed to the Loom. When she nodded her agreement, he put the coins into another saddlebag. Then he rode over to the stump and placed the jingling bundle on top of it.

'There are one hundred gold coins left in there,' he said.

The Loom indicated to one of the mercenaries near her, and he walked over and felt around the inside of the bag with a finger.

'Full of gold. No silver or copper. Should be about right,' he said abruptly.

Ahren saw a scar around the man's neck which seemed to have been the result of a noose. This scoundrel had, it seemed, cheated death on more than one occasion and seemed neither nervous nor fearful. The rest of the troop of mercenaries seemed similarly relaxed. The apprentice was beginning to understand why they weren't fighting, and he was pleased that everything was being done in such a civilized manner.

The ringleader bowed in an exaggerated manner and stepped out of the way. 'May you reach your destination safely,' she said in a generous tone. The crossbows surrounding them were lowered even if the mercenaries remained on red alert.

The travelling party slowly rode out of the deadly circle and soon the bandits were out of sight behind a bend in the path.

'That all ran very smoothly,' said Trogadon in a strangely approving voice. 'There's nothing better than watching people who know what they're doing.'

'Don't count your chickens before they're hatched,' said Uldini in a dark voice. 'I've thrown a little magic net. If they don't follow us, we're in the clear.'

Ahren looked inquiringly around the group, but nobody apart from Khara seemed to be aghast or even angry at the fact that they had just been held up by bandits. Finally, Ahren could contain himself no longer. 'Did you calculate on something like this happening?!' he blurted out.

'Let me put it to you like this. It happens often enough so you should be ready for it,' answered Falk stoically. 'You have an adequate amount of money ready in a separate bag. You ask for a bit of pocket money, so you won't starve on your journey, so it looks as if you've given them all your money, and you keep a cool head.'

131

Ahren persisted: 'So that wasn't all our money?'

Jelninolan shook her head. 'Each of us has a little pouch in our travel bag - you do too. Imagine if the horse with all the money in its bags got lost or was stolen. The experienced traveller *always* divides up his possessions.'

'And if she'd wanted to have our horses?' thought Ahren out loud.

'That's the difference between a normal highwayman and a genuine bandit. The bandit will only take so much, to give you the opportunity to survive and at worst dream of revenge. The highwayman is greedy, and it always ends up in a fight,' explained Trogadon. He pointed with his thumb over his shoulder in the direction of the ambush. 'They didn't want to fight, just earn a bit of money. That was just one hundred gold coins without pain or danger to life.'

Ahren was irritated by the lax, almost friendly manner with which the dwarf described the rabble of ne'er-do-wells, but before he could speak Uldini began to scold.

'Blast it! Now they've run through my magic net. They're following us', he said sourly.

The faces of the travellers darkened. 'I hate it when they're greedy. Damned amateurs!' blurted Trogadon. His respect for the mercenaries seemed to have lessened significantly, And Ahren had the impression that the dwarf was taking their disappointing behaviour personally.

'Well, we're on horseback and they're on foot. Should we flee?' asked Falk curtly.

Uldini shook his head. 'I'm sure they know the area inside out. If we gallop off, they'll know that we've smelled a rat, and they'll cut us off at some point of their choosing.' He pointed a little down the track where a few dense bushes were standing close to its edges. 'We'll turn the tables on them', he said.

'An ambush? Are you sure?' asked Falk as he contemplated the scene.

'It's our best chance of getting out of this tricky spot we're in,' argued Uldini.

Falk shrugged his shoulders. 'Fry them when they get to us.'

'Or we can use Tanentan,' added Ahren hopefully. He was eager to avoid a fight.

'Not a good idea. I sense solitary Dark Ones all over the hills around us. The southern end of the Borderlands is another two days' ride away' interrupted Jelninolan.

Falk grimaced. 'They'd sense the magic and discover us easily, wouldn't they?'

Both magicians nodded, and the old man gave a deep sigh. 'Right then, the old-fashioned method. Could you at least create a few shields against the arrows?'

Jelninolan considered for a moment before answering. 'Only for a few heartbeats. Any longer and the Dark Ones would sense us too easily.'

'That's long enough,' said Trogadon cheerfully. 'They only have one volley with the crossbows.' The dwarf's mood had brightened considerably once it had become clear that there was going to be a fight, and Ahren worried about the warrior's priorities.

'Right, then. We don't have much time,' said Uldini urgently.

They rode quickly up to the bushes, and Jelninolan led the horses deeper into the forest to keep them out of sight and free from injury. Trogadon and Falk crouched down on the left of the path in the undergrowth, Ahren and Khara did the same on the right. The plan was that the two Forest Guardians would pepper the mercenaries with arrows as soon as they appeared, and the close-combat fighters would make sure they had enough room to continue shooting for as long as possible. Uldini and Jelninolan would maintain a safe distance and protect their fellows for short periods with magic if the crossbows started shooting at them.

Falk issued his instructions: 'Remember, boy: as precisely and as quickly as you can. Give them no chance to entrench, otherwise they'll end up dividing into groups in the forest and trying to wear us down, and the magic won't last long enough to protect us.' Then he disappeared into the greenery.

Ahren was nervous and slightly nauseous. He had become familiar with using his weapon against Dark Ones, but he still found it difficult to shoot at people even when there was no alternative. The Void had helped him on previous occasions, but now he couldn't find the necessary concentration to reach the trance which protected him from his feelings. His connection with Culhen still caused considerable interference. The wolf was crouching in a patch of long grass and waiting with excitement.

Only intervene when somebody needs help, Ahren communicated to the animal as he sought out the optimum position in the shrubbery, from where he had a good view of the path while remaining hidden from the enemy. He took an arrow from his quiver and practised drawing it on the bow. Then he snapped a few branches out of the way so that he could draw the weapon unhindered. His face was glistening with sweat and his hands were shaking. His fear of being attacked by mercenaries was mixed with his fear of having to kill them, and they both combined into a ball of emotions which threatened to debilitate him altogether. Ahren had been injured often enough to realise that every battle was a gamble, which could cost him or his comrades their lives. Certainly, Jelninolan's healing magic was helpful, but even the elf was unable to cure an arrow in the head or a knife in the heart.

He was all too aware that Khara was looking at him critically as she crouched stock still a half a pace away in the undergrowth with Wind

Blade in her steady right hand. There was nothing he wanted more than to have the Void back, to be able to reach it. But Culhen's hunting instinct, awakened by the tension in the others and the first smells of the approaching mercenaries, nipped the young man's every attempt in the bud, leaving him an emotional mess in the shrubbery. The twittering of the birds welcoming the arrival of spring with their song was just as surreal to him as the curious squirrel that Ahren could see two trees away. The little animal was looking at him sceptically, doubtless asking itself why there was an odd-looking animal crouched in the bushes and bathed in sweat.

Ahren frantically tried to think of what he could do to avoid a bloodbath, but he just couldn't think of a way of dodging the skirmish. He felt just as helpless as he had a few weeks previously when he had led Sven into exile. He bit his lips and looked over at Khara again. She looked back at him and rolled her eyes.

'What's wrong?' she asked in an annoyed voice.

'How can you stay so calm?' he asked urgently. 'Aren't you afraid? Do you love killing that much?' he hadn't meant to sound so accusatory, but his frustration rolled off his tongue more scornfully than intended.

Khara's admonishing hand gesture indicated that he should keep his voice down. 'We've no time for this,' she hissed.

Ahren thought that was the end of their conversation and was surprised not only by her speaking again, but also by what she said.

'Use one fear against the other. Do you want us all to survive? Then overcome your fear of death by your concern for our well-being.' She held his look. 'That's how I survived the arena.' Then she turned her eyes to look forward, and Ahren did the same.

The young Paladin's dilemma continued to intensify when the first mercenaries came into view. And when Falk shot off the first arrow, he only raised his own bow hesitatingly.

One of the mercenaries dropped to the ground, severely wounded, and then Ahren had a brainwave, which was like a rock rising up in the middle of his emotional maelstrom. It connected Khara's advice with Falk's pragmatism, Trogadon's directness, Jelninolan's goodness and Uldini's tendency to dramatise. Somehow the influences coming from his companions seemed to unify into one solution within him, a solution that fitted in with Ahren's ideals, even if the apprentice now had to be more coldblooded than he had ever been before in his life.

Ahren aimed and let fly an arrow, which landed exactly in one mercenary's thigh. The man collapsed immediately, screaming and holding his injured leg, but Ahren was already shooting at the next figure. The mercenaries hadn't yet reacted – the shock of being themselves targets of an ambush seemed to have frozen them temporarily.

What are you doing?!' screamed Falk as he saw Ahren sending two more attackers crashing to the ground with arrows in their legs.

'Trust me, master. Aim at their thighs!' shouted Ahren with as much self-confidence as he could muster.

The mercenaries now raised their crossbows, and after three more arrows from the Forest Guardians they began peppering the bushes on either side with crossbow bolts.

The bolts were just about to hit Ahren and Khara in their hiding places when the air flickered for several heartbeats in front of their covers and the bolts fell harmlessly to the ground.

'Magic!' shouted one of the mercenaries and they dived sideways in an effort to protect themselves.

Ahren knew that correct timing was essential for his plan to succeed. If the battle took too long, he would never manage to get as far as their ringleader. He then leaped out from the undergrowth, shooting off a steady stream of arrows in an effort to wound as many mercenaries as possible in their legs.

'Ahren!' screamed Falk, flabbergasted, but the apprentice ignored him and continued to pepper the figures hiding behind trees and shrubbery.

Ahren counted mentally how long it would take to reload a crossbow, so that he could figure out how much time he had for the next stage. He would have to be quick. There were nine wounded mercenaries on the ground in front of him, crawling to safety, their faces the picture of agony.

'Loom!' cried the young Paladin. 'Break off the attack and put your weapons down! Then we will give you enough healing herbs to treat your wounded!' Ahren kept his instruction brief to give the ringleader enough time to consider his demand before her people had reloaded their crossbows. He forced himself into appearing full of self-confidence and withstood the urge to scan the trees for the tell-tale glittering of bolt tips.

It was true that Uldini or Jelninolan could protect them with magic again, but that would only alert every Dark One in the vicinity and they would be on their track in no time at all, meaning all his efforts at avoiding further bloodshed would come to nought.

Nothing happened for several heartbeats, and Ahren tensed himself up to throw himself sideways to avoid the first bolts.

It was then that the scrawny woman in her red-white garment came out from behind a tree, her eyes shining at him in a mixture of rage and amusement. 'What gave you the idea that we're going to let you go after you've badgered my people like that?' she asked scornfully.

The young Paladin picked up on the undertone of hesitation in her voice, and that, combined with the fact that none of the mercenaries had shot at him yet, gave him hope. 'We're in the middle of nowhere here. Nine of your companions are wounded and arrow wounds become infected very quickly. How many are you going to lose to gangrene? How long will you have to hold out in a cave somewhere or in an abandoned farmhouse before they regain their strength? And how many of them will never be able to walk properly again?' During those last words the image of Sven came back into his head, and he had to force himself to remember that he was doing this in order to save everyone present and not just the lives of his companions.

The Loom hesitated, her eyes darting left and right at the wounded mercenaries around her. 'How do you know I won't just cut the throats of everyone here and recruit new people with the booty I'll have taken off your corpses?,' she asked coldly.

Ahren swallowed hard. He had no answer to that and he hadn't counted on anyone being so cold and calculating. He spoke immediately, not giving his fear a chance to gain the upper hand. 'So, are you telling me that your people mean so little to you that it makes no difference to you if one of my companions sets fire to the bag of herbal medicines?' He shouted out his last words as loudly as he could, in the hope that Uldini would understand his bluff.

The Arch Wizard stepped out of the undergrowth with the aforementioned bag while the skinny woman was biting the inside of her cheek and considering what to do. A little flame was dancing on top of Uldini's free hand and was already beginning to lick at the outside of the leather. The Ancient's theatrical leanings were of great benefit to Ahren at that moment, and there was no doubt they were effective.

'Your people will be standing again in three days, in four they will be walking. Within a week they'll have fully recovered,' said Ahren firmly. 'Or we'll take our chances in battle and see who's victorious.'

The Loom pursed her lips and for a moment nobody spoke. The twittering of the birds could be heard mingling in a grotesque manner with the groans of the wounded, while the spring aromas of the plants were overlain with the sickly smell of spilled blood.

Finally, the Loom put her dagger away and nodded once curtly.

Ahren felt dizzy with relief, but forced himself to remain perfectly still, maintaining the determined look in his face.

'You all come out and take the bowstrings off the crossbows. Then we will place the bag on the path and ride away,' he said in as commanding a voice as possible.

'Agreed. You drive a hard bargain, boy, considering your age,' acknowledged the Loom with reluctant respect. 'What's your name?'

The young man was now the picture of serenity. He gave a little smile and said simply: 'My name is Ahren, and I am the Thirteenth Paladin of the gods.'

Chapter 8

'I am the Thirteenth Paladin and I keep fainting.' Ahren heard Uldini behind him, uttering the same jibe for the umpteenth time.

Ever since they had left the befuddled mercenaries behind them Ahren had been subjected to different variations of his pronouncement, each one more outlandish than the last. Even the normally kindly Jelninolan took part, and the forest, which was thinning out now, echoed to the laughter of the travelling party. They were knocking great fun out of the fuming apprentice, as they travelled along, taking advantage of the last rays of the afternoon sunshine to travel an extra few miles.

'Maybe that's enough now,' chortled Falk finally. 'We should stop teasing him and be thankful that he's finally admitting who he is.'

'But I had another great one ready!' protested Trogadon in an exaggeratedly offended voice.

It was clear to Ahren that the jibes were really only a way of the others expressing their relief at the close shave they had just had with the ambush, but he was sick to the back teeth of being the butt of their jokes.

He rode ahead of the group so that they wouldn't see the look of fury on his face, and he prayed quickly to the THREE to give him more patience.

The countryside began to open up before him as he left the last trees of the forest behind. The trade track they were on wound its way through softly rolling grasslands, and the steadily undulating horizon was silhouetted by occasional farmhouses.

At last there was no more sniggering to be heard, and Jelninolan took advantage of the silence to ride up to Ahren in order to speak to him.

'Your idea was truly brilliant and because of it no lives were lost. I really am proud of you.'

Ahren spun his head around and examined the elf's face closely, thinking there might be another jibe coming his way. But he only saw deep warmth in her look. Reassured, he quickly murmured something in a low voice before facing forward again.

'The boy is becoming as vain as his wolf,' interjected Trogadon with a laugh. 'From now on we're going to have to clap in admiration at every one of his ideas.'

Ahren was about to protest, but when he glanced down at Culhen, who was trotting beside him with his tail in the air and looking up at his master haughtily, he wondered about how much truth there might be in what the dwarf had said. He just needed to be thankful that his plan had been effective. Falk, Uldini and the others didn't expect praise every time they did something successfully. The apprentice was happy with what he had done, and he realised he should be satisfied with that.

'On the other hand, we don't have any healing herbs now,' said Falk thoughtfully. 'And guess who's going to replenish our supplies?'

There was no need for Ahren to turn around. With a tired sigh he slid off his horse and set off to explore the edge of the forest behind them for arrowroot while the others waited for his return.

That evening they made themselves comfortable under a large weeping willow that had been visible to them for some time in the hilly grasslands. Ahren had noticed that for the previous few miles the grass was becoming considerably shorter and hardier than in the rest of Hjalgar.

'We're going to reach the Northern Steppes of the Sunplains soon,' his master had explained to him. 'There isn't much water there and very little grows. You're seeing the first signs of the typically barren vegetation.'

The young Paladin had replenished their herb supplies to some extent during the course of the afternoon, and during supper he couldn't help noticing out of the corner of his eyes that the others were observing him in a strange way when he wasn't looking directly at them. He pondered over this for a while until it dawned on him that they were now looking at him with a certain amount of respect. Khara alone looked at him in exactly the same way as before, but that was no surprise to the budding Forest Guardian.

'That was a good tactic of yours today,' said Uldini suddenly after a prolonged silence. They were all sitting around the campfire. The others in the group nodded in agreement, but then the little Arch Wizard gave a melancholy sigh. 'Too bad that your efforts were in vain,' he added.

Ahren pricked up his ears. 'What do you mean?' he demanded.

Uldini waved his hand in a vaguely northern direction. 'A horde of Low Fangs seem to have picked up the scent of the mercenaries. They'll all be dead before dawn,' he answered with mild regret in his voice.

Before anybody could say a word Ahren had leaped up and was running to his horse.

'Well done, Uldini,' grunted Falk as his apprentice swung onto the saddle and galloped off without saying a word, back the way they had come. 'Give the boy some light before he breaks his neck,' shouted Falk over his shoulder to the Arch Wizard as he himself ran towards Selsena.

With a curse Uldini lit up his crystal ball, which he always had under his cloak, and sent the artefact floating towards the galloping apprentice.

'If only I'd kept my trap shut!' cursed the Arch Wizard before following the others' example and riding after Ahren.

The darkness and Ahren's mediocre horsemanship made his precipitous departure more dangerous than he had anticipated. Even though he was sticking to the trade route they had followed during the day, no sooner was he back in the forest when he was encountering bends and low-hanging branches coming out of the blackness that he had to swerve around to avoid being knocked off his horse. He looked over gratefully at the glimmering ball which the Arch Wizard let fly beside him, and without which he couldn't possibly keep up his present speed – at least, not without breaking his neck in the process. The others were riding close behind him. The apprentice was all too aware of the fact that they were better horse-riders than him, and that they could easily have taken the lead or cut him off. But they seem to have come to an agreement that he should be at the front for now, and for a heartbeat the young Paladin granted himself a swashbuckling smile, only to be met by a treacherous branch that nearly swept him to the ground.

Ahren became completely disorientated and lost all sense of time as he galloped through the night, and the unfortunate horse under him grew increasingly exhausted.

'We're almost there!' shouted Uldini after what seemed like an eternity. 'Another ten furlongs and then a hundred paces into the forest towards the west.'

Ahren nodded determinedly and ran through the options in his mind. 'Are we still ruling magic out?' he asked curtly.

Uldini nodded with a look of apology. 'Unless you want to be fighting for the next three days. The place is teeming with Dark Ones that would be able to sense our magic. The light magic is the maximum we can allow.'

Ahren's brain was working feverishly, and he could hear fighting echoing into the peaceful forest from a westerly direction.

'It's now or never, lad!' cried out Trogadon exuberantly beside him, and the dwarf practically fell off his horse before disappearing into the trees with a loud battle cry. Then they all stormed after him and all thoughts of a tactical plan were forgotten.

The battle unfolded remarkably smoothly. It was the first time Ahren had seen how the enemy reacted when it was surrounded, and he made a firm promise to himself never to end up in a similar situation. The Low Fangs turned frantically hither and thither as Trogadon, Khara and Jelninolan ploughed into them and began striking at the startled enemy. The dwarf's mighty hammer whipped the contorted bodies, only a moment before under the thrall of the dark god, through the air as if they were nothing more than rag dolls. Simultaneously, the flowing movements of the two female fighters were snapping bones and cutting off any limbs that were reaching towards them. The mercenaries, who up until that point had been caught in a hopeless rearguard action, seized the moment and bore with their blades into the backs of any Low Fangs who had turned to face the new danger. Then there was Falk, galloping in atop Selsena, a whirlwind of hoofs and deadly blows as they milled into the Low Fangs' left flank.

Ahren, inexperienced in this type of attack, didn't join in with the others, but surprised by the sheer force of his comrades' attack, remained behind in the undergrowth. From there he peppered the Dark Ones to the right with arrows, where there was least chance of hitting one of his friends by mistake.

Culhen remained by his side, growling uncertainly at the Low Fangs, ready to attack any that dared to come too close.

Uldini floated above the battle, from where he had an overview of what was unfolding and could anticipate possible dangers with lightning speed, calling out commands to his companions when necessary.

It took less than twenty heartbeats for the course of the battle to turn in their favour and the Low Fangs were wiped out between their two advancing fronts.

Ahren stopped shooting when he realised that he might injure one of his own, and instead watched the final moments of the battle, relieved that he could see no sign of injury to any of his friends. Four of the mercenaries, however, were lying spread-eagled, motionless on the ground and with terrible injuries. Even from where he was standing Ahren could see that they were beyond help.

'Ahren! To your left! A Moonrunner! Don't let it escape - we need it alive if possible!' The apprentice heard the voice of Uldini, whispering magically into his ear.

The young Forest Guardian looked to his left, but at first he could see nothing. He peered around a tree that was blocking his view and only saw a fox, crouched in the meagre greenery of a stunted bush.

Ahren was about to look further when the fox spun its head around towards him. Horrified, Ahren saw eight tiny red eyes, arranged in a broad semi-circle on its head. Unusually large ears pricked themselves up in alarm and pointed in his direction, and a peculiarly broad mouth revealed small pointy teeth which sparkled like razor-sharp knives.

Before the young Paladin had time to react, the Moonrunner had spun around and scampered away, faster than any fox Ahren had ever seen. He looked at the Dark One in shock, then reacted instinctively by mentally shouting at the wolf, *Attack!*

The wolf reacted with lightning speed, emitted a terrifying howl and raced after the fox-like creature.

Three heartbeats later and the two of them were out of sight. Ahren closed his eyes in order to concentrate entirely on his sensation of the wolf. Suddenly, a branch in the undergrowth snapped beside him. A Low Fang that must have been hiding there threw itself with a snarl at him. It clearly had every intention of using its quadripartite tooth-filled mouth, which took up half its face, to tear the apprentice's throat to shreds. Ahren threw himself to the side and let out a scream of terror just as Trogadon's hammer whizzed past him with an almighty whistling sound before smashing the attacker with full force into the nearest tree. The brittle crunching of bones echoed unmistakeably through the forest and the Low Fang landed in a broken heap on the forest floor.

Trogadon trotted past the stunned apprentice and winked at him. 'Don't try that until you've had plenty of practice,' he whispered conspiratorially. 'If you miss your target, then you'll have spectacularly disarmed yourself, and if you hit a friend by mistake it'll be embarrassing or even a little dramatic.'

Ahren wasn't sure if Trogadon was speaking from experience and considering how closely the hammer had whizzed by him, he really didn't want to know the answer.

He gave the dwarf a nod in gratitude and closed his eyes again to concentrate fully on Culhen. He sensed the excitement of the hunt pounding through his friend's veins, and the graceful interplay of muscles as Culhen followed the zigzag course of the Moonrunner as it tried vainly to shake off the big wolf.

The wolf's joyful anticipation as he neared his prey was increasing with every heartbeat, and when Ahren felt the exhilaration of a hunt about to be successfully concluded, he hurriedly pushed his thoughts through to the triumphant wolf.

Don't kill it! Bring it here! He commanded with all the power he could muster. The creature seemed to be important for some reason, and so he made every effort to follow Uldini's wishes.

Culhen transmitted a mixture of incomprehension, disappointment and a deep sense of having being wronged, and Ahren was surprised at how deeply the wolf was affected by this demand for his booty.

The apprentice calmed him down. *You really wouldn't want to eat it anyway. It's a Dark One.* To underline his words, he transmitted an image of a particularly disgusting Dark One.

The wolf obeyed in a sulk and trotted towards Ahren with the badly injured Moonrunner in his mouth.

Relieved, the apprentice withdrew into his own thoughts and opened his eyes. The battle was over, all the Low Fangs were dead. The mercenaries were treating their wounded, with Ahren's friends helping them as much as possible. Jelninolan was performing a little magic charm on one of the badly injured, and Uldini floated down from the sky to Ahren.

'And? Do you have it?' he asked breathlessly.

The apprentice nodded and pointed behind him into the dark. 'Culhen caught him and is coming now. If I'm reading his thoughts correctly, there's still a bit of life in the Moonrunner, but not much.'

Uldini rubbed his hands gleefully. 'I'll just need a few moments, but it might really be worth it.'

'What's so special about this Dark One?' asked Ahren curiously. He'd never heard of Moonrunners before, and they didn't seem particularly dangerous.

The little figure stared at him in astonishment before giving a disapproving shake of his head. 'What's that good-for-nothing master teaching you anyway?' he asked in a biting tone.

147

Ahren was about to protest, but Uldini cut him off with an imperious wave of his arm. 'Save your breath, I can answer the question myself. There haven't been any Moonrunners for over five hundred years. HE, WHO FORCES must have created new ones shortly before your Naming, using the strength he had sucked from you. If he was already awake enough to successfully force new Moonrunners into existence, then we have to be doubly thankful to Tlik. Who knows what else HE might have let loose in the world?'

Ahren cleared his throat, and Uldini understood the hint. 'Moonrunners are the most effective scouts and harbingers of the dark god. They see and hear practically everything that's going on around them. They can communicate with every Dark One they meet, and Doppelgangers like to use them as messengers. If this one had escaped, it would have informed the next Doppler it met of our presence.'

Ahren shivered at the thought of having one of those mighty opponents on their heels. The Doppelgangers were treacherous and very intelligent, and every time Ahren had been the focus of a Doppler's attention, he had been in fear for his life. Their elaborate strategies were second to none.

Culhen stepped into the milky magical light emanating from Uldini's crystal ball, which was now floating peacefully above the Arch Wizard's shoulder. The limp body of the fox-like creature was hanging from the wolf's mouth, and it was barely breathing.

'We have to be quick now,' said Uldini and reached out for the little scout. Culhen twisted his head and growled at the childlike figure.

'Culhen, behave yourself!' ordered Ahren, sharply. The Ancient's face looked thunderous, and the last thing the young Forest Guardian wanted was for the grumpy Arch Wizard to cast Culhen on top of the next tree in a fit of pique.

The wolf gave Ahren an offended look before carelessly dropping his booty onto the ground. Then he snorted, raised his nose in the air and stalked away to the mercenaries' rucksacks, which he proceeded to sniff for titbits.

Uldini had meanwhile leaned over the half-dead Moonrunner, and now he placed his hands over the animal's head and listened almost prayerfully. Then he turned around and looked at the others. 'Jelninolan, I need you here. You're far better at reading animals' minds. I've broken through its defences but can't make head or tail of what I see.'

The elf came towards them, accompanied by Trogadon and Khara, both of whom looked curiously down at the fox.

'A harbinger of death!' hissed Khara in terror, and Wind Blade seemed to leap into her hand of its own volition before Uldini had the chance to push himself between girl and fox.

'We have to find out what it knows,' he shouted commandingly, and Ahren placed his hand carefully on the girl's sword-arm.

She gave him a furious look and shook him off but made no further effort to attack the Dark One.

'There must have still been Moonrunners all these years in the Eternal Empire, perhaps under a different name,' murmured Falk quietly in reaction to Khara, who had undoubtedly recognised the creature. Uldini nodded with a thoughtful look.

'We really don't know enough about what's going on there,' said the little Arch Wizard in an uneasy voice.

Jelninolan was now bent over the badly scratched body of the harbinger and was listening to the creature's memories. 'It hasn't received any clear orders since it's been created. The Adversary seems to have been too weak to issue them.'

An audible sigh of relief could be heard among the group. This was tangible proof that the goblin Tlik's magic had knocked their enemy back for six.

'It met a Glower Bear on its travels, who informed it about us. It seems the monster is hunting us down.' She looked into the concerned faces around her. 'He's the same one that attacked us in the ruins during the Naming ceremony. Maybe he hasn't got over the fact that we slipped through his grasp. This Moonrunner was supposed to track us down and report where we are.'

Ahren gasped when he heard that. The almighty beast had been tormenting him in his dreams every night. 'Are Glower Bears that intelligent?' he asked fearfully.

Uldini shook his head. 'Jelninolan is translating the animal's impressions in all too human terms. It would be more correct to say that he has fixed us in his mind as his prey. But yes, they are clever enough to rope Moonrunners into their plans.'

Falk scratched his beard thoughtfully. 'That's not good. One of those monsters hunted me during the Dark Days. It was a she-bear. She hunted me for two years and she would keep reappearing whenever I was alone or vulnerable. I was constantly on the run until I finally lured her into an ambush.' There was pain in the eyes of the old Forest Guardian. 'I lost more than a dozen knights that day, veterans one and all, and all good friends.'

Uldini turned around uneasily and looked out into the darkness. Ahren half-expected the beast to rush in on top of them, but all was quiet except for the groans of the wounded. Ahren felt a tension building up between his shoulder-blades as he tensed up at the thought of their dangerous pursuer.

Jelninolan straightened up. 'I can't make out anymore. The Moonrunner is dead,' she said in a mournful voice. She bent down and closed the lifeless eyes of the fox-like creature before turning and heading back to the wounded mercenaries where she washed and bandaged their wounds.

Ahren looked over at the elf. He too yearned to save as many lives as possible from the grotesque deeds of the Adversary, but there was no doubt that she paid closer attention to the animals of the world than he did. Every Dark One that she had to kill in her quest for victory over the Adversary was a creature that could not be freed from his power. It was true that Ahren was more pragmatic in this respect, and had fewer scruples when it came to killing an onrushing Dark One, but he understood her pain nonetheless. The four dead mercenaries were weighing heavily on his conscience, and as the Loom came towards him, he could see the pain of loss in her eyes.

'You really are a Paladin, aren't you?' she asked, coming straight to the point.

Ahren gave a tired nod. 'Not only me. There's my master over there, Dorian Falkenstein. Doubtless you've heard tales of his deeds.'

Falk gave a faint smile and slapped his powerful left hand down on the dumbstruck woman's shoulder. 'You fought well. Too bad that you're wasting your talent,' he said grimly and gave her a severe look.

The mercenary turned away from the hard stare of the living legend, who only that morning had been the object of her ambush.

Ahren almost felt sorry for her, but now was the perfect opportunity for him to reveal his plan for the future of the mercenaries. 'You will compensate us for our help, won't you?' he said in as confident a voice as he could muster.

151

The Red and White Loom stared at him in disbelief. 'But of course. We don't have much gold, but...'

'It's not gold I'm looking for,' interrupted Ahren, taking advantage of the mercenary's irritation. 'I want your fealty.'

Everyone within earshot gasped, and Ahren continued quickly. 'The Dark Days are going to return, and more quickly than anyone wants. We need seasoned warriors and we can't afford to be fighting amongst ourselves.' His voice was becoming louder as he tried to make himself heard by all the mercenaries as well as to forestall any angry protest from his master. 'I am Squire of the Falkenstein Barony in the Knight Marshes. As such I am entitled to small troop of soldiers. I choose you.'

There was immediate uproar as everyone talked loudly across each other. Falk planted himself squarely in front of his apprentice and drew himself up to his full height. 'A word, *Squire!*' he snarled in a low, threatening voice and pulled Ahren by his ear behind the nearest tree. 'Have you completely lost your mind?' he hissed quietly, and a vein on his forehead pulsed angrily.

Ahren made a soothing gesture with his hands. 'They are good fighters, they stand up for each other, and they have the courage to take on Low Fangs. We need people like that,' he said quickly. 'These people can surely think of something better to be doing than lying in wait in a damp forest for the next traveller, so that they can pilfer some money off him to keep the wolf from the door.' And he pointed emphatically at the mercenaries who were standing there in shock and chattering loudly about his offer. Half of them were completely perplexed, the other half certainly seemed hopeful. 'We can send them to Falkenstein. Captain Greycloth can knock some sense into them there. You said yourself that Falkenstein was completely undermanned with only four guards, and that we needed more armed men and women. These are veterans here. If we give them responsibility, a roof over their heads, something to eat and a decent wage, don't you think they'll be thankful and become good soldiers?' Ahren held his breath. Falk was still looking daggers at him, but Ahren could see that he was thinking about what the apprentice had said. He took a step back, and out of the corners of his eyes he could see the mercenaries gesticulating wildly as they argued and pointed repeatedly in the direction of the two Paladins.

'Very well,' said Falk finally. 'If they all agree, it's fine by me. But every one of them has to swear fealty to Falkenstein and recognise Greycloth as captain-in-command, or not one of them will set foot on my land without fear of having it cut off.' The old Forest Guardian's voice was raw with disgust, but Ahren gave a thankful nod, nonetheless. He wanted to rush over to the potential recruits, but Falk grabbed his wrist in an iron grip.

'That was the first and last time you will do anything like that again without having discussed it with me first. I am your master, your accursed liege, and as a Paladin I am more than eight hundred years your senior. Do we understand ourselves?'

Ahren nodded hurriedly. 'Good', growled the old man. 'Because if we adopt every Johnny-come-lately that tries to kill us, my barony will be bursting at the seams before the year is out.'

Ahren released himself from his master's grip, before the old man had a chance to change his mind. He trotted over to the mercenaries in order to lay down the conditions of their new way of life before their leader. Much to his surprise his offer unleashed another heated debate, and he withdrew perplexed to the edge of the squabbling group of men and women.

Uldini approached him with a grin. 'Things not going according to plan?' he asked sarcastically.

Ahren scratched the back of his head in bafflement. 'I thought they'd be delighted,' he complained, baffled by their reaction.

'You're demanding that they give up their freedom, something that mercenaries attach great importance to. And don't forget: we're riding towards a conflict that has only arisen because a troop of mercenaries, namely the Blue Cohorts have put their foot down and are defying an Emperor. It's in their nature to contradict – otherwise they would have become good little soldiers,' said Uldini with a smile.

'Are you telling me that the Blue Cohorts are going to be just as difficult to persuade?' asked Ahren uneasily.

Uldini looked up at him in amusement. 'An elite unit betrayed by their employer and led by a stubborn Paladin?' He laughed uproariously. 'I've no doubt at all they will follow you like brave little lambs,' he concluded sarcastically.

'Gather this rabble together first. We have to move on and quickly, as long as that Glower Bear is breathing down our necks. It's true that the creatures only travel at night and are not particularly quick, but on the other hand they are extremely durable,' he added quickly once he had noticed that Ahren was making no attempt to involve himself in the mercenaries' dispute.

Ahren looked down at the childlike figure and could see a calculating glimmer in his eyes, as if the Arch Wizard was putting him to the test and was trying to find out if he was up to dealing with the situation he had brought about himself.

The apprentice squared his shoulders and marched energetically up to the Red and White Loom. 'Have you reached a decision regarding our offer?' he asked with as much authority as he could muster.

The woman with her blond hair shaved at both sides bit the inside of her cheek thoughtfully, a gesture which made her more human in Ahren's eyes. 'Personally, I am in favour of it. I believe both you and your master, but there are still a few among us who consider you to be nothing more than imposters who are good at fighting,' she said regretfully.

Ahren frowned and placed his hands on his hips in irritation. Why were these people so stubborn? The young man had been so proud of his plan, and now this? His eyes scanned the clearing in search of inspiration. Some of the mercenaries were in the process of burying their fallen comrades. Jelninolan and Khara were treating the wounded. Falk and Uldini were standing beside each other deep in quiet conversation, and Trogadon was standing among the mercenaries talking shop and cracking jokes. Culhen was nowhere to be seen, but Ahren could feel through their connection that he was still in a sulk because Ahren had taken his booty away from him. Then he spotted Selsena and he had a brainwave.

He quickly walked over to the Titejunanwa and pressed his head towards hers. A wave of affection flowed over him, which also seemed to contain some kind of question. Ahren realised to his own surprise that he seemed to have acquired a feeling for Selsena's empathetic communication too. He indicated to Selsena that she should follow him, and the Elfish charger trotted with curiosity alongside the young Paladin.

He led Selsena into the middle of the sceptical mercenaries. 'I think this might persuade you that we are who we say we are,' was all he said before unstrapping Selsena's head armour. With the headpiece removed it was clear to all the onlookers that they weren't looking at a horse in impressive armour, but rather a real-live unicorn. Ahren remembered how impressed he had been the first time he saw Selsena, and he hoped that the presence of a magical figure, who for most people only existed in the old tales, would persuade the doubters among them.

Awestruck faces looked at Selsena's mesmerising head with its bone plate, its spiral horn glittering white, and the smaller razor-sharp lower horns. Some of the veterans even had tears in their eyes, and a dumbfounded silence hung over the clearing. Then Selsena stood up on her hind legs and let out a shrill whinny, shaking her mane and kicking the air with her hooves.

Culhen, who had been watching the proceedings from the undergrowth, let out a deep, terrifying howl and trotted over to Ahren's side. There was no way he was going to let the unicorn have all the limelight.

The mercenaries around them sank to their knees until only the Loom was left standing in front of Ahren. She stretched her hand out towards him, her eyes continually darting back towards Selsena. 'I think we have an agreement,' she said drily. Silently but gratefully Ahren shook her hand.

The travelling party spent the rest of the night on horseback, slowly retracing the steps they had taken the previous day. The mercenaries had headed towards the north, after promising to take the quickest route to Castle Falkenstein. Uldini had given them extra gold for the journey with gritted teeth and had pointed out that he wasn't made of money.

Ahren ignored the Arch Wizard's protest and basked in the knowledge that he had transformed twenty highwaymen and women into sixteen followers. The four dead mercenaries saddened him, but he was beginning to understand that there were battles where he couldn't guarantee that all his comrades would survive. His good mood evaporated, and he fell into a melancholy rumination as he considered how many more he would see die before his task was finally achieved.

'Such a sad face, lad?' the cheery voice beside him was so loud that he almost fell off his saddle. Trogadon had ridden up beside him unnoticed, and now he grabbed the unsteady Forest Guardian by the shoulder and steadied him with a spirited laugh. 'Careful, Ahren,' he snorted merrily. 'What an inglorious end it would be if you fell off your horse and broke your neck. Especially now that you're beginning to make a name for yourself.' The twinkle in the dwarf's eye took the bite out of his sarcastic tone, and Ahren couldn't help giggling as his mood improved.

'Tell me what's bothering you,' said the warrior, and now he was being serious. 'Your little trick worked brilliantly, and you should be singing out your happiness into the night.'

Ahren frowned. 'I was thinking how many lives our war has yet to claim,' he answered in a gloomy tone. He pointed back to where they had left the mercenaries. 'Sixteen are still alive, but four didn't make it. What will happen in the Dark Days that are coming if only four out of five survive? How many are going to die?'

Ahren felt a lump in his throat and fell silent while Trogadon played thoughtfully with one of his beard plaits. 'The only advice I can give you is this,' said the dwarf warrior in an unusually grave voice. 'Concentrate on trying to keep the loss of life to a minimum, and take heart with every life you save. If you concentrate completely on the dead, then you won't be able to help the living.' He gestured with his large, calloused hand towards where they had helped the mercenaries. 'You did something amazing today. Enjoy it. Take satisfaction from it. Draw strength from it so that you will be ready for the next battle you will undoubtedly face. Only in this way can you always give your best and not fail in your mission.' Trogadon's customary merriness and light-heartedness had returned, and he began singing a lewd song that Ahren had heard him sing so often it no longer made him blush. The dwarf gestured to him to join in, and so Ahren sang, albeit hesitatingly, along to the chorus. The squat warrior gave a nod of approval and belted the next verse out into the forest and gradually Ahren's spirits rose. Soon they were bellowing exuberantly together about the assets of the pretty miller's wife and her three daughters.

Uldini observed the carry-on and shook his head. 'If their caterwauling doesn't frighten off our pursuers, then I really don't know what will,' he whispered to Falk spitefully, but he too was humming along and a moment later had joined in the song.

'Well, if we fail in our mission, we can at least earn a living as the evening entertainment in a tavern,' muttered Uldini poisonously to himself, once the ladies too had joined in. Culhen, infected by Ahren's exuberant joy, let out a triumphant howl.

Chapter 9

The further south they travelled, the more barren the landscape became. The forests of Hjalgar gave way to bushy hills, whose vegetation became ever sparser until only occasional trees and low thorny bushes bedecked the low elevations. The countryside seemed to be yielding to an invisible, all-oppressing power, and was becoming flatter all the time. The green turned to brown, and the sand, which was everywhere, found its way into every crack and fold of their clothing. Farmhouses or any other signs of humanity were now few and far between.

Had Ahren the time to look at his surroundings, he would undoubtedly have found them depressing. But Falk still hadn't forgiven him for his solo actions, neither for his impetuous ride back to the endangered mercenaries, nor for his later push to employ them in his service. A merciless training programme was now the order of the day for the apprentice, one that was aimed at the young Forest Guardian's two weaknesses: riding and maintaining patience.

Then there was also the sword training on horseback, where Khara always had the upper hand. He could just about parry her thrusts, but a counterattack was out of the question.

Falk's advice was both simple and depressing: 'With your limited riding skills you're faced with two options if you're attacked while on horseback: use your bow or fall off your horse and fight on foot. If you try fleeing or pull your sword, any half-decent rider will knock you off your horse no problem by catching you from behind or throwing you off balance.'

Despite the hard words, his master stubbornly tried to give him an understanding of the interplay between man and horse. But to little effect.

Those workouts proved frustrating, but the other half of the day was worse. Falk had brought the old leather ball along that he had used at the beginning of Ahren's training, and now he introduced the diabolical object in a most creative and malevolent manner. Its purpose seemed to be to both torture the apprentice and to test his patience to the limit. Ahren's task was to shoot an arrow at the ball as soon as Falk threw it into the air. Under normal circumstances hitting it would prove no problem, but the catch was that his master might wait half the afternoon before flinging it the first time! By the time that happened Ahren would be bathed in sweat, and his hands and back knotted with tension from holding the bow and arrow at the ready, having done nothing but watch the small, hateful object as his master tossed it lightly from one hand to the other. Then to top it all off, when it was finally hurled through the air, Ahren would miss three out of five times. He was ready to burst into tears with rage.

After two weeks Jelninolan finally took pity on him by riding up to him and explaining to him what he had to change. 'You tense up too much because the task is taking all your attention,' she began, and Ahren stared at her with a look of incomprehension. Jelninolan gently took the bow out of his shaking hands and gave him a reassuring look. 'The trick is to remain calm. A bow shouldn't be constantly extended, or it will become loose through wear and tear. The same applies to your body and your mind. It's like what Trogadon tried to explain to you, except that he was talking about your feelings and your soul.'

Just at that moment Falk tossed the ball over his shoulder, and Ahren, still completely tensed up, let out a warning cry. But the elf had already reacted. With a relaxed, almost lazy movement she let the arrow fly and it hit the ball in mid-air slap in the middle, before nailing it into the dusty ground.

Culhen pounced on the leather and brought the practice object back to Falk. Ahren had been continually developing his connection with the wolf and could formulate the most basic wishes subconsciously. Falk gave the animal a good-natured slap and Ahren turned to look at the elf again as she gave him back his bow. 'You're missing the Void, and that's no bad thing. You had become too dependent on it as if it were a crutch, and that has held back your progress. It suppresses your feelings, but it would be better if you could master your emotions yourself.' She pushed a finger into his chest and looked at him forcefully. 'You have to learn to carry out actions from a position of calm. You just need to focus at the moment of action, and this transformation from waiting to acting must be seamless.'

The young Paladin looked doubtfully at her. 'How is that supposed to work?' he asked in a voice that sounded sulkier than he had intended. These mind games really annoyed him and his young spirit longed for action. 'And how could that possibly be good?' he added grumpily.

'Swarm Claws!' shouted Falk and threw the ball, hitting Ahren's head. Befuddled, Ahren held his burning face and stared accusingly at his master.

Falk looked back at him, his face serene. 'A Swarm Claw attacking from the sun's shadow, might give you a heartbeat's more time than that, but then you're dead because it will have cut your throat. Plus, there are over a dozen equally quick Dark Ones out there. You have to be ready at all times and yet without wearing yourself out,' he said in a surprisingly gentle voice.

Ahren was on the point of exploding with rage. Every time he thought he was making progress, another more difficult lesson would appear before him, which made everything he had learned before seem easy as pie!

'Khara has spent half her life fighting, but even she has to keep practising so that she can master her reactions perfectly,' added Jelninolan. She could see the young man's face darkening.

Ahren paused for a moment. The one-time slave girl had stiffened up at her mistress's unintended rebuke and she was blushing.

Somehow Ahren felt responsible. 'I'm much slower than Khara. When she's fighting, she almost seems to consist of water or air,' he said as a compliment, hoping that her mood would improve. Unfortunately, it ended up sounding grumpier than he had intended. Still, he saw a triumphant smile beginning to form on Khara's face before he turned away.

Falk and Jelninolan glanced at each other and the priestess raised a questioning eyebrow. Falk merely shrugged his shoulders. 'At least he's learning a few things, even if only slowly.'

Then they both laughed, leaving a confused apprentice behind them. He wondered what exactly it was he was supposed to have learned.

The grime was getting in everywhere. In Ahren's nose, in his ears, in every cranny of his body, even where he was saddle-sore. Every intake of breath tasted of dust, and they had all tied strips of cloth around their faces to stop the fine particles from going into their lungs. The land through which they were riding now was even drier now, and with the exception of the few bushes, pushing their dried branches up through the poor topsoil as if they were the last remaining living creatures, there was hardly any vegetation to be seen. The brown surface of the lifeless earth stretched as far as the eye could see, and water in this part of Jorath was a rare and precious commodity.

Uldini and Falk had, before they entered this inhospitable region, purchased all available provisions from the farmers at outrageously high prices, and filled every waterskin they possessed to the brim. Now Ahren understood why. The horses' heads drooped even before the sun was at its zenith, and the young Paladin was eternally grateful to the animal that carried him through this wasteland without once complaining. The thought of having to travel through the Plains for days on end was a nightmare, and he hoped he would never be stranded without a horse in such a place. Culhen was becoming increasingly irritable and unbearable with all the dust that was gathering in his fur, and every evening, out of pure necessity, Ahren was resorting to brushing his friend's fur by the campfire and ridding him of the worst of the dust. At least that way he had some respite from the constant nagging of the animal in his head. Conversation among the travellers was at a minimum and almost exclusively took place on windless nights around the campfire when it was possible for them to take the cloth from their mouths and breathe normally.

'Why do they call this country Sunplains?' asked Ahren on one such occasion. 'It's not particularly warm, and you hardly see the sun on account of the dust clouds. Dirtplains would be a more suitable name.' He spat some dust out and immediately regretted his decision when he felt his mouth constricting with the dryness.

'Good point,' interjected Uldini morosely. He turned to the apprentice, casting a distrustful look over the barren landscape as he did so. Its blurred outlines didn't look any more attractive in the deepening darkness. 'This part of the Sunplains is widely known as the Dead Hills. A big battle took place here in the Dark Days. It was, to be exact, one of the three main battles waged in an effort to drive the armies of the Dark Ones towards what are now the Borderlands. That was after the fall of

Geraton, and just twenty summers before we finally managed to chain HIM, WHO FORCES under the Pall Pillar.' Uldini coughed for a moment and when he spoke again his voice sounded raw and rough. It comforted Ahren to know that even the ageless Arch Wizard could be afflicted by something as banal as dust. 'Damned dirt!' he cursed. 'If we didn't have to worry about this Glower Bear, I'd take action against it.'

'Don't!' warned Jelninolan. 'I can sense that he's still on our trail. We don't want to make it easier for him to find us, do we?'

Uldini looked angrily at the elf but silently followed her advice.

Ahren gave a slight nod. 'You wanted to say something about the Dead Hills?' he asked, steering the Arch Wizard back to the original topic.

Uldini nodded and pointed at the shallow, undulating hills around them. 'All this was once a respectable green spot of land. Not a paradise but there was water, there were little woods and green bushes, and the earth was as smooth as silk. A powerful High Fang cast a dastardly charm once it became clear that he was going to lose the battle and his army. He used the essence of his own soldiers to lay waste to the surrounding countryside.'

Uldini paused and Ahren realised to his own surprise that the hard-nosed Arch Wizard was fighting hard to control his emotions. Two heartbeats later and the childlike figure had everything under control again.

'It was the most horrific bloodbath,' the Arch Wizard continued. 'Every single Low Fang and every Dark One perished on the spot. Their blood seeped into the ground beneath them and caused a powerful, supernatural earthquake. Faults with razor-sharp edges appeared, whole rivers and lakes were swallowed up by the earth and the vegetation withered within moments. Any of us who hadn't fallen down a fissure or been impaled by a jagged earthwork had to run for his life and flee into greener climes, while this swathe of country reared up into a fight to the death and killed anyone foolish enough to remain. All our supplies were destroyed by the earthquake, and as the countryside offered neither food nor water, there was nothing left for us but to retreat. It was true that we had defeated the Dark Ones, but the last spell of the High Fang set us back many summers.'

Uldini fell silent, and Ahren thought over what he had heard. In order to distract himself from the abominations described and remembering through Uldini's choice of words something that had been puzzling him, he decided to ask a harmless question. 'Why do you always count time in terms of summer, and we do it in terms of winter?'

Uldini didn't answer. He seemed to be caught up in the old, terrible memories. Much to Ahren's surprise it was Khara who responded.

'I asked Jelninolan the same questions when I was learning to master the Northern language. It's down to the weather. Winter is the hardest time of the year in the north, and that's when most people die, in the south that happens during the summer. In Middle Jorath both terms are in use.'

Ahren nodded in gratitude. He was glad that he wasn't the only person who asked such banal questions. 'What became of the fissures and the jagged edges?' he asked to nobody in particular. 'There are only hills here.'

'The greatest enemy of all overpowered them', answered Jelninolan wistfully. 'Time itself. It's always very windy here as I'm sure you've realised. Over the centuries the wind carried away the earthworks and filled in the fissures. Land heals itself, divides up its burdens until finally everything balances out.' She picked up a handful of the brown earth and let it slide through her fingers. 'I can sense the memory of life in the earth already. As soon as the water returns, life will too.'

'Then the land won't have to wait long,' interjected Trogadon laconically, interrupting the rapt silence that Jelninolan's speech had initiated. 'The waterways of Waterheart are no more than four leagues distant if I'm not mistaken.'

Everyone looked at him, some in amazement, and the others with curiosity. 'You mean they've penetrated that far already?' asked Uldini in disbelief.

Trogadon let out a guffaw. 'You should spend more time on important things and less on politics. I've spent the last five winters in a tunnel and know the state of play better than you do.'

Uldini grunted something incomprehensible and Ahren leaned over to his master. 'What are they talking about?' he asked quietly.

Falk hesitated. 'The view is so unusual that I don't want to spoil the surprise', he said finally.

Ahren wanted to press him further, but his master was unyielding. 'Look on it as a good exercise in patience,' he said in a firm voice as he reprimanded his pupil.

He knew there was no point in pestering the others with questions concerning the waterways of Waterheart, having only brought on another lecture from his master with his thirst for knowledge. And so, he glumly settled down to sleep, cuddling Culhen, who sent his friend comforting thoughts until they both finally fell into a slumber.

Falk was proven right. Words couldn't come anywhere near enough to describing what they encountered the following day, and the apprentice doubted he would have believed his master, had he attempted a description. They were sitting on their horses and were looking down from one of the higher hills onto a construction, which earlier that morning had only been a narrow strip on the horizon. The stone construct had gradually become bigger, and finally Falk had led them up to higher ground. From there Ahren could at last make out what they were looking at.

A kind of wall led straight towards them, except that it wasn't a wall at all. A kind of broad channel was held aloft, many dozens of paces high, by a succession of curved arches. Water flowed along the channel, some of which flowed down at regular intervals where it flowed into canals on the ground, which led away from this peculiar wall. Narrow green bands of sparse vegetation shimmered in the pallid sunlight, which had, in this part of the world, to constantly fight its way through a veil of dust.

'What is that?' asked Ahren cautiously. Was he imagining things, or was the wall becoming gradually higher, the further away it went? Perspectives seemed to be playing tricks on him, and every so often he would squint with one eye, but the effect remained the same.

Trogadon gestured to the sight below. 'What you see below represents one of the two great virtues of the Sunplainers. They are masterful cultivators of the land. What you see there is a water channel, which carries the priceless liquid from Waterheart to here in the Dead Hills. In this way new life can be created, and the earth can become fruitful so that it will finally serve as farmland. We're going to follow this road back to its source, and you will see how much the Sunplainers have already transformed the land.'

Ahren was stunned by the dwarf's answer and he looked at him carefully to see if the squat warrior was pulling his leg. Trogadon's expression was serious as he continued to speak. 'We dwarves helped with the initial planning and built the first hundred paces. We taught the people of the Plains how to continue the construction themselves. There were a few accidents to begin with and the occasional pillar collapsed, but if I look at this little section here, I can see that they've got the *hang* of it.' He pointed at one of the load-bearing arches of the waterway and laughed heartily at his own witty words.

Uldini pulled a face, but Jelninolan admired the view in front of her and was astonished. 'I never thought that people could champion nature to such a degree,' she whispered.

'Wait a while and you might reconsider your opinion of us. The population of the Sunplains is constantly increasing and they are in urgent need of new farmland, otherwise they wouldn't give the Dead Hills a second thought,' said Falk drily.

Uldini frowned and nodded. 'One problem is that our empire has become too big. We can't transport foodstuffs quickly enough from the eastern border to the south before they rot, and that's why we need the farmland in the Dead Hills, which was taken from us that time.'

This information made Ahren dizzy. Crops could be transported a very long way before they started to go bad. 'How big are the Sunplains?' he asked in irritation.

'Last spring, before I headed off to find you, the distance from the Sun Palace to the southern foothills was a good four hundred leagues. I don't doubt the border has pushed further south since then though,' said Uldini thoughtfully. 'Because the second virtue of the Sunplainers, as Trogadon has so euphemistically phrased it, is their thirst for conquest. We are good farmers and tenacious warriors. Quite an ignoble combination, as Middle Jorath has found out over the last three thousand years.' Ahren wasn't sure if the Arch Wizard was conscious of it, but his voice betrayed an element of pride.

'Until the arrival of the Eternal Empire,' interjected Falk with a smirk, and Uldini's face darkened.

'You mean until Quin-Wa decided to transform the western territories into her own private playground and establish a belligerent feudal state?' he snapped back.

'Exactly,' answered Falk with a satisfied grin. The old man enjoyed nothing more than to disconcert the eloquent Arch Wizard.

Uldini didn't respond as he turned his horse towards the waterway, spurred it forward, and trotted off.

'He'll make mincemeat out of you someday, old friend,' laughed Trogadon before moving off too.

'Maybe,' answered Falk, and shrugged his shoulders. Infected by Trogadon's good humour he added, 'But it will certainly have been worth it.'

The thundering sound of the cascading water was deafening as they rode along the stone construction. Ahren didn't see any other travellers, but a rough track led along the foot of the pillars, which were sunk into the ground at intervals of sixty paces. Every hundred paces a small waterfall, left and right of the waterway, cascaded to the ground from where it was directed into the surrounding land.

When they rested for the night, Ahren saw the first animals in a long time. They were grazing by the canals in the weak light of dusk. Ahren had never seen such sylphlike slim animals before with their serpentine horns, and in spite of the animals keeping their distance, he tried to sneak a closer look. He saw a small herd, and they were drinking from one of the waterways that led the water away and chewing on the tough grass at its banks. The air was much clearer here, the dust being bonded through the increasing moisture of the land. For the first time in weeks he could see stars in the night sky.

Everyone had stored away the cloths that had protected their mouths, and the first lively discussions in ages filled the air. Trogadon was entertaining Jelninolan with his usual racy tales from his mercenary days, Khara had insisted on brushing Culhen and Jelninolan was keeping watch over the Plains. Uldini and Falk were talking shop and were at that moment discussing the length of the waterway. Ahren had learned that its principle rested on the simple fact that water always flowed downwards. His eyes had not been deceiving him when he had seen the stone construct for the first time. It descended almost imperceptibly with every pace, ensuring that the water reached the dried-up plains.

'Why does it just peter out?' interjected Ahren.

The two looked at him in surprise as if they hadn't expected him to be listening in.

'This isn't its actual end,' said Falk absently. 'Whenever a section of land has recovered, a few of the sluices at the front are closed, and the waterway is built on a little more, so that the water can be transported further.'

'Won't the beginning of it just dry out again?' asked Ahren doubtfully.

Uldini shook his head. 'It's not as simple as that. Because of the plant growth, the earth can store much more water before it seeps down into the deeper strata. Even the weather changes once the vegetation has come back, and it begins to rain more often. One of the other Ancients penned a long treatise on the matter but I never read it. To sum up: once we've helped a tract of land get back up on its feet, the first farmers settle in the newly developed areas, where they sink wells and cultivate the land. You'll see it in the next few days,' finished Uldini.

Ahren nodded and looked out into the night. He breathed the slightly tangy air, which smelled faintly of the new-growing plants, deep into his lungs and he enjoyed the light, cool breeze on his skin. The following days, dust-free and with fresh water aplenty, promised to be less stressful than those that had gone before.

The next few days were the toughest in moons. Falk seemed determined that Ahren would make up for the hours they had lost on their journey through the Dead Hills in double quick time. He ensured that Trogadon put him through his paces when it came to muscle training, Khara thrashed him with Wind Blade, and Jelninolan overwhelmed him with balancing acts – everything of course while he was on horseback – and to top it all, his master showered him with information concerning the animals and plants of the Sunplains.

Being under such pressure, Ahren was only vaguely aware of the changing landscape. The dry dust was gone, and more and more green covered the ground. In the distance Ahren could see small, modest farms and people working the fields.

On the fifth evening of their journey along the waterway, Ahren was wearily settling down in his sleeping place when he heard a most peculiar sound. A deep vibration accompanied by a rumbling that was becoming louder. At first Ahren thought it was a protracted thunderclap. Jelninolan and Falk peered out into the darkness, and then indicated to the others to remain perfectly still. Ahren did as he was told, and suddenly their encampment was engulfed in chaos.

As if from nowhere, dozens of gazelles were storming through the stone archway, under which the travellers had planned to sleep. Ahren saw the wide, terrified eyes of the graceful animals galloping straight towards them, only to swerve around them at the last moment. The noise was deafening, almost paralysing, and Ahren stood stock still and watched in horror as the herd trampled through their encampment, galloping between them in terrified flight.

'Don't move or they'll throw you to the ground and that will be the end of you! Trust that they'll shimmy around you!' called Falk, pleading with his companions. His voice could barely be heard in the whirling chaos of hooves. Ahren could see Trogadon, like a coiled spring, standing at the ready with his hammer held high, eyeballing any animal that came too close. Uldini had simply levitated over the fray, and Khara had taken up a defensive position in front of Jelninolan in order to protect the elf. Ahren found it extraordinarily difficult to follow Falk's command and not move, but his master appeared calm and collected, like a rock in the broiling surge. It seemed like a miracle to Ahren that not one of them was swept along by the herd or trampled under their hooves.

Finally, the last animal passed through, and a ghostly silence lay over their encampment once the noise of the herd died away in the distance.

'Anybody hurt?' asked Falk, and everyone shook their heads. 'Good,' he grunted. 'The trick is to stay calm. The animals always find their way around you, provided you let them.'

Ahren knew through his connection with Culhen that the wolf was fine, and at last he could relax a little. The wolf had instinctively avoided the herd, but Selsena on the other hand, who was standing in the middle of their encampment, radiated displeasure. The Titejunanwa was not used to having her personal space invaded by others jostling her impetuously. It seemed to be a new experience for the age-old animal.

Falk patted the flank of the Elfish charger, but Jelninolan looked uneasily out into the darkness. 'What was it that frightened them so much?' she asked fearfully, and her eyes glazed over.

'Be careful. Think of the Glower Bear,' warned Uldini, who was beginning to concoct a charm.

Suddenly Jelninolan became ashen-faced and she shouted, 'Sicklehoppers! Everyone up the pillars! Now!'

Uldini reacted immediately by floating up to the top of the waterway, while Falk cursed and quickly gathered the most important paraphernalia from their devastated encampment. Selsena let out a terrified whinny and galloped out onto the Plains, and Trogadon yanked the dumbstruck Khara to the imposing pillar on her left which soared unperturbed into the night sky.

Falk turned with blazing eyes to his apprentice, who was standing in a daze. 'Culhen should follow Selsena as fast as his legs can carry him! And you, don't just stand there! Climb! Go, go, GO!' he roared at the top of his voice.

Ahren spun around, raced to the other pillar on his right and tried to get a foothold on the rough brickwork. The surface was damp with the fine spray coming from the nearby waterfall, and the young Forest Guardian struggled to get a good grip. Simultaneously he sent Culhen such a sharp order, that the wolf let out a yelp and proceeded to hare after Selsena, who was disappearing at full gallop on the Plains.

Ahren still hadn't managed to climb upwards when Falk appeared beside him and began to ascend. 'Stop dawdling, boy!' he snorted and pulled himself upwards with all his might. The old man clawed relentlessly at any rough parts the bricks offered him, seeming to ignore the lacerations his violent climbing technique cut into him.

Ahren gritted his teeth and copied his master. His heart was pounding in his chest, and a thousand questions where racing through his mind. What could have caused his companions to panic in this way?

He tried to suppress the pain of the cuts in his hands. The rough stone was tearing into him with every claw-like grasp. He looked over his shoulder, hoping to recognise something. He could see shadowy outlines of figures the size of fully grown horses, only somewhat longer and curiously misshapen. They seemed to mysteriously appear out of the darkness, only to disappear a moment later. Finally, Ahren understood what he was looking at. The creatures moved forward by hopping, and they were able to leap high and far. Ahren could see iridescent wings, shimmering red, and oddly shaped, dead-looking black eyes.

Falk was now several paces above him, screaming at Ahren: 'For the love of the THREE, get your act together, Ahren! You're still within their range!'

As if in confirmation, the young Paladin heard a high humming sound and felt a blast of air as one of the creatures leaped within a hair's breadth of him. Ahren saw a fragmentary silhouette of the creature, which reminded him of a plump praying mantis with its grotesquely thick hind-legs and four sickle-like arms, whose sharp edges stretched out in front of it. Its stumpy wings were just broad enough to enable the Sicklehopper to glide several paces though the air before falling to the ground again.

Ahren swallowed hard and redoubled his efforts to scale the life-saving stone pillars. He could hear another humming sound coming from his right, and then whirring loudly behind him. Ahren pressed himself into the pillar instinctively and held his breath. There was a sharp bang as one of the Dark Ones sprang over him, its sickle narrowly missing the young man before scoring a deep scrape in the pillar. Little pieces of broken stone rained down on Ahren, and he looked down at them for a heartbeat in silence as they tumbled into the depths below. If one of those things were to hit him, he would be sliced in two. His Elfish armour would not help him a whit.

Sobbing with fear Ahren clambered higher. Every muscle in his back was burning, his arms were becoming exhausted, and his fingers were riddled with cuts. He heard the banging sound again and again as the

Sicklehoppers glided by, attempting to gash him and his friends, scoring scrape after scrape into the massive stone pillars. He heard the terrible death whinnies of the horses below as they were torn to ribbons by the fearsome Dark Ones. Ahren screamed out his fear as he scaled upwards, trying to get beyond reach of the creatures. At last his hand grasped thin air. Blinded by tears and dust he had reached the top of the pillar. Falk pulled him upwards with a groan, grabbing him by the forearm and yanking him unceremoniously and heaving him like a bag of flour into the water-filled channel. The cold water closed in over his head and he rose to the surface, gasping for air – the water had not only washed away the dust in his eyes, but also the panic in his mind.

Ahren noticed that he was being gradually carried away, and so he quickly stood up to avoid being pulled down one of the drains of the waterway. They were just about twenty paces above the ground and he certainly didn't want to be washed down to the Sicklehoppers. The young Paladin rubbed his burning hands, whose cuts were being gently numbed by the cold water.

'Has everyone survived?' he gasped. The thought that one of his friends might have been torn to shreds by the sickles of these insect-like Dark Ones made him shiver and feel nauseous.

Falk frowned. The moon was shining brightly on the clear water of the artificial stream, which rippled cheerfully and steadily along the waterway. Their travelling companions could be seen as shadowy outlines some fifty paces downstream.

'I think everyone has managed to make it up,' said Falk and started moving. He splashed through the water to their companions with Ahren following, who prayed he would find them all unharmed. He quickly checked his connection to Culhen. The wolf was fine, but was still running after Selsena, who was leading him further and further into the

175

Plains, away from the dreadful danger that had burst in upon them so unexpectedly.

Ahren saw that Uldini was floating unscathed above the stream and looking down at a prostrate figure being tended to by Jelninolan. It was Trogadon who was lying on the channel's edge, one pace in width. The apprentice was relieved to see Khara, passing a rucksack over to the elf, who was nursing the injured dwarf.

They arrived over at the others, and the young man saw that the dwarf had a gaping wound, a cut which stretched across his back. The warrior was letting out a torrent of curses and looking angrily at the cut in his old chainmail shirt, which was almost divided in two. He tossed the useless piece of armour over the edge and closed his eyes in sadness, while Jelninolan worked his back with a tincture that sent up steam whenever it touched the wound. If the dwarf was feeling any pain, he certainly wasn't showing it.

'Blasted fleabags of excuses for animals! That was my favourite chainmail shirt!' he scolded aloud, and Falk shook his head disapprovingly.

'I've been telling you for moons to kindly wear your namesake's shirt. That would undoubtedly have protected you, and you wouldn't be looking like a burst dwarf sausage,' he said, scolding the warrior without the smallest hint of pity in his voice.

Their friend had won the right to wear the name and the artefacts of the old dwarf hero Trogadon. Among these was the chainmail made from Deep Steel, but within no time at all, the stubborn Dwarfish warrior had simply shoved the valuable piece of equipment into his rucksack because it chafed his chest, or so he said. Falk had repeatedly tried to change his mind, but until this evening Trogadon had preferred to wear his own tattered chainmail which had been corroded by the gastric acid of the Orc

Worm. Against his own wishes, he pulled the ancient chainmail from his bag. 'If my chest hairs are scrubbed off, you'll be to blame,' he said sulkily.

Jelninolan placed her hands on the treated wound and whispered a little spell which pulled the edges of the cut together. The dwarf gave a groan and threw the elf a distrustful look. 'It doesn't seem so painful when you heal the others,' he grunted suspiciously.

She glared at him with scornful eyes. 'Firstly, it's extremely difficult to apply magic to Pure Ones. Secondly, I can only perform weak magic or we'll be sitting ducks up here for Swarm Claws. And thirdly, I hate having to heal wounds that could have been avoided. So, at the very least *put on that stupid shirt!* Her last words sounded just like a whip lash, and even Ahren flinched.

Trogadon lifted his arms in a conciliatory gesture and proceeded to force himself into his famous namesake's armour with comic theatrical effort.

'Everybody else uninjured?' Jelninolan looked at her companions and they all nodded although they were all gently rubbing their sore hands. Satisfied, Jelninolan tended to their cuts and while this was taking place Falk communicated with Selsena.

'She'll meet us a little further south, and in the meantime, she'll take care of Culhen,' he began and was interrupted by a terrifying bellow which split the night air, and which Ahren recognised immediately.

'The Glower Bear!' he cried out in alarm and reached for his bow.

'Nothing to worry about, he's still some distance away,' said Jelninolan in a placatory voice. 'We have a good head start on him.'

'Then it's decided', announced Uldini firmly. 'We're staying up here.' Ahren looked aghast at the Arch Wizard who was making a sweeping gesture.

'Look around you. The stone edges are wide enough to walk comfortably during daylight, and we're safe up here, not only from the Sicklehoppers but also from the Glower Bear. And considering he's so near to us already, Jelninolan can also use magic to keep an eye out for Swarm Claws. That's the best strategy,' said the ageless Arch Wizard as he listed off all the advantages of his plan before folding his arms in front of his chest.

The others understood that his decision was not up for discussion and were too exhausted to contradict him, so they nodded and lay down on the broad flagstones that bordered the artificial river left and right. But while Ahren lay there and looked at the stars above, he couldn't help worrying. What would happen if he turned over in his sleep? If he was lucky, he would just get a soaking, but if he rolled over in the wrong direction, he would plunge into the depths. Without giving it a second thought he tied himself firmly to the much heavier Trogadon with a rope, as the dwarf looked on, chuckling. Ahren lay down again, reassured, and was delighted to see that the others were following his example by securing themselves to each other so that in the end they looked like a comical pearl necklace, lying in a row along the stone slabs and drifting off to sleep.

Chapter 10

They travelled carefully under the bright spring sunshine along the edge of the stone canal, which quietly and steadily distributed the life-giving water down onto the plains below, reawakening the dead landscape and bringing it back to its previous vitality. Ahren absorbed every detail of what was unfolding before his curious eyes. The channels below stretched in straight lines away from the waterway, only to divide into many smaller offshoots and ended up in enormous islands of plant life situated sometimes ten, fifteen, or even twenty furlongs away. In the beginning, there was often only one tiny farmhouse near one of these artificial oases, and the vegetation was wild and primeval, but the further south they rode, the more the picture changed. The vegetation in the oases had been cultivated, and many farmhouses stood at regular intervals in the middle of the neatly arranged fields.

Ahren was in awe of the Sunplainers' ability to plan and implement their ideas and of the way they had won back this barren part of their country.

One day flowed into the next. They travelled along the waterway during the sunlight hours, and at night they rested on its edge. Jelninolan kept a lookout for Swarm Claws and Uldini cast a weak disguise charm, which was enough to delay the Glower Bear by erasing their traces.

'Why didn't he do that earlier?' asked Ahren one morning as Uldini incanted the charm again.

Falk scratched his beard while he considered an answer. 'I'm no expert, but as far as I know, its effect is only limited and very temporary. As if you were ploughing up the earth in an effort to hide your footprints.

It causes momentary confusion, but in the long run it becomes easier to track you. Uldini has calculated that the bear will fall for the trap for another three nights at most, but then he'll be breathing down our necks.'

Ahren looked at the farms, which were now no more than five furlongs away, with concern. The thought of the bloodshed that their pursuer could wreak on the land dwellers filled him with horror.

His master followed his look and laid a comforting hand on his shoulder. 'There's no need to worry. A hunting Glower Bear is decidedly single-minded. We are his prey. As long as nobody attacks him, he will ignore everybody around him. The beasts can travel for weeks without food, and if this one gets hungry, he can help himself to the domestic cattle that are grazing on the surrounding farmland.' He pointed towards the south. 'And apart from that, the land is becoming more and more densely populated, and it won't be long before we meet the first patrols. If Uldini announces himself and reports who's on our heels, they'll send a complete legion to corner him. That will chase him away for the time being.'

'What's a legion?' Ahren had heard the term before but couldn't make head or tail of it.

'The army of the Sunplains is divided up into legions, and each one consists of one thousand soldiers,' said Falk matter-of-factly.

Ahren blinked and tried to comprehend that number. Even on King's Island he had never seen more than two hundred soldiers in one place, and a single unit here contained a thousand?

'Didn't Uldini say that the 17th Legion was besieging the Brazen City?' he asked awestruck.

Falk nodded. 'But don't be fooled. Thirty years ago, the Sunplains celebrated the creation of the 50th Legion. There could well be more by now.' He noticed the disbelieving face of his apprentice and pointed at the surrounding fields. 'Why do you think they need all that food? Their stomachs get hungry just as quickly as ours do, but they have to feed tens of thousands of soldiers, who have been having their heads bashed in by the Eternal Empire for more than forty winters.' Falk gave a spit in disgust and became silent.

Ahren tried to imagine all the legions on one field, but the picture was too vast for his imagination. He wanted to ask more questions, but Falk forestalled him.

'Why don't we use this wonderful location for a few balancing exercises? First, you have to jump from one side of the canal to the other a hundred times while we march onwards. By the time you've done that, I will have come up with some more ideas.'

Ahren swallowed hard as he looked at the artificial stream, three paces across. He had to leap across it, but without overdoing it and being carried over the opposite edge. He wiped his sweating hands on his legs and chanced his first jump.

His master wanted to kill him! Ahren was in no doubt about that. Falk had ordered him to perform daredevil stunts up on the canal throughout the day, and later on he had put Khara onto him, who subjected him to a succession of sword thrusts and kicks from which he had great difficulty defending himself on the restricted stone space. Finally, darkness had mercifully closed in and the others had settled down to sleep after their cold supper.

Ahren was still nibbling at a hard piece of cheese and looking forward to the fact that they would soon be able to replenish their food supplies. He missed Culhen terribly. The absence of the wolf from his thoughts felt almost the same as if he had lost a limb. Falk had explained that his friend and Selsena were seeking out a safe route to the south and were covering their tracks to prevent the bear from finding them – to avoid all their efforts being in vain.

The apprentice couldn't wait to embrace his four-legged friend again, and he even intended to put up with the wolf's slobbery licks across the face. As long as he didn't fall to his death beforehand thanks to Falk, of course.

The young Paladin stood up with a groan and stretched his back. Then he noticed a movement to this right. He froze for a moment, and then realised it was Khara. She was sitting a little bit away on the edge of the canal with her legs dangling beneath her. He wasn't sure if it would be better to leave the secretive girl alone – after all he had the unerring knack of saying the wrong thing to her, and the thought of antagonising the swordfighter while he was half a pace from the abyss struck him as being far from wise. But he was in a restless mood and really wanted company, and so he decided to take his chances.

He cleared his throat as he approached her, hoping to prevent any misfortune, and when she looked at him with her dark, melancholy eyes, he sat down cross-legged beside her. A gentle breeze blew the aromas of plants and animals up to them and gave Ahren a feeling of familiarity. The waxing moon floated large and brightly in the sky and few clouds hid the stars. Dots of light from the farmhouses could be seen here and there and everything was covered in a blanket of peace and quiet. It was still cool at night but not uncomfortable, and if Ahren hadn't been in fear of his life for the whole of the previous day, he would certainly have enjoyed this moment.

However, instead he let out a bitter sigh. 'For some reason Falk seems to be intent on my meeting a premature death', he said in a jocular manner.

Khara looked at him with her sad eyes before grimacing. 'I was only thinking how jealous I am of you, and then you go and say something stupid like that. You're pitiful.' The hostility in her voice was unmistakeable and Ahren flinched in shock, not understanding what he had done to her again.

She turned her head and looked out into the night, and then she continued to speak in a voice so quiet he could hardly hear her. 'I wish I had a teacher like yours', she murmured sadly. 'He pushes you to your limits and beyond, ensuring that your skills increase a little with every passing day, and he always keeps an eye on you. Today he paid respect to your ability by making you confront the possibility of falling into the depths. He trusted that you would become used to the fear of death, and yet you still moan and groan like a little boy who's being dragged unwillingly across the market square by his mother.'

Ahren was glad that the night was hiding his blushing face. The ex-slave had survived a difficult upbringing with considerable pain and constant danger of being killed. Although he had been told before about her situation, he still couldn't fully comprehend it. His complaining could only sound pathetic to her ears.

'But you have Jelninolan', he interjected, steering her away from his own crassness, as well as offering her a little comfort.

The girl shook her head. 'She's my mistress, not my teacher. That's the difference. I serve her, I'm not her student.' Then she looked guiltily over at Ahren. 'Don't misunderstand me. I'm eternally grateful to her. But I've learned everything about the art of sword-fighting that she can teach me. She helped me regain my sense of balance and my flexibility, but she's not a swords-mistress.' She sighed bitterly and pointed at him. 'All I have is a little boy who I have to teach to walk while all he wants is to be cosseted.'

Ahren took the insult quietly on the chin. He didn't know if it was peculiar to Khara, or if it were typical of all the inhabitants of the Eternal Empire, but her tendency to make comparisons that hit the mark, but yet were hurtful at the same time, was difficult to swallow. The young swordsgirl fell silent and turned away from him again.

Ahren rattled his brains for a suitable reply. He had never really put himself in her shoes, not least because their experiences and ways of seeing the world were so different. However, he could certainly identify with her desire for self-improvement. This was something he had felt himself ever since Falk had lit the fire of ambition in him. Ahren might groan over each individual exercise, but so long as they didn't actually kill him, he wouldn't have missed them for the world. Now he understood why Falk had wanted to adjust the training course. The old man had included Khara, and the girl had positively blossomed. He bit his lip thoughtfully.

'What would you like to practise if you wanted to continue your...your training?' he asked haltingly.

'I would really love to learn how to handle a Whisper Blade correctly,' she said after a moment's consideration.

Ahren shivered when he noticed how passionately Khara spoke of deadly weapons.

'What is a Whisper Blade?' he asked.

Khara stood up and quietly collected her Wind Blade and then his from their sleeping quarters.

Then she began making slow, supple turns, at the same time carefully carrying out circular thrusts and stabs with both weapons. 'The Whisper Blade is the counterpart to the Wind Blade. It's shorter and lighter, and always used as a supplementary weapon,' she explained, all the while continuing her elegant blade dance. Then one of the blades scraped the stone and she stopped abruptly. Annoyed with herself, she passed Ahren his blade and pointed at the score on the stone, while looking at their companions to see if any of them had been awoken by the noise. 'That was the "Dance of the Waking Student," a warming-up ceremony. You see what happens if you try it with two Wind Blades,' she whispered in supressed rage. 'The dimensions of the second blade are all wrong, and so one can't practise the routine properly.'

Ahren nodded although he was confused and put Wind Blade back in its scabbard. He knew how difficult it was to get weapons from the Eternal Empire, so he understood the swordsgirl's situation a little better. He thought again of Falk's attempt to support her, and he decided to try something out.

'Maybe I can help you,' he said uncertainly. 'Just tell me how and where I should attack you, and at least then you will be able to hone your skills with Wind Blade.' Hardly were the words out of his mouth, when he realised how miserable his offer sounded, but in spite of this Khara examined his face critically. She waded into the water without saying a word and immediately took up a low, defensive position. 'Jump with the blade over my head and make a straight downward slice,' she blurted.

Ahren was somewhat taken aback, but he got himself into position and did as he had been asked. Khara turned away when she was under him and tried to swing Wind Blade upward in one elegant movement, managing however only to slip and end up under the surface of the water. Spluttering and gasping she came back up again, and Ahren was surprised to see that she seemed neither angry nor disappointed. She beamed at him with blazing eyes and pointed to the stone edge.

'Again!' she commanded quietly, and the young Forest Guardian obeyed.

As he was preparing to attack again, he noticed that the cold water had soaked Khara's tunic in a very noticeable way. He leaped forward, trying in vain to concentrate on his technique, and to keep his eyes focussed on the task in hand. He had a terrible feeling this was going to be a very long night for him.

Ahren struggled through the next day completely exhausted. Khara had been bursting with enthusiasm, and so he had trained with her until almost dawn, while she restlessly carried out a succession of complicated manoeuvres. The girl had been remarkably cheerful by her own standards, and now he realised to his own surprise that he couldn't get her smiling face out of his head, as well as other images of her that he tried not to think about. Of course, their nightly activity hadn't remained hidden from the others for long, but nobody had made any particular comments on the matter. Both Falk and Jelninolan had looked at him proudly but without saying a word, while Trogadon had winked at him lewdly and smiled in a manner that caused him to blush on the spot.

Mercifully, his master held back with his commands, probably out of concern that his apprentice in his present state might really topple off the canal, and so he hammered more theoretical knowledge into the mind of the would-be Forest Guardian.

'Sicklehoppers were once common or garden grasshoppers, hard enough as that is to believe. HE, WHO FORCES altered them further and further until they became true killing machines. Luckily, he lost the run of himself as always,' said the old man frankly.

Ahren looked at him in surprise, but it was Jelninolan who continued the explanation. 'Creation follows a delicate balance, something that the Adversary simply does not understand. What you don't realise is that the Sicklehoppers were once even more deadly. Their leaps were more precise but lower, and they were considerably more flexible and swifter.' Her eyes suggested that she was remembering something dreadful. 'However, the dark god wished to make them even stronger and better – but he went too far. Their hind-legs are now too heavy and powerful for the rest of their bodies, and while it's true they can now go further with each hop, they've nonetheless lost their precision and speed. They also have to eat four times as much as before, and so they lie for a long time in a so called "prey sleep," while they wait for an appropriate prey to approach nearby.' She paused and thought for a moment. 'If HE, WHO FORCES had stopped tinkering around with them at the right time, I really don't know if we could have won the war.'

The thought of facing an even more dangerous form of Sicklehopper, and on a battlefield without any pillars for fleeing was difficult for Ahren to imagine. Then it struck him that he might have to face these Dark Ones in future battles. Bungled or not, the present version of the grotesque grasshoppers was enough to make his heart sink.

'When am I going to receive my magic Paladin armour,' he asked as he thought of the ease with which the Sicklehoppers had sliced through the dwarf's chainmail.

'We'll see if I can get hold of the right material and a suitable blacksmith,' growled Trogadon cheerfully. 'I think you'll just have to be patient though, until we reach Thousand Halls. Deep Steel is not easy to work, and difficult to find outside the dwarf territories.'

Ahren nodded and let his fingers glide along his Elfish armour. The apprentice was not even sure he wanted to get rid of it so quickly. He had become so used to his armour that he only took it off when he was bathing or when he believed himself to be perfectly safe. The light leather plates, which moved so easily, had become a second skin to him, and when they were travelling, he could even sleep in the armour and still wake up refreshed. Trogadon was the only other one of them who managed to do that in his chainmail, but Ahren believed that the indestructible dwarf would be able to rest squeezed in between two jagged rocks, and still belt out a rowdy drinking song the following morning. Uldini relied totally on his magic to protect himself, and Jelninolan took off her ribbon armour at night. Falk would sleep in his leather jerkin and generally only put on his knightly armour when he was expecting trouble and was preparing for close combat. Then his eyes fell on Khara, who was walking beside him on the other side of the canal. She was only wearing a thin green tunic of Elfish material.

'But wouldn't it be a good idea for Khara to get some armour too?' he suggested. For some reason the thought that the girl might be injured, perhaps badly, made him uneasy.

Jelninolan nodded vigorously. 'Because of the trouble with Sven, I completely forgot to make something or to send out an order.' She looked at Khara apologetically, and the young girl blushed.

'Not necessary, mistress. I have to be very quick anyway. Armour would only slow me down,' she said quickly.

'Fiddlesticks!' replied Uldini, interrupting the conversation and causing general consternation. 'There are enough things out there that are faster than people or take more than a thrust of a sword to make them breathe their last. And anyway, you're a distraction for one or other of us if we have to be worrying about your safety.' He then glanced over at Ahren, who made every effort to appear impassive. 'There are any number of merchants in Waterheart. One of them is bound to have something that will satisfy your requirements.' The Arch Wizard was speaking once again in a tone of absolute authority, and Ahren turned to his master.

'Am I imagining things, or has he become very decisive recently,' he whispered to the old man as quietly as he could.

Falk smirked and pointed out towards the farms and the roads that were beginning to give the area an air of civilisation.

'We're here in his country. He is the Chief Advisor and Arch Wizard to the Sun Emperor and strictly speaking the second most powerful person in this enormous empire. The surroundings are doubtless reminding him of just how important he is.' He pondered for a moment, then bent down conspiratorially towards Ahren. 'Did you know that he has his own tower? Tall and slim and very white and with a golden roof?'

'A tower?' asked Ahren in surprise and far too loudly.

Uldini stared daggers over his shoulder towards them, and Falk quickly straightened up and gave an amused grimace.

'We'll talk about it another time,' he said sardonically, and within a few heartbeats the Arch Wizard and the Paladin were having one of their regular verbal duels.

They travelled southward along the waterway for another week. The land became greener and greener, the farms larger and larger, and the fields broader and broader. They were stopped four times by patrols who ordered them to clamber down immediately, but every time Uldini floated down to them and subjected them to such a barrage of orders that they bowed deeply and carried them out immediately.

The sun was growing stronger, and the afternoons were so warm that they now stopped at regular intervals to cool down by the artificial river.

One morning just before noon, Uldini raised his hand and turned back to face the others. 'This evening we cross the Sword Path. From that point on we should be safe from the Glower Bear, and also from other Dark Ones. And anyway, I have given instructions to every patrol we've met. At this point there's bound to be a whole legion with long spears and heavy crossbows hunting the beast. It's time we were travelling like normal people.'

By this point the stone canal was over fifty paces high, and so Uldini created a Floating Charm which brought them all safely down to the ground.

'How can you be so sure we won't meet up with any more Dark Ones?' asked Ahren, who had been made uneasy by the open use of magic after they had been followed for so long.

'The Sword Path is the main trading route from the Sun Palace to the deep south of the Plains,' interjected Trogadon. The dwarf had hummed nervously during the downward float, and he seemed quite relieved to be back on firm ground. When the Sunplains began to expand past Thousand Halls in a southerly direction, it was nothing more than a simple army track, but the bigger the empire became, the broader the road got. Now it's the main artery of the Sunplains. Whole legions and enormous supplies of provisions such as food, tents, boots or spare pieces for armour are sent southward, while expensive, exotic goods make their way up north. I'm talking about dates, spices and cotton. There is no road in the Plains that is better protected.'

'That sounds good,' said Ahren cheerfully, but Falk smiled and gave him a box on the head.

'Don't be cheerful too soon, lazybones. We're only crossing the Sword Path. Waterheart is ten leagues further south.' When the old man saw the disappointment on his apprentice's face, he softened and added: 'Uldini's escort party will be waiting for us there, and if the present Sun Emperor is anything like the ones I knew, then it will be very comfortable for us from that point on.'

The Arch Wizard rubbed his hands. 'Then we'll have civilisation at last. I can hardly wait,' he called out, and for once sounded just as young as he looked.

Jelninolan snorted scornfully. 'What you call civilisation is pure decadence to us.'

'I had to put up with your cloth houses, so you'll just have to bear the occasional silk cushion', countered the Arch Wizard benevolently.

Ahren listened as Uldini described the advantages of his culture, and he felt a tickly sense of pleasant anticipation. If only half of what he was hearing were true, he would be in no hurry to leave it again.

The night was beginning to set in, and the first stars could be seen in the evening sky. Not for the first time, Ahren was standing still, staring like a clodhopper. He thought back to Three Rivers, and then to King's Island. Those two places had impressed him, but nothing compared to the Sword Path. It was neither ostentatious nor lofty, but rather simple and, well, *big*. The apprentice was looking at a ribbon that was at least fifty paces wide, constructed of hardened clay tiles, that stretched in a straight line from east to west. Tower-like constructions lining the colossal supplies route at intervals of ten or fifteen furlongs could be seen in the fading light of the sinking sun.

'Sentry towers,' whispered Trogadon to the speechless apprentice. 'If there's trouble anywhere, then horns are blown as signals, and they are passed from one tower to the next. Every ten leagues there's a little garrison, whose soldiers immediately march into action if they hear the alarm. We could set up camp here and we'd still be safer than anywhere we've been over the last two moons.'

Uldini turned around to the dwarf. 'I had hoped it wouldn't be necessary,' he said in a disappointed voice. 'There are comfortable lodgings for travellers near the garrisons, but it's too dark already, so we really are better off staying here for the night.'

The Arch Wizard gestured to the others to follow him, and they crossed over the road with its narrow well-tended slab-joints, and the stone felt surprisingly even under Ahren's feet. He was familiar with a similar road quality from King's Island, but he had never expected to find something similar in the middle of the Steppes. He studied the road in both directions. 'There's nobody to be seen apart from us. Is it used so little?' he asked.

Trogadon shook his head. 'The law states that merchants may not use the Sword Path at night.' He pointed at the Arch Wizard, who was floating ahead of them. 'Which is why we're crossing the road now, when it's empty.'

They arrived at the other side of the tiled surface, and Uldini pointed at a path, eight paces wide, that ran along the waterway towards the south.

'The way to Waterheart,' he sighed wistfully. 'So near and yet so far.'

Falk laughed and slapped him on the back, so hard that the Arch Wizard flew forward. 'We'll get there tomorrow and then you'll have all your luxury again. Grant Jelninolan and me one more night in the fresh air, you old fox.'

The robed figure nodded reluctantly. 'It's better this way,' he said, more to himself than anyone around him. 'It would be a big how-do-you-do for them if they had to open the gates for us at night.'

Jelninolan took out the last of her supplies and created a sumptuous meal for them. When they arrived in Waterheart she wouldn't need to be providing for the travelling party for some time. Fire was allowed again, and so Ahren enjoyed toasted bread with melted cheese, into which the elf had cleverly rolled the rest of their dried fruit. The whole thing was perfected by the addition of herbs that Falk had gathered along the way that afternoon, and the food was more full-flavoured than anything Ahren had ever eaten before.

If the wild plants were already that tasty, then the cultivated fields of the Sunplains surely had to result in more culinary delights. Ahren was munching yet another piece of bread when he suddenly experienced the familiar feeling of joy, hunger and the urge to hunt in his mind.

Ahren? he heard Culhen calling, and when the apprentice answered, he was overwhelmed with a sensation of joy. He could sense the wolf racing along to be with his friend as quickly as possible. The young Forest Guardian was about to tell Falk that their companions were approaching, but he could read from the overjoyed look on the face of the old man that Selsena had announced herself too.

Ahren waited for the moment when he would embrace his true wolf and glanced over at the little that was left of the evening meal. Culhen might well have missed him too, but it would take him a while to forgive Ahren for having eaten all around him.

Ahren woke up in the middle of the night to the ground vibrating. He was immediately awake. He freed himself from Culhen in his panic, who was lying low and growling, his nose towards the Sword Path.

The sensitive nose of the wolf had already picked up the source of the vibration, and Ahren, images of another herd in flight or an attack of Sicklehoppers filling his imagination, was relieved once his eyes followed where the wolf was looking, and he recognised what had caused the deep rumbling noise. Dozens of torches lit the night sky and cast a flickering light on hundreds of soldiers, marching in ordered rows along the Sword Path. The sight was awe-inspiring, but there was no threat in the disciplined quiet and calm regularity of their marching. Ahren would never dream of standing in the way of this ever-advancing mass of bodies, but he was certain too that the army would take no notice of him or his like as long as he left them in peace.

The steps became louder as the armoured soldiers came closer, and soon his fellow travellers too had woken up. Trogadon and Uldini simply turned away again. Jelninolan and Falk stayed lying down too, but they watched the performance with thoughtful looks. Khara however, just like Ahren, had sprung up and stared in terror at the approaching fighting force. Ahren realised in a flash that the one-time slave could still, in theory at least, be seen as the enemy, since she came from the Eternal Empire, with whom the Sunplainers were at war.

Instinctively he went over to her and put a reassuring arm around her shoulders, turning at the same time so that her face was hidden in his shadow. For a moment he feared that she would break his arm for this approach, but the girl remained still and joined him in watching the soldiers as they passed the travellers.

Ahren saw men and women in leather armour which went down to the knee and was surprisingly thick. A steel plate was sewn onto the chest, protecting the vital organs, and their leather helmets encompassed their whole faces, and also covered their necks. Broad wooden shields with metal rims were tied to their backs and each soldier held a spear in one hand and a short sword on their belts. Row after row of soldiers marched quietly and determinedly past, their eyes facing forward, their feet moving in unison. The travellers felt the ground quake as the troop, one enormous unit, passed their encampment, marching on until they disappeared into the night.

When the soldiers were no longer visible, Khara quickly released herself from Ahren's arm, not without twisting it painfully, and went silently over to her sleeping quarters. He looked after her somewhat irritated, but then Falk distracted him.

'Quite impressive, a legion like that. Don't you think?' he asked in a conversational tone. He pointed with his chin towards where the army had disappeared. 'That's why the Sword Path is taboo for merchants at night. In this way the troop movements can be carried out unhindered, and with the armour they have on, marching at night makes more sense than during the heat of the day.'

Ahren imagined that there were over fifty of these enormous units, and the realisation that the army of the Sunplains was really that big made him dizzy. Then he raised his voice. 'If we have that many soldiers, then the Dark Days will be over quickly, surely?' he asked hopefully.

Falk raised his eyebrows. 'You really should know better by now, Ahren. Firstly, most of these soldiers are stuck in a dogged war of attrition, and secondly, we need the Thirteen Paladins. Everything else is just decoration.'

Ahren blinked in disbelief, and after a moment of thinking, Falk corrected himself. 'That was a little bit of an exaggeration perhaps, but it does hit the nail on the head. If we have many warriors on our side, we'll find it much easier to contend with Dark Ones, who might appear in greater numbers in the future. Tlik gave us a breathing space, but in half a dozen winters HE, WHO FORCES will finally awaken, and then everybody needs to be ready, armies and Paladins alike.'

He looked firmly into Ahren's eyes. 'But don't fool yourself. If necessary, we can manage without the armies, even if it means large tracts of Jorath will be devastated. Without the Paladins however, we will lose, no matter what our military strength is.'

Ahren curled up under his blanket again and pulled Culhen in beside him. He listened to the powerful heartbeat of the wolf and thought perhaps Falk was right. But if he had the choice, he would still rather have the legions supporting him when he went into battle against the Adversary, rather than have to cut his way alone through the enemy ranks.

Chapter 11

As soon as Ahren woke up the next day he noticed the little table mountain to which the waterway led.

From which it springs, he corrected himself mentally. The elevation before him had to be Waterheart, the settlement which was the source of the water they had been following for the previous few weeks. He stretched up his neck curiously but couldn't make out any houses or other buildings from this distance.

He gobbled down his breakfast excitedly and quickly set to work doing the little tidying up jobs, so they could break camp more quickly, whether it was rolling up the mattresses or quenching the fire.

'Your apprentice is very lively this morning,' said Trogadon teasingly.

'There was too much talk about luxury. No wonder he's got off his backside,' said Falk, taking the same tack.

Ahren bit his tongue and continued packing his rucksack. Then he belted it on pointedly and looked at the others serenely.

'Shall we?' he asked innocently, and when the others saw that he wasn't going to react to their jibes, they relented and packed their own belongings. Ahren smirked inwardly and decided to remember that tactic. Maybe in that way he could put an end to the endless teasing which, in his opinion, he was far too often subjected to.

He walked alongside his master and decided to ask a few questions that had been weighing heavily on him for some time now.

'How far do the Steppes that we are travelling on now extend?' he asked. He started with something innocuous. He'd ask the trickier questions once the old man had warmed up a little.

'We can hardly call them steppes really, can we?' suggested Falk mischievously, and pointed at the farms surrounding them, whose occupants were working the fields. There were only a few brown patches here and there, where the land had retained its barren form. 'These are the offshoots of the Dead Hills. Further east the earth is wet, fruitful and easy to work. The spell that created the Dead Hills didn't reach that area.' He looked over at the table mountain. 'The spell ended there, and also of course, the steppes. The rock that you see there is actually not that old for a mountain. All the water that was flowing underground that time had to come out somewhere, and so the mass of rock was pushed upward. The result is Waterheart.'

'And what's it like down in the south, behind Thousand Halls?' interjected Ahren with another harmless question. His master was in an expansive mood, and Ahren was going to make full use of it.

'First there's a desert as long as it's wide, in which the unprepared die of thirst in no time at all. It takes two weeks to pass through it if you follow the Sword Path. If you deviate from it, you're as good as gone. Beyond it lies countryside both beautiful and forbidding, consisting of sand, dust and oases. Hence the name of the empire, whose plains are so varied and marked by the sun. The Sunplainers are proud of this variety and intend to expand it as far as the Ice Fields in the south and the Green Sea to the north-east.' His voice had taken on an anxious tone. 'I always forget how much this nation tends towards expansion. If Quin-Wa hadn't attacked them, the Sunplainers would probably be at war with every large nation of Jorath and might well have already swallowed up the smaller ones.'

Now they were coming to the more exciting themes. 'Was that maybe why she declared war on the Sunplains? To stop their expansion?' he pressed. He found it hard to come to terms with the fact that the Eternal Empress was a Paladin and also one of the Ancients, and yet at the same time she provoked a bloody war that had been going on for generations already. It was true that the Paladins had experienced hard times, and he had learned from Falk's past how far they had fallen, but creating an empire in order to attack another one was a different kettle of fish from drinking too much and hiring yourself out as a mercenary, as Falk had done.

His master pondered Ahren's question. 'Maybe that really was one of her reasons,' he said cautiously. 'Quin-Wa always had the tendency to do three things with the hope of getting fifteen different results. Her ruthless efficiency seems to be reflected all over the Eternal Empire.' He looked over at Ahren. 'The truth is, we really don't know. She could just as easily have been driven by boredom. The centuries can come to feel endless - I can tell you that much.'

Falk winked at him as he said this, and Ahren knew his master well enough to realise that the old man wasn't going to expand on this point any further, so the young Forest Guardian came to the point that was concerning him the most. 'What will we do if Justinian refuses our help as go-betweens, or he has Bergen executed in spite of everything?' he asked anxiously.

'We'll rebel against him,' said Falk in a hard voice. Bergen is one of us, one of the Thirteen. We need him in the war against HIM, WHO FORCES. Uldini would rather tear down the mountain on which The Brazen City stands than lose another Paladin. That was what I tried to explain yesterday. If the worst comes to the worst, it's just we Thirteen

Paladins against the rest of the world, but without the Thirteen of us, we're powerless.' His voice was quiet and flat and Ahren shivered.

The young man's determination to save as many innocent beings from the consequences of the Dark Days that lay before them would be much more difficult to implement than he had anticipated. He pondered for a while and tousled Culhen's neck-fur absently. The wolf had been walking close to him all morning and kept looking up at him with his loyal eyes.

Finally, they approached the low mountain with its flattened summit, and Ahren could see in the distance a wrought-iron barred gate. It guarded a tunnel which seemed to lead directly into the mountain, but the gate was raised for now. An ox and cart were coming out of the entrance, as the group of travellers climbed steadily up the path. The tunnel was square-shaped, a good dozen paces wide and equally high.

'Is Waterheart a dwarf enclave?' he asked confused.

Trogadon laughed heartily and shook his head. 'No son, but first impressions can be misleading, I'll give you that. After the Pall Pillar was created, the Plainers asked us to assist in building their city and the waterways. That's why everything looks a little Dwarfish.'

Ahren's ears pricked up. 'Did you say water*ways*? You mean there are more of them?'

'Three in total' answered the dwarf warrior. 'The northern one – you know that one already. Then there's the one that leads east towards the Core Country, and the last one, which carries water south into the middle of the desert.'

Ahren looked to the horizon left and right of the mountain. He squinted and could finally make out a construction to the east that seemed to wind its way through the countryside at a surprisingly flat angle.

'That one doesn't reach as far as the northern one, and the land dips very slightly towards the east. Which is why it's so dainty' added Trogadon, seeing Ahren's doubtful expression.

As they approached the tunnel, the mountain began to dominate their view, and Ahren realised that the rock rose two furlongs, while its width stretched a good ten across. The steep rock-face was remarkably smooth, and when they finally arrived at the tunnel, the apprentice saw that the mountain looked as if it had been pressed upwards out of the ground.

When the travellers reached the entrance to the mountain, a dozen sentries at the gate bowed respectfully in front of them. The officer in charge, who had recognised Uldini immediately, gave a signal, and instantly seven enormous sedan chairs appeared from the dark opening. Each of them was carried by eight muscular young men, who lowered the sedans right in front of them so that none of the visitors needed to take an unnecessary step when climbing in.

Ahren stared at the vehicle in disbelief. 'Are we supposed to climb in and allow ourselves to be carried?' he asked Falk in a low voice. A horse and cart were already luxury enough for a Forest Guardian like himself. Being carried by the muscular strength of other people was just too embarrassing to contemplate.

Falk gave an affirming nod. 'I know what you mean. I don't like it either. But this pompous form of transport befits Uldini's station here, as does all the other deference and luxury that we're going to enjoy. We want as many dignitaries as possible to believe his news of the Thirteenth Paladin's return, so we'll just play along with it and strengthen his authority.' And with a look of disgust on his face, the old man sank back into the extremely plump, white satin pillows, which almost swallowed him up, forcing Ahren to suppress a grin.

Selsena, on the other hand, seemed to be quite offended at the fact that Falk had abandoned her back in favour of the sedan, and the displeasure that she emitted confirmed her displeasure. Culhen seriously considered jumping up and joining Ahren in the sedan, but the apprentice threw the lazy wolf a warning look until his four-legged friend gave up the idea and trotted along faithfully beside him. Ahren chuckled until he noticed Khara and Jelninolan admiring the muscles of the semi-naked sedan-bearers. At which point his merriness vanished. While they were being carried into the rock, he watched the young swordsgirl keenly until Trogadon, who was being carried alongside him, had seen enough.

'If you really want to, I can show you how to look like those men there,' he said conspiratorially, and pointed at the panting and sweating bearers, who were struggling under the immense weight of the dwarf, while casting envious looks at their fellow-bearers, who were carrying much lighter loads. 'A little exercise every day, and your muscles will expand in no time.'

Ahren blushed a deep red and turned his head away in embarrassment. 'I don't know what you're talking about,' he grumbled quietly. And for the rest of the journey he deliberately studied the stone walls of the tunnel, which didn't prevent Falk and the dwarf from laughing merrily at him.

The tunnel led them steadily upwards in a wide, serpentine movement, only dimly lit by the torches that hung on the walls. When they finally came out into the daylight again, Ahren had to shield his dazzled eyes from the strong midday sun, which was burning down on them from a cloudless sky. As he was becoming accustomed to the light, he also noticed how much warmer it was here in the city. Within ten heartbeats, the sweat was running down his back inside his armour, and Ahren hoped he would soon be able to dress more suitably. He was now doubly embarrassed by the fact that the poor unfortunate servants still had to carry him through the streets of Waterheart in this oppressive heat. His nostrils filled with strange aromas: spices that were completely unknown to him mixed with the mineral smell of a large body of water. He rubbed his eyes once again and suddenly he was able to make out more than mere outlines. Now that he could see Waterheart in all its glory, he was truly amazed.

The table mountain must have been a volcano at one time, he realised. An enormous lake filled most of the crater he could see in front of him. Little whitewashed houses with flat roofs were pressed into the rock. They stood beside each other in neat rows, taking up every available bit of dry land in several concentric circles around the lake. The narrow, intertwined streets between the houses, as well as the three main roads, were the only means of moving forward, and many of the residents seemed to travel through the city in little boats that crisscrossed the lake. There were little cockleshells with room for only one person, and bigger boats with up to six people or laden down with essential goods. A constant noise reverberated in the crater, caused by three small artificial tunnels that had had been carved at water level into the rock wall, and from which gurgling lake water continually disappeared. This had to be the source of the waterways, and Ahren felt a deep respect for the ingenuity of the Sunplainers. They had suffered dreadful misfortune when the Dead Hills had been created, but rather than leave, they had used the effects of the spell to slowly bring life back into the land by using the water from the charm-created lake. In the middle of the lake, Ahren could see the unmistakable rippling of a strong current, and he was sure that was where the water was pushed upward, which would later flow away in the three artificial canals. The young man looked happily at Trogadon and Falk, who grinned back at him, knowing exactly how he felt.

'Everyone is overcome the first time,' growled the dwarf, who was moved himself. 'It was about a hundred years ago when I was here first. We were chasing a few bandits. You were with us, weren't you?', he asked Falk.

Ahren understood that he was referring back to their shared experiences as mercenaries, but the old Forest Guardian shook his head.

'That must have been after my time. The last time I saw this place the second waterway had just been built, and there were a lot fewer houses around. There's hardly enough room to swing a cat now,' he grunted, and wiped the sweat from his beard. 'I'd forgotten how hot it is here.'

Falk was right. There wasn't a breath of wind within the enormous rock basin, and the dark volcanic rock seemed to attract the heat of the sun. The sedan bearers continued steadily onwards and carried them down towards the water's edge. The air was much more bearable here, and Ahren noticed that the houses directly on the water were much larger and more luxurious than their narrow, dustier counterparts in the upper rows. It seemed as if properties on the lake were much sought after, and he could understand why as he drew the cool, refreshing air deep into his lungs.

The sedan bearers finally stopped in front of a large property, one of the few multi-storeyed buildings in Waterheart. An overhanging balcony dominated the top floor of the enormous house. It offered the visitors cooling shade as they stepped out of their sedans. Four servants in blue and white uniforms bowed in a ripple effect in front of them and gestured, without saying a word, to the travellers that they should enter the house. Selsena was led to a comfortable stable.

Ahren noticed much to his irritation that two of the four servants had very dark skin, and a third one had the same light-yellow tone as Khara.

'Don't tell me they're slaves,' he said indignantly to Falk, but Uldini immediately intervened and reassured him concerning his misgivings.

'No, they're not. The Sunplainers have conquered large tracts of land over the years, and the reason they are so successful is the simple fact that the conquered peoples enjoy the same rights afterwards, like the original Plainers with their pale skin and curly hair. Half of the Sun Emperor's team of advisors come from the southern countries, two are from what once were provinces of the Eternal Empire, and one even comes from the Jungles although they don't officially belong to the Plains.' The Arch Wizard shrugged his shoulders nonchalantly. 'You can accuse my people of making many mistakes, but they certainly aren't vindictive. If someone turns up, they are always welcome and can participate in whatever occupation they wish.'

Ahren looked curiously at the servants, who were now leading them up a narrow spiral staircase to the first floor. The young Forest Guardian had only seen a few doors inside the house, but they were all open, presumably to let as much fresh air as possible circulate throughout the house. The furnishings were remarkably modest when compared to the opulent exterior of the property - which reflected the property-owner's wealth. Whoever lived here clearly kept luxury to a level that wasn't ostentatious. They were led through a cloistered courtyard which had spacious bedrooms left and right. Then they reached the large balcony where a stocky man of about fifty winters was sitting, wearing an airy, loose-fitting garment whose wide sleeves and trouser legs suggested that their host was still in his sleeping garb. His dark hair was plaited in the fashion of the little folk, and for a moment Ahren wasn't sure if he was looking at a very large dwarf or a small, squat human.

'I'm delighted that you've finally arrived.' The man approached them beaming and opened his arms in a welcoming manner. 'I had them searching everywhere for you, but you were nowhere to be found until I finally heard reports of some crazy people walking along the waterway.' He gave a practised bow in front of Uldini and winked mischievously at the Arch Wizard. 'Then I knew that our all-powerful master had returned.'

Uldini rolled his eyes before quickly embracing the stranger. Ahren raised his eyebrows in surprise at the unfamiliar friendliness of his normally tetchy travelling companion, but the Arch Wizard turned towards them and made a formal gesture towards the stocky man.

'Allow me to introduce Akkad tul Balan to you. He is one of the Ancients, and I would describe his as a sluggish whale in a bay of sharks. He covers my back because there are few Ancients senior to him and so he can issue instructions in my place.'

Akkad gave an indulgent smile. 'I see you as my friend too, for which I am grateful.' The man spoke in a peculiarly sing-song manner which Ahren found both warm and soft, and the gentle reproach towards Uldini in his voice contained genuine warmth.

Jelninolan stepped forward and embraced the little man. 'It's been an eternity, Akkad. How are your family?' she asked warmly.

'All are happy and well. After Pulatan departed from us ten years ago, I got to know my Walina.' He sounded like a shy youth as he continued. 'She is heavy with our second child and I can hardly wait to see her again.'

Jelninolan looked at him wide-eyed. You're married again? Are you never satisfied?'

Akkad shrugged his shoulders in embarrassment. 'I have a lot of love in my heart and I don't like being alone. The joy at sharing my life with them outweighs the sadness that comes with the knowledge that I will outlive them as I have all the others.'

Falk scowled, but stepped forward too and shook hands. 'What number wife are you on now? The twenty-fifth?'

'Forty-eighth,' replied Akkad calmly. 'Not all of us Ancients lead a life of loneliness.'

Ahren saw that Falk had tensed up even more. 'Not all of us have a choice,' he replied coldly and then turned away to look from the balcony down onto the lake.

Akkad sighed quietly. 'Is it really that hard for him to accept the happiness others might have?'

'He's a good man, who only wants what's best for everyone!' interjected Ahren in an angry tone. His original positive feelings towards the man had changed to a deep disgust, born of his loyalty to his master.

'You're reminding him of what he himself has lost,' said Jelninolan in a low voice, but Akkad's attention was now focussed completely on Ahren.

'You must be the Thirteenth Paladin, who Falk discovered in the back of beyond. Welcome to Waterheart. I will do everything in my power to help you on your journey,' he said in a strangely formal voice, and bowed before the incensed young man, this time without a hint of mischief in his eyes.

The Ancient seemed to be completely unfazed by Ahren's anger, and the young man, who was disconcerted by this reaction, stammered a few words of thanks. The relaxed manner of his opposite had a disarming effect, and now the young Paladin understood why Uldini had described him as a whale. The man's presence seemed to fill the balcony with an unusual calmness, and any resentment was like water off a duck's back.

Ahren was relieved when their host turned towards the others to greet them. Khara presented her usual impassive face, while Trogadon grasped the man's forearms firmly. They both looked almost like brothers, and they were in spirit, although not blood-related. Trogadon expressed his joie-de-vivre through laughter and song while Akkad did so through a steady calmness as if he were a second sun, bathing those around him in a warm golden glow. They looked deep into each other's eyes, and Ahren was convinced that he had just witnessed the beginning of a beautiful friendship.

Then Akkad released himself from the dwarf and turned with a curious look towards Culhen, who up to this point had remained at the entrance to the balcony sniffing around him. The wolf had smelled something he couldn't find, and Ahren sensed a rising irritability in his friend.

The stocky Ancient was smiling at a joke that clearly only he understood. 'I see you can still smell my snack, am I right?' he said, teasing the large wolf. Then he made a flinging gesture with his hand and a large roast appeared in the air, flew in a wide arc and landed directly before Cullen's front paws.

Both Ahren and his companion were stunned by the food, but the wolf's reflexes were decidedly faster than those of the young man. The young Forest Guardian was still gaping in amazement as the wolf bit into the meat, which he started feasting on greedily, rolled up into a ball in a corner of the balcony.

Ahren blinked and tried to make sense of what he had seen when Akkad did another graceful bow in front of everyone.

'Show off,' snorted Uldini.

Their host smiled. 'That wasn't showing off. *This* is,' he said airily as he lifted both hands and whispered something which Ahren couldn't understand.

Large marble benches with silk cushions and high arm- and backrests rose up from the floor, a canopy of shimmering blue appeared in the air above them, and a table, laden with fruit and joints of meat, golden cheeses and steaming hot bread materialised in their midst. With a final click of the Ancient's fingers, a large carafe of deep-red wine along with seven goblets came into view on the afore-mentioned table.

'Ahren, my dear friend, how many times, have I told you to keep your mouth closed when you're amazed by something?' scolded Uldini. 'How are people supposed to take the Thirteenth Paladin seriously if he goes around looking like an idiot?'

The young man quickly snapped his jaws shut and looked at Akkad almost fearfully. 'Did you just create all that out of nothing?' he asked in an awestruck voice.

The Ancient shrugged his shoulders. 'One of my favourite spells. I call it "lunchtime with good friends." Do you like it?' he asked coquettishly. 'Try the wine,' he added with childish glee. 'I've just composed the magic for that.'

'Oh, we two are really going to get on like a house on fire,' said Trogadon with a satisfied sigh, as he began filling one of the magic plates with an outrageous amount of food.

Jelninolan had a critical look on her face and she picked one of the grapes up between her fingers. She examined it carefully, put it in her mouth and slowly began to chew. Then she smiled in satisfaction and nodded appreciatively at Akkad. 'You've improved considerably since the last time I tasted your handiwork. Congratulations.'

The magician clapped his hands gleefully. 'If an Elfish palate is satisfied, then I am too. Stone, metal and wood is one thing, but food has cost me a lot of time and effort.' He sat down on one of the benches and created a plate laden with delicacies, which he began to feast on.

'Now that your food really tastes good, you're going to get even fatter,' prophesied Uldini scornfully, but his sarcasm had absolutely no effect on Akkad's unflappable demeanour.

Ahren eyed the feast mistrustfully before going over to Falk, who was still leaning on the balcony balustrade and staring down at the glistening lake.

The afternoon sun was gradually losing its intensity, and a refreshing breeze wafted through their hair. Ahren closed his eyes and enjoyed the peaceful moment. The sound of the waterways provided a calming background, and the shouts of the busy residents of Waterheart created an almost homely atmosphere, a faint echo of the village square in Deepstone, when everyone gathered to celebrate the Spring Festival.

'Why don't you like Akkad? Is there something I should know?' asked Ahren after some moments of silence.

Falk glanced at him, then looked back onto the water. 'No, there's nothing he can do about it, really. I'm just different to him in matters of the heart. When Miriam died that time, a part of me died too. Something that I will never be able to get back. He, in the meantime has buried forty-seven wives, and yet still has the strength to fall in love again.' Falk hesitated. 'Somehow it doesn't seem right to me. As if his love has lost something in value.' Behind them, Trogadon was just telling a lewd joke which made everybody laugh, and Falk took a deep breath as he tried to control his emotions. 'Akkad remains true to them and he stays by their side until they pass away. He behaves impeccably and seems genuinely sincere towards all of his wives.' The old man shook his head. 'I just find it very hard to understand how people can behave so differently in such fundamental matters.'

The thought came to Ahren that his master was clinging to his grief like to an old security blanket. It had taken several years of living together at close quarters, and Ahren having a near death experience for his master to open up enough to tell him of his wife who had been murdered, and of their daughter. The cantankerous Forest Guardian had buried his grief so deeply within himself, that there hardly seemed to be room for anything else. Now that he himself had a companion and knew how this deep connection felt, Ahren was convinced that it was only Selsena who had prevented his master from losing his mind altogether. The young man was relieved that Falk had recovered enough in the ensuing centuries to finally give a shy young village boy the chance to become his apprentice.

Being unfamiliar with affairs of the heart, and preferring to keep his conjectures to himself for the time being, Ahren decided to steer their conversation in a different direction. 'If he's had that many wives, how old is Akkad actually?' he asked, genuinely baffled. If the Ancient had really accompanied each of his wives until they die, then he had to be older than Jelninolan!

Falk shrugged his shoulders. 'We don't know precisely. There's a persistent rumour going around that he's the first person that the gods revealed the secrets of magic to. That was at the beginning of the Dark Days.'

'But the Dark Days were only eight hundred years ago,' replied Ahren.

'The end of the Dark Days, yes. Their beginning was many, many winters before that. The Wizards were the first attempts of the gods to protect their Creation from the control of HIM, WHO FORCES. The

Paladins appeared much later. What is described in a few brief paragraphs in the godsday school actually refers to dozens of centuries full of battles and bloody deeds.' He pointed over at Uldini. 'He took the trouble of trying to find out how long the Dark Days actually were. But he didn't succeed. Whole civilisations were wiped out in the wars, and the calendars were changed at least three times during those epochs – so far as anyone can tell.'

Ahren was aghast as he considered how many must have died over such a long period. 'I'm surprised that there was anyone left in the end that was capable of fighting,' he said stunned.

'It wasn't battle after battle,' replied Falk. There were always breaks when each side recovered its strength. One of those pauses is said to have lasted for over a century.' He shrugged his shoulders again. 'The truth is that most of them you see here are spring chickens who only started fighting when the Paladins already existed. I don't even want to imagine what it was like earlier.' He placed an arm on Ahren's shoulder. 'Enough of this depressing talk. Akkad is a good man and I just have to get that into my thick skull.'

As he walked back to the others with his apprentice, he whispered one last piece of information into Ahren's ear. 'Regarding his age, the following might give you a vague idea: none of us know to which people he belongs. His tribe must have been wiped out before Jelninolan was born.'

Ahren sat down on a marble bench and studied the elderly-looking, stocky man who was just at that moment enquiring of Jelninolan what the latest news from Eathinian was. His cheek bones were a little higher than those of a normal person, his skin had an olive tone, and his greying hair was still flecked with a deep-black hue. The host sensed that Ahren was looking at him and he turned towards the young man. 'Please help yourself,' he said and pointed to the dishes. 'It's completely safe and has enough durability to satisfy your body before the magic dissolves.'

The young Forest Guardian frowned in puzzlement, and Uldini laughed aloud. 'His creations last two or three days, then they dissolve into thin air. Akkad has specialised in conjuring things up, but creating out of nothing something that remains is the prerogative of the gods.'

Akkad nodded and seemed not the least insulted. This revelation made the magician more human somehow, and Ahren found himself relaxing a little. He looked over at Culhen, who was lying there snoring with a very large stomach. He decided to follow his friend's example and began helping himself to the wonderfully aromatic food.

The afternoon gave way to a mild evening, while the travelling companions ate, drank and sang. Uldini, Jelninolan and Akkad exchanged information concerning the other Ancients. Ahren didn't understand much, but he heard with a certain amount of satisfaction that Elgin's misguided ambition, and the Illuminated Path's trap into which that Ancient had fallen, had ensured that for the time being the other Ancients were following Uldini's instructions and had abandoned their customary power struggles. The fact that that the Court Wizard of King's Island had almost fallen victim to his own ambition and at the same time unwittingly played into the hands of the enemy was warning enough for the other ageless Wizards.

'What exactly are you doing in Waterheart?' enquired Uldini. 'Wasn't it your plan to slip into the Eternal Empire unnoticed, and to check and see if everything was in order?'

Akkad frowned. 'I didn't make it beyond ten leagues. Anyone who is capable of performing magic is spotted immediately, thanks to a finely woven magical web which covers all of Quin-Wa's empire. I've never seen anything like it. It must have taken decades to weave.' He shook his head and ruminated. 'At least she was polite. A messenger came to me one morning and asked me to leave the Eternal Empire forthwith or my safety could no longer be guaranteed. I understood the subtle hint and turned around immediately. That was the end of my expedition.' He spread out his arms. 'At the border I was apprehended by a legion and they brought me here. I'd always wanted to study the waterways anyway, so I stayed for a while. I wanted to see if I could carry out some refinements, and I'm currently working on a few promising ideas. When I heard that you were on the way here, I kept an eye out for you, but you must have been shielding yourselves.'

'Glower Bears are not to be taken lightly,' said Uldini curtly.

'What sort of refinements?' interjected Ahren. The man was still a mystery to him.

The plump Wizard grinned. 'I like tinkering with things. If I think up an improvement or a new construction, I simply conjure it up and then test it out for as long as it exists. I do that until I've perfected it and then I have it built using real materials.'

Ahren was more than a little surprised and found himself re-evaluating the sensual-seeming man, who apparently expended his energy trying to improve the lot of his fellow citizens.

'But enough about me,' cried out the cheerful inventor. His friendly eyes turned towards Khara, who had spent most of the time sitting in silence. 'Your mistress has informed me that you grew up in one of the arenas. She said you escaped before it was decided in which cage you had to go?'

Khara nodded shyly. Suddenly her previously relaxed attitude had vanished. She was hiding once again behind her veil of hair, and her shoulders were tensed up. Ahren was tempted to hit the plump Wizard in the face but held himself back.

'What do you mean by that?' asked Trogadon irritably.

Jelninolan's lips were now no more than a thin line across her face. 'The arenas are more than a spectacle for the masses,' she said in a strained voice. 'The fighters are sorted out. They are then sorted into different cages, depending on their capabilities. The best are put into a golden cage. They are then collected and serve in the elite divisions. The most unscrupulous are put into a black cage. They become the Night Soldiers of the Empress – assassins one and all. Anyone who has just managed to remain alive unscathed is put into iron cage, and they end up in the normal army. The rest are already dead by that stage or wounded so badly that they are thrown into a wooden cage.' She was silent and although Ahren feared the answer, he asked the question anyway.

'What happens to those in the wooden cage?'

Khara turned her face, still hidden behind her silk-black hair, towards him. 'Anyone who can work, goes into the mines. And anyone who is pleasingly built, is brought into the sleeping quarters.' Her voice was almost inaudible. 'For breeding purposes.'

Ahren gasped and looked pleadingly at the others, hoping that somebody would tell him that he had misheard. He sat there in awkward silence while an uncontrollable hatred for the Eternal Empress began to take hold of him. 'And you just let her get away with that?' he snarled. 'She is one of us, and yet she allows such terrible things to happen in her empire. Why didn't the Ancients tear her from the throne ages ago?'

Uldini's face hardened, his eyes blazing black. 'Overthrowing Quin-Wa would throw all of Jorath into a war of attrition which would result in the deaths of tens of thousands. On the other hand, there are a maximum of twenty such arenas in the whole of the Eternal Empire. In other words, we would manage to rescue a couple of hundred poor souls but cause dreadful bloodshed in the process. I know you don't want to hear that, but it isn't the right approach. Sometimes you can't solve things by taking the direct route.'

Ahren wanted to protest, but Akkad raised a commanding hand.

'Uldini is right,' he said. 'The Ancients have been sending bards into the Eternal Empire over the last few decades, and they sing tales of freedom, runaway slaves, and the futility of senseless killing. As a result of this a third of all the arenas have closed down because the spectators have stayed away. We shouldn't just start wars because we don't like certain traditions. In a century they will have been wiped off the face of Jorath anyway.'

Jelninolan looked at the two darkly, and Ahren could see that the Ancients were at odds over this matter. He found the long-term strategy of bringing the arenas into disrepute both cold-hearted and calculating, but he had to accept through gritted teeth that it made little sense to save a few hundred by sacrificing tens of thousands. He looked guiltily over at Khara, but the one-time slave ignored him, and Akkad continued.

'There is no shame in having run away,' he said in a quiet voice, and Ahren was surprised to see Khara shrink back again at those words. It had never occurred to him that the girl would have feelings of guilt regarding her flight. But she had very strict ideas when it came to her honour, which he hadn't been able to fully grasp yet.

Akkad, on the other hand, seemed to know the rules perfectly. The Wizard stood up and pointed to a part of the balcony that was clear of objects. 'You are familiar with the Ritual of Worthiness?' he asked in a strangely severe voice.

Khara nodded and tilted her head slightly as she observed him uncertainly.

'Then get to it girl, I don't have all evening,' he commanded.

Khara leaped to her feet and made her way over to the free space that the Ancient had indicated.

Ahren was totally confused, and the others weren't much better, but Khara seemed to be full of energy and almost eager for whatever it was Akkad had in mind.

He barked out a command in the language of the Eternal Empire, which Ahren guessed had to be something like 'begin' or 'start.'

Khara gave a deep bow and began to speak. 'I am Khara, the daughter of Winji, property of Xantukai, Lord of the Guitu Arena. I petition my worthiness.'

The girl's head remained bowed until Akkad responded forcefully. 'The request is granted. Explain your worth.'

Khara straightened herself up and fixed her eyes on Akkad with a suddenly self-confident look. 'I am trained in the weapons of the army,' she began in a loud clear voice that could be heard fifty paces away. 'I was selected for combat with Wind Blade, and I was proposed for Whisper Blade. I have taken part in forty-three fights and won thirty-seven of them. Eight of them were single-combat, and I was victorious every time.'

Akkad nodded but he looked bored. 'That's all well and good. Let's see what you can do.' He performed a few intricate hand movements and suddenly Khara was dressed in leather armour and in her hands she was holding Wind Blade and also a much smaller, though similar-shaped weapon which Ahren took to be Whisper Blade.

Khara only paused briefly with the weapons in her hand before beginning a quick succession of thrusts and parries against an invisible opponent. Her movements were graceful and fluid, like water wending its way wherever it found a gap.

Ahren still didn't know what to make of the performance, but the relaxed look on Khara's face indicated that she enjoyed doing whatever this routine was.

He looked questioningly over at Falk, who merely shrugged his shoulders before continuing to watch the drama in front of him.

After what seemed like an eternity, Akkad lifted his index finger and Khara immediately went into a bowing position again.

'What is the most dangerous opponent you have ever defeated?' he asked firmly.

The swordsgirl paused for a moment before she answered: 'A Sicklehopper.'

Ahren gasped and a murmur filled the room as the others reacted to Khara's revelation.

Akkad wasn't deterred. 'An audacious claim. Show me how.' He performed some more mystical hand movements and for a moment Ahren held his breath for fear that the Wizard would really conjure up a Dark One. What appeared, however, was an enormous straw puppet in the shape of one of the grasshopper-like monsters.

Khara closed her eyes and concentrated. Then she went into a low defensive stance, her knees bent, Wind Blade hidden behind her back, Whisper Blade put away.

'The Sicklehopper had sliced open my two comrades but had lost one of its wings in the process. Its hops were now shorter and less energetic. I was the smallest and so I was allowed to attack last, which was lucky for me. As the Sicklehopper leaped towards me, it landed a pace too soon, and I seized my chance.' She jumped demonstratively forward and began an amazing dance with Wind Blade, directing it past and behind the puppet. Deep cuts slashed through its right jumping leg and it was clear that the Dark One would have been practically incapable of further movement. Undaunted, Khara leaped on top of the practice dummy and rammed Wind Blade as far as it would go between the shoulders of the imaginary being. Then she twisted the weapon, causing maximum injury, before she pulled it out and made a dramatic rolling jump, which she finished by landing elegantly on the floor. The swinging movement brought her back up into her bowing position.

'The Sicklehopper collapsed there and then and I was declared the victor. That was the evening I was proposed for Whisper Blade. The evening I managed to flee.'

'Anyone proposed for this weapon need fear neither the iron nor the wooden cage. So why did you flee?' The question struck like a whiplash.

Khara stayed stock still. Her voice was barely audible as she answered. 'The black cage would undoubtedly have been my fate, but I did not want to be a night soldier, murdering others in their beds.'

Akkad clapped his hands once, the Sicklehopper dummy vanished and Khara came up from her bow. The Wizard rubbed his chin thoughtfully while the one-time slave looked at him, almost pleadingly.

'I have made my decision,' he announced loudly. 'I pronounce your worth to be fifty Imperial Gold Coins.'

Jelninolan leaped up in rage, but Khara let out a whoop of joy which caused the elf to stop in surprise.

'I shall pay your owner your value. Your service to me will begin immediately. You will guard this property until the morning of the eighth day of the fourth moon of the year 731 after the founding of the Eternal Empire. Then your time in this house will be over.'

Khara bowed hurriedly and disappeared on feather-light feet, as if she were practically floating, to within the house.

Jelninolan stood as tall as she could, shaking with rage, and looked down at the plump, smiling Wizard. Ahren was convinced now that the man had to be thousands of years old. Nobody he knew would risk being confronted by the priestess in her present mood, and both Falk and Uldini looked seriously concerned.

'What have you done?' demanded the elf in a tone that Ahren recognised. He'd heard it before in the seconds before she had punished Sven.

'Use your head, girl,' hissed Akkad to her, and he looked at her with real scorn.

'What day is it? And I'm talking about the Imperial Calendar,' he demanded severely.

Jelninolan looked unsure and her rage melted under the Ancient's self confidence.

'Seventh day, fourth month in the year 731', she finally said meekly.

'There you go,' grunted Akkad, pleased with himself. 'It will be the most expensive night sentry I'll have ever employed, and that's saying something, but tomorrow Khara will be yours again.'

'Just what was all that about?' asked Ahren suspiciously. The very thought that somebody bought the girl, even if only in pretence, made his blood boil.

'The worth that slaves from the arena give themselves is the compensation that is due to their master if they leave the arena. The worth of the slave is calculated by the buyer and is based on their achievements. The more they are worth, the higher the status of the slave. At fifty Gold Coins, Khara is now one of the best in the Brazen Kingdom. I'll send a messenger tomorrow who can get the money to Xantukai using middlemen.'

Ahren still didn't understand. The Wizard would really be paying? 'But why?' he asked.

Akkad sat down and took a sip of wine before continuing. Jelninolan followed his example although she was still far from relaxed.

'This is how it is: We all have different notions of ourselves, some good, some malign. Jelninolan sees herself primarily as a priestess rather than as a force of nature. Uldini enjoys the role of statesman.' He pointed at Falk and himself. 'Your master is unable to shake off the mantle of sacrificial lamb, and I can't get the image of a young shepherd out of my head, who happened to say the wrong prayer at the wrong time and then got a visit from the THREE.' His finger pointed over at Trogadon and Culhen. 'He still has the outcast in his bones, and your wolf doesn't want to grow up. I'm sure there's also a picture of yourself that you don't want to, or can't let go of, isn't that so?' His piercing eyes seemed to penetrate through Ahren's skull, and the apprentice instinctively thought of the timid son of the village drunk, an image that was always there at the back of his mind, influencing the way Ahren saw and dealt with the world.

He nodded and Akkad continued. 'What I'm trying to say is that we can only partially influence the way we see ourselves. In Khara's case though it was easy to solve the dilemma. She was still hanging onto the notion of herself as a contemptible, worthless fugitive, without a right to her own life. I've helped her to see herself as a young swordsgirl who has bought her freedom and who has earned herself a place in the world – away from the arenas. If I could only help each of you the same way with fifty Gold Coins,' he finished with a wistful sigh.

A silence came over the veranda and Akkad clapped his hands, at which the canopy vanished. They all looked up at the twinkling stars which decorated the heavens above them. Nobody spoke a word. Everyone considered their own visions of themselves, which were either spurring them on or holding them back.

221

Chapter 12

The contemplative mood of the previous evening was replaced by a boisterous atmosphere at the following morning's breakfast, not least because of the fancy dishes that Akkad had conjured up: iced strawberries with cream, warm apple pie, and over half a dozen exotic fruit that Ahren had never seen before, and which their host assured them came from the Southern Jungles.

Everyone helped themselves, relishing the meal until Akkad looked critically at the position of the sun. 'That should be enough,' he murmured, more to himself than anyone else. 'Khara, you can come up now. Your watch has finished.' The young woman had guarded the entrance to the property right through the night, ignoring all distractions and keeping one hand continuously on Wind Blade. Ahren had hoped to speak with her before going to bed the previous night, but she had ignored him, and so he had retired with a sigh of frustration.

Within a few heartbeats, the one-time slave appeared on the veranda and bowed before Akkad, who stood up and gestured commandingly to the others to follow suit. They quickly stood up, and Ahren was curious to see what would happen next.

The Wizard clapped his hands once, and Khara straightened up, seeming completely calm on the outside, but her eyes burned with a longing that surprised the apprentice.

'Khara from the Guitu-Arena, I hereby discharge you honourably from my service. You have served well and conscientiously, and as a sign of your status I present you with this Blade-Pin, by which everyone can see a free warrior is standing before them.' As he was speaking, he reached under his loose clothing and pulled out a small white glittering hairpin. He gave a slight bow and handed it to her.

The swordfighter took the slim little object with shaking fingers and bowed in response before skilfully and swiftly tying a knot in her hair with it.

She looked at the others proudly and sat down on the marble bench without saying a word. Ahren looked at the girl in amazement. She seemed to have been transformed in front of their very eyes. Her back was as straight as a post, her eyes were calm and confident, her hair which she had used so often over the previous moons as a protective veil, was now neatly tied except for a solitary strand falling over her right ear. The effect of all this was striking. It seemed to the apprentice that a completely new person was sitting opposite him, and when he smiled at her and he received a smile in return, Ahren decided that he really liked this new Khara.

Ahren hated the new Khara. They had a short training session after breakfast, and the apprentice was aghast to realise that the young woman was expressing her new self-confidence by mercilessly and unhesitatingly taking advantage of all of his failings in the art of swordplay. He sat bent over at the water's edge, washing his cuts and bruises in the clear volcanic lake, trying to come up with an excuse for withdrawing his offer to become her training partner without losing face. With his tongue he jiggled a tooth that had come loose thanks to a sharp backhander. If he was to continue being abused like a manikin, he would literally lose face, and he was quite sure he would still need that for future purposes. And anyway, he only had the one face, and he was actually quite fond of it.

Laughter filled his spirit as Culhen reacted to his angry sarcasm. *Khara good girl. Very strong. And fast. Much better than you*, he shared with the young Paladin, who was at that moment awkwardly cooling his left eye by ducking his head half under the water.

Ahren got his revenge by imagining a scrawny white wolf looking sadly at his empty feeding bowl. *If I'm really that bad, then it looks like I won't be able to supply you with food in the future*, he shot back darkly.

Culhen let out a terrified yelp and pressed his wet nose into Ahren's chest. The apprentice rubbed along the bridge of his friend's nose with a smile and was amazed at how big the wolf had become. Culhen's shoulders reached up to Ahren's stomach already. The Elfish animal blessing that Jelninolan had spoken over him had seemed to have caused another growth spurt. Ahren hoped that the wolf would stop growing soon or nobody would regard him as a normal animal. Already he could be described as *exotic* at best, and Ahren feared that when the wolf was seen for the first time, he might be mistaken for a Dark One on account of his size.

'That can become a real problem,' said Ahren quietly and tickled Culhen behind the ear. The wolf let out a contented growl.

'This is where you've been hiding then,' said Falk, coming up behind them. 'Are you licking your wounds? Khara marched by me so triumphantly, I thought to myself you must really have been through the mill.'

Much to Ahren's surprise, there wasn't a hint of sarcasm in the grey-haired man's words. He nodded without turning around. 'She was clearly in a celebratory mood,' he mumbled. Apparently, a tenderised boy is part of the proceedings.'

Falk laughed at the young man's dry humour. 'It's good you're accepting it with dignity.' He looked Ahren up and down. 'It's not that bad. The main thing is, you've learned something.'

Ahren wanted to retort that his only aim had been to enable Khara to train with her weapons, but he bit his tongue. However painful it was, the young woman had pointed up some of his weaknesses and told him how he could overcome them. She had cleverly combined her own exercises with his learning. He narrowed his eyes and abandoned any hope of renegotiating their agreement.

'Do you know what the healing herbs are like in this region?' he asked instead, and Falk slapped him good-naturedly on the back. 'It will all work out,' he said, acknowledging his pupil's stoic acceptance of the situation. 'Come on now, our escort is here, and we want to depart.'

Ahren nodded and poured water over his head one last time. He really didn't feel any compulsion to be covered in the dust of the road again and had nothing against staying another day in this peaceful place. He examined the boats on the water for a moment, and spotted a seagull, hanging over the water like a little black dot. There was something strange about the animal...and as the dot grew rapidly bigger, Ahren realised it wasn't an animal that was approaching them.

The arrow was flying at high speed towards him, and the young man was so surprised he couldn't move. Falk, however, followed the eyes of his apprentice and reacted with all the experience of a canny veteran.

'Down!' he screamed in warning and yanked Ahren to the side.

The young Forest Guardian was swept to the ground as Falk threw him downwards, and then there was the sound of a dull thud followed by a horrible crunch. Falk screamed in pain and began cursing.

Ahren spun around and saw to his horror that a thick arrow was stuck in his master's chest, just under his right shoulder. The force had carried the wide arrowhead out the other side, and blood shot out both the entry and exit points created by the cross-shaped warhead. To Ahren's horror, Falk's face was already pale and his curses were becoming quieter. The shaft of the arrow had not sealed the wide channel of the wound, and his mentor was rapidly bleeding to death.

Overcoming his panic, Ahren embraced the old man so that he wouldn't fall to the ground and thereby dislodge the arrow. He placed the flat of both hands on the two wounds, the shaft between index and middle finger, and he pressed with all his might. His training as an archer had taught him that blood loss was his greatest enemy at this point, and in his thoughts, he sent Culhen off to get help - Selsena was already letting out a shrill whinny.

Ahren breathed a sigh of relief. The Titejunanwa must have already felt Falk's pain and she would alert the others.

'Hold on, master!' he cried out, his voice agitated, and he looked at his master's eyes, normally so severe, but now becoming glassy. The blood was still spluttering between his fingers, and so he pressed with more effort, causing Falk to groan in pain.

'It almost seems as if you're enjoying this, boy,' he gasped, and Ahren gave him a tortured smile.

'Don't talk,' he ordered, but Falk simply shook his head.

'Sniper,' he whispered and pointed to where the arrow had come from.

Ahren's brain was racing as he realised that a second projectile could come flying at any time and searched feverishly for any tell-tale black dots in the sky.

'I can't move you, you'll lose too much blood,' he gasped in a sobbing voice. Falk's face was now ashen in colour and Ahren looked back and forth between the lake and Akkad's property. What on earth was keeping the others?

'Over here! Over here!' he screamed again and again until Jelninolan and Uldini finally came running out of the house. Selsena galloped around the corner at the same instant. She had stayed the day and night in a comfortable stable at the back of the property, but now she stormed scornfully off along the waterfront in order to get at the miscreant on the other side of the crater as soon as possible.

The two wizards were casting charms even as they were approaching, both of which hit Falk simultaneously. A blue light caused the old man to immediately go limp, and a red shimmer covered the two wounds, causing the blood to congeal within a heartbeat.

Ahren misinterpreted the slack body for a moment and painfully blinked away his tears, his hands still pressed firmly below his master's shoulders. He was fighting hard to contain his rising panic.

Trogadon and Khara also arrived from the house, followed by Akkad, who was gasping for breath.

'What's happened,' shouted Uldini imperiously, whose floating magic had enabled him to be the first beside the injured man.

'He's been hit by an arrow. There must be a sniper lurking somewhere on the other side of the lake,' gasped Ahren. 'He's lost too much blood. Do something!' the young man knew he had to hold his nerve, had to be heroic and calm, but by now he was covered in his master's blood, and only a few heartbeats earlier they'd been joking around and laughing, and now he was lying there, and...

He felt a sharp slap across his cheek. 'Pull yourself together,' commanded Jelninolan. 'You're in shock, but you're no good just babbling...'

Ahren looked at her in irritation, but then the penny dropped. He had clearly been on the point of losing his self-control. He looked down at Falk, whom he was still clasping. The wounds had stopped bleeding and were covered in a thick crust, but his master's face now looked more dead than alive.

When Trogadon had heard Ahren's warning that a sniper was wreaking havoc, he had run back into the building and now he came storming back out carrying Falk's shield. The dwarf positioned himself in front of them and shielded them effectively with the piece of Deep Steel.

'The magic sleep has calmed him. His heart is pumping much more slowly now, but he's still lost a lot of blood,' said Jelninolan in a concerned voice. 'We have to get the arrow out, Uldini, without opening the wound up further. Any ideas?'

The small wizard merely grunted and pointed at the wood, which was immediately turned into ash. A little trickle came from the wounds, and then the surfaces crusted over again.

Jelninolan's eyes opened wide in amazement, and she gave a nod of approval. 'You'll have to teach me that trick sometime,' she murmured.

'My own invention,' snapped the childlike figure. 'I was shot at once. After an experience like that you think long and hard about suitable magic.'

'Can you not create a magic shield to protect us?' interjected Ahren.

Uldini shook his head and pointed at the remains of the arrow. 'Too much force. Arrows like that have been created to penetrate magic shields. Maybe we could make one strong enough if we didn't have to save Falk's life, but as you can see, we have more than enough to do as it is,' he snorted snappily.

'I can help there,' said Akkad, and immediately a solid brick wall several paces broad and tall appeared, providing a solid defence against further attack from the air. Blindsided, Trogadon dropped the shield and staggered backwards as the magic construction appeared right in front of his nose. 'A little warning would have been nice,' he grumbled as he knocked curiously against the solid stonework. 'Could have been built by the dwarves themselves. We'll be safe behind this alright.'

Uldini and Jelninolan were now bending over Falk, both placing their hands on the wounds of the old Forest Guardian. Ahren had made room for them and was now only supporting his master's upper body so that the two magicians could work undisturbed.

'Now gentle and steady,' whispered Jelninolan. 'The new tissue has to knit from the middle; otherwise Falk will be hunchbacked later.'

'Then he'd be even more unbearable, and we certainly don't want that,' quipped Uldini cynically, and Ahren gave a sigh of relief on hearing the black humour of the dark-skinned Arch Wizard. If Uldini was using taunts, then Falk was out of immediate danger, for the time being at least.

The simultaneous incantations caused the edges of the wounds to knit together, and fresh pale skin formed over the once gaping holes. Jelninolan whispered one last charm, then took her hands away and gave a grim smile of satisfaction. 'Three weeks rest and he'll be as good as new,' she announced, exhausted. She looked at the Arch Wizard, who was similarly bathed in sweat. 'I have to admit that now I'm only too pleased we're going to be travelling with a luxurious escort party. That way we can transport Falk without doing him any damage, and we can improve his health further with more charms.'

Uldini bowed ironically, but when he answered, his voice was serious. 'We should get going immediately. The assassin may well be able to hide easily enough in Waterheart, but it will be a different kettle of fish on the Sword Path.'

Ahren stared at Uldini in disbelief and was aghast when Jelninolan agreed with the magician.

'You've only just patched him up and now you want to transport him in a bone-shaking cart?' He was almost overcome with agitation, and Jelninolan slapped him on the cheek a second time.

'Pull yourself together now!' she shouted. 'We don't just make a decision like that on a whim. His wounds have been healed. The problem now is that there is too little blood in his veins. No magic can help there, and we just have to let Mother Nature take her course. We can only give our support so that things move along more quickly. He needs the right food and plenty of rest, but the journey won't kill him.' She glanced over at Uldini. 'Regarding the bone-shaking cart, you're a bit off the mark there too.'

Uldini grinned suddenly and looked for all the world like a little boy. 'Let it be a surprise,' he sniggered.

Their farewell from Akkad was deep-felt but muted. Uldini had already transported Falk to the tunnel that would lead them out of Waterheart using floating magic. The others were saying goodbye to the plump Ancient, who finally waved them off with tears in his eyes. Ahren would have preferred to stay by his master's side, but Uldini had told him in no uncertain terms that he needed to stay in the protection of the group. The arrow, after all, had been intended for him, and as Selsena had found no sign of the assassin, the danger of an ambush was very live. Trogadon remained constantly at arm's length from Ahren, the Deep Steel Shield always at the ready.

They nervously and carefully negotiated the few paces from Akkad's house to their escorts. When Ahren saw what awaited them, he was flabbergasted. An obscenely large box wagon drawn by a dozen oxen towered over them. It reminded him of a house to which someone had attached wheels by mistake rather than a means of transport.

At least fifty soldiers were standing to attention and looking at them expectantly. Uldini peeked out of one of the large entrance doors on the side of the carriage, and gestured to his companions to approach.

'Falk is covered up safe and sound in one of the bedchambers. Come aboard and we can head off.' The Arch Wizard rubbed his hand along the thick wood of the outer wall. 'A small charm will be sufficient, and we'll be perfectly safe inside this beauty.'

Eager to see his master and the inside of the carriage, Ahren was the first to climb the high step which had been placed outside the doorway.

Uldini made room for him with a courtly nod, and Ahren stood at the entrance, rooted to the spot. The furnishings were nothing short of opulent, and carefully selected so as to provide maximum comfort in minimal space. Silk cushions bedecked cosy wooden benches, shelves on the walls held wines, soaps and even perfumes. A round table provided enough room for eating, and two doors suggested further similarly furnished rooms.

Uldini indicated to the farther door. 'Falk is lying in there. You can have a look if you want, but don't wake him.'

Ahren nodded, walked through the living room and carefully opened the door. Three narrow beds dominated the room, which was lit by narrow slits of light – something that Ahren had also noticed in the other room. Falk was lying in a deep sleep on the bed to the left of the door, and only his ashen face betrayed the torture he had gone through earlier in the morning. Ahren quietly closed the door again before glancing into the other room, which was similarly furnished. The others had climbed on board by now and Uldini pointed to the sleeping quarters. 'The ladies will be with Falk, Trogadon and I will squeeze into the other one and Ahren and his oversized wolf can sleep here in the main room,' he announced.

Ahren considered this for a moment before shrugging his shoulders. He would rather sleep on the floor beside his friend than not have Culhen with him. The wolf nudged him gratefully with his nose, and the apprentice struggled to suppress his tears. The events of the day had shaken him to the core, and he needed some peace and quiet to come to terms with them.'

Uldini rubbed his hands and closed the door behind Culhen.

'Does the wolf have to stay in here? It's going to get decidedly cosy,' said Trogadon cheerfully.

'As long as there's a sniper hiding out there, we're staying in here,' answered Uldini in a steely voice. It's going to take us roughly three weeks to get to the foot of Iron Peak, the mountain on which the Brazen City was built. That's where we'll finally meet my Emperor Justinian and hopefully, we can nip this disastrous business in the bud. Make yourselves comfortable because this is going to be our home for the next while.'

Ahren was already on the point of losing it. They had only been travelling in the rolling prison for three days, and the apprentice had the feeling he was going to explode. There was hardly room to move. Falk was sleeping his way back to health and unavailable to teach him new things, while the others were all uneasy in their own ways. Trogadon had positioned himself in the coach box with Falk's shield, and was keeping his eyes peeled for the sniper, or so he said, but Ahren knew an excuse when he heard one. Uldini and Jelninolan were constantly monitoring Falk's condition, and would speak magic charms over the sleeping figure at regular intervals. Culhen did nothing but complain to Ahren that he was bored, and Selsena, who trotted along beside the carriage, overwhelmed them with either waves of concern or disapproval. The Titejunanwa was clearly unhappy at their decision not to actively hunt down the scoundrel that had shot at Falk. That left Khara, who was totally wrapped up in training with Whisper Blade for as long as it existed. Akkad had warned her in advance that the weapon and armour he had charmed into existence would only last for a few days, and so the young woman used every free moment to brush up on her skills with her second weapon. And as there wasn't enough room in the carriage for two people to train, Khara claimed all the free room for herself.

Ahren withdrew into a corner and spent the days wrapped up in his own thoughts. He decided during the third day that this enforced quiet and self-reflection were not doing him any good. Time and again his thoughts would focus on the moment Falk had thrown him to the ground in order to protect him from the oncoming arrow. Had he only reacted more quickly himself or noticed the danger earlier, Falk would not have been wounded. He was filled with self-doubt and haunted by accusations against himself, and his train of thought was simply too complicated for the wolf, and as a result his companion was of no comfort to him. On the contrary, now the thought kept striking him that he had been responsible for the wolf being poisoned, and his accusations against himself developed into self-loathing.

Ahren tortured himself for his actions against Sven, his lack of horse-riding skills and for his inability to prevent Tlik from sacrificing himself. It mattered not a whit that he knew he really couldn't have done anything to save the fay-creature. He was sliding into a dark despair without even noticing as he brooded in the corner of the carriage.

It was in the morning of the fourth day and Trogadon was almost halfway out the door when he noticed the murderous look Ahren was giving to all and sundry. The dwarf squatted down in front of the apprentice and disregarding the young man's loud protests, he seized Ahren's chin in a vicelike grip and looked deep into his eyes.

'You're clearly suffering from cabin fever,' the dwarf grunted as he examined the apprentice.

233

'Leave me alone!' snarled Ahren as he tried to free himself from the strong fingers which were painfully pressing in on his jaws.

Trogadon's demeanour darkened, something Ahren had rarely seen in the normally so cheerful warrior. The effect was sobering and calmed him down sufficiently for the dwarf's words to penetrate through to him. 'It's not unusual for you to be feeling this way. Up until now you've had too much success without things going wrong, and now that things are uncomfortable, your doubts have seized their opportunity. That happens to everyone who risks his own life and those of others.'

Ahren stared at the grey-haired dwarf in amazement. The warrior had managed to boil down the hell he was going through to a perfectly normal emotional process that could befall anyone.

Trogadon released the apprentice's chin and straightened himself up. His piercing eyes twinkled down on Ahren while he pointed his calloused paw towards Khara.

'Do you think she did everything correctly in the arena? Or do you think I did when I was a mercenary? Nobody can make their way through life without making mistakes. You can only try to do things better the next time.'

Ahren nodded weakly while he tried to assimilate the lecture he was being given. His mind was still a maelstrom of thoughts and feelings.

Suddenly Trogadon laughed out loud. 'Whenever I have the wish to be young again, I look at you, and then I'm happy again that I've already experienced some of the nastier things in life.' He winked at the young Paladin. 'I really know nothing about the whole Forest Guardian thing, but I'm pretty sure a bit of movement will do you good.' The dwarf rummaged around in his large rucksack and pulled out two fist-sized black spheres, each with a small handle attached. He held them out to

Ahren, and when the apprentice took one in each hand, the young man almost toppled over. Those things were much heavier than they looked!

'We'll concentrate on strengthening your muscles while your master is out of commission. You won't need any room, and the effort will clear some of the chaos in your head.'

While Ahren continued to struggle with the heavy spheres, Trogadon explained to him how he was to lift and lower them, sometimes in front of his body, sometimes behind, then to the sides and even above his head. Ahren was sweating in no time at all and after a while, Trogadon allowed him a break.

'Have a rest, think about how you can do things differently in the future, and then start with the weights again. Keep repeating the process until your arms are falling off. Then you'll feel better,' he said in a cheerful voice. The dwarf leaped out of the carriage door, which slammed shut behind him, leaving an aching Ahren, who threw himself into the exercises the warrior had prescribed him.

Things slowly began to improve. Ahren's mind began to become clear over the following days, even though he could hardly move his arms and legs by time it was evening, and parts of his back were hurting that he had never known existed before. Trogadon's advice had ensured that his self-doubts were transformed into ambition, and Ahren had concocted a plan for improving his abilities. What had begun on the ship the previous year was now blossoming into a firm determination. From now on he was going to face challenges independently and head-on, and so overcome his limitations. That time he had practised increasing the tension in his new bow, but later his ambitions had gone into hibernation, shaken by his experiences among the dwarves and in Kelkor. He had simply reacted and listened to Falk's commands, but hadn't set his own goals. It was hardly a surprise he felt so lost, now that the old man wasn't telling him what to do.

Strangely, now that Ahren had made this decision, he felt freer than ever before. He took advantage of the pauses that the weight training enforced to peek out through the vents in the walls at the scenery and people of the Sunplains.

Throughout the day, the Sword Path was filled with trade caravans going in both directions – massive carriages drawn by oxen and horses. He saw Sunplainers of all varieties dressed in exotic garb. Some of them had Uldini's dark skin, others resembled Falk and his skin-tone, and then there were others who surely must have originally come from the Eternal Empire. Additionally, he noted in-between hues, all of which were eloquent testimony that the ancestors of these people must have come from widely varied areas.

The travellers' garb was also multi-variant: white tunics that reached down to the ground and held onto the shoulders by metal buckles worn by both men and women; airy flowing white garments just as Akkad had worn; and clothing that Ahren was used to from his homeland. Then there was all the different headgear, the most exotic variety seeming to consist of a single scarf which the men and women had wrapped around their heads presumably as protection against the sun.

Rich green fields stretched as far as the eye could see to the left and right of the broad path. Ahren saw long vineyards that put all the ones he had seen in Hjalgar or the Knight Marshes into the shade. He saw wheat fields that looked like endless seas of gold. And every so often, there were groupings of almost square, white-washed houses that had been built in unusually regular proximity to each other. There always seemed to be groups of four, six or eight of these properties, each group sharing an inner courtyard, decorated with colourful plants and the occasional fountain. The clusters of houses were like little islands among the cultivated fields. The Sword Path itself was lined at regular intervals by sentry towers, each manned by three sentries who kept a critical eye on the people passing by, as well as the surrounding fields. Ahren saw the enormous bugles, one on each tower, and was astounded by the logical implementation of order that seemed to underlie everything in the Sunplains. Everything had its fixed place, but even though the inhabitants seemed contented, Ahren found his surroundings somehow rigid.

Every night they slept in a secure courtyard belonging to one of the wooden barracks which lay one from the next at intervals of roughly a day's journey. Even then, Uldini would not allow them to leave the carriage unless it was to answer the call of nature. Ahren learned to value these few solitary moments of calm, even if the danger of a missile flying at him from out of the dusk made him hurry.

After a week, Falk woke up sufficiently to do little more than merely slurp at the broth Jelninolan had prescribed for him. Ahren was by his side in an instant and immediately started stammering an apology, but Falk cut him off.

'You would have done the same for me,' he said in a weak voice, and that was the end of the matter as far as the old man was concerned. He asked about the rest of the group and then fell back to sleep.

Frustrated, Ahren returned to the main room where Khara was practising some slow movements without her weapons.

'Stand beside me,' she said in a commanding tone, and Ahren stopped himself from uttering a sharp rejoinder. The swordsgirl's new-found status had brought with it a bossiness that he didn't want to submit to without a fight. But in view of the fact that these were the first words she had spoke to him in days, he really didn't want to fight.

'Copy me,' she said quietly and began to stretch her hands in front of her in slow, flowing movements. Ahren followed her instructions, and step by step they went through a series of almost meditative body positions which loosened his tired, protesting muscles and calmed his spirit.

Finally, they finished the exercise routine and he turned to Khara. 'What *was* that?' he asked curiously.

'It's called *The Twelve Greetings to the Sun*. Actually, you do it after getting up in the morning, but if you're stuck in one place, as we are now, it helps to keep the body supple.' A shadow came over her face. 'We used to practise it up to a dozen times a day in our cells on the days between the fights.'

Ahren swallowed hard, still unsure as to how he should respond whenever she talked about the hard times she had gone through in her childhood. While he was still trying to find the words, she ordered him up. 'From the start again,' she said, and Ahren followed, only too happy to comply.

A routine slowly developed in their confined, rolling refuge with every passing day while Falk grew stronger and Uldini and Jelninolan decreased the amount of magic they performed on the old man.

'We've strengthened him as much as the human body allows, and soon he'll be back to his old self. But I think it would be best if he sat out the next ambush.'

'Ambush?' asked Ahren tensely. The image of the arrow flying towards him came back into his mind yet again, and he immediately broke into a sweat. 'You think there might be another attack on us here?'

Uldini shook his head gruffly. 'Don't be silly. *We* are the ones who are going to perform an ambush on our arrow-happy friend. Jelninolan and I have been experimenting over the last few days, and we're sure that we can protect you in a massive magic shield capable of stopping one of those heavy war arrows. As soon as the assassin reveals himself, Culhen can take up his scent and lead us to him. We'll need one of his projectiles that the wolf can sniff, and seeing as I turned the old arrow to ashes, we'll have to provoke another shot.'

Culhen looked at Ahren with his head tilted and then let out a quick bark that echoed horribly in the compact space.

I can do that! heard Ahren in his head. Somehow his friend's voice sounded clearer than usual. It seemed that the wolf too had used his time of enforced unemployment to sharpen his understanding, although Ahren wondered quite how he had managed it.

I listened, said the wolf, answering his thoughts. *Ever since I've been in this travelling cave, I've been in your head all the time and have been learning the sounds that create images.*

Ahren looked into Culhen's eyes in surprise and could see the same intelligence that he was familiar with in Selsena's. He ruffled Culhen's fur and left his hand lying on his friend's broad back.

'Culhen says he's ready,' he announced proudly and was met with surprised looks.

Jelninolan wove a little magic charm and gave a cry of disbelief. 'Their connection is complete at last. I never even noticed.'

'High time too,' said Falk in a quiet voice. The old man was sitting with him although he was still pale, and his voice hadn't regained its customary power. 'It's enough that Ahren is slow off the mark, we don't need his wolf taking forever to pick up the basics.'

Ahren was all too familiar with the laughter that followed, but the fact that Culhen was joining in was a little hard to take.

They spent three hours huddled together, planning the best way to implement their ruse. Finally, they had put together a very solid plan.

Uldini loosened one of the rear wheels with a tiny spell so that it slipped off the axle late the following afternoon. Even though the travellers had been expecting it, they were still literally shaken about the place by the 'accident.' The escorting soldiers immediately got down to work, trying to repair the damage, but Uldini's clever magic ensured that it would take them some time to get the wheel back on properly. And so they presented the classic picture of the stranded carriage, as the sun began setting behind the horizon. As soon as the light conditions hid the magic shield which protected the two Ancients, Ahren jumped out of the carriage and walked stiffly to the next bush as if he urgently needed to answer the call of the wild.

The apprentice loosened his tunic and squatted down in the undergrowth so that the assassin would literally catch him with his pants down, and he felt like the goat tied to the stake as bait, which came up in every story about bad monsters. His pulse was racing, and his throat was tightening as he waited for the murderous arrow, which would hopefully be stopped by the magic.

Just as the demoralising realisation came into his head that not one of the goats in any of these stories had lived to tell the tale he heard a high whizzing sound and a heartbeat later he was thrown forward by a hard bang between his shoulder blades. Ahren felt the tip of the arrow pressing into his skin before it was stopped in its tracks by the magic shield. He couldn't breathe when he realised what a narrow escape he'd had, and he almost forgot to perform the one action that was required of him in their ruse. He quickly let out a death rattle and then remained as still as possible.

The soldiers ran around wildly, some of them forming a protective wall around him, not having been let in on the secret, so that everything looked as convincing as possible. Then Culhen leaped out of the carriage and with an extended theatrical howl, indicating his grief for his fallen friend, and rushed to Ahren in order to sniff the supposed body. Although Ahren felt the vain wolf was taking things a little too far in his performance, it certainly seemed to persuade the guards who shrank back. The animal quickly sniffed the attacker's scent and a satisfied *I've got him* was transmitted into the mind of the apprentice.

Be careful was the message Ahren sent back to his friend, but Culhen had already whipped around and was sprinting so quickly, he seemed to be flying over the ground. Uldini simultaneously floated out of the carriage and soared into the air at lightning speed, all the time following the white wolf's eyes.

Ahren gave up his charade as it had to be clear to the assassin by now that he had been caught in a trap, and he turned around nervously, making sure he was protected by the shield of one of the soldiers. The scoundrel was already trying to flee for safety, but the young Paladin had already experienced enough revengeful creatures not to rule out the possibility of the attacker shooting off another arrow rather than turning tails.

Be careful that he doesn't shoot at you, he transmitted after the wolf, and then closed his eyes in an effort to dive into the wolf's mind.

The picture he could see was surprisingly clear. It was as if he himself was racing through the nearby fields. Culhen's nose was following a faint scent, which looked like a black ribbon leading directly through the air to a little hill just a hundred paces away. The wolf saw a movement behind a large tree and ducked into the high grass behind a fallen tree trunk. A dark outline whizzed over him as the assassin's arrow shaft narrowly missed him, and the wolf howled and gave his rage free rein. He stormed up the incline and caught sight of a figure dressed in black with a strange looking bow retreating several paces, with its free hand sliding towards a dangerous looking hunting knife.

Culhen was preparing to leap when the figure pulled the knife out, and Ahren's heart almost stopped beating as he called out to the wolf not to jump. At that instant a flash of light lit up the evening sky and blinded his friend. Culhen broke off his attack in confusion, shaking his head wildly while Ahren instinctively rubbed his eyes. The animal's nose was picking up the smell of burning flesh, and when Culhen's eyesight returned to normal, he saw a smoking glimmering bundle of charred flesh, beside which was a knife and the strange looking bow.

Relieved and disgusted at the same time, Ahren freed himself from his friend's thoughts, and the wolf's howl of triumph echoed across the Plains while Uldini was already flying back to the apprentice's side.

'You know it really does one good to exercise one's magic muscles every so often,' he said in a smug tone. 'Although somehow I think our one-time assassin would have a different opinion.' He laughed darkly, and Ahren could see in the faces of the guards who were standing there that they found this side of the Arch Wizard just as unnerving as Ahren did. The young man knew that it was the destructive power of the battle magic that was speaking out of the childlike figure, but he still had an uneasy feeling in his stomach.

The others too came out of the carriage having heard the wolf's victory howl. Falk was leaning heavily on Trogadon and became even paler when he saw the arrow lodged into Ahren's back.

'Everything is fine,' called out the young Paladin reassuringly, and yanked the long shaft out of the material of his tunic, ignoring the stab of pain as the arrowhead slipped out of his skin. 'Nothing more than a scratch.'

Reassured, Falk nodded and Trogadon laughed in relief. 'Then maybe you should pull up your trousers now, what do you think?' the dwarf called out cheerfully.

With ears burning, Ahren followed the warrior's advice as quickly as possible and then stood up with as much dignity as he could muster.

'That worked well, didn't it?' interjected Jelninolan and seemed to be grimly satisfied. If she was disturbed by the assassin's grisly end, she was hiding it very well. It seemed that the elf's gentleness had limits too.

Khara stood beside her mistress and bowed slightly in Ahren's direction. 'That was very courageous,' she said, and Ahren decided to take the meagre compliment without reply. At least she hadn't commented on his dropped trousers and he considered that to be progress of sorts.

Some of the soldiers had salvaged the mortal remains of the assassin, but Uldini's magic had unleashed so much destructive power it had charred the body from within so they could only look for clues from the clothing. They quickly found a few Sunplains coins and a folded piece of paper describing Ahren in great detail and offering a reward of five hundred gold pieces for his death.

Trogadon gave an appreciative whistle. 'That's a tidy little sum. No wonder the chap was so stubborn. You should watch yourself more carefully from now on, lad.'

'Luckily we don't have to worry about that for now,' snorted Uldini. 'That was a contract killer, no common or garden highwayman. They don't go bounty hunting. The risk of months of work coming to nought at the last moment by a rival getting to the target more quickly is too great. So, there was only one on our heels. Nobody else is going to be bothered with it until the news of his death gets around.' He grinned darkly. 'And if the manner of his death spreads too, that might well put off any potential imitators.'

'And if it doesn't, then it's my turn next,' interjected Trogadon and he stroked his hammer. 'Alma and I have a few little ideas about what we could do to a fellow like that.'

'Alma?' asked Falk in disbelief. 'You're really calling a priceless artefact of your folk, one that has survived over the centuries, Alma?'

The Dwarf shrugged his shoulders in a deliberately nonchalant manner. 'Of course, I could have called her Deathshadow or Backsquelcher, but they sound too pompous to me, and they don't roll off the tongue. And anyway, the real Alma was a dwarf I courted once. Boy, was she able to mete it out! I woke up three days later in a disused mine shaft, and it took a moon before the ringing in my ears died down.' He stroked the head of his weapon. 'So now you know why I really think it's a good name.'

While everybody else was laughing uproariously, Ahren was thinking how nice it was to have escaped the dangerous threat of the assassin. For now, at least.

Chapter 13

The headwind caressed Ahren's face, the spicy scents from the surrounding fields tickled his nose in a most pleasant manner and the sun left a warm sensation on his skin. The rumbling of the wagon beneath him had become a familiar sound. It was mixed in with the shouting and talking of the merchants and farmers, travelling beside them.

Ahren had made himself comfortable on the roof of the carriage enjoying every second of his newfound freedom outside in the fresh air. Culhen's appearance on the Sword Path had put half of the horses and oxen into a panic, almost causing a large-scale pile-up, and now he spent his time in the nearby fields, sniffing around as they moved along.

The young Forest Guardian heard the clip-clop of hooves and looked to his side. It was Falk riding alongside on Selsena. The enforced idleness over the previous weeks had been difficult for the old man too. He was wearing his Paladin armour and carrying the shield that Trogadon had presented to him that time. 'Better safe than sorry,' was all his master had to say on the matter, and Ahren suspected that the memory of his injury was still too fresh in the mind of the indestructible old man. He didn't want to risk riding along unarmed. The apprentice instinctively scratched the point where the arrow had hit him between the shoulders, and he couldn't blame his master's desire to wear protective armour.

'I heard that you were busy during my recuperation,' said Falk once Selsena was in position beside the carriage. The Elfish charger was emitting rays of overwhelming joy at the fact that she was able to go for a canter with her master, and Ahren had to smile at the storm of emotions as he answered.

'Trogadon helped me,' was all he said. He really didn't want to talk about the first days of their journey, and anyway he was quite sure that the dwarf had given the old man all the necessary information.

Falk nodded in acknowledgement. 'I think we should relax your training a little. You've learned enough by now to be able to train on your own, and if you need to know something, or if I can help you along, just come to me. Conversely, if I notice you're neglecting a particular aspect of it, I'll point it out to you.' He studied Ahren keenly. 'How does that sound?'

The young Forest Guardian was dumbstruck and simply nodded. His master was showing enormous trust, and Ahren was determined not to let him down.

'Good,' growled Falk. 'The next while is going to be more turbulent anyway, so take every opportunity you can find to practise.' He looked intently at the young man. 'I think you're beginning to realise why we're constantly driving you to improve.'

Ahren nodded enthusiastically. 'I'm not just protecting myself, but also others,' he said keenly. The images of the attack at the volcanic lake were going through his mind, and he heard the sound of the arrow as it tore through Falk's body.

'You understand then,' responded the old man calmly. 'The next time I expect it will be *you* getting *me* out of the line of fire.'

Ahren almost burst out laughing, but then realised that Falk wasn't joking. His master was being very clear with him: it wasn't a matter of *if* one of them might be in mortal danger, but *when*. And Ahren had better be prepared for the occasion. They exchanged silent looks. Then Falk rode off and Ahren swung himself down into the carriage to get his weights.

Ahren spent the following days growing accustomed to his new-found freedom by developing his training techniques in various ways. He would shoot from the roof of the carriage at targets he had mentally selected such as corncobs or branches of trees, then order Culhen to fetch the discharged arrows. He also invited Khara up to practise swordplay with him. It didn't take him long to realise this was a mistake, because the young Paladin still hadn't developed sufficient balance to handle the combination of rickety carriage with the movements during combat. After he had almost tumbled from the roof three times, they had agreed on an evening lesson on solid ground. Nevertheless, that bungled training session had taught him quickly and clearly what his limits were, and he was grateful that his master had given him the opportunity to try it out.

He could have carried on training in this manner for weeks, but finally they left the Sword Path and turned onto a trading route five paces across, which both carriage and honour escorts completely filled. Ahren could already make out the mountain range where Thousand Halls, the kingdom of the dwarves, was situated. Iron Peak, the mountain on whose top the Brazen City was situated on the eastern foothills. According to Uldini they would arrive there in several days. It was then that Ahren noticed, much to his surprise, that the thought of meeting his Emperor again was making the ageless Arch Wizard nervous.

While they gradually ascended into the mountains, Ahren asked himself what sort of a man could command such respect from the Ancient.

The encampment of Justinian III, the Sun Emperor of the Sunplains and the most powerful man in Jorath (depending on whom you asked), looked like a newly built city. Ahren stared in amazement at newly constructed walls, whose mortar still wasn't dry, and at a squat little palace in the centre, which was still imposing, despite its improvised nature. Of course, there were also hundreds of tents at the periphery of the camp, but what really astounded Ahren was that a complete building had been constructed in the middle although the Emperor had no intention of spending even a summer in this spot.

Uldini looked particularly embarrassed when he noticed the apprentice's reaction. 'My Emperor doesn't believe in holding back. But that's part of being Emperor of such a huge area. Do you remember the barons that the king of the Knight Marshes, Senius Blueground had to keep in check because they were constantly challenging his authority?'

Ahren nodded at the memory of the troubled king whose kingdom they had saved from civil war.

'It's ten times worse here. The Sunplains are a juggernaut, which has become so big that if you killed the Emperor today, you would still be able to collect taxes in his name in the south of the empire next summer, because nobody would have heard the news yet. He has to plan every step precisely, and show his strength at every opportunity, because there are hundreds of senators who would gladly replace him.' He pointed at the constructions. 'There are many little cities like this all over the country. Over forty advisors accompany the Emperor on his journeys. The business of state never rests, and Quin-Wa's spies are everywhere. It would be highly irresponsible to rely on thin tent walls under the circumstances.'

Ahren nodded in a daze. He tried once more to imagine the sheer size of the Sunplains, but it was simply too much. Only the magnitude of this improvised city gave him a sense of the empire whose ruler he was about to meet.

While the carriage was being led from sentry post to sentry post, its interior was a hive of activity. Everyone was making sure they looked immaculate in their best clothes, and Ahren was amazed to see that even Trogadon was trying to make himself as presentable as possible. Ahren quickly followed their example, and when the carriage finally came to a halt, he had to force himself not to stare in astonishment at his companions.

Uldini looked as ageless as ever in his black robe, as indeed did Jelninolan, who had slipped into her green Elfish finery again. Falk on the other hand had dressed himself in the full regalia befitting Baron Dorian Falkenstein and every inch of his Deep Steel armour glistened in its characteristic whitish sheen. Khara was wearing a short green tunic that Jelninolan had given her while her hair had been artfully tied up in a knot which made her look more mature and dignified. Ahren had decided on his Elfish ribbon armour in order to give him a martial look – after all, they had to persuade the Emperor that the apprentice was indeed the newly named Thirteenth Paladin. Selsena was wearing her armour of course and Culhen had been brushed until his white fur was hanging as smooth as silk. The noises he had made in the apprentice's head while he was being groomed were almost indecent, and Ahren decided he would have to have a word with this wolf about his behaviour or he would never brush him again.

Uldini examined them with an eagle eye and then gave a curt nod. 'It will have to do. I would have liked to have made more of an effort, but Justinian will know that we've just completed a long journey and he will make allowances for our shabby appearance.'

Ahren gave a nervous laugh, but nobody else joined in. Surely the Arch Wizard wasn't serious? Before he had a chance to enquire further they were on the move. He had been informed in no uncertain terms that from this moment on he should not speak unless requested, and so he followed the group with his lips firmly sealed.

The young Paladin remembered well their visit to King's Island where Uldini had almost casually floated into the king's hall. This time there was no sign of that jovial attitude in the Arch Wizard, and the others' formality almost made him afraid. When he considered that their intention was to stop the ruler from taking further action against Bergen, the signs were looking rather ominous.

They were led through a large lobby area with more guards than guests. Although Ahren could see enough wealth to fill a small treasury, the people who were standing around took absolutely no notice of the costly wall hangings with golden borders, the crystal goblets and silver plates, not to mention the furniture made of ebony. Their attitude suggested that the furnishings here were only on a modest scale. But he also noticed, much to his delight, that both he and Falk were being examined with great interest. He suppressed a haughty grin and went instead for a modest smile which unnerved everybody he looked at.

Uldini looked at him out of the corner of his eyes while he floated in front of them. 'Not bad at all, but don't lay it on too thick. If you intimidate them too much, you might quickly turn them into enemies.'

The Arch Wizard's comment brought Ahren down to earth immediately and he quickly brought his facial gestures under control, even though it struck him as ridiculous that he could have so much power over these people. He stayed close to his master, who had a polite smile fixed on his face which never changed during their procession to the main hall.

Much to Ahren's surprise he spotted a few dwarves and even two elves among the royal household, and they, for their part, were looking intently at Jelninolan and Trogadon. The elves' eyes were drawn to the artefacts of the legendary blacksmith which the warrior had been allowed to carry since he had earned the Ancestry Name, while the elves made a little hand gesture towards Jelninolan, which she acknowledged with a polite nod.

'We're lucky,' she murmured quietly. 'The Elfish ambassadors say the Emperor is in a good mood today.'

They reached a pair of large double-doors at the far end of the Main Hall which swung open dramatically to reveal a surprisingly small room. It measured ten paces by ten and was therefore only a quarter the size of the Main Hall and without any furnishings whatsoever, except for a large throne. Sentries lined the walls with their spears held at the ready, so that the travelling companions walked into a ring of steel spear heads, which put a big damper on Ahren's self-confidence.

Justinian III, Emperor of the Sunplains sat on a bare throne, surrounded by his guards and examined the visitors keenly. His skinny body was covered by a yellow tunic with silver and gold thread worked through it and held in place on his left shoulder by a golden buckle in the shape of the sun. Ahren guessed that the figure in front of them was at least thirty winters old. His thin face with its deep-green eyes was dominated by a golden headband with zigzag edges which suggested stylised rays of sunshine.

'Welcome to the Sun Court,' intoned the ruler with a strangely raw voice, as the doors locked behind them. The bodyguards closed the gap and they were now trapped in a ring of pointed spears.

Ahren shifted nervously from one foot to the other and asked himself if these weapons would ever be lifted again.

Uldini sank down on one knee. The others followed his example and Ahren hurriedly followed their lead.

'My Emperor', began the Arch Wizard in a formal voice. 'It does me good to see you again. Allow me to introduce my companions.' Uldini's hand pointed from one to the next. 'This is Jelninolan from Eathinian, one of the Ancients; Baron Dorian Falkenstein, a Paladin of the Gods; Trogadon from the Silver Cliff, bearer of an Ancestry Name; and Khara, a free swordfighter, freshly recruited from Akkad's retinue – you know him well.' Ahren was amazed by the Arch Wizard's ability to leave out certain facts, which lent a completely new reality to the truths he spoke. Finally, the childlike figure pointed towards the apprentice. 'And this here is Squire Ahren, the Thirteenth Paladin of the gods.'

The room was deathly silent, and Ahren had to admire the discipline of the bodyguards, who hid their surprise superbly, with only a hint of movement from the spears.

Completely different to the Sun Emperor. 'The Thirteenth, you say? Really?' he called out. Strangely, his voice was filled with scorn and Ahren feared for the worst. 'Well, at least that explains why my valued court wizard leaves the empire in the lurch during a crisis AND DISAPPEARS INTO THE WIDE BLUE YONDER IN THE MIDDLE OF THE NIGHT!' The last words were more of a roar than an exclamation, and Ahren wondered, insofar as he was able to think at all, how this weedy man could produce such a loud sound. But mostly the apprentice was shaking like a leaf. The man's voice suggested that he was clearly used to giving orders and Ahren asked himself if Justinian had ever been confronted with the word 'no'. And indeed, what might have happened to anybody who had dared to contradict him.

Astoundingly, Uldini seemed able to defy his master's rage. 'Oh Emperor, unfortunately my departure was unavoidable. I had to travel along magic ways to save the Thirteenth, or he would have been killed. A pack of Fog Cats were hunting him down, sent by HIM, WHO FORCES.

Had I arrived an hourglass later, he and therefore all our hopes would have been lost.'

Ahren remembered back to that fateful night, but the Emperor seemed only marginally placated. 'If he really is a Paladin, then he should have been able to handle a few ridiculous Fog Cats,' he said harshly and eyed Ahren critically.

'Please remember that at that point he was neither named, nor educated. A foal is never left to the hyenas, your majesty.'

Justinian gave a disapproving snort and made a hand gesture ordering them to stand up. 'Well, at least that explains your company.' He pointed at Trogadon and Jelninolan. 'They are his Einhans, I take it?'

'Your Majesty has been well informed,' responded Jelninolan with a courteous nod and a smile, which up until then had melted everybody's heart.

'I wasn't talking to you!' snapped the ruler imperiously. 'And of course, I'm well-informed. Every godsday pupil knows the stories.' His eyes turned towards Uldini again. 'And he's definitely the Thirteenth?' he probed.

'Yes, my Emperor,' answered Uldini in a firm voice. 'I swear to you on my life. The Naming was unambiguous. The wolf is his companion animal.'

The wolf, who up to that point had pressed himself against Ahren's leg and made himself as small as possible, tilted his head when he heard his name and gave a questioning whine. Ahren stroked his fur and sent him calming waves, while the wolf radiated back sensations of a trap snapping closed.

'You, Ahren, step forward!' ordered Justinian curtly, and the young Forest Guardian had to summon all his courage so that his legs obeyed.

253

He paused one pace in front of the Sun Emperor and couldn't but admire the man's charisma. He only knew that feeling of absolute power from Uldini whenever he threw off his cloak of insignificance and revealed all the power of his magic. But this man in front of him was only mortal and yet he produced the same effect. It was dawning on the apprentice that he was standing in front of one of the world's most powerful men.

'So, you stole my most important advisor and opened the floodgates to disaster,' began the skinny Emperor. 'It seems as if you Paladins manage to conjure up trouble wherever you go.'

Ahren wasn't sure if this complaint was an invitation for him to speak, and so he remained quiet. He really didn't know how to respond to this accusation anyway.

His opposite number clicked his tongue impatiently. 'Talk, why don't you! My time is limited. I have an empire to govern, a war to win and a siege to end.'

Ahren desperately looked for something to say. He had hoped that the monarch only wanted to let off steam, but it seemed it was down to the apprentice to make their request. He took a deep breath and hoped his voice wasn't trembling too much.

'Your Majesty, Arch Wizard Getobo was indeed in the right place at the right time that night. Without him, I and my home village would most probably have been extinguished. Ever since that time, he has accompanied me without fail, and saved us from harm on more than one occasion. With his help, an early return of the Adversary was prevented last winter, giving the peoples of Jorath several years' grace, during which time they can prepare for the Dark Days to come. I don't know what he could have done from your court, but I can assure you that the long term damage to your empire would have been far greater, because I would not be standing before you, and the free peoples would be without the protection of the Thirteen.'

Ahren fell silent. All in all, he was quite proud of his little speech, and the Emperor stared at him thoughtfully before turning to Uldini and doing the same. His face still expressed the deepest displeasure and the apprentice was painfully aware of the speers that surrounded them.

Finally, Justinian exhaled violently and threw his arms in the air in the most un-majestic manner. 'Have you any idea of the position you put me in? My Court Wizard and closest advisor disappears without so much as a by-your-leave, so that every second-class intriguer gets the idea I might be vulnerable. Since you vanished, I've had to thwart over two dozen plots against me, and more than half of them ended in bloodshed. Because of you, I listened to that idiot Falturios and tried to bring the Brazen City under my control. I needed to show a sign of strength, instead of which I have a debacle hanging around my neck, which, if it isn't resolved, will lead to my downfall faster than Quin-Wa could ever have managed it.'

The monarch's outburst had caught Ahren completely on the wrong foot. He carefully retreated until he was beside Falk, keeping his eyes fixed on Justinian as if he were looking at a dangerous Dark One.

'To be perfectly honest, I'd really like to have you all locked up while I check out your story through a third source,' continued the monarch as he leaped up from his throne. Ahren could see that the skinny man was getting into a terrible lather. He looked pleadingly over at Uldini, who looked disconcerted and then suddenly straightened up.

'With all due respects, your majesty, that really wouldn't help matters. We think we are in the position to help you solve your issue with the Brazen City should you so wish,' he said hastily.

Justinian, who was pacing up and down, stopped abruptly. 'You expect me to forget about your dereliction of duty and instead let you solve the problem you yourselves have helped to cause?' He laughed bitterly. 'I always thought you were cleverer than that, Getobo.'

Ahren saw how Uldini struggled to bite his tongue. It seemed he had expected less resistance from his Emperor and being reprimanded like that really rubbed the Ancient up the wrong way.

Uldini cleared his throat and tried again. 'If we can manage to get the Brazen City to back down, then my temporary leave of absence from your court should surely be of no interest to anyone. I am truly sorry that I left without saying a word and it was never my intention to leave you in the lurch, Justinian. But if I hadn't gone, we would now be discussing how we could prevent an insane god from destroying your empire.'

Uldini's addressing his monarch by name hadn't escaped Ahren, but the sun emperor seemed not to have taken any notice.

After a moment Justinian gave a deep sigh. 'Very well then', he said. 'You help me to face the music that you yourself composed, and if you succeed, then I will forgive you. Otherwise, I'll throw you out of my empire and raze this city of unruly blacksmiths and traitors off the face of the earth.'

'That went rather well,' said Uldini quietly and rubbed his hands with satisfaction.

'Well if that's the case, I don't want to be around when an audience with the Emperor goes badly,' replied Trogadon with raised eyebrows, and Ahren silently echoed his sentiment.

They were standing in the entrance lobby, having been led out of the Emperor's hall and were separated from the courtiers by sentries.

Justinian had explained that he had other state business to attend to and that he expected them at supper later.

Ahren was happy to comply with anything which meant they could get out of the circle of spears that had increasingly been getting on his nerves. Now he was ruffling his nervous friend's fur while listening to the others.

'We've jumped the first hurdle anyway,' Falk was saying. 'According to the letter of the law, Justinian was well within his rights to throw our little wizard friend here into the dungeons or even have him executed for treason.'

The hairs stood up on the back of Ahren's neck when he heard that. 'But he'd never have succeeded!' he blurted out angrily.

'Of course not,' said Uldini patiently. 'If I had escaped using magic though, then we would have been banished from the Sunplains forever. We need Justinian and his armies for what we are going to be facing in the oncoming Dark Days. Endangering his well-being, and that of half the royal household would not have helped us a whit.'

'And we would all have been in mortal danger,' interjected Jelninolan. 'You've experienced what damage a single arrow can do at the wrong moment.'

Ahren shivered and Falk laid a comforting hand on his shoulder.

'There's one thing that annoys me,' said Uldini ruminatively. 'Falturios supposedly pressurised the Emperor into capturing the Brazen City. The man is over seventy summers old and would never have an original thought, even if it hit him in the face.'

They all fell silent, and Ahren couldn't help remembering the tense situation they had drifted into in the Knight Marshes the previous year. 'Is there any way this Falturios could be working for the Adversary?' he asked in an uncertain voice.

'I can't imagine so,' said Uldini frowning. 'For all his faults, his loyalty to the throne is unquestionable. I myself vetted him several times using magic.'

'Until you were gone,' interrupted Khara. Since they had arrived in the encampment the young girl had tried to make herself as invisible as possible. Her intervention in the discussion was all the more surprising, thought Ahren.

Uldini shook his head slowly. 'I still can't imagine that old Falturios has been turned,' he said finally.

Then Ahren heard something in his head: *A man with many faces has been here*. He looked down at Culhen in surprise. The wolf was sitting on his hind-legs and was sniffing the air curiously. *I smell something strange – as if many people were standing on the exact same spot.*

It took Ahren a moment before the penny dropped. 'Is it possible that a Doppelganger took Falturios's place when you were gone? Culhen says he can still smell him.'

Uldini's face went pale and everyone instinctively reached for their weapons. He and Jelninolan quickly cast a secret spell before nodding in embarrassment. The little Arch Wizard let out a curse, and Jelninolan explained quietly: 'A Doppler *was* here, no more than two days ago.'

Ahren tickled Culhen proudly between the ears while Uldini continued scolding.

'That makes sense,' he said finally. 'My guess is that the gambit of provoking Justinian to take action against the Brazen City was planned long ago. The Doppler simply waited until I had left the court before fomenting chaos and casting his bait.' The Arch Wizard looked miserable.

'Even you can't be in two places at the one time,' said Jelninolan in an attempt to comfort him.

'We need a plan and quickly. Justinian wants to hear from us how we propose to solve the problem with the Brazen City,' said the Arch Wizard urgently.

There was a constant flurry of attendants and officials coming and going from the Emperor's audience room, and all the while the travelling companions were thinking up plans which were discussed, adapted and finally abandoned again. When the double doors were finally opened again for them to enter, they were no wiser than they had been at the beginning of their discussions.

At least the food was good, thought Ahren to himself. They were sitting at the table, which was covered in a white cloth, and which had been placed in the room when they had entered for the second time, laden down with all sorts of food. Uldini was playing for time by politely asking the Emperor about current affairs in the Sunplains, while the others enjoyed their food and whispered quietly among themselves as they desperately tried to find a suitable plan.

At last Uldini sighed and came to the point. 'Oh Emperor, we believe that you were taken in by an enemy's advice when you decided to take control of the Brazen City. A Doppelganger was roaming here until yesterday.'

Justinian's face went pale. 'Falturios announced yesterday that he was going to withdraw from my service on account of the humiliation he felt after having advised me badly.' Then the monarch's face went red with anger. 'You really threw me to the wolves, Uldini.' At that very instant Culhen cracked a bone he was enjoying, which gave the ruler's accusation an added authority.

The Arch Wizard's face betrayed his feeling of guilt as he raised his arms in a placatory manner. 'An unforgivable mistake which will not be repeated, your majesty. But For right now though, we need to concentrate on tidying up this mess if you don't mind me saying.'

Justinian threw his cutlery on his expensive plate and the clanking sound echoed through the room. 'Damn it, Getobo! I have absolutely no room to manoeuvre! Bergen and the Blue Cohorts have disobeyed my direct command, the Triumvirate of the city are refusing to eat humble pie, and if I withdraw the soldiers now, half the senate will attack me. Then we'll lose the weapons delivery from the Brazen City and Quin-Wa's armies will overrun us faster than you can say the word "retreat" in the next few years; and if what you're saying is true, we're going to need every man and woman available for when the first horde of Dark Ones approach my empire.'

'This is how I see it,' began Jelninolan in a soft voice. 'Diplomacy is the only answer. We can negotiate on your behalf.'

Justinian gave a sort of disgust but continued to listen.

'Trogadon here is the holder of an Ancestry Name. The Brazen Clan, who make up a third of the Triumvirate, will listen to him. The Irenius noble family have always been loyal to your empire. If Uldini comes along as your court wizard and offers them an amnesty, they are certain to listen to your proposals. Falk, as a Paladin, can prove to them that the dark god is awakening, which will also help in negotiating a compromise with the Brazen City. Which leaves only the founders of the city, the Regelstens, to be persuaded.'

Justinian silently considered her suggestion before replying in a quiet voice. 'What about Captain Olgitram and his Blue Cohorts? They are traitors and are unlikely to give in so easily?'

Falk cleared his throat and began to speak. 'If we can present Ahren to him, he'll understand that the time has come for him to dedicate himself to his primary duty. If you could grant him and his people an amnesty…'

'Absolutely not!' thundered the Sun Emperor and slammed his hand on the table. If I pardon my renegade advisor, the population of the Brazen City, the Blue Cohorts *and* their captain of all their transgressions against the empire, there will be wholesale anarchy. The disparate areas of the Sunplains get along so well together *because* of the rule of law. And the laws apply to everyone. I can't let everyone who defies me go free. Out of the question!'

Jelninolan, Falk and Uldini were all about to object, but the monarch raised his hand in a commanding manner. 'You may submit the following offer: If the city surrenders, I will pardon its population; Captain Bergen will be imprisoned until such time as I need him, at which point he can happily take on the Adversary – but his Blue Cohorts are to be executed for treachery.'

Again, the others wanted to protest, and again, the Emperor stopped them.

'This offer is very generous, given the circumstances. Only twenty-four soldiers will lose their lives, the rest will escape scot-free. You will get your Paladin when the time is right, I will get my weapons, which, by the way, I need urgently on account of the Dark Days that are to break over us. You have one week to persuade the Triumvirate, and after that I will have to assume that they are not in agreement, and the same applies to the renegade Paladin. Should that be the case, following the deadline, I will capture the 17th Legion by force and execute anybody who resists. If Bergen refuses to agree on account of his pride, then you are better off looking for a new Paladin anyway.'

His tone brooked no contradiction, reflecting the Sun Emperor's iron will, and they knew that no further compromise was forthcoming. Their supper continued in icy silence, and even Culhen was relieved when the Emperor finally released them, and they left the room with its table still full of delicacies.

Chapter 14

'Well, that's put the cat among the pigeons!' raged Uldini once they were back in their carriage. They would be departing the following morning and so had decided against other accommodation. Time was of the essence, and they needed to come up with a strategy now that the Emperor had given them an ultimatum. 'What were you thinking of?' he asked Jelninolan in an angry tone.

'Nobody else had a better idea,' she responded coolly. 'Capture Bergen and take him out of the city? Dissolve the Triumvirate? Neither of those would have been possible without causing a bloodbath. Neither of those would have ensured Bergen's co-operation. Or have you forgotten already why exactly we're here?' She pointed a finger at Uldini. 'The Paladin is the central figure. He is the person who has to join up with Ahren and Falk in their war against the Adversary. We need a diplomatic solution!'

'And how is that going to work if Justinian has Bergen's priceless cohorts – his family – executed?' added Falk darkly. 'Bergen is at best an idealist and at worst a stubborn mule. He's never going to agree to those conditions.'

'But the Triumvirate will,' insisted the elf obstinately. 'At least that way we could prevent an attack on the city. Justinian has only blocked the Mountain Way for now and surrounded the city. If he starts introducing catapults, well...' Her voice faltered and nobody wanted to develop her argument.

'So, we have to persuade this Bergen to at least negotiate,' said Trogadon.

'Good luck with that,' snorted Uldini. 'According to the Emperor's reports, he's entrenched himself somewhere in the city with his people. Whoever is giving him shelter, is also hiding him from the Triumvirate. As long as he's not found, he can't be extradited, and if the whole city is declared an enemy, then the paltry Brazen City guard will need the help of the Blue Cohorts in their defence against the attacking legion.'

'Then we'll split in two,' said Khara suddenly, and everyone turned to look at her.

'How exactly?' asked Jelninolan in a friendly manner, cutting off Uldini before he had a chance to reject the idea out of hand.

'We have to persuade two independently operating groups to work with us, and we have only a week. If we go to the Triumvirate first, we'll be seen as emissaries and Bergen won't show his face. If we speak to the Paladin first, having slipped into the city, the Triumvirate will consider us spies.' She brought both her hands together and then separated them dramatically. 'If we split up, then we can persuade both parties simultaneously and bring them to the negotiating table. If we can first get them to agree to talk, then we'll already have made considerable progress.'

A silence descended on the room as everyone contemplated Khara's suggestion. Ahren thought the concept to be both brilliant and frightening. They had never split up before, and the very idea terrified him.

'I would have to be in the official delegation,' said Uldini out loud. 'And Jelninolan would attract far too much attention as an elf, so slipping in unnoticed is out of the question for her. She'll come with me. And then we need a Paladin to persuade the Triumvirate that this conflict must come to an end, so that we can concentrate on the real danger.'

'The boy can go with you,' said Falk quickly, but Jelninolan shook her head.

'Bergen has to see the Thirteenth,' she said forcefully. 'You and he locked horns too often before you left. He'd see red and wouldn't listen to you. Ahren must find him. You, on the other hand, are famous enough to be recognised as a Paladin by the Triumvirate immediately.'

'But we can't just send the two children off on their own,' interjected Trogadon. Both Ahren and Khara looked daggers when they heard how they were being described, but they both remained silent. 'I'll go with them. A third of the citizens are dwarves, and I can easily pass myself off as a mercenary, and the same applies to Khara and Ahren. We'll mingle with the locals and seek out this Bergen. We can persuade the Brazen Clan as soon as all parties are at the negotiating table.'

Ahren was quite dizzy at the speed with which the plan had been formulated. It would be the first time he'd be separated from his master.

'We will enter the main gate with great pomp and ceremony, with emissary flags and all the usual paraphernalia, and meanwhile you three can slip into the city unnoticed. We'll deal with the Triumvirate while you look for Bergen, who'll hopefully be trying to avoid us,' explained Uldini, and Trogadon nodded his head in agreement.

Khara seemed pleased at the fact that her suggestion had been taken on board, and it seemed as if it was only Ahren who felt uncomfortable the idea of them splitting into groups. 'Is there no other way? One where we can all stay together?' he asked meekly.

Falk placed a comforting arm on his shoulder. 'You'll manage it alright. Anyway, Trogadon and Khara will be watching out for you. You find Bergen, reveal yourself to be a Paladin and bring him to the Triumvirate. Then we'll all be together again, and we can think up a plan for getting out of this in one piece.' The old man's wrinkled face creased into a crooked smile. 'You've always wanted to save everybody, and that's exactly what we're all about here.'

Ahren's eyes opened wide in surprise. He'd never thought of it like that. He looked around at the encouraging faces of his companions.

'Right then', he said, 'let's slip into the Brazen City.'

They set off early the next morning, hoping to get to the foot of the mountain as quickly as possible. Towards noon they reached the broad path in the rock, which wound its way upwards and would lead them to the top of the Iron Peak. Ahren had looked up now and again at the roofs of the houses peeping out over the squat city walls. Smoke could be seen rising up from more than a dozen locations behind the walls, thick swathes that combined into a heavy cloud in the skies above. At first Ahren thought the attack on the city had begun already.

Falk set his mind at ease, however. 'They're just the fires from the forges. The Brazen City is full of blacksmiths and traders, and both groups are too stubborn to be put off doing their work by a siege. I've no doubt the black market is flourishing, which must be annoying Justinian.'

The path was steep and full of hairpin bends now, there were soldiers encamped everywhere, setting up fortifications and digging trenches. The Iron Peak was impassable on the other three flanks, with this being the only route up, making a siege easy to implement. Ahren could see why Justinian favoured that approach.

'He also wants to capture the blacksmiths using as little force as possible,' whispered Trogadon, after Ahren had shared his thoughts with the dwarf. 'It's pointless fighting for a city and then capturing it after it's been reduced to rubble.'

'Why don't you tell those people over there?' interjected Falk drily and pointed at the level ground they had just crossed. They could see a large group of soldiers busily constructing enormous catapults, the advance party preparing for the attack which would inevitably take place in six days if their plan failed.

'My Emperor is rather impatient, unfortunately,' Uldini sighed. 'And the voices that say this whole conflict is a mistake are growing louder. He has to negotiate or he's going to lose all his support in the senate.'

'Why are all the rulers we meet continuously under pressure? You'd think that being the head of a kingdom would mean having more freedom in what you do,' said Ahren, who was finding it difficult to breathe. They were moving forward at a challenging speed, and the steep incline of the path was nothing to be laughed at.

Uldini, who was contentedly floating in front of them, laughed sarcastically. 'You really should know better. Doing what you want in a tyrannical manner can sometimes be pretty reckless. Quin-Wa seems to have the hang of it alright, but then she is one of the Ancients.'

'Don't be getting ideas into your head,' added Jelninolan with a laugh, but then resisted from teasing him further as she needed to conserve her breath.

They reached the last bend in the path when darkness fell, so Uldini ordered them to stop.

'We can't go any further together,' he whispered. 'This is where we'll split up. You slip along the city wall in that direction and find yourselves a secluded spot. We'll go through the city gate late in the evening and arouse as much excitement as we can.'

Everyone nodded, but Ahren's throat was bone-dry. He turned to Falk, who slapped him silently on the shoulder and gave him an encouraging smile. Ahren swallowed hard, pulled himself together and followed Trogadon and Khara, who were waving goodbye to the others. Culhen gave a quiet yelp but remained by Jelninolan's side. The priestess was going to camouflage the wolf with some magic and smuggle him in. The wolf would be unable to scale the city walls, but once inside he could find his own way to Ahren.

We'll see each other before this night is over, Ahren comforted his friend.

Be careful – a pack divided is a pack endangered, he heard in return, and the apprentice groaned. He really would have to have a word with Culhen about his lack of tact.

Night had well and truly fallen. Luckily, there was cloud cover. Ahren, Khara and Trogadon were crouched by a large rock on the edge of the plateau upon which the Brazen City lay. The apprentice couldn't make much out in the darkness apart from the city wall a stone's throw away, which stretched up a good five paces, dividing them from the first houses that were built close behind it.

'The city grew too quickly over the last few winters, and obviously the inhabitants never expected an attack,' whispered Trogadon, examining the wall. 'The houses are too tall and too close to the defensive structure.' He winked at his two young companions. 'I bet you a big purse of gold that at the end of this conflict the Triumvirate will commission the building of a higher city wall.'

'That's fine by us,' murmured Ahren absently.

He was following the others in his mind by pushing his way into Culhen's head. Falk was riding on Selsena – every inch a knight and Paladin – while Uldini floated in front of them, surrounded by fiery flashes of light. Then the Arch Wizard created a magic fanfare sound that was so loud Ahren could hear it from his hiding space with his own ears.

The three had crept a good five furlongs along the city wall until they had found the rock, which would serve as a hiding place. Ahren could hardly imagine how loud it must be at the city gate itself. Very loud if the ringing in Culhen's ears was anything to go by.

'Hear ye, hear ye, citizens of the Brazen City! The right hand of the Emperor, Uldini Getobo, Chief of the Ancients and beloved of the gods, has been sent to lead peace negotiations! Open the gates and let hope and friendship enter!' The magically strengthened voice of the Arch Wizard echoed through the night air.

'A bit kitschy, don't you think?' whispered Ahren with a giggle.

'Lady Jelninolan likes to make a good entrance whenever she gets the chance', whispered Trogadon, grinning.

Khara cleared her throat forcefully, and the others stopped their sarcastic jibes. They were relieved to see the sentries on the walls disappearing as they marched quickly towards the city gates.

'Now or never,' hissed Trogadon and began running forward.

Ahren and Khara quickly followed, and the young Paladin couldn't resist a smile as he felt the excitement within, and his heart pounding faster. He knew that Khara wanted to race him to the wall and so he increased speed. They quickly passed the dwarf who looked at them in surprise. Ahren would have won, but for the swordsgirl jostling him and slamming her hand on the stone wall before him. She threw him a triumphant look and he glared at her as Trogadon arrived, shaking his head.

'Take this a bit more seriously if you don't mind,' he chided, almost inaudibly. 'If they capture us, we'll be treated as spies or an advance party. Which means they'll use their weapons. Do you understand?'

They both nodded sheepishly, so Trogadon decided to leave it at that. The dwarf pulled out a grappling hook and threw it with impressive ease over the wall. He gave it a short tug, there was a faint noise of steel on stone, then Trogadon tensed his muscles and indicated to them to start climbing. 'I'll hold the rope taut, so that you can climb up more quickly. Tug the rope once when the coast is clear' he instructed in a whisper.

Ahren wiped his sweating hands on his trouser legs. Suddenly everything was all too real and tangible. They were going to break into a potentially hostile settlement – and without the aid of magic. No protective shield to give them cover, and no healing magic.

While he was still trying to summon up his courage, Khara was already making her way nimbly up the rope, and within a few heartbeats she disappeared over the parapet. Trogadon gave him a signal and Ahren began his ascent. The rope felt raw under his hands as he steadily climbed upwards. His training with Trogadon's weights had paid off, and soon he was up at the parapet. He was about to swing himself over when he heard a noise to his right. It sounded like a shrill whistling, and indeed, there was a sentry, walking along the wall and whistling a simple melody with more enthusiasm than talent. Ahren didn't dare to move but looked along the parapet to see if there was any sign of Khara. The girl was cowering in the shadow of a merlon three paces to his left, waiting intently for the sentry to disappear again. Unfortunately, the man didn't do her that favour, and kept walking towards her. Ahren watched in frustration as Khara slowly reached for Wind Blade and he shook his head almost imperceptibly. Her eyes were seeking out his, and he could see their wild, questioning look. The sentry was now almost parallel to Ahren, and the apprentice quickly ducked behind the stone edging and prayed that the whistling man wouldn't notice the grappling hook. The whistler walked by him much to Ahren's relief. His fingers were burning with the effort now, but he knew he had to hold out for just a little longer. Any moment now the distance between the sentry and Khara would be so small that he would have to discover her. Ahren had to act. He had no time to swing over the parapet behind the man, so he did the first thing that came into his head.

He started to whistle too.

The footsteps above him stopped and he heard how the sentry let out a surprised sound and turned around to where the apprentice was hanging. Now the armed guard would undoubtedly see the grappling hook, and Ahren hoped that Khara would react quickly enough to prevent the man from cutting the rope to which Ahren was attached.

While he was wondering whether he should swing himself upwards or slide back down, he heard a short, muffled scuffle, followed by a strangled gasp. Ahren quickly pulled himself over and spotted Khara, who was kneeling on the ground behind the collapsed sentry with her lower arm in a merciless choke grip around the neck of the blindsided man. The eyes of the unfortunate sentry were rolling up in his head. Then they closed and the whole body went limp. Ahren stared at the young fighter in horror.

'He's only sleeping. Tomorrow he'll have a headache, but that will disappear quickly,' she whispered to him reassuringly.

Ahren gave her a grateful look before tugging on the rope so that Trogadon would know that the coast was clear. The young Paladin didn't want to push their luck in case one of the sentry's mates appeared.

'You keep watch, and I'll check to see how the others are getting on' he whispered and immersed himself in Culhen's spirit.

The city gates were now wide open, and over sixty guards were greeting Uldini and his companions in a decidedly chilly manner. The features of the soldiers only softened when they recognised Falk, and at least he was given a polite reception.

There was something strange with the perspective. Culhen seemed to be sitting on Jelninolan's arm, but that was hardly possible. The wolf's body felt somehow *denser* than normal. Culhen reacted to his friend's thoughts and looked deliberately downwards. Ahren saw the skinny little legs and the curly hair of a poodle. He had to really pull himself together to stop himself from exploding with laughter. It seemed that the elf had transformed Culhen into this harmless creature so that nobody would associate the while wolf with the emissaries later on.

There will be consequences, growled Culhen in his master's mind. Ahren tried to think of comforting thoughts, but as he couldn't laugh for fear of revealing his and the others' location, his merriment came across as bellowing laughter in Culhen's head.

Before the wolf could react, Jelninolan whispered into Culhen's ear. 'The charm will only last for a few moments. Off into the alleyways with you.'

The transformed wolf leaped out of her arms and raced off in the direction she had indicated. Jelninolan cried out in a wailing voice: 'Come back, Fiffi, come back!' Ahren quickly withdrew from his friend's mind before he completely lost his self-control.

Suppressing the urge to laugh, he opened his eyes and saw Trogadon rolling up the rope and looking at him questioningly. 'They're inside and Culhen is on his way here,' he said, smirking.

The dwarf refrained from asking any more questions and led them down one of the narrow stairways that were spaced at regular intervals along the wall.

We're here! Ahren sent forth the call and within ten heartbeats Culhen came leaping around the corner of a house, every inch the noble white wolf.

The young Paladin spread out his arms in welcome, but his friend stopped a few paces from him, sat down and growled at his master.

'What's going on here?' asked Trogadon in amazement.

Ahren could control himself no longer and the sulky wolf was the last straw. He collapsed into a helpless, laughing heap and babbled repeatedly: 'A poodle! Our Culhen was turned into a silly poodle!'

Chapter 15

After Ahren had pulled himself together, Trogadon led them deeper into the besieged city. The clouds still covered the night sky, and a light breeze carried the strange smells of the Brazen City towards them. Ahren tasted the bitter taste of cold smoke on his tongue, coming from the city forges, but there were many other scents he couldn't identify. The apprentice had been concentrating on their secret incursion, so it was only now that he become aware of the buildings surrounding them, which were lit up at regular intervals with oil lamps hanging on the walls. He saw the familiar building style of the Sunplains, except the almost square-shaped whitewashed buildings were more compact here, being squeezed in together, and giving people little room to walk between them. Ahren calculated that there was hardly space for a handcart to transport goods on the narrow streets. 'Why is everything so tightly packed?' It's terribly impractical.'

The dwarf stroked his long plait and paused for a moment to look around. 'The last time I was here was more than fifty winters ago. That time, there were individual houses in this part of the city. The rest of the buildings were warehouses. The shortage of space is recent. I'd imagine that the Brazen City just kept growing, but space is limited, so they're building more densely all the time. Even though the Sunplainers who live here believe strongly in tradition, they're going to have to break with their custom for good or ill and build upwards.' He looked around again and then they moved on. 'I wonder if the blacksmiths' quarter is still the same. But we'll look tomorrow. Now, we'll find a place to stay for the night. It's late, and we should look for the captain in the morning light before we start soliciting the help of creatures who ply their trade at night.'

The dwarf's statement irritated Ahren. Nobody worked during the night in Deepstone, not counting the tavern-keeper. He was just about to ask Trogadon what he meant when he spotted an unusual building set between the low whitewashed houses with their little square windows. It stuck out like a sore thumb, like a bear among cows. The oblong, contoured structure built with enormous beams reminded Ahren of a capsized ship with its keel in the air. One end of the roof ridge was decorated with a playful carving, containing strange square-like images. Long, gently bending beams formed an unusually rounded roof, with only the very bottom of the building being made of bricks. The house was over a dozen paces long and rose twice as high as the brave little white buildings to either side. An iron torch-holder was affixed to each corner of the building, whose smoky torches produced an unruly smoky light, lending the house a wild, untamed appearance.

Ahren turned to the others and could see in Khara's baffled face that she too had never seen a structure like this before.

Trogadon chuckled quietly and gestured them to carry on walking. 'That's a longhouse in the style of the Ice Islands. When the Regelsten Clan landed on the coast here that time in search of new lands, they brought their building methods with them. There were a few skirmishes with the Sunplainers but finally they were allowed to settle up here on this mountain. Much to the surprise of the Plainers, the Ice Landers were thankful for this patch of land, because they didn't freeze off their...fingers..., not like in their native land,' said Trogadon after a little glance at Khara. 'They brought their own blacksmith arts with them, which was far superior to that of the locals. Because Thousand Halls is only a fortnight's march from here, and we dwarves are always interested in people who are skilled at wrought-iron work, we very quickly reached an agreement that was beneficial to all parties. Ever since then, Thousand Halls has delivered ore or finished steel, which is then turned into weapons.'

'Why don't the dwarves sell their weapons themselves? Why the circuitous route?' asked Khara. The young woman was expressing her curiosity more since she had gained in self-confidence, and Ahren was glad that he was no longer the only one asking the seemingly silly questions.

'Tradition,' said Trogadon, and shrugged his shoulders disparagingly. 'Thousand Halls doesn't sell Dwarfish weapons to non-dwarves. This rule was first implemented during the brief war between the little folk and the humans. We dwarves have very long memories, and this prohibition on arming the enemy is still in existence.' He snorted ironically. 'On the other hand, we love wheeling and dealing, so there wasn't too much opposition when the first resourceful dwarves realised there was no law forbidding them from selling the ore.'

They walked on, and the longhouses became more frequent, rising like hills between the smaller buildings of the Sunplainers.

Trogadon pointed at one of them as he continued to speak. 'The family always live together in the longhouse, and by that, I mean the whole family – grandchildren, aunts, cousins, you know what I mean. That continues until the building is overflowing, at which point they build another one, some of the family move there, and the whole process begins again.' He shook his head dismissively. 'It's not my way of living. I had to stay in a longhouse one winter. All those people in one room, laughing and arguing with each other. It was the loudest winter I'd ever experienced. And I'm a dwarf who loves the sound of the hammer hitting the anvil, so you can imagine what a racket they made.'

Ahren looked longingly over at one of the wooden roofs. He had only his drunken father as family, so the thought of having a longhouse filled with relatives who looked after each other, laughed, sang and argued with each other sounded very tempting to him. Khara seemed to be thinking the same thing and they shared a look, each acknowledging what the other was feeling. Culhen pressed himself against Ahren's hip and expressed his sympathy with his friend, once he had picked up on his master's sadness. The apprentice quickly tickled the wolf on the head and assured the animal that he would never feel lonely with Culhen by his side.

The dwarf had led them purposefully towards the centre of the city where the buildings were now gradually becoming bigger and more elaborately decorated, without losing the essential quality of the Plainers' building methods. They had hardly seen a living soul up until this point, and so Ahren was startled when an inebriated man came around the corner of a large building and staggered along, using the wall of the house as support.

'I think we'll find a tavern around here,' said Trogadon with cheerful anticipation in his voice. 'They always have sleeping quarters available.'

Indeed, it wasn't long before they came upon a brightly lit building from which could be heard the babble of laughter and talking.

Trogadon stopped and turned to face the others. 'Now, you're going to have to be very careful. Even if everything seems very orderly and mannerly, there is a siege mentality here. I can sense that the mood is calm but tense. Which is why there are so few people out on the streets.' He lifted a warning finger. 'If we give the impression that we don't belong, it could turn nasty very quickly. So, no stupid questions in there. We are one of the small companies of mercenaries, trapped in the city because of the unexpected siege of the Brazen City. Culhen is our guard-wolf. Many mercenaries have guard-animals in their ranks, whose sense of smell can anticipate ambushes. We've been employed in another part of the city up until now, and this has been yet another boring evening, and we want to blow our pay. Is all that clear?' he raised his eyebrows and stared at them so long with his questioning eyes until they both nodded in agreement. 'Great,' he said enthusiastically. 'Then let's go get a drink.'

The tavern was full to bursting, and it was only thanks to Trogadon's broad shoulders and his willingness to push his way past people when necessary that they managed to grab themselves a table in the corner. Ahren and Khara sat there, trying to hide their uncertainty while the dwarf went off to get something to drink and to organise their accommodation. The tavern was bustling with the usual Sunplainers, but also with men and women from the Ice Islands, who also had nothing else on their mind apart from trying to forget the fraught situation they had been caught up in for several moons. Ahren had already met with one of their kind before – the blacksmith Falagarda from Three Rivers, but he still found it hard not to stare at them. Very few of the Ice Islands men were less than two paces tall, and they were all muscular and broad-shouldered, while the women were a little smaller and more sinewy. Their clothing too took some getting used to, for although it was cold up here on top of the mountain, they were scantily dressed and yet, still sweating. Ahren could see a lot of naked flesh, and it was only when Khara gave him a mock-disapproving look that he forced himself to stop looking at one of the younger women of the Ice Islands.

Trogadon pushed his way to their table carrying three tankards and set them down in front of their noses. 'They have Dwarfish stout here!' he cried out enthusiastically. 'Pity we're only spending another six days here; I'd have liked to stay longer.'

Ahren sniffed at the head on top of his tankard and recognised the familiar aroma of the brew he'd already tasted in the Silver Cliff. The patrons in the tavern reeked rather, and so Ahren enjoyed the malty smell of the beer and held his nose close to the tankard, taking a sip every now and again. He sensed how Culhen smelled the aroma through their connection and was sneezing. He had asked his friend to stay outside in one of the alleyways and wait for them. The tavern was full enough as it was, and the big wolf would have caused too much of a furore. His friend was lying in the shadows of one of the unlit houses, keeping an eye on the tavern door.

The three companions sat there with their tankards (Trogadon was already on his fifth) and listened as unobtrusively as possible to the conversations going on around them. The main subject of discussion was, of course, the arrival of one of the Ancients in his function as an emissary of the Emperor. It was said the visitor had a Paladin in tow. Hope that the end of the siege was in sight was mixed with fear that this was a ruse of the Emperor, so that the city gates would be opened, and he could march in unhindered.

They quickly got the impression that Bergen was some kind of local hero because he had foiled the initial plan of the Sunplainers to capture the city in a surprise attack.

'This is going to be trickier than I thought,' whispered Trogadon. 'It sounds as if the citizens of the Brazen City are four-square behind Bergen. Even if the Triumvirate decide to extradite him, I can't imagine the citizens putting up with that. There's more likely to be a rebellion in the city.'

Ahren's face went pale and he quickly gulped down more beer. He really hoped Uldini and the others would be able to persuade the city rulers to accept the Emperor's conditions, but not before the three of them succeeded in finding Bergen. Otherwise, they would unwittingly have turned the Brazen city into the lion's den.

***

Uldini chewed the inside of his cheek, unsure of how to proceed and then let out a frustrated groan. 'We're not getting an audience with the Triumvirate before tomorrow evening. They're probably going to spend the whole day discussing what position they're going to take regarding peace talks.' He listlessly kicked against the ornamented stool that was in his way in the opulent guest quarters they were staying in. 'I really hate dealing with small committees. They are too few to make it possible to get away with a secret bribe, and yet too many to actually agree on a common position.'

Falk turned away from the window through which he had been studying the sleeping city. The principal building of the city, in which they were housed offered extensive views, and the old Forest Guardian had been looking down onto the dimly lit streets and alleyways, asking himself where his apprentice was and if he was keeping safe. He reacted to the Arch Wizard's tirade with a laconic shrug of his shoulders. 'We have enough time to win them around to our point of view before Ahren appears with Bergen in tow. We can't enter into any meaningful negotiations before that anyway,' he said.

'I still think we should persuade them to serve that stubborn old mule to us on a silver platter,' grumbled Uldini.

Falk shook his head wearily. 'You've never really understood how much the Night of Blood affected us. It cost us our families and our final victory, as well as damned us to loneliness with endless waiting for the Thirteenth to finally appear. Do you really think Bergen is going to lift a finger for us if we drag him to the Pall Pillar in chains? Keep in mind that we have to do far more than gather all the Paladins together. They'll have to want to help us too.'

Uldini was on the point of uttering a sharp rejoinder when Jelninolan stepped into the room.

'We've a bigger problem than I'd expected,' she began. 'I cast a magic net to get an overview of things. There's a Doppelganger in the city.'

The two men looked at her in horror.

'Are you absolutely certain?' whispered Falk fearfully.

Jelninolan nodded, her face furrowed. 'Probably the same one who took Falturios's place.'

'Uldini's fingers sparked with darts of light as he moved towards the door. 'Is he here in the building?' he asked belligerently.

'No. somewhere in the northern part of the city. He noticed my magic net and is hiding. At least we know he's here,' answered the priestess.

'Yes, we do,' said Falk uneasily. 'But Ahren and the others have absolutely no idea.'

***

At last the tavern began to empty, and Trogadon gestured that it was time to leave. Ahren was exhausted. He too had listened closely to the chatter in the hope of picking up information regarding the whereabouts of Bergen or the Blue Cohorts. But if any of the guests knew anything, they weren't foolish enough or drunk enough to say anything, and Ahren understood why. The local Sunplainers, represented in the Triumvirate by the Irenius noble family seemed to be in favour of peace at any price with the Emperor, while the Ice Landers allied with the Regelsten Clan saw things differently.

The landlord of the tavern gave Trogadon a battered key, and the dwarf gestured to his companions to follow him. They went to the rear of the building where a narrow wooden staircase led up to a weathered door. Ahren called Culhen mentally and the wolf came bounding towards him. The apprentice had bought an over-priced piece of meat from the landlord, which he tossed to his friend. Culhen caught the spoils in his mouth and gulped it down in two bites. Then he licked his mouth and looked up expectantly at his master.

That's all my friend. There isn't any more, I'm afraid, he said apologetically. *We're in a besieged city. You're going to have to diet over the next few days for good or ill.*

You always take me to the best of places, replied the wolf drily, and Ahren's mind boggled.

'Everything alright?' asked Trogadon, who had noticed the apprentice's reaction.

'Culhen is making great progress with his vocabulary. Unfortunately, he seems to be adopting more and more of Uldini's humour.'

Khara put a hand on his shoulder in mock sympathy and then climbed the stairs with a laugh, while Culhen gave an annoyed snort and pushed past his master.

Don't be jealous now, reverberated in Ahren's head, and the apprentice wished they were back in more innocent times when they communicated with each other using images. He went behind the others and wrinkled up his nose when he stepped into the musty corridor with its piles of rubbish and smell of unwashed bodies. There were two doors on either side, and the dwarf walked slowly and quietly to the rear door on the left. He pushed the key into the lock, turned it and pushed the door open with his shoulder.

Scowling, he entered the room with the others following behind. The room was little more than a tiny cell with a single narrow bed, lit by a small oil-lamp. There was a single miserable hole in the wall for air which could hardly be called a window, and the musty smell was appalling. The three looked at each other, none of them looking enthusiastic at the prospect of sleeping there.

Culhen sniffed once demonstratively, then turned on his heels. *I'm sleeping outside,* was all he communicated, and ran down the stairs where he curled up at the bottom.

Ahren was tempted to follow suit, but Trogadon shrugged his shoulders. 'Better here than on the street. I'm sure the cut-throats roaming outside will leave an enormous wolf alone, but we wouldn't get away scot-free.' He pushed the resistant door closed with a curse and locked it from the inside. 'This room is really only designed for one person. The siege is slowly revealing its unpleasant side.' The dwarf pointed to the bed. 'Khara, that's where you're lying. The two of us will sleep on the floor. I'm too big for it anyway, and Falk would make short shrift of Ahren if he claimed the only bed as his own.' The warrior lay down on the spot, blocking the door, using his rucksack as a pillow and putting his hammer beside him within reach. If anyone attacked them tonight, they would have to deal with the dwarf first.

Khara curled up on the bare bed, and Ahren lay down on the floor beside her with Wind Blade by his left hand. A low snoring sound could be heard from next door, and after Trogadon had put out the light, Ahren lay in the dark with his eyes open and considered the tricky situation they were now in, finally dropping off to sleep through sheer exhaustion.

Ahren was woken up the next morning by a scream, and he instinctively had Wind Blade in his hand by the time he leaped up, as if he'd been stung by a Needle Spider. Trogadon and Khara were looking at him in amazement. It was then the young Forest Guardian realised the scream had come to him through Culhen's ears. He closed his eyes and saw an elderly lady making her escape from the wolf, who was yawning. His friend was not used to people around him reacting negatively, and looked at the terrified woman, his emotional world a whirlwind of irritation and annoyance.

I'm not surprised, with your bad breath, teased Ahren. He pushed past Trogadon and opened the door. 'Culhen is frightening the natives. I'd better go to him,' he said and left the tiny room.

The air in the passageway was actually refreshing compared to their tiny room, and as he stepped onto the wooden steps, he gratefully inhaled the fresh mountain air, which only had a hint of the smoke coming from the many forges, which were starting to spew their fumes into the early morning air.

He hurried down the stairs and embraced the wolf, who was still sitting there confused. *What was wrong with her?* he asked sulkily, and Ahren wondered how he could explain to Culhen gently that many people saw him as a threat. Up until now, they had spent a lot of their time in the wilderness or among groups who accepted the animal, but his friend had undergone another dramatic growth spurt since then, and no magic would be able to camouflage him as a sheepdog in the way that Jelninolan had done the previous year in the Knight Marshes.

'Alright then,' he said loudly. 'We'll try it like this.' He imagined a picture of a little girl who was just coming around the corner and almost running into Culhen – only it wasn't Culhen – it was a snarling red-eyed, nasty version of the animal.

His four-pawed friend whimpered. *But that's not what I'm like at all!* he complained.

I know that, and our companions know that. But strangers see a starving wolf ready to eat anything, whether its prey has two legs or four, said Ahren in an attempt at lightening the theme. He looked lovingly into the amber-coloured eyes of the wolf, who was looking back at him, his head tilted quizzically.

Culhen gave an offended bark, but the feeling of sadness disappeared from Ahren's head. *It's not my fault that you people are scaredy-cats,* he sulked, butting Ahren with his head, almost knocking him to the ground.

'You're right,' said Ahren laughing and embraced the animal again. 'Come on, we'll look for something to eat.'

Culhen gave a bark of joy, and Ahren commanded him to stay by his side.

Trogadon had just come out the door at the stop of the stairs, and he raised his hand in warning. 'We'd better all stick together until we know our way around here.' Then he quickly came down the stairs, followed a moment later by Khara.

Ahren smelled the stench coming from his companions and pulled a face. 'Do I smell the same?' he asked worriedly.

Like a dead rabbit from last week, was Culhen's prompt reply.

The smell didn't seem to bother Trogadon. 'We have to pass ourselves off as mercenaries, and they don't smell of roses. And anyway, I'd imagine that washing facilities in the city are beyond our price range by now.' He scratched his head thoughtfully. 'Illnesses inevitably break out if a siege lasts any length of time, and then it gets nasty. We should try and find our friend as quickly as possible. You know who I'm talking about.'

Trogadon was about to lead them to the marketplace in the middle of the city but was stopped by a patrol that had just come around the corner. An old lady was cowering behind the guards. She pointed accusingly at Culhen. There's the monster!' she cried out fearfully.

How about putting your best paw forward now? Ahren asked his friend, and the wolf obeyed unwillingly.

The large animal threw himself in front of the startled guards, rolled around on his back and looked at them with wide eyes, panting, as he presented the soft fur of his stomach to be tickled. Ahren sensed that the wolf's self-worth had increased along with his understanding, and the apprentice could feel that these overblown theatrics were distasteful to his friend.

Khara had to turn her face, unable to suppress a giggle, and Ahren struggled to remain serious as he addressed the leader of the troop nonchalantly. 'Oh, he's harmless as long as nobody attacks us.'

Trogadon seized on what Ahren had said and followed the same tack. 'He always manages to get our pay raised during negotiations because he looks so ferocious and could do the job of a night watch.'

The captain nodded and hissed a warning to one of his men, who was bending down to tickle the wolf. 'Then it seems we just had a misunderstanding here. Pangram's mercenaries in the north barracks even have a tiger with them, but he stays in his cage at least. Make sure you keep the animal with you, so we don't have any more false alarms. The populace is likely to overreact to animals straying about the place,' he said brusquely, and then the soldiers let them pass.

Culhen leaped up onto his paws and trotted cheerfully by Ahren's side, playing the well-behaved pet as long as the guards could still see them. They could hear a lively discussion among the soldiers before their leader finally said in a loud, annoyed voice: 'No, we are not getting ourselves a wolf, and there's an end to it!'

Trogadon looked over at Culhen and grinned. 'I think you might have created the job of Guard Wolf. Congratulations!'

Culhen craned his neck superciliously and deliberately looked in the other direction. *Please inform the dwarf that I am going to piss in his boots this evening,* he said firmly and sniffed the air.

'Did he just say something?' asked Trogadon curiously, noticing Ahren's reaction.

'Nothing important,' mumbled the apprentice, hoping the wolf wouldn't be so unforgiving as to carry out his threat.

They walked through the awakening city, and Ahren was amazed to see so many people looking as if they had nothing better to do than stare distrustfully out of their windows at the passers-by on the streets. But then the penny dropped. Normal life had been severely affected by the siege and many of the people were now unable to work, so they were surviving on their savings. The young man thought back to the large amount of money they had handed out the previous day for food and lodgings, and he realised it would only be a matter of time before tensions in the Brazen City would reach boiling point.

They finally reached the first broad street that Ahren had seen in the city, and when he craned his head, he could actually see the city gates. He looked in the opposite direction and spotted a tall building with four floors at the end of a large marketplace. It had the same square form and whitewashed walls as the other houses in the Sunplains style around it, except that it also had a wooden porch reminiscent of the longhouses. Broad steps led down into a tunnel in front of the house, which Ahren looked at with interest.

'Don't be so obvious! We belong here, remember?' hissed Khara in a low voice as she poked him in the ribs with her elbow.

The young Paladin started in shock and quickly looked away. 'What sort of a stairway is that?' he whispered to Trogadon, without looking back at it.

'It leads to the Brazen Clan. The dwarves that do trade with people decided at one time to stay here. First only a few, then more and more, until finally they founded their own clan. They're all traders through and through. They buy the ore or Dwarf Steel from Thousand Halls and they sell it in front of the Place of the Smiths. They save the dwarf kingdom from having to haggle with the people. It's the ideal situation for Thousand Halls because they don't have to deal directly with the humans, which is why they value the Brazen Clan so highly.'

Ahren raised his eyebrows in surprise and Trogadon snorted. 'We dwarves are nothing if not pragmatic, and this city has been built as a result of mutual self-interest of the various parties. Of course, we've settled down here over the years, because we're never going to pass up such a good trading opportunity.' He craned his neck and looked around. 'This is the main street. This is where the traders used to sell nuts, fruit and other goods from the Sunplains, but it looks as if there's nothing left to sell.'

Ahren saw the many weathered market stalls and could easily imagine how it was in normal times with the stallholders calling out their offers loudly.

Culhen tested the air with his nose. *I smell something to eat,* he said excitedly and looked towards the city centre.

A row of people could be seen, along with a few dwarves, all standing in a long line, which led to a longhouse situated a little out of the way at the edge of the market.

'There seems to be food there,' said Ahren, pointing at the waiting citizens.

Trogadon grunted in agreement and they wandered over to stand in line. Culhen attracted some attention, but Ahren patted him demonstratively on the head and soon the interest died down.

I'm going to bite you on the hand sometime, said Culhen, annoyed that he had to take on the role of lap wolf again. *Just for the fun of it.*

Ahren sensed that the vain animal's pride was being severely injured, so he tried smothering him with loving thoughts. *Once we're out of here I'll buy you a complete cow,* he said reassuringly, but not even this temptation could cheer the wolf up.

'You're talking with Culhen again, aren't you?' asked Khara. Ahren frowned. 'How do you know that?'

Khara giggled. 'Firstly, you look even more stupid than usual,' she said in a teasing voice, 'And secondly, you tilt your head when you're doing it.'

Ahren was stunned. He'd noticed this quirk with Falk, whenever his master was talking to Selsena, but he was completely unaware of the fact that he had been doing the same thing. On the other hand, he thought it was useful that the others would know when he was communicating with the wolf.

While the queue was moving forward at a snail's pace, Ahren eavesdropped on the people who had lined up behind him.

'It's getting more difficult to get food every day,' said a woman with a little child in her arms in a concerned whisper.

'It will all work out, Elvira,' replied her husband hopefully. 'The Emperor has sent an emissary, and there's a Paladin with him. Two of them are already in the city. They're certain to protect us.'

At first Ahren thought that he had been discovered, but then it struck him that the man must have been referring to Bergen. The confidence in the man's voice warmed his heart, and he swore to himself that he would help to fulfil the man's expectations in so far as it was possible.

He spent a large portion of the time they were waiting, pondering over the situation until suddenly there was a tumult in front of them. They were still twenty paces away from the entrance to the longhouse when the scuffle broke out, and several of the people queuing were knocked to the ground. Two men from the Ice Folk were coming out through the entrance with a fuming man held between them. This person had curly hair and the pale skin of the Sunplainers from the Heartland. They dragged him several paces onto the street and tossed him carelessly among the waiting citizens.

'It's disgraceful!' screamed the man, whose white tunic was torn and covered in dust. 'How can you just double the price like that?' His voice cracked as he walked along beside the queue. 'Five gold coins for one bowl of stew?' he shouted at the top of his voice and pointed dramatically at the longhouse. 'How long are we going to put up with it? The Ice Landers are using this critical situation to make themselves rich at our expense!'

There were murmurs of agreement, and many were appalled to hear the price they were expected to pay for their miserable meal.

The man continued complaining, but as he was passing them, Trogadon quickly yanked him towards them and whispered something into his ear. He also pressed a few coins into his hand, and the man quickly walked away.

The dwarf noticed Ahren's questioning look and leaned in towards him. 'I gave him three gold coins, told him to stop his yelling and to politely join the queue again later. The last thing we need is a loudmouth inciting the people to riot.'

At last they reached the entrance to the longhouse and Ahren caught a glimpse inside. People and dwarves were sitting on long wooden benches eating. The walls were packed with personal belongings to make room for the needy. Over a dozen Ice Landers were standing at the other end preparing cauldrons of stew, which they poured into large bowls to the clinking of coins. Each customer also received a large piece of dark bread. Anyone who didn't want to eat in the hall went out through a door at the back, making room for the next hungry mouth to feed.

Ahren smelled the tangy aromas coming from the large cauldrons, and his mouth watered. By the time it was their turn, he was absolutely ravenous, and Culhen was dripping saliva onto the straw-covered floor in a most inelegant manner.

A plump woman with chubby cheeks and grey hair gave them a friendly look. Although she was at least sixty winters old, she was still a good half a head taller than Ahren. 'My. But you have an impressive Ice Wolf, my dear,' she said joyfully. 'I've only heard about such animals from the stories of my ancestors, from when our Clan lived in the cold north.'

Annoyed, Culhen was about to re-enact his performance as the puppyish, tame little wolf by rolling about on his back, but Ahren stopped him. *You can allow yourself to be admired here,* he invited his friend. The wolf didn't need to be asked twice.

Culhen immediately sat bolt upright, bared his fangs and finally let out a long howl which echoed around the hall. Half of the guests dropped their spoons, and everyone turned around in shock, but the Ice Landers laughed and clapped their hands as if Culhen had just performed a couple of somersaults.

The old woman came around the cauldron and embraced the astonished wolf in a bear hug. Ahren was sure that he heard Culhen's shoulders crack and ignored his strangled cry for help. *You wanted to be treated in the manner of the big bad wolf, so you can hardly complain now.*

The Ice Lander went around to the back of her cauldron again while some of the braver guests made a move to embrace the wolf in the same manner. Culhen let out a low growl and the outstretched hands were quickly drawn back again.

Enough is enough, he said with as much dignity as he could muster and ignored Ahren's laughter which was echoing in his head.

The old Ice Lander filled their bowls with generous portions and gestured to the travellers to sit down. 'I'll get a few scraps of meat for your wolf,' she said in a conspiratorial voice.

And so they sat down and dived into their meal, which proved to be just as tasty as it had smelled. It only took a few spoonfuls for Ahren to realise how wholesome it was, and he revised his original opinion. One portion like that, you could easily manage until the next day. He was enjoying the remains of it when the old woman returned to them and threw a heap of scraps in front of the wolf. The scraps looked far from tasty – unless, of course, you were a wolf.

Culhen set about consuming his portion in an instant, and the old woman looked at him with a well-meaning smile. Then she became serious when she laid a calloused hand on Ahren's cheek. She bent down until her mouth was right beside his ear. 'If you love your wolf, get him out of the city as soon as possible. In a few days we'll have to resort to cooking the innards, which nobody here wants to have yet. And it won't be long before people will be eyeing your friend, not as a ferocious beast, but as a feast for two dozen people.'

Ahren stared at the old woman, his face a picture of disbelief mixed with shock. Was she really serious? Could people really go that far? The sadness in the woman's eyes was certainly real, and Ahren stood up abruptly. 'We mustn't waste any more time,' he said in a flat voice, and there was something in his face that persuaded his companions to follow him without saying a word. Culhen gulped down a last portion of liver and they went out the back door of the longhouse and went over to a quiet part of the market square. One or two stallholders were offering food at exorbitant prices, and the meagre portions reminded the apprentice that soon all the food would be used up.

'What did the woman say to you?' asked Trogadon in a concerned voice.

'That Culhen could be in danger soon,' answered Ahren in a horrified voice. 'Why did none of you warn me?' he asked forcefully. 'Why did nobody tell me that they might try to eat him?!'

'We're all risking our lives,' said Trogadon calmly. 'If they'd caught us on the city walls yesterday, we'd have been done for. And if we trust the wrong people, we might end up with our throats cut,' continued the dwarf, in a tone that suggested he was talking about the weather. 'The trick is, not to let it come to that. We're all going to face danger again and again during our journey. I thought that was obvious to you since the arrow pierced through your master's chest.'

Ahren nodded. 'It was just the thought that someone might want to eat him that really bothered me,' he said with anger in his voice.

Khara laid her hand on his forearm. 'If they want Culhen, they'll have to get past all of us first,' she said soothingly, trying to calm the outraged Forest Guardian, who nodded defiantly.

And I prefer to eat than be eaten, interjected the wolf coolly, baring his teeth.

Ahren burst out laughing and Trogadon nodded contentedly. 'Now we've sorted that out, we need to plan our next move,' said the warrior quietly. 'Most of the Plainers who are supporters of the Irenius family are in favour of extraditing Bergen, which means we can take it as given that the Blue Cohorts will not be hiding out in any part of the city heavily populated by Sunplainers.'

'Would they be with the dwarves?' asked Ahren and gestured towards the enormous staircase.

Trogadon shook his head and pointed at the large building with the wooden porch. 'That's the main building in the city where the Triumvirate meet, and those steps are the only entrance to the Clan Halls of the dwarves. 'They'd have to have smuggled the Blue Cohorts directly under the eyes of the guards across half the market square to get to the steps. And anyway, humans are not allowed into the Clan Halls. So, I can't imagine that having happened.'

'Which leave the longhouses,' suggested Khara.

Trogadon nodded. 'They could easily find refuge in one of them. There are also a few warehouses on the edge of the city, but if I were a betting man, I'd put my money on the longhouses.'

'And it has to be one where there aren't so many Plainers,' interjected Ahren.

'The blacksmiths' quarter,' said the dwarf without hesitation. 'There are countless Ice Landers living there, but hardly any Sunplainers. Anyone unconnected with blacksmithing avoids the area because of the constant fumes.'

Ahren was beaming. At last they had a plan they could follow!

The others seemed similarly optimistic and Trogadon rubbed his powerful pawss together. 'Then let me introduce you to the Brazen City forges.'

Chapter 16

Everywhere was smoke and noise and fire. At least that's what if felt like to Ahren, as he couldn't walk five paces without being hit by the heat of a large blacksmith's fire, blazing up with every blast of the bellows. Then there was the thunderous hammering of the muscular men and women, working the fiery steel into shape with heavy tools. Everything more than ten paces away was no more than a blurry outline, the smoke from the chimneys having gathered together into a thick cloud of smog, pressed in by the unfavourable wind blowing onto the mountain top.

Khara and Ahren tied up their kerchiefs to cover their noses, and Culhen sneezed repeatedly. Only Trogadon seemed perfectly at home, grinning broadly. 'How I missed the song of a good blacksmith's hammer,' he said wistfully. 'As long as you stay around here, you should be safe,' he called out loudly in an effort to be heard above the din. 'It may be loud, filthy and hot, but this is where honest work is done, and only paying customers tolerated. No pick-pocket would be foolish enough to try anything here among the Ice Landers with their hammers at the ready.'

Ahren understood that Trogadon's statement was intended to be both comforting and a warning, and he nodded keenly.

'Then I suggest we split up,' shouted the dwarf. 'We'll all try and find out information regarding the whereabouts of the Blue Cohorts or Bergen, and we'll meet here again this evening. But don't stray from the blacksmiths' quarter!'

Ahren watched Trogadon and Khara uncertainly as they disappeared down different side streets, leaving him behind with Culhen.

It stinks, complained the wolf, and sneezed gain.

'Let's see if we can find a spot where the smog isn't so thick,' said Ahren loudly, and they both made their way towards the city wall to the east. Falk had taught him many things about the wind and the weather, and he was going to implement one of the things he had learned. The wind was blowing in an easterly direction. Since the blacksmiths' quarter was also east, Ahren knew that it would be calmer just at the city wall, which meant the smoke wouldn't be pushed downwards to ground level as much.

They wandered slowly between the large longhouses with their forges snugly placed beside them, each with three or four Ice Landers working away. With the larger pieces, such as shields or two-handed swords, they worked in pairs, bringing the hammers down at speed on different parts of the glowing steel, one and then the other, in a hypnotising rhythm. The rapid clanking was quite melodious, and the Forest Guardian observed in awe, how the pieces took on a form under the skilled hammer blows of the powerful craftsmen and women. And it wasn't just weapons and shields he saw being made. Everyday objects too, such as hooves and nails, hinges and simple rods – a huge variety of things, and everything top-quality.

At last they reached the wall of the city, and Ahren was relieved to see that his theory was borne out. It was true, there was still some smoke on account of the gusts of wind, but it was far less intense, and Culhen radiated his gratitude.

We can stay here by the walls for a while and see if we can find out a little more about Bergen, said Ahren. *But if we're not successful, we'll have to head back towards the centre of the city.*

And so they marched along the stone wall, and Ahren tried to ask the blacksmiths as innocently as possibly if they knew anything about the whereabouts of Bergen and the Blue Cohorts. Unfortunately, the young man was not particularly skilful, and although Culhen always ensured an initial friendliness, the people always clammed up as soon as he mentioned the mercenary unit.

The day dragged on and Ahren became ever more frustrated. At one point he thought he spotted Khara, a blurry outline in the distance, but the smog descended before he could be certain. The afternoon was almost over and Ahren had traipsed around every forge in the area without unearthing a single piece of useful information. He was now an expert on the current prices of weapons made of normal or Dwarf Steel, but that was of absolutely no benefit to him.

I could chew on one of them, suggested Culhen unhelpfully, and Ahren gave him a severe look until he realised that the wolf was cracking a joke. He was just slapping his friend playfully on the head when he noticed a forge that seemed remarkably undermanned. There was a solitary young Northman standing in a sweat at the fire, trying to work a short sword while also occasionally operating the bellows and shovelling the coals. He looked almost comical in his efforts and he certainly didn't look as if he had time for small talk, but Ahren sniffed an opportunity.

'Are you all on your own here?' he asked, opening the conversation as he stepped towards the Ice Lander. The man's smooth face had seen no more than twenty summers, and his pale-green eyes suggested tiredness but also a willingness to talk. His blond hair was tied up at the neck in an untidy knot and for a moment Ahren was reminded of Holken when he had still been working in his father's forge. He suddenly felt a pang of homesickness and almost missed the blacksmith's answer.

'Uncle Faldir is ill and has infected half of the longhouse,' he said, panting, as he quickly brought the hammer down, and then reached for the bellows. 'So, I have to work all on my own.'

Ahren stepped in beside him and began operating the bellows at regular intervals. It took all his strength, but the blacksmith gave him a thankful smile.

'That's really decent of you, but slow down, or the fire will get too hot,' he said as he hammered again.

'No problem. I'm not doing anything else today anyway,' said Ahren innocently.

'Were you let go?' asked the Ice Lander sympathetically.

Ahren nodded quickly. 'Exactly. I had sentry duty, along with Culhen here.' He pointed to his friend, who was playing the role of proud predator again. 'But our employer couldn't afford to feed us anymore,' he added.

'I've never seen you here before; you must be employed by the merchants in the west quarter, am I right?' Ahren nodded again. He thought it best to just agree with the craftsman's suggestions and then fill in the gaps through his answers.

'Long shifts, poor pay,' he said, repeating the standard complaint he had heard from Trogadon every time he talked of his days as a mercenary.

'It's no different here, believe me,' said the young smith breathing deeply. He was smoothing one side of a short sword with skilful hammer blows. Then he turned the piece over.

Ahren shrugged his shoulders in as casual a manner as he could manage. 'Didn't matter to me. The only important thing was getting enough to eat for me and my wolf.'

The blacksmith lowered his hammer and gestured to the small shovel beside the pile of coal. 'Two scoops in the fire please,' he said and wiped the sweat off his brow.

Ahren grasped the shovel and did as he was told, at which point sparks and flames flew in all directions.

'Slowly but surely,' laughed the blacksmith, and put out the spark that had landed on his arm. 'You don't want to set fire to half the city.'

Ahren's eyes opened wide in shock and he dropped the shovel, which amused the blond man even more.

'I like you, and I like your wolf.' He thought for a moment before continuing. 'I've a suggestion: as long as I'm here on my own, you can lend me a hand. I can't pay you, but you and your friend will get food every day. What do you think?'

Ahren hesitated and considered the offer. He was doubtful that the tactic he'd been using up to this point would yield success when it came to finding out the whereabouts of the Blue Cohorts. Maybe it would be beneficial if he won over the trust of this Ice Lander over a period of one or two days and kept his ears open in the meantime. And in this way, he could ensure that both he and Culhen would be taken care of, which would mean Trogadon could save a few of his coins.

'Agreed,' he said and stretched out his hand. 'My name's Ahren.'

'Vandir,' said the smith, as they shook hands. Ahren noticed that the blond man's hand was raw and calloused, and his own – though well used to hard physical work – felt much softer in comparison.

'Then help me finish this trinket here before it gets dark. If you don't make a complete hash of it, then you can come again tomorrow morning early,' said Vandir, and they began working the blade.

Culhen rolled himself up into a ball in a corner of the room where there was less smoke, and whenever Ahren made a mistake, he would send his master some friendly advice.

The young Paladin couldn't miss the self-satisfied tone in the wolf's thoughts, but he bit his tongue and put on a brave front. His friend had been forced to play the lap wolf several times already that day, so it was understandable that he was enjoying the role-reversal – even if Ahren was more than a little annoyed.

They finally finished the work on the sword, and Ahren was bathed in sweat and covered in grime. His lungs were burning, and his breath smelled of smoke.

Vandir gave his handiwork a critical look and then put it aside with a satisfied look. Ahren too, felt a certain pride when he saw the sword, even if his contribution to its creation had been limited.

'Not bad for your first attempt,' said the Northman to Ahren. 'But make sure you're standing in a better position tomorrow, so the wind isn't blowing into your face all the time or your lungs will give up.'

Ahren gave a tired nod and promised to return the following morning. Then they said goodbye and he headed back to the others while Vandir closed up the forge and disappeared into the longhouse.

Ahren ground his teeth and looked up to the sky. It was already dark and the time he was supposed to have met up with his friends had long since passed. He could only hope that they were still waiting for him.

***

Falk and Uldini were pacing nervously. An adjutant of the Triumvirate was supposed to have collected them from their room at dusk, but nobody had made an appearance.

Jelninolan, who was laboriously trying to charm a poem onto a piece of parchment, looked up in annoyance and rolled her eyes. 'You two are driving me insane!' she hissed. 'Calm down and settle yourselves. How are you going to engage in negotiations if you're like cats on a hot tin roof?'

'Time is running out,' said Uldini in a strained voice. 'And the fact that they haven't called us yet, means they're not in agreement with each other.'

'You're a wily politician. You should be used to waiting around', said the elf emphatically.

'But this time the negotiations are deadly serious,' replied Uldini with irritation. 'It's one thing to put gentle pressure on a couple of barons or senators to keep things nice and peaceful. If it works, fine and dandy, and if not, well, you just get on the right side of the victor. But here we're dealing with something much more important – we're laying the foundations for the oncoming Dark Days. Without the support of the Brazen City, the Sunplainers will lack the necessary weapons. Any diplomatic mistakes made now will be impossible to fix again in time.'

'Very well then, get yourself in a tizzy if you want,' said the priestess. 'But why are *you* pacing the room like a Fog Cat caught in the sunlight?' she asked Falk. 'You have more staying power than the rest of us.'

Falk looked darkly at her. 'I'm worried about Ahren and the others,' he admitted. 'It's getting quite unpleasant out there. Food is becoming scarce, as well as work. Diseases are beginning to break out, and I overheard one of the guards say that Justinian has proclaimed that all smuggling is punishable by death. Probably because he wants to increase the pressure.' He gestured to the city outside lying in darkness. 'There's an ever-increasing danger of chaos taking hold of the city, thanks to the lack of a black market – and our four friends are in the middle of it, trying to track down an elite troop that doesn't want to be found.' He let out a bitter sigh. 'And I'm stuck here playing the Paladin.'

Jelninolan jumped up and slammed her fists on the table. 'You *are* a Paladin, for the love of the THREE! It's high time you started to remember that. This here is no role, no disguise you can put on and take off at will. Even Ahren has come to understand that better than you!'

Falk was stunned by the outburst and looked dejected, while Uldini laughed sarcastically.

'Auntie, your powers of motivation before really important events are...well...unique.'

She was about to respond to the Arch Wizard when there was a timid knock at the door.

'Understood,' said Falk, and he scowled at the elf as he went across the room to answer the door.

A liveried servant, wearing a tunic and bearing the tripartite coat of arms of the Triumvirate, stood at the door with his impassive face and gave an elegant little bow. If he had overheard any of the argument, he certainly wasn't showing it. 'Esteemed gentlemen, gracious lady: The Triumvirate of Brazen City is ready to receive you now,' said the man, straightening himself up again and smiling at them under his turban. 'If you would follow me please?' Without waiting for an answer, the servant moved off with graceful steps, and the three companions followed him impatiently.

Uldini spoke quietly and gave them his last few instructions. 'Remember that the Regelsten Clan speak for the progeny of the Ice Landers, the Irenius family represent the resident Sunplainers, and the Brazen Clan are dwarf representatives.'

Jelninolan gave a bored nod. 'Don't annoy the dwarves, be polite to the Plainers and persuade the Regelstens' she rattled off. 'We know the tactics.'

'We also have to find out where they stand beforehand' added Uldini quickly, as they walked down the last few steps of a broad staircase. They were surprised to discover that the meeting room of the Triumvirate was only one floor below their lodgings. To their left was the entrance with its two guards that they had been led through when they arrived, and to their right were brass-studded double doors. These swung open and revealed a comfortably furnished room with wall hangings. In the middle was a round table with room for no more than ten guests. On the far side of the table, and with considerable space between them, sat three people, who were looking at the newcomers curiously.

On the left was a dwarf with a mane of jet-black hair, which was thick and wiry, even by the standards of the little folk, and which refused to be tamed no matter what effort was taken, as was evident from the many unruly strands. A tall, middle-aged woman, clearly from the Ice Islands, sat in the middle and looked at them with deep-blue eyes, her blond hair plaited around her forehead. She was wearing the leather apron favoured by blacksmiths, which was engraved with the Brazen City insignia. A dark-haired, slim beauty was sitting to her right, diminutive in stature whose neat appearance reinforced her natural elegance.

The servant bowed and then announced in a melodious voice as he waved his hand from left to right: 'If I may introduce the rulers of the Brazen City to you – Xobutumbur of the Brazen Clan, Windita Regelsten and Palustra Irenius.' Then he turned around and pointed at the guests: 'Here we have Uldini Getobo, Emissary of the Sun Emperor Justinian III and Commander of the Ancients, Jelninolan from Eathinian, also an Ancient, and Baron Dorian Falkenstein, Paladin of the gods.'

The Triumvirate arose as one and gave a sustained, low bow.

'Well, that's a good start,' whispered Uldini cheerfully.

The three straightened up and Palustra cocked her head and smiled at Uldini. 'Our deference is towards your achievements as Ancients and as Paladin, not towards the Emperor for whom you are speaking today.'

'You have sensitive ears,' said Falk in surprise, as he and his companions sat down.

'Good ears are useful in our position,' she said and gave the old Forest Guardian such a charming smile that he couldn't but respond in kind.

'Has the youth on the throne finally come to his senses and realised that it was reckless and idiotic to tear up a centuries' old alliance and to reward our loyalty with treachery?' growled Xobutumbur.

'That's a rather harsh summation of the events…' began Uldini but Windita cut across him.

'Perhaps the esteemed emissary would like to clarify how the actions of the Sun Emperor can be interpreted in any other way?'

The Arch Wizard shifted about uncomfortably on his chair until Falk finally shook his head.

'Leave it, Uldini. Not even you can make a silk purse out of a sow's ear,' he interjected with a growl. 'You are completely in the right with your accusations,' he said bluntly, causing Uldini to let out a gasp while the three city representatives looked at each other in surprise.

'But perhaps it might be easier for you to understand this mistaken policy, once you've learned that it was none other than a Doppelganger that whispered the idea into the Emperor's ear,' continued the old man calmly.

Uldini let out a groan of frustration and closed his eyes. 'Why don't you just join them and sit on the other side of the table,' he said wearily. 'Then at least it's clear as to who stands where.'

The dwarf leaned forward, his recalcitrant beard scratching the table loudly. 'You really expect us to believe that story? Your Emperor makes a complete dog's dinner of his surprise attack, and now, after all these moons, it's really the fault of some Doppler?'

'And even if it's the way you say it is,' Palustra interjected vigorously, 'it wasn't the Doppelganger who ordered the attack, it was the Sun Emperor. And he's clearly decided to carry on with the siege, instead of issuing an apology.' Her lovely, brown eyes were now hard and cold, and the warmth had disappeared from her demeanour.

Jelninolan's voice was almost inaudibly quiet when it interrupted the ensuing silence. 'We only discovered the presence of the Doppler once Uldini had returned to the Sun Court.'

Perplexed, the Triumvirate members looked at each other. 'We shall need to discuss among ourselves whether to accept your words, because they will have a long-term effect on any further negotiations,' said Windita finally, and the other members of the Triumvirate nodded in agreement. 'We shall speak to you again tomorrow,' she concluded.

Uldini wanted to protest, but Falk and Jelninolan held him back. They stood up, bowed and dragged the protesting Arch Wizard out of the meeting room.

No sooner were the double doors closed behind them than Uldini pinned Falk against the wall using magic and whispered into his ear furiously. 'What exactly were you thinking of?' he said, growing more furious with every heartbeat. 'You bring the Sun Emperor into disrepute, you reveal that he was manipulated by a Doppelganger, and make absolutely no attempt to present the story from his point of view. Do you really want us to fail?'

Falk couldn't move, but his fury was evident in his voice. 'Think about it, you numbskull! Everything that the three of them said in there is true. Justinian made a pig's ear of it. Telling them about internal political pressure or insubordinate senators would have changed absolutely nothing. Anything they would have heard would only have confirmed their belief – that the Sun Emperor betrayed the Brazen City for his own benefit. Now at least they know that he didn't have the crackpot idea himself. If they believe us that a Doppler has his finger in the pie, at least they will listen to us when we bring up the subject of how we are going to act against HIM, WHO FORCES. And that, in the final analysis, is why we're here.'

Uldini reversed the spell as Jelninolan was laying her hand on his shoulder. 'He's right,' she said softly. 'Of course, we have to get everybody on our side, but that will only work if we can concentrate their minds on the Dark Days that are inevitably approaching us. The fact that they are all united in their disgust regarding Justinian's treachery is quite exceptional. Not even Palustra showed any hint of offering forgiveness.'

The Arch Wizard snorted angrily and floated up to their room. 'I really hope your gambit works, because if they don't believe our story about the Doppelganger, then in their eyes we're nothing but a pack of liars, and the negotiations will be over before they've even begun.'

They retired to their quarters without saying another word. Falk took up his position by the window, stared into the night and wondered how his apprentice was managing out there.

***

Ahren breathed a sigh of relief when he spotted the silhouettes of Khara and Trogadon in the torchlight of the longhouses. It had taken him a while to find his bearings in the unfamiliar surroundings, and to locate their meeting point. As he and Culhen approached, his companions turned and caught sight of him, and he could tell they were not happy with his delayed appearance.

'Where were you?' asked the dwarf, irritated. 'We've been standing here forever, kicking our heels, and I was really beginning to get worried about you.'

'I managed to get myself a job at a blacksmith's,' said Ahren defensively. 'Nobody wanted to talk to me about Bergen all day long, so I thought I might try and win the trust of an Ice Lander.'

Trogadon was about to continue scolding, but then paused. Khara too seemed to be considering what he had just said and held back with her rebuke. 'You know something', said the warrior, 'that's not such a bad idea.' He looked at Ahren thoughtfully. 'I think I'll copy your plan and give it a go too. Any smith around here is bound to happily employ a dwarf.'

Khara seemed somewhat baffled and shrugged her shoulders. 'They were all very friendly to me, even if nobody had anything important to say about the Blue Cohorts. I'll visit everybody I had longer chats with tomorrow again. Maybe somebody will let something slip.' She didn't sound particularly convinced herself, but neither Ahren nor the dwarf had any better ideas, and so they started heading back towards their lodgings. They crossed the deserted market square with its dilapidated stalls and burnt-down torches, lending the area a gloomy tone.

Trogadon was looking around him alertly, a hand on his weapon, which was hanging from a loop tied around his back. 'I really don't like this. It seems the night watch are beginning to neglect their duties, or the stock of torches is running low. One way or another we're like sitting ducks here. Every respectable citizen has long since gone to sleep in the safety of their homes.' He threw an irritated look at Ahren who shrugged his shoulders apologetically.

They quickened their steps and entered a narrow lane which led directly from the market square to their lodgings. Suddenly they were confronted with six figures, all holding sharp knives or thick cudgels.

'Damn it,' said Trogadon, and stood still. Ahren took a step backwards and took his bow from his shoulder, while Wind Blade made a scraping sound as Khara pulled it from her scabbard. Culhen went into a crouching position and emitted a continuous low growl.

The six figures approached them silently, staying all the time in the shadows, making it more difficult for their potential victims to make out their movements.

'You've bitten off more than you can chew!' shouted Trogadon loudly. 'Get away from here while you've still got the chance!'

The attackers neither answered nor slowed down, and the dwarf cursed quietly. 'Stupid, desperate or greedy, it makes no odds. They're faster than me, so we'll just have to go through them.' He pulled out his hammer and weighed it in his hands. 'Do your best not to kill them, or we'll have the city guards breathing down our necks.'

Ahren put his bow back with a curse and took out Wind Blade instead. It was too difficult to see for him to be certain that his shots wouldn't be fatal. He was going to have to improvise. Khara pulled the scabbard out of her belt and held it in her left hand, which Ahren found puzzling.

The bandits were almost upon them. Trogadon took a step backwards so that they would be fighting in the light of a torch. 'Hold Culhen back. If anyone gets savaged by a wolf, the word will spread faster than it takes Culhen to swallow half a pig,' he instructed Ahren. And then the fighting began.

Stay back! The apprentice ordered his wolf. Just then a gaunt man, dressed in tatters entered the flickering light and aimed a large cudgel, flecked with dried blood, at the young man. The Forest Guardian took a step back in surprise and just managed to parry the unexpected weapon. Whoever the person standing in front of him was, he had been in more than his fair share of fights. Ahren could see hunger in the man's sunken eyes, and he figured his attacker hadn't eaten in a long while. He almost felt sorry for the man, but then the cudgel swung towards him again, nearly connecting with his shoulder. Ahren turned in towards the blow, steered the weapon aside with Wind Blade, and pushed his shoulder into the man's chest while at the same time kicking his enemy's standing leg sideways with his own shin.

The move was as effective as it was simple. The man's mouth made a surprised O-shape, and he fell over like a tree being cut down, landing with a thud on his back. Ahren finished the man off by hitting him in the head with Wind Blade's pommel. There was no chance of his attacker getting up again. The bandit groaned, his eyes rolled around in his head and he lost consciousness.

Ahren heard a noise behind him, and when he spun round, he saw a little woman standing over him, a crooked dagger over her head, ready to attack. Her triumphant smirk was wiped off her face by Culhen leaping on her back and throwing her forward. Ahren reacted immediately by rising up from his crouched position and smashing his free fist with an upward motion into the chin of the staggering woman. She collapsed on the ground like a sack of potatoes and Ahren was in doubt that her fight was over.

Thanks, big lad, he quickly transmitted to the wolf. He took a deep breath and had a look around him, holding Wind Blade in a low defensive position in case of any unexpected attack.

Trogadon was standing with his foot on the chest of his fallen enemy, who was making ever weaker attempts at trying to hit the dwarf with his cudgel. If the warrior felt the blows on his leg, he certainly wasn't showing it. He was holding the weapon-hand of another attacker in a vice-like grip and Ahren could hear the dreadful sound of crunching bones as Trogadon tensed his muscles and squeezed the unfortunate's hand around the grip of his own weapon. The dwarf then head-butted the screaming man and Ahren saw a few teeth flying through the air, followed by the defeated bandit, once the dwarf had let go of his hand. The other attacker had now lost consciousness due to lack of air. Trogadon examined him briefly, before lifting his leg off the man's chest.

Khara was dealing with the enemies in her own merciless manner. She parried their blows with Wind Blade, using the wooden scabbard as a blunt sword, slamming it down on outstretched arms and legs, causing their bones to crack. Her two attackers were soon lying on the ground, holding their broken limbs and groaning while the swordfighter quietly put her weapon into its scabbard, before fixing it onto her belt again.

Trogadon examined the scene with a disappointed look. 'Was that all? Oh well,' he said slowly, 'we're fine and they're all going to survive, so all-in-all an enjoyable little skirmish.' He gestured his companions onwards. 'We should keep moving though, in case the noise attracts any more vultures. And anyway, you should always stop when you're ahead.'

As they hurried to their lodgings, Ahren asked himself how many more desperate souls would be created by this siege, and when the facade of civilisation, still visible during the day, would finally begin to crumble.

Chapter 17

They all had a restless night, though free of further fighting. Ahren had hardly slept a wink – he was too on edge following the brief, brutal confrontation. He couldn't get the images out of his head of the single-minded desire to kill he had seen in the eyes of the cutthroats. They were no Dark Ones, nor were they professional highwaymen and women; instead, they were desperate inhabitants of a city under siege, running out of food and seeing no other way out of their predicament than going on the hunt at night. Ahren was relieved that nobody had lost their life, but still, he couldn't help asking himself if it had been a mistake to be so merciful. Perhaps someone else would fall victim to their weapons the following night. He comforted himself with the thought that they would hardly be ready for action again in the foreseeable future, and if he and his friends were successful, the siege would be lifted in five days time anyway.

If they were successful. It made him dizzy to think how much depended on Bergen being found. In spite of the dreadful effects of the siege, most of the residents of this city were trying to live their lives as normally as possible, and that made Ahren more determined. He wanted to save the old North woman who dished out the food to the hungry, not to mention Vandir, who had so willingly given him work. And then there was the Sunplainer couple with their young child standing behind him in the queue, and all the people and dwarves who wanted to do their best for the community in spite of the dreadful circumstances, and who weren't just thinking of themselves.

Ahren had caught a brief glimpse of how much worse the situation could get, and he was certain of one thing: if the citizens of the Brazen City started fighting amongst themselves, then the peaceful co-existence of so many different cultures would be shattered, possibly never to be repaired again. He simply had to find Bergen!

At last the first rays of light shone through the air vent into the tiny, shabby room. Ahren threw off his blanket quickly and got to his feet.

Trogadon was still snoring heavily, but Khara was staring at him, her eyes wide awake. She couldn't have slept well either, and when she stood up, she grimaced. 'How can a bed be too soft and too hard at the same time?' she whispered in annoyance, as she rubbed her aching back. 'Is there anywhere at all I can practise *The Twelve Greetings of the Sun*?' she asked doubtfully.

Ahren frowned. Even if the Brazen City didn't officially belong to the Sunplains, it had been delivering weapons for decades in the war against the Eternal Empire. He couldn't imagine that a traditional performance from the Empire would go down to well in the present fraught atmosphere. The apprentice was about to shoot down her idea when a thought struck him. 'Come with me,' he whispered, and they climbed over the dozy dwarf, who blinked at them and mumbled something that sounded like 'I'll be with you in a bit.'

The two of them went out onto the wooden landing, and Ahren turned to face Khara with a grin on his face. He then interlinked his hands in the form of a stirrup and looked up. 'The roof is just above us and it's nice and smooth. We won't be disturbed up there.'

Khara nodded happily, and using his stirrup, pulled herself up the wall and onto the roof in a flowing, graceful movement.

The young Forest Guardian tried jumping up after her in a far less delicate manner, finally managed to grasp the edge of the roof with his fingertips. He was about to slip down again, but Khara grasped him by the arm. He pulled himself up with a groan and rolled over onto the roof.

'Well, we really need to practise that,' he panted and got up onto his feet.

Khara giggled. 'Good idea. If Falk saw you doing that, you'd be spending the week clambering up the sides of buildings.'

The girl was probably right, and Ahren realised that this was another thing he could practise independently. 'Thanks for the suggestion,' he mumbled with a sigh, and got into the starting position for the Sun Greeting.

Khara did the same, after correcting his foot stance. Then they remained in that position for one hundred heartbeats of total stillness. The sounds and smells of the city hardly reached them up there, and the weak light of the first rays of sunshine lit a sea of whitewashed roofs around them, interspersed with the elegantly curved wooden roofs of the longhouses, which gave the appearance of cows among a flock of grazing sheep.

Then the sun crept over the city walls, and everything was immersed in a golden sheen. Khara used that moment to begin the slow movements, which loosened her muscles and sinews and induced a deep concentration. Ahren imitated her actions and his spirit was filled with contentment. Even Culhen seemed to be getting something out of it, because the apprentice could feel the wolf relaxing in his sleep at the bottom of the wooden staircase.

Ahren breathed in the morning air deeply. It was still clear as the forges were only now firing up, the smoke from the chimneys having not yet dispersed. He turned his head to the left at the Tenth Greeting and saw that Khara was as completely relaxed in her movements as he was. The sun was shining off her jet-black hair and a thin layer of perspiration made her exotic face shimmer. It struck the young Forest Guardian that he felt drawn to her more strongly than he wanted to admit to himself and was relieved when the next greeting meant looking away from her again. He suppressed those emotions, allowing himself to be carried away by the peaceful harmony of the movements, but a persistent echo of his feelings for the young swordswoman remained, even when the session was finally finished.

Khara beamed at him happily. 'You had a good idea there for once,' she teased, and he smiled in embarrassment.

All of a sudden, he felt that his arms and legs were too long, that they refused to co-ordinate properly. And his mouth was terribly dry. 'I'd better get to Vandir before he thinks I'm trying to skive off work,' he said quickly, and he almost fell off the roof in his hurry to get away from the young woman and the confusing feelings she had released in him. He quickly slipped over the edge of the roof, hung on by his fingertips and then let himself drop, falling heavily on his hands and knees – as if this was his first day training as an apprentice Forest Guardian.

Cursing quietly to himself, he called for Culhen, who sprang up immediately in order to follow his confused friend.

Is everything alright? asked the sleepy wolf, sensing the turmoil within Ahren.

Yes, Ahren responded curtly, trying to concentrate on the work that awaited him so that Culhen wouldn't find out what was troubling him.

In spite of his best efforts, he couldn't resist one glance back. There was Khara, standing on the edge of the roof with a hurt expression and looking at him with a scowl.

By lunchtime Ahren was thanking all the gods that he had become a Forest Guardian, and not a blacksmith. He would rather take on Dark

Ones any night than stand in a forge, day in, day out, doing the most backbreaking of work.

Vandir had greeted him cheerfully that morning and they had set to work. Ahren had to keep the fire blazing, add coal with the heavy shovel, and operate the bellows at the same time, while the smith worked away on a mighty steel hammer. Time and again the Ice Lander would issue a barrage of instructions, ensuring that the fire would be the right temperature for that stage in the process. Sometimes it had to be really hot and blazing, other times glowing and low; sometimes the apprentice would have to take burning coal out of the forge, or he would work the bellows until he was panting as loudly as the leather monster he was struggling with.

Ahren didn't have a moment to ask the blond man questions, and by the time the sun was at its zenith and adding to the heat of the fire, the apprentice was asking himself if he would ever find out anything about Bergen before he melted away to nothing or his heart gave up.

Vandir announced it was lunchtime, just as Ahren was ready to collapse.

The powerful smith gave him a sympathetic grin. 'The first days are always the hardest. Then it gets better. Wait here while I get some food and water. I'd invite you into the longhouse but the fever is rampant among the family, and I don't want you to get sick.'

'Are you not afraid?' asked Ahren in surprise, but Vandir gave a dismissive wave.

'I've had it already, so it's hardly likely to do me any harm,' he said casually. 'But my uncle and my cousins are really suffering' he added glumly. Then he disappeared inside, returning a short time later with a chunk of cheese and some roast pork. He put the food, whose tempting aromas made Ahren's mouth water, unceremoniously down on an upended water drum, and they both helped themselves. Ahren gave a contented sigh with his mouth full. Then he mentally heard a coughing sound.

Haven't you forgotten something? asked Culhen in an offended voice. *Like, for example, a loyal, starving wolf, who's making every effort not to feed on the gentlemen sitting in front of him?* Culhen's words were accompanied by a low growl, and the apprentice looked at Vandir apologetically. He laughed heartily and reached into his leather apron, pulling out a bundle wrapped in cloth. He opened it up, revealing meat scraps which must have been part of the pig that the young men were currently devouring. The smith threw the chunky leftovers onto the ground and Culhen jumped on them with a delighted yelp, undermining the previous dignity he had been trying to maintain.

The three of them sat together outside the forge on the quiet street, contentedly munching their food. The sound of clanging hammers from the other forges echoed around them in a strangely reassuring manner, seeming to suggest that all was in fact, well in the Brazen City.

'Why are all you blacksmiths still working away?' asked Ahren curiously. He wanted to use the opportunity to start a conversation, and he was also puzzled by the fact that not a single customer had dropped into the forge.

Vandir looked up in surprise and stopped chewing. 'You've never taken an interest in politics then?' he asked, amused. 'The Triumvirate are buying all the weapons we produce. Either the siege ends peacefully, and the warehouses are full, which means trading can begin again, or the city will need them for defence purposes.' He scratched his head and pondered. 'It's really strange – we felt so secure over all these years. There were probably only two dozen weapons in the rooms of the city guards until the conflict began, because we had the mercenaries from the Plains to protect us.'

Ahren's heart missed a beat, and he bit into his piece of cheese to disguise the surprise on his face. This was the first time that anybody from the city had mentioned the Blue Cohorts off their own bat, and the young man hoped desperately that the smith would continue speaking. But Vandir didn't grant him his wish, and so Ahren tried to innocently develop the theme. 'Did you get to know them?' he asked casually between two bites of his food.

Vandir nodded and his face beamed. 'They were often to be seen around here in the blacksmiths' quarter when they were looking for new armour or needed repair work done. Three-Finger Jarla always bought directly from us – she never went through the dealers. She always says why not pay the craftsmen and women directly. She has a good eye for quality, and thanks to her, three long swords from our family forge are now in the possession of the Blue Legion.'

The blond smith's eyes were full of pride, and Ahren couldn't help but grin. Here was somebody who was proud of his craft, and placed value on working with his hands, and that was something that Ahren could only admire. The job of Forest Guardian went largely unnoticed in peacetime. It was only when a settlement was under attack from Dark Ones that you could achieve success and prove yourself if you defended it successfully, and of course your own life was in danger at such a time.

All of a sudden, the life of a blacksmith seemed much more attractive. Vandir could look back on his day's work every evening and hold what he created in his hands. That had to be a good feeling, thought Ahren wistfully. Now he understood how much it must have hurt Trogadon that the dwarf tradition had forced him to leave the blacksmith's life and spend his days with the Mountainshield Clan protecting the long tunnels of the Silver Cliff.

Vandir put aside his food and Ahren cursed inwardly. He'd almost missed his chance to sound out the smith due to his daydreaming, and so he chewed as slowly as possible to win himself some time. 'Who's Three-Finger Jarla?' he asked in a voice that he hoped sounded bored. 'I've only heard of Bergen, the leader of the Blue Cohorts.'

Vandir stood up and stretched. 'Their armourer. She's Bergen's right-hand woman, and she makes sure that everyone has what they need to survive the next battle.'

'Does she only have three fingers or how did she come by the name?'

'No, she's not maimed,' said the smith, laughing and shaking his head. 'She says she's only met three men that are fit to hold a candle up to her in battle, and somehow that's how her nickname came about.'

Ahren nodded and put the remaining bread into his mouth. He was considering how to formulate his next question when Vandir thwarted his plans.

'Come on. We have to get going again,' he said. 'Food prices have shot up again today, and I if don't finish this long sword, I won't be able to employ you tomorrow.'

Ahren leaped up dutifully, and they spent the rest of the day working on the slender weapon. While it was taking more and more shape, Ahren congratulated himself on the fact that gaining the trust of the smith through hard work was beginning to bear fruit. Vandir and his family knew the Blue Cohorts, and hopefully the apprentice would glean more information from the young craftsman the following day.

***

The fiery red sun was setting behind the horizon, and the west was basking in a light of burning gold.

'It's as if the land were on fire,' whispered Falk. 'Is it an omen?'

Uldini scowled and followed the direction of the old man's eyes, before rubbing his own face. 'By the THREE, I know you're worried about Ahren, but you're going too far now. Trogadon is with them and Khara has a sensible head on her shoulders. They'll get the boy out of any scrape he manages to get himself into.'

Jelninolan glared at the Arch Wizard, who was delighting in the Forest Guardian's misery. 'Don't listen to the bold, cynical Ancient. He's only jealous because none of the protégés he had over the centuries turned out to be worth the effort he put into them,' said the elf, calming the old man.

That wiped the smile off the childlike figure's face. 'That was not very nice, Auntie. I just don't have a talent for it.'

'As well as no patience. Just like you have no compassion or understanding for others' failings,' she added sharply.

Uldini closed his mouth, cocked his head and nodded. 'Point for you,' he said simply, then floated over to the opulently stocked wine rack where he poured himself a goblet of Liebhügler, an expensive and much sought after brand, and one which the Arch Wizard had been paying close attention to ever since they had arrived in the Brazen City.

The priestess was now standing beside Falk, and she placed a reassuring arm over his shoulder. They both looked out at the magnificent sunset playing out before them. The wind had mercifully carried away the smoke from the forges during the day, and there was only a faint layer hanging in the air, like the memory of a cold night at the beginning of a morning in spring.

'We're doing our share, and the others are doing theirs. Your best way of helping Ahren is to make sure that the Triumvirate listen to him and Bergen as soon as they appear here. They have to get the big picture or their attitude to the siege will overshadow everything, and their resentment will only ensure Justinian's victory.'

Falk grimaced and turned away from the natural wonder outside. 'Easier said than done. I'd feel much better if we knew whether they believed our news about the Doppelganger or not.'

''We're going to find that out soon enough', said Uldini drily. 'A servant is coming.' Since having been surprised the previous day during their argument, the Arch Wizard had cast a small magic net which informed him of anybody approaching the door. Their negotiating position was tricky enough as it was, and at least they could now be certain that nobody was listening in on them.

The servant knocked, and the Emperor's emissaries were in the hallway outside within a heartbeat, as if they had been waiting behind the door the whole time. The servant's eyes opened wide in amazement and yet he still managed to bow gracefully as Uldini floated past him.

'The Triumvirate await your presence,' stammered the baffled man and Falk slapped him on the back as he passed him.

'We know the way already,' he simply said while Jelninolan gave the poor servant an apologetic look.

'Forgive my companions, they always get restless when they're confined in a small room for too long.'

The trio went briskly down the stairs, leaving the flabbergasted servant in their wake, and went through the front hall to the meeting room, which Uldini opened with a wave of his hand. Hardly had the companions stepped inside, when he closed the heavy doors again, causing the servant to give a little painful yelp. The poor man's nose had been caught for a moment by the doors that he had intended to close himself, before being totally wrong-footed by the magic.

'Was that really necessary?' hissed Jelninolan quietly.

'Yes,' said Uldini with a self-satisfied chuckle. Then he spread his arms out and floated to his seat. 'A very pleasant evening to you all. I trust your deliberations have been fruitful?' he said as a greeting to the three representatives of the Brazen City, none of whom took any notice of the pompous nature of his arrival.

'Indeed they have, worthy emissary,' answered Windita as she looked at him critically with her blue eyes. The Ice Lander had tied up her hair with silver clasps this time, and now she was wearing leather armour instead of the smith's apron. Her appearance was now considerably more martial than on the previous day. Xobutumbur and Palustra looked the same as the evening before although the golden evening sun highlighted the beauty of the dark-skinned Sunplainer even more strongly.

The Triumvirate waited until everybody was sitting, before Windita continued. 'We've come to the conclusion that what you were saying is true, Baron Falkenstein. We know that some of your actions over the last few centuries were...questionable, but you always spoke the truth when it came to the Adversary.' She indicated the dwarf on her left. 'Xobutumbur has further pointed out to me that you are considered a friend of the dwarves. That is no small achievement for a human and adds more weight to your words.'

'Also, the presence of the august Ancient Jelninolan only makes sense if there really is a Doppelganger behind this conflict,' interjected Palustra. 'We could simply see no other reason for Eathinian to involve itself in this dispute.'

Jelninolan politely bowed her head and Falk gave a sigh of relief.

'Lucky again, old man,' growled Uldini sulkily, before continuing in mellifluous voice. 'Can I assume then that we are looking forward to finding a peaceful resolution?' he asked.

The blond leader nodded. 'We have come up with a few conditions and then we will forget about your Emperor's trespasses and resume normal trade', began Windita, but immediately Falk raised his hand energetically.

'Now that you believe us, there's more you need to know. The Thirteenth Paladin has been named and the Pall Pillar will fall. The Dark Days are going to come upon us again, and we're going to need every Paladin if we're going to be victorious.'

A deathly silence filled the hall as the Triumvirate sat there in shock and stared at Falk in disbelief.

'I solemnly swear that when we get out of here, I will never let you near a negotiating table again,' said Uldini angrily to the old Forest Guardian, who had folded his arms with determination, and was now leaning back in his chair.

'They said themselves, I don't lie when it comes to HIM, WHO FORCES', said Falk serenely, turning not just to the Arch Wizard but also to the Triumvirate. 'And Jelninolan and you can confirm what I've said. Beautiful and all as the Brazen City is, two Ancients and a Paladin don't turn up simply to discuss who should control the forges of the city. We're going to need the weapons that are being produced in our war with the dark god, and I really don't care whose coat of arms is going to decorate the city flagpole.'

Windita went pale at these blunt words, and Xobutumbur seemed to be about to explode. Palustra was the only one of the three who accepted Falk's rationale without batting an eyelid.

'Baron Falkenstein is not saying this to insult you,' interjected Jelninolan in a soft voice. 'We only want to impress upon you how much is on the line in this conflict, which has been stirred up by an agent of the Adversary. The Paladin Bergen simply must stay alive, and the forges of the Brazen City must remain untouched, or our chances of defeating HIM, WHO FORCES will sink dramatically.'

'This changes everything,' said Palustra quietly. 'We have to revise our demands.'

'We most certainly do,' interrupted Xobutumbur. 'You need us. You've just said it yourselves. Which means we can demand whatever we want.'

Windita shook her head violently in disagreement. 'We will not act against the wishes of the THREE.'

An argument erupted, which the blond Ice Lander put a stop to within a few moments. 'We're going to have to discuss the matter amongst ourselves. I propose that we met again tomorrow evening and we resume negotiations.'

Both Uldini and Falk groaned, and so it was left to Jelninolan to respond. 'We will happily appear here again tomorrow. Have a good evening.'

She skewered her two companions with a look, and they followed her unwillingly out the door, leaving the Triumvirate squabbling quietly in their wake.

'At least they know the whole truth now,' said Falk when they were finally back in their lodgings. 'Hopefully they'll have reached the point tomorrow where we can have decent negotiations.'

'Hopefully,' said Uldini sourly. 'There are only four days until Justinian sounds the call to battle, and there are too many open questions.

Once the rocks start flying around our ears, nobody is going to listen to us.'

Nobody had an answer to that, and a heavy silence descended on the companions, which remained for the rest of the evening.

***

Ahren groaned uncomfortably as he lifted the spoon of thick stew, which Trogadon had purchased from the innkeeper for a little mountain of gold. Every muscle in his arm and back was burning, and he felt as if he was back in the first days of his apprenticeship with Falk. He scattered a few crushed leaves from his bag of herbs into the bowl and dutifully continued to eat. The healing plants would help his body sufficiently so that he would be able to continue helping Vandir the next day.

Trogadon looked at him and grinned. 'I recognise your body posture. You've got Bellows' Back. That'll clear up after a few moons, believe me.'

'Luckily it won't come to that,' groaned Ahren, struggling with a trembling hand to get the next spoonful to his mouth. 'In five days time, we'll either have been successful or there'll be war.'

'Be quiet,' warned the dwarf in a serious voice. 'If the wrong ears hear us, the whole city will be after us.'

They both looked over at Khara, who was sitting and drinking with a few Ice Lander smiths, and they all seemed to be having a very amusing time. 'She's made friends quickly,' remarked Trogadon and Ahren nodded grimly. He was far from pleased at the way she was smiling at one of the tall smiths. The fact that he was battling with every spoonful himself, didn't exactly improve his mood either.

'Poor lad,' said the warrior when he noticed Ahren's look. Trogadon stroked his beard for a moment before continuing. 'You've really picked a hard nut to crack.'

Ahren's ears reddened, but he didn't respond to his partner's statement, continuing instead to struggle with his stew.

'And if you don't want to talk about it, that's fine too,' said Trogadon serenely. 'But I know something that will put some pep in your step. I got myself as a job as a blacksmith today. And as a reward for my work, I'm going to be allowed to make a little weapon out of Dwarf Steel. What would you think of a nice new dagger?'

Ahren thought for a moment and was considering declining the offer. The dagger was an absolutely last resort when it came to fighting, and it struck Ahren that it might be a waste, if the dwarf was to put all that time and effort into something that hopefully Ahren would never need. But then he had a brainwave, and he explained in detail how his dagger was to be formed.

The warrior raised his eyebrows and then shrugged his shoulders. 'If that's what you want – it's your dagger,' he said sceptically.

Ahren nodded tiredly as he unceremoniously slurped down the rest of his stew. 'I'm going to bed,' he stated grumpily, glancing over at Khara, who was laughing a little too merrily and coquettishly. 'Tomorrow's going to be a hard day, and it's too loud in here.' Even to his own ears, what he said sounded too much like sulking, but Ahren was too tired to think of a better excuse. Culhen shoved himself beside his master, and the apprentice tickled the wolf's fur gratefully.

I can bite him if you like, offered the animal, who was looking at the smith that Khara was making eyes at. Ahren gave a weary smile.

Thanks for the offer, but he's here with his pack, the apprentice responded. *There might be too many of them.*

Culhen stood still and stared at the Ice Lander, who was whispering something into Khara's ear. The wolf seemed to be listening to his inner voice. *You go ahead,* he said drily, and disappeared under Trogadon's table again.

Ahren was surprised, but was going up the stairs nonetheless, when he suddenly heard an uproar from down below.

'The beast pissed in my boot,' screamed the voice of a young adult, and Ahren saw Culhen bursting out of the inn barking loudly, before disappearing down a darkened alleyway. The apprentice had arrived on the top step when four of the tall customers burst out of the tavern and looked around furiously. Khara's knight in shining armour was among them, and he was angrily shaking out his dripping boot, which even Ahren could smell. Ahren quickly disappeared into the room and sent Culhen all his love and affection, and the wolf answered with a loud, triumphant howl, which echoed through the night.

No matter what happened, he and Culhen would always be together, and with this reassuring thought, Ahren drifted off to sleep.

Chapter 18

Something had changed. While Ahren strode through the streets of the Brazen City towards Vandir's forge, he saw many residents with distrustful and irritated faces, holding their purses or possessions closely. Food was becoming even scarcer, and he heard whisperings that several murders had been committed the previous night – the victims having been robbed or their homes plundered. Several people looked angrily at Ahren and Culhen, and one old woman spat at his feet. 'Parasitical mercenaries.' she hissed and scurried away.

They're all smelling of fear and hunger, was the message he received from Culhen, who deliberately held his nose upwind.

'They're running out of provisions,' said Ahren quietly. Suddenly, he had a sick feeling in his stomach. Hopefully, Vandir wasn't infected by the general mood, or all of Ahren's efforts over the previous few days would have been in vain. He picked up the pace and was relieved to see the blacksmith giving him a friendly wave when he arrived at the forge.

'Now that's what I call dedication. The sun has only started to rise, and you arrive for work in double-quick time. Have you caught the blacksmithing bug or are you running away from something?' he asked with a laugh.

Ahren responded half-heartedly, because the craftsman had hit the nail on the head without knowing it. Ahren had slipped out of the room as early as possible so as to avoid Khara. He was just too confused by his own feelings, and her behaviour the previous evening spoke volumes. He didn't stand a chance against her Northmen admirers. He thought it was clearly best not to be alone with her until he had figured things out. He sighed to himself when he realised that he was subconsciously following Falk's instructions for stalking a Dark One, and somehow it was apt. Khara was at least as dangerous and decidedly less forgiving.

Vandir clicked his fingers in front of the apprentice's eyes. 'What's going on in your head?' he asked, concerned.

'Just the mood in the city,' Ahren quickly responded. 'It seems that mercenaries like me are no longer welcome since this morning.'

The blacksmith frowned. 'There's hardly anything left to eat, and the siege weapons on the Plains at the foot of the mountain are ready for action.' He gestured with his chin towards the city wall nearby. 'Have a look for yourself and you'll understand why everyone is on edge.'

Ahren walked the few paces to the wall and climbed the steps to get a look from the parapet. A city guard was standing nearby, but took no notice of him, concentrating instead on the sight below, which made Ahren gasp when he saw it.

More than three dozen siege weapons had been drawn into position on the green Plains. The louring clouds which threatened a heavy downpour, added to the menacing atmosphere created by the enormous catapults, anchored to the ground by man-sized pegs, the buckets of their long arms holding rocks as big as fattened sheep, ready to be hurled up towards the city. Even though the distance was considerable, Ahren had little doubt that the projectiles would reach their target. Little wonder that the mood in the Brazen City had changed. He needed to make contact with Bergen as soon as possible, or countless people would lose their lives in this senseless conflict!

He ran down the steps and towards Vandir. 'This is madness,' he said forcefully. 'Justinian needs the smiths; he can't use catapults!'

The Ice Lander shrugged his shoulders stoically. 'I assume he simply wants to tear down the wall so his legion can gain entry. As long as the city walls hold, we can pick off his soldiers as they move up the switchback.' There was a note of concern in his voice too.

'Will Bergen and the Blue Cohorts fight if it comes to the crunch?' Ahren asked. This was no time for subtlety, and he had a sick feeling in his stomach now that he fully comprehended that they would soon be caught up in the middle of a battle that nobody had wanted.

Vandir nodded emphatically. 'They're staying hidden for the time being because they don't want spies or traitors to have any idea of where they're quartered. Bergen has experienced enough sieges to know how to minimise risks to himself and his people.' The blond man's voice still sounded full of admiration for the commander, and Ahren hoped that someday people would speak in the same way of the Thirteenth Paladin.

'That's enough chit-chat for now,' said the smith. 'We need to work while we can. Who knows how many days we have left?'

I know, thought Ahren darkly and he exchanged a glance with Culhen. The wolf sent him back calming thoughts and settled down in a sheltered corner, where he could keep his eyes on the forge. *In case anybody causes trouble,* Ahren heard in his head, and he gave an almost imperceptible nod. Then he got down to work, while the wolf kept an eye on the pair.

The day dragged on, Ahren's muscles ached, and the passers-by glared in at him as they walked past the forge. He wondered how Khara was getting on. The girl was still trying to befriend people, and he was unsure whether she would continue to have success now that the mood had changed for the worse. His concern for the swordfighter increased, causing him to lose concentration. So much so, in fact, that he almost missed the figure wearing a deep-blue cloak, approaching from the city wall and beckoning to the blond blacksmith.

Ahren kept his head down, trying to see more out of the corner of his eyes while mechanically operating the bellows. The stranger seemed to be a woman, and he identified blue leather armour peeking out occasionally from under the heavy cloak. Trogadon had described the normal garb of the Blue Cohorts in great detail to Ahren and Khara, and the apprentice was convinced he was now looking at a member of the mercenary troop they had been searching for since their arrival in the Brazen City.

His heart was pounding, but he pulled himself together and looked down at the coals.

Can you pick up her scent somehow? he asked Culhen.

The wolf stretched contentedly and yawned. *No problem,* he responded calmly, before bounding over to the two, clumsily and excitedly, tail waving, every inch the skittish puppy. Except that this puppy was over one pace tall and had long, gleaming, white fangs. Still, Vandir laughed and tickled Culhen's head, while the wolf, apparently curious, rubbed up against the stranger's leg. She flinched, but then patted the wolf, who then proceeded to bury his nose in her pockets, as if looking for a treat.

The woman finally pushed the wolf away, laughing in a sonorous alto voice. 'That's enough now,' she said with an amused laugh, and Culhen trotted off obediently and curled up in his corner again.

That was far too easy, was the self-satisfied message Ahren received from his friend. *I'll find her no matter where she goes.*

Vandir and the mercenary talked for another while before the mercenary disappeared behind the longhouse.

Should I follow her? asked Culhen excitedly.

No. You'll be able to follow her scent this evening, won't you? was Ahren's quick response.

Of course, responded the wolf, and sorely aggrieved, buried his nose into the fur of his tail.

Ahren rolled his eyes but left it at that. He went back to his work and waited for the afternoon to turn into evening. His plan was to find the Blue Cohorts' hiding place with the help of Culhen's nose, and then return to Trogadon before nightfall when the streets would be too dangerous. As soon as the evening began to set in, he began sighing and rubbing his back obviously. At last Vandir looked up from his work with a concerned look.

'It's been a hard day's work today,' he said sympathetically. 'We'd better stop before you break in two. Same time tomorrow?' he asked.

Ahren nodded keenly, said goodbye, and went over to Culhen, giving the appearance they were going to take the familiar route home. They were hardly out of sight of the longhouse when the wolf changed direction to see if he could find the scent of the woman in blue.

His nose in the air, the wolf trotted down a street parallel to the one they had just been on, and finally arrived at the city wall. *Have it!* he said triumphantly and led Ahren along the inside of the protective wall, sniffing the ground intensely all the while. The stranger must have used the wall as cover, and so they ran alongside it in a northerly direction, until they finally arrived at a large wooden, weathered-looking warehouse, wedged in between three longhouses and the city wall. He spotted a remarkably large number of Ice Landers, who were standing around outside the longhouses, and Ahren's instincts told him they were more likely to be guards than walkers taking the evening air.

He signalled to Culhen to duck down and did the same himself. Crouched in the long shadow of the wall, Ahren looked carefully at the longhouse. Thick old timber beams hid the inside, and the doors appeared to be very sturdy in comparison with the rest of the ramshackle building.

Ahren gave a silent whoop for joy, believing he had found Bergen's hiding place. He would need to make certain before telling the others. If this was only a storage depot for a pile of expensive weaponry, and they entered without authorisation, then at best they would be unable to get any more information, and at worst, it could come to physical combat. They had only one chance of finding Bergen, and so the young Forest Guardian decided to risk having a look inside.

The warehouse had a few small windows just under the roof through which he could possibly peek. They were hardly bigger than air vents and so entry would be impossible, but they were sufficient to his purposes. If he kept to the city wall, and climbed the back wall of the building from the narrow alley around the back, then nobody would spot him. With a little luck, he would see something inside and then return to Trogadon and Khara.

Stay here! he ordered Culhen. *You're too big and too conspicuous to slip in unnoticed.* The wolf was now very imposing and had become a much more powerful fighter, but the flip side was that it was becoming increasingly difficult for him to remain invisible.

Right, then, muttered Culhen grumpily.

Ahren moved forward warily, only proceeding when the guards were looking in a different direction. With every step, the nervous feeling in his stomach increased until he was finally past the longhouse. He was giving Culhen a warning look over his shoulder, when he spotted the wolf's concern. The apprentice was now surrounded by guards, and there were too many of them for the wolf to be of any assistance if the apprentice were discovered. Driven by his protective instinct, Culhen crawled a few paces forward, and Ahren had to use all his willpower to instruct the animal to lie perfectly still.

Then he crept onward until he finally reached the back of the warehouse. He gave a sigh of relief. The distance between the city wall and the building was no more than two paces and there were no torches hanging on the wall, so he was invisible in the long shadow. He stretched his fingers and prepared to climb the seven paces up to the little square holes above him.

Just as his fingertips had found a precarious hold in the wooden wall, he heard a noise left and right and Culhen's warning voice popped in his head.

Above you! echoed through his head, and as Ahren looked up he saw two figures, who must have been lying on the city wall, from where they had kept an eye on the back of the warehouse unnoticed. They jumped nimbly down to him and in no time at all he was trapped between them.

An ambush! shot through his head as he grasped Wind Blade. *Fetch the others!* the apprentice ordered Culhen and spun to his left to dodge a heavy blow, while the attacker used his crony's feint to hit Ahren hard on the back of his head with something heavy.

The young Forest Guardian hit the ground like a sack of potatoes, everything went black around him. The only thing he could hear was Culhen's anguished howl.

***

Falk tilted his head while they were sitting with the Triumvirate, while Uldini was trying to persuade the three city representatives. Their reception this evening was less formal and cool than previously, but the negotiating partners had requested the Arch Wizard to present the Sun Emperor's demands, a request that Uldini granted at great length and in even greater detail. The old Forest Guardian had hardly been listening, but now he was staring intently into space.

'What's wrong?' whispered Jelninolan, who had noticed his expression.

'Selsena thinks she's picked up a signal from Culhen,' said the old man, his face creased into a frown. 'The wolf was too far away for Selsena to be certain, but she's uneasy about it – and so am I.'

'Culhen's probably just hungry,' joked the elf half-heartedly, but her voice betrayed her own concern.

'Can you track him down with a spell?' asked Falk urgently, but Jelninolan shook her head. 'I could, but then the Doppelganger would find out where the target of the magic is hiding. I wouldn't like him to discover where Ahren is. If the boy is too far away, then we'd be running the risk of the Doppler getting to him before we would.'

Falk frowned and Uldini cleared his throat before continuing. 'So those are the conditions under which Justinian, Emperor of the Sunplains, is willing to put an end to the conflict. He hopes that in the light of the greater dangers posed by the Adversary, you are willing to agree to them.'

Xobutumbur roared with laughter and drummed the table with the flat of his hands, his face the picture of bitterness. 'Well that's a fine ultimatum! His treachery doesn't come off and now we're supposed to deliver the mercenaries who have stood bravely by us. We are to turn ourselves into traitors so that we can all negotiate as equals again?' he spat out.

'And he's using the dark god as leverage,' said Windita in disgust, backing up the dwarf.

Only Palustra seemed to give the proposal serious consideration although her face suggested rejection. 'We should present our demands and see how the negotiations develop,' she finally suggested.

Windita nodded and looked gravely at Uldini. 'We demand free access to the Eastern Sea harbour so that we can sell our wares to the peoples of other harbours. We also reject any further occupation by mercenaries of the Sunplains, as we will now be responsible for our own protection. The price of weapons will increase by one tenth, and those made from Dwarf Steel by one fifth. In return your fine Emperor will not have to make an official apology, and we will present an agreed statement referring to the matter as an unfortunate "misunderstanding."'

Uldini gulped, and his eyes shot from one member of the Triumvirate to the next as he considered the consequences of their demands. 'And what about Bergen and the Blue Cohorts?' he asked cautiously.

'Considering the whole episode was a misunderstanding, they cannot be seen as traitors and therefore cannot be executed. It should be left to them to decide whether to stay or to go,' said Palustra smoothly.

Uldini blew out his cheeks, then turned to his two companions for advice. 'Their suggestion of proclaiming this quarrel to be a misunderstanding is excellent. It would be a way for Justinian to save face and forget about executing the mercenaries, but the rest is utopian. We can't fulfil all of their demands,' he said quietly.

Falk rolled his eyes in disgust and prodded Uldini in the chest. 'Then think of something else. We want to save Bergen, the Cohorts and the blacksmiths. The rest is incidental,' he whispered in a hard voice. 'If everyone is happy afterwards, well and good, but now it's vital that everyone will be able to fight when the Dark Days come upon us.'

Jelninolan nodded, while Uldini chewed his lower lip as he considered what to do next. Then he turned back to the Triumvirate and the serious bargaining began.

Falk closed his eyes in annoyance and asked Selsena to investigate Culhen's emotions further. Hopefully the Titejunanwa could find out what was going on out there.

***

'Where's he hiding himself?!' said Trogadon in an exasperated voice. He and Khara were sitting in the taproom of the tavern as they did every evening and were looking at the door intently. Darkness had set in some time earlier and there was still no sign of Ahren. The dwarf absently took another sup of beer while Khara sat there, her body appearing calm, but her face betraying concern.

'Maybe he's been attacked,' she said finally. 'I got a lot of hostile looks today, and even people who were drinking with me yesterday are avoiding me today. Anyone who isn't native to the Brazen City is now being looked on as the enemy.'

Trogadon snorted. 'I already know the rules of sieges, thank you very much. If you don't belong, you're the first to perish,' he said, grumpily putting down his beer. 'There's nothing for it. We'll have to go find him, even if we risk being attacked ourselves.'

Khara nodded and was up in an instant. She was clearly not half as relaxed as she had let on.

Trogadon looked her up and down. 'Damn it, girl, we haven't bought any armour for you yet, have we?' he said grimly, and she shook her head.

'I looked into it yesterday, and can collect it from the blacksmith tomorrow, but until then I've no protection.'

Trogadon shook his head angrily. 'It was obvious, we should have...' he began, before being stopped in his tracks by Culhen, who leaped into the taproom gesticulating wildly so that all conversation in the room stopped and several swords were drawn.

Trogadon stood up quickly, upending the table in the process, and caught Culhen by the collar, dragging him towards the door. 'No need to be afraid – he belongs to us,' he called over his shoulder, pulling the excited animal out of sight of the customers.

Khara followed hot on his heels and went down on her hunkers to calm the wolf down. 'Good boy, Culhen. What's up? Is there something wrong with Ahren?' she implored, and the wolf started barking wildly again.

'That's not going to work,' growled Trogadon, but Khara raised a placatory hand.

'He's much more intelligent than a normal wolf,' she said and put Culhen's head between her hands, looking deeply into his amber eyes. 'Calm down now, or we won't be able to help you. Bark once for yes and twice for no. Understood?'

The wolf immediately barked once and Khara gave a grateful nod. 'Has Ahren sent you to us?' she asked. Another bark.

'Does he need help?'

'Woof!'

'Is he injured?' she probed.

The wolf hesitated.

'Has he been attacked?' interjected Trogadon.

'Woof.'

'Right then,' said the dwarf firmly. 'Show us the way.'

The white wolf spun around and disappeared at lightning speed down an alley with Khara nimbly following and Trogadon struggling behind and snorting for air.

***

Cold water tore Ahren from his dreamless state and he immediately had a painful headache. With a groan, he made a move to feel the swelling on the back of his head, but his hands were tied painfully together, and any attempt to stand was futile as his feet were bound to the legs of a chair. He tried to open his eyes but was blinded by a bright light and so he closed them again with a groan.

'You gave his brain a good rattling there, Tontur', said a deep woman's voice, which Ahren recognised immediately. It was the woman who had visited Vandir. 'How are we supposed to question this spy if you've cracked his skull?'

'You're too kind-hearted, Jarla,' said a hard, buzzing voice directly beside Ahren's right ear. The apprentice tried to shrink away but was painfully prevented from doing so by his fetters. 'We're going to have to slice off a few bits of him anyway in order to get him to talk.'

'Slice off?' squeaked Ahren in a panic. He swallowed hard and a feeling of nausea came over him. He tried opening his eyes a second time but gave up. 'I'm not a spy,' he stammered, but then he felt a firm hand under his chin and, to his horror, a cold blade on his right ear, painfully stabbing his skin.

'I think this might be a good place to start. He can hear our questions with his left ear anyway,' continued the heartless voice, and Ahren's eyes filled with tears of terror. He had never felt so helpless before, and nothing in his training had prepared him for a situation like this. He searched mentally for Culhen, but either the wolf was too far away, or his head too battered to be able to hear his friend.

'I'm no spy!' he screamed. 'I am a Paladin and I'm looking for Bergen!'

This was met with uproarious sarcastic laughter from all around him. He was well and truly trapped and over a dozen voices were cackling among themselves. Finally, the hubbub died down. The blade was still lying on his ear and the danger of it being sliced off if he made the slightest movement was all too real.

'So, you're a Paladin then?' cackled the hard voice in mock merriment. 'Then tell us how *that* came about.'

In his panic, Ahren started babbling about everything he could think of. His training under Falk, the discovery that he was the Thirteenth Paladin, the journey through the Knight Marshes, and the revelation that Falk was really the Paladin Dorian Falkenstein. He babbled for as long as he could, in the desperate hope that the hand holding the sharp knife to his ear would not begin to cut. Deep in the back of his mind was the hope that Culhen would have found his friends, and the longer he kept speaking, the better chance there was that they could save at least some of him. He shuddered and carried on yapping.

He told of how he had visited the dwarves, and of how he had finally been Named, and that they were now trying to free Bergen from the present mess the Paladin now found himself in, and that they were attempting to negotiate peace between Justinian III and the Brazen City.

'That's enough,' announced a warm-sounding voice which resonated with authority. The blade immediately disappeared from Ahren's skin and with two quick cuts he was freed from his fetters. Ahren heard a metallic sound directly in front of him and when he cautiously opened his eyes and blinked, he could make out a lantern being moved away, which the henchmen had placed right in front of his face.

A comfortably dim light filled the room, and the apprentice realised to his relief that he could now keep his eyes open without feeling any pain. He looked around and saw two dozen men and women, all dressed in deep-blue, positioned in a rough circle around him. Most of them were hunkered down on the dirty floor of the dilapidated room, and many of them were performing their everyday duties – most of which seemed to be connected with their armour. Some were mending holes; others were polishing their boots or sharpening their weapons. A small fat man with a crafty look on his face was just putting away his sharp-looking knife. and Ahren was certain that this was the mercenary who had just been threatening him. The apprentice carefully felt the apple-sized bump on his head and looked daggers at his torturer, who shrugged his shoulders apologetically before grinning greasily.

In spite of his terror, Ahren was about to launch into a tirade, but was prevented by the comforting voice coming from a dim corner of the room. 'Please forgive Tontur; he plays the blackguard with too much passion. We've discovered that fear of pain is generally much more effective than pain itself.' The speaker came into the light as he continued to speak. 'Which is why we almost always find out the truth without inflicting permanent injury on the person. I suppose I really haven't forgotten who I once was.'

Ahren was staring at a tall, broad-shouldered Ice Lander, whose blond hair was streaked with grey, and whose otherwise handsome face had lines of deep sorrow and weariness. Blue eyes, almost colourless, examined Ahren intensively, and Ahren looked back, captivated. The man's beard was decorated with a few short braids, and the apprentice's eyes were drawn as if by magic to the man's breastplate, shimmering with the white sparkle of Deep Steel. A heavy axe of the same material could be seen extending upwards from behind the man's right shoulder as he bowed slightly. 'Allow me to introduce myself,' he said quietly. 'My name is Bergen Olgitram, commander of the Blue Cohorts and Paladin of the gods.'

***

Trogadon smashed his hammer in frustration against the wooden wall of the abandoned warehouse in which they were standing. Everywhere there were tell-tale signs that a crowd of people had been living here until very recently – but now it was empty. The residents of the surrounding longhouses had withdrawn quietly into their homes and hadn't prevented them from entering the warehouse. Now the dwarf knew why,

'They've moved on,' cursed the dwarf, and hammered the wall once again, causing the beams to grind against each other.

'I wouldn't do that while we're inside if I were you,' said Khara nervously, stepping out onto the narrow street.

Trogadon followed her example and called over his shoulder. 'Culhen, try to follow their scent. It stank so much in there that even I can't forget the stench.'

A heartbeat later, and the wolf was out the door, nose to the ground, and leading them deep into the darkness of the Brazen City.

***

'Enough!' thundered Xobutumbur and threw his goblet against the wall. 'Whenever we're on the point of making progress, you come along with your supposed war against the Adversary!' The heavy chair fell with a crash to the ground as the dwarf stood up. 'If you want to have any decent negotiations, you need to prove your story. Until you present your Thirteenth Paladin, you're nothing but a pack of liars that have allowed yourselves to be manipulated by a treacherous Emperor.' He shook his fist and the vein on his temple pulsated. 'Deliver a message to that snake in the grass. Tell him that he's welcome to try and attack us. Thousand Halls has heard our appeal for help, and we've received permission to use Deep Fire. His legions will drown in blood and heat on the side of the mountain!' The dwarf stormed out of the room, leaving the three companions shell-shocked in his wake and the two female members of the Triumvirate, who had also stood up, looked on somewhat shamefacedly.

'His choice of words may have been a little drastic, but essentially he's correct,' said Windita politely. 'You do owe us some proof if we are to completely abandon our conditions. Our people look up to us. If we surrender unconditionally to the Sun Emperor, we will be torn asunder by a furious mob and in the end, there will be war anyway.'

The two ladies bowed their heads slightly, then followed the irate dwarf, leaving the stunned emissaries behind them.

'Where did that outburst come from?' asked Uldini in bafflement, and Falk laughed bitterly.

'You're really asking that? You picked apart and undermined almost all of their demands and didn't offer them anything in return except for sparing their lives,' he said forcefully.

'We either serve the Brazen City to the Sun Emperor on a silver platter or we sacrifice the Blue Cohorts – you know that yourself,' hissed Uldini in response. 'And Bergen is doubtless attached to his surrogate family. Because of this, I'm trying to conduct negotiations in as thorough a manner as possible, so that Justinian allows them all to go free.'

'We need Ahren,' interjected Jelninolan simply, before the two were able to start squabbling with each other again.

'And we can only present him once he's found Bergen,' groaned Uldini. 'Don't you just long for the old days when we only had to slaughter an army of Dark Ones?'

The three companions trotted back to their lodgings lost in thought, and Falk resumed his watching position at the window, warning Selsena again to listen out for any emotional signal from Culhen or Ahren.

***

Ahren let out an almost hysterical laugh as the gigantic man straightened himself up again. 'You were damned difficult to find,' said the relieved apprentice. 'We've travelled a long way to help you.'

Bergen raised his eyebrows in amusement. 'And how is a young lad, still yet but an apprentice, going to help me? I've taken on the mightiest ruler in the area because I refuse to betray either my principles or this city.' He turned around and was going to leave the room, but Ahren wouldn't give way.

'I am the Thirteenth Paladin, and HE, WHO FORCES will re-awaken. That is a truth you cannot run away from. My master tried to and he failed as well,' he said forcefully.

Something in either Ahren's tone or choice of words caused the captain to pause. He turned back and looked Ahren up and down. 'Where is your armour? Where is your weapon of Deep Steel? Where is your companion animal?' he snarled at the young man. 'You are nothing but an imposter!'

Once again, he turned, and Ahren struggled for words, when a woman with a face like toughened leather and pitch-black hair flecked with grey, interjected. 'He had a damned big wolf with him, Captain. Completely white and remarkably strong.'

Ahren recognised the speaker's voice. That could only be Three-Fingered Jarla, the armourer of the unit. 'Culhen is my companion, blessed by HER, WHO FEELS. I don't have my armour or my weapon yet because we had to improvise at the Naming. I am a Paladin and I am speaking the truth.' Then he added quietly: 'I've seen them. You know who I mean.' Ahren's mind flashed back to the moment he had caught sight of the sleeping gods, and when Bergen spun round and looked him in the eye, the expression on the captain's face changed. For an instant the rough lines on his face seemed less sad, his shoulders not quite so tensed. Then the moment was past, and Bergen straightened to his full height.

'You will stay with us tonight as our guest. We will give you food to eat and something to drink, and no-one will touch a hair of your head while I consider what you have said. Do you give me your word of honour that you will not flee?'

Ahren nodded, and Bergen seemed satisfied. Inside, the apprentice was jumping for joy at having got through to the Paladin, at least to some extent. And although the young Forest Guardian had promised not to flee, he was sure that his friends would soon find him, and they could all persuade the mercenary together.

***

Culhen sneezed violently, then sneezed again. He was overcome by a sneezing attack and found it impossible to stop. Trogadon had to drag the helpless animal away until he finally calmed down. They had just been following the scent that Culhen's nose was tracking so well, and then from one moment to the next, Culhen was incapacitated.

'Sneeze Weed,' groaned Trogadon. 'Clever little swine. They were prepared for Culhen and covered their tracks by laying this ingenious trap. They've scattered it everywhere.'

Culhen whined and was about to rub his nose with his paw, but the dwarf caught it in an iron grip. 'Don't scratch or it will be sore. It will be alright, son.'

'So can we go around the outside and take up their scent again later?' asked Khara hopefully.

'Unfortunately, not. Culhen's nose is out of action for a while. The poor chap won't be able to find his own backside for the next few hours,' said Trogadon grumpily. Then he shook his head. 'I suggest we forget this plan and try the other one.'

Culhen barked his support, Khara nodded, and they set off towards the city centre, Culhen repeatedly being shaken to the core by violent sneezes.

'I know it isn't easy, but could you try to be a little quieter?' whispered the dwarf nervously, holding hard onto his hammer. 'It's the middle of the night, and you're positively inviting...'

More than a few figures stepped out of archways, alleyways and darkened corners. They had weapons in their hands and hungry, greedy looks on their faces.

'...trouble', said Trogadon, wearily finishing his sentence. He quickly calculated how many opponents there were, then reached a conclusion. 'Right then,' he whispered. 'You and Culhen are agile. Run to the others and tell them the news. I'll follow you.'

Culhen sneezed out an objection, and Khara's face spoke volumes as she drew Wind Blade.

The bandits came closer, and when they saw Khara, some of them let out a greedy, cheerful whoop of joy.

The dwarf rolled his eyes and spoke to the stubborn young woman. 'Of course, you can cut some of them into pieces, but Culhen won't be any help if he has to keep sneezing, and you certainly won't be helping Ahren,' he implored. Then he loosened his shoulders and tested out his hammer, swinging it in wide arcs, which caused the cutthroats to slow down.

'Now go!' he snapped. Khara hesitated for a moment, then ran off down a side-alley, followed by the sneezing wolf.

The dwarf stared after them with a look of satisfaction and then began to sing quietly as his attackers approached. He raised his weapon and let the hammer swing down in time to the music, as the first of the bandits thrust his knife forward.

***

Falk's eyes were beginning to close and he decided to go to bed. A last glance down on the dimly lit square revealed that there were no souls out, apart from the nightly scavengers, looking for anything edible or valuable enough to be exchanged for foodstuffs. He almost thought he caught a glimpse of Culhen's white silhouette stalking along the edge of the square, but then he wearily shook his head. His imagination had been playing too many tricks on him over the previous few days. He turned around. He was tired and thought the best thing to do would be to lie down. The following day was going to be long.

He sat down on his bead with a groan and was about to take off his boots when he felt a sudden jerk in his body that caused him to leap back on his feet.

'Selsena!' he shouted. 'She's telling me that Culhen is terribly agitated. She senses terrible concern!'

He ran to the window and looked out. The white spot hadn't moved, and now Falk was certain that the wolf was biding his time, waiting for the moment he would not be observed, to race between the scavengers and reach them. Three paces and Falk was at the door, which Uldini was quick-witted enough to cast a spell on, preventing the Forest Guardian from storming out.

'Think, numbskull! Do you really want to go running out there in your linen shirt and boots?' said Uldini urgently. 'Get your armour and weapons. Jelninolan and I will deal with those dubious characters on the square for now. Our current position is no secret anyway, so it makes no difference if the Doppelganger senses our magic.'

The elf had already magically put on her ribbon armour and was holding her fighting staff in her hand. She pointed it down towards the square and immediately all the torches round about blazed to fiery life. Every inch of the market square was lit up by blazing flames, and all but the most obdurate scavengers left the open area of their own accord and sought refuge in the darkness of the surrounding alleyways.

Uldini gave a nod of appreciation. 'Very effective.'

'Sometimes the simple solutions are the best,' responded Jelninolan modestly.

In the meantime, Falk struggled into his armour, combining centuries of experience with reckless force, and willingly enduring bruises and abrasions in his desire to prepare as quickly as possible for their departure.

'We'll wait downstairs,' said Uldini drily, and the two Ancients quickly left the room while Falk secured his breastplate. Cursing, he snapped the lower cannons onto his forearms before hurrying after them, past a stammering servant who had already failed to halt the two experts in magic.

The old man came out of the main building, almost in full armour but for the last few touches, and then he was ready. Culhen hurtled towards them, whimpering with joy at having found them, and the Forest Guardian spotted Khara, who was waving them towards her from one of the side streets. Uldini and Jelninolan quickly flashed a few thunderbolts across the square which chased away any of the stragglers, before they all ran over to Khara who was waiting for them with Wind Blade drawn.

'Selsena is going to be fuming that she missed all the drama,' grumbled Falk when he'd caught up with the others. 'but if I take her out of the stables now, that will slow things down even more.'

Everyone sensed the warhorse's anger at these words and Falk scowled. 'Oh dear, this is going to be fun,' he predicted, and then turned to Khara. 'Where are the others?'

'Ahren has disappeared and Trogadon is fighting with a few scoundrels,' gasped Khara.

'First the dwarf, and then we'll talk about the others,' commanded Uldini and they set off.

Khara led them at breakneck speed through the dark and narrow streets of the Brazen City. After a while, they heard a dwarf song echoing into the night, and they increased their speed.

Uldini, who had been flying in front of them, soared unceremoniously up above the buildings. 'He's over this way,' they heard a moment later, the Arch Wizard's voice having taken on a curious undertone.

Falk felt a lump in his throat and gasping, he called out Trogadon's name as he turned the corner. The sight that presented itself left him rooted to the spot.

Trogadon was sitting with several nasty stab wounds on his arms in the middle of a circle consisting of bandits who were all lying on the ground, more or less incapacitated. The Forest Guardian saw countless smashed up weapons, and just as many broken bones. The dwarf warrior was sitting on his upended hammer, which served as an improvised stool, and he was breathing heavily while still continuing to sing.

'He's not reacting to me,' said Uldini with a look of concern as he waved his finger in front of the dwarf, who seemed to be looking through him as he sang on.

'That's a battle hymn of the little folk,' said Falk quietly. 'He has to sing it through to the end, and then he'll come back to himself. It helps the dwarves to remain concentrated and numbs the pain. Unfortunately, they tend to hit out at everything that isn't a dwarf when they're in this state, so I'd stop waving around that finger if I were you.'

Uldini pulled back his finger at lightning speed and his eyes widened in surprise. 'And I thought that was only a myth.'

Falk shook his head. 'For obvious reasons, they only use these songs when they're alone or among themselves, so that they don't injure any allies. Trogadon was alone, and so he decided it was worth the risk.'

Jelninolan looked at the dwarf with concern. 'Is there anything we can do for him?'

'You can heal him if you like. When he comes out of the trance, he will certainly feel those cuts,' replied the Forest Guardian pragmatically.

The elf nodded. She and Uldini set to work, healing the singing dwarf, while avoiding any quick movements or standing directly in his line of sight. Falk watched their tortuous manoeuvrings for a while with a wry grin, before helping Khara bind up the bandits with their own belts and securing the few weapons that hadn't been damaged.

'He must have deliberately aimed for their weapons,' said Falk in wonderment.

There were nine battered and bruised figures lying on the ground, a royal household of cripples, who had paid their tribute to the still-singing dwarf.

'Luckily the wounds weren't that deep. The force of the stabs was lessened by the thick skin of our dwarf friend,' said Uldini, once they had finished with their healing. 'I really wish he's stop that singing now,' he added with irritation.

Jelninolan turned to Khara. 'Are you alright?' she asked.

Khara nodded and Falk interjected. 'Where's Ahren?' he demanded. Now that Trogadon was safe, the Forest Guardian's concern for his apprentice's safety came bubbling to the surface.

'He was set upon at one of the old longhouses and taken away, that much we know. But Sneeze Weed was scattered on the scent and Culhen couldn't follow it,' said the girl.

'Oh, you poor thing,' said Jelninolan, and tickled the wolf, who was whimpering quietly.

Falk let out a sigh of relief. 'At least we know he's still alive.'

'And how do we know that?' asked Uldini, irritated.

'Culhen would be behaving differently if something bad had befallen Ahren,' said Falk darkly. 'Then, a little Sneeze Weed would be the least of his problems.'

The wolf gave him a guilty look and then let out a low howl, but Falk played down the issue. 'Now it's time for some magic to lead us to him. I don't want to depend on their magnanimity when it comes to letting him live.'

'He said this morning that he was hot on Bergen's trail,' said Khara in a concerned voice.

Falk thought for a moment. 'That sounds like him alright, but we need to find Ahren now anyway. I wouldn't like to leave him alone with that honour-obsessed mule. The boy is difficult enough as it is. Who knows what other nonsense Bergen will put into his head?'

Uldini waved his arm energetically. 'We're not doing any more magic here. The Doppler undoubtedly knows where we are now, and there are enough desperate souls here he could have hunt us down. We'll go back together to our lodgings, and tomorrow we'll cast a beautifully branched charm net which will search the city slowly and quietly. The Doppler will sense us alright, but he won't locate the target of the charm so easily.'

Falk looked uneasily, but Jelninolan interjected reassuringly. 'We're practically begging to be attacked here by scavengers, and it wouldn't be a good idea for the city guards to find us with a pile of beaten up citizens. We can't do anything here without using magic, and that might just put Ahren into more danger. Culhen can't smell him now anyway, as his nose is out of commission.'

Falk nodded doubtfully, and at last the dwarf stopped singing.

'How do you feel, old friend?' asked Falk with concern.

The warrior glanced at the others, then at himself, and laughed. 'What do you think? Nine cut-throats and I didn't get a single scratch.'

Falk grinned and pointed at Uldini and Jelninolan. Then he indicated the many indications of newly knitted skin on the dwarf's arms.

'Damn it!' grumbled the dwarf in jest. 'I'll do a better job next time.'

'It's high time we disappeared,' said Uldini urgently. 'We'll get some sleep and tomorrow we'll track down our missing apprentice.'

They all headed back to the security of their lodgings with queasy stomachs, thinking about the young Paladin held captive somewhere in the city.

Chapter 19

A good night's sleep behind him, Ahren examined the mercenaries around him as he sat on the ground in the big room. Their pieces of armour all shared the same deep-blue colour, but that was where their commonality ended. He saw men and women, old and young, leather armour and chainmail, steel-plating and naked torsos; there was so much variety underneath all that blue – almost as if everybody was trying to hold onto their own individual identity. Ahren recognised three people from Hjalgar, five Sunplainers, three Ice Landers, four who had to be from the Southern Jungles, and even several Clansmen from Kelkor and the Green Sea. He saw nobody from the Eternal Empire however, and Ahren asked himself if this was only a coincidence. He yawned and wondered what was keeping his friends. He had lain awake during the night, expecting their imminent arrival, had imagined Falk and Uldini sternly lecturing the stubborn Paladin Bergen, and then Jelninolan softening the captain up with her gentle persuasion. But nobody had come. The night had ended and Ahren had gained nothing but a feeling of overwhelming weariness.

The mercenaries had been very friendly to him in their own gruff manner, following his terrifying interrogation. And although he had been shaken to the core by the nature of his examination, the apprentice found it very hard to remain angry with them.

Tontur was a different story. Ahren looked daggers at him whenever he came into view, but the mercenary ignored the young man for the most part and so Ahren nursed his grievance in silence.

'He's used to that, you know,' said a deep contralto voice, and Ahren looked up at Three-Finger Jarla, who was holding two steaming mugs, one of which she handed to the young man. She indicated over to Tontur. 'He always takes on the role of the evil torturer, and with good reason,' she continued.

Ahren took the mug sceptically and sniffed the brew distrustfully, but immediately recognised the characteristic aromas. 'Wolf Herb and Life Fern,' he said gratefully, and took a big gulp, only to immediately scowl. It tasted much more bitter than normal.

Jarla nodded in approval. 'You have a good nose and an equally good palate. You certainly cut the mustard as a Forest Guardian if you can pick out those herbs so quickly.'

Ahren shrugged his shoulders nonchalantly. 'If you have Falk as your teacher, you have to learn how to nurse your body back to health very quickly.'

'Falk?' repeated Jarla in surprise, and Ahren quickly corrected himself.

'Dorian Falkenstein. Falk is the shortened version,' he explained.

Jarla gave an ironic laugh. 'And here I thought I was something special because I'm on first name terms with a Paladin, but a little snotty-nosed brat like yourself can address one of them using his nickname!'

Ahren was about to protest but thought it best to let the matter drop. The fact that the woman thought he might be important might be useful if he needed to prove himself to Bergen. 'You wanted to tell me about Tontur,' he said, changing the subject.

'Yes, you're right. He used to be a fairground performer, and a very good one. Made the mistake of courting the wrong woman, whose husband, a spoiled nobleman, punished him by making him gargle acid. Tontur survived, but that was the end of his singing voice, and also his means of earning a living. Bergen picked him up off the street and he became one of us. The fat lad can tell a really good story, and he's a very believable villain, isn't he?' She raised an eyebrow and gave Ahren a quizzical look. He nodded sulkily, an unforgiving expression on his face, nonetheless.

'Don't be angry with him. The more persuasively he can terrify people, the more quickly they begin to talk, and the less we need to encourage things along.' She slapped her right fist into her left palm and Ahren swallowed hard. 'The mercenary's life is not an easy one. Hard work and a lot of bloodshed on both sides. And if you're out of luck, your employer betrays you instead of paying you. So, we take care of ourselves, and that means interrogating spies from time to time,' she continued.

'I'm not a spy,' responded Ahren automatically.

'Of course not. We know that now. Thanks to Tontur.'

Ahren understood what she meant, but he still wasn't ready to forgive the man who had made him feel so helpless and vulnerable.

'Your first interrogation?' asked Jarla, who seemed to know what he was thinking.

Ahren nodded silently. His shame at having spilled the beans so quickly was written all over his face.

'Everyone sings like a canary the first time. Don't believe everything you hear in the heroic sagas. Surviving an interrogation is something you have to learn, just like everything else. Things like willpower or the principles of honour or duty help of course, but without practice you really don't get very far,' said the woman. Ahren stared at her in disbelief. He really didn't know which was more incredible: the fact that you might be willing to undergo interrogation training or that being a hero wasn't enough to get you through the questioning.

Jarla patted his cheek in a grandmotherly fashion. 'I don't want to rob you of your illusions; I just want to tell you that you've actually done very well. You didn't reveal anything that might put others' lives into danger; you didn't beg for your life or exchange your freedom for somebody else's. This makes you more courageous than most people.' She finished speaking and went towards the door, leaving Ahren to think about what he had heard. But then she turned and added: 'Oh, and Bergen won't be back before midday. So, you can sleep for a little longer.'

Ahren nodded and followed her advice. If he had to persuade Bergen and his hardened mercenaries, then he should at least do it fully rested.

***

'Please hurry!' implored Falk. He'd hardly slept a wink during the night and pressured Uldini and Jelninolan until they finally cast their magic net. But it was taking far too long to track Ahren down as far as the old man was concerned. In spite of the roominess of their lodgings, it felt uncomfortably full in the room, but nobody wanted to leave the group. The women had finally decided to commandeer the connecting bathroom for themselves and declared it a man-free zone.

Now the elf was sitting on the carpet, legs crossed, and in a trance-like state. She had both hands placed on Culhen's head, who sat with ears pricked, but with his tongue lolling, and he looked as if he were about to fall asleep. The priestess had given in to Falk's persistence and cast another charm which would enable her to ascertain Ahren's condition through Culhen's connection to the apprentice.

'Leave her alone,' said Uldini. 'She has to perform her magic very slowly or the Doppler will discover his whereabouts. Just imagine you had to draw your bow inconspicuously under the eyes of a Dark One, then you have a rough idea of what she's trying to achieve.'

'Would you like to teach me a little more sword-fighting?' suggested Khara diplomatically. 'I could do with limbering up and I still find it very hard to parry your back-hand thrusts.'

Falk nodded absently, and it was only when he was walking towards his sword that he realised what she was up to. 'Very clever, young lady,' he grunted, but still reached for his broadsword.

'I'll get you as soon as she wakes up,' said Uldini reassuringly. Trogadon had gone back to the smith where he had hired himself out as part of his disguise, where he hoped to pick up some information about Ahren's whereabouts. That meant the Arch Wizard would be keeping his eye on the elf and the wolf on his own – and he was quite happy about that.

Falk and Khara went out into a little inner courtyard with a fountain and flowers, and a path running around it, edged on the outside by a series of playful archways. Jelninolan had discovered it the previous day and had sat their meditating before they had negotiated with the Triumvirate.

'It's a little tight but the challenges that it creates make it all the more interesting', said Falk, casting a critical eye over the space and drawing his sword. He breathed in the scent-filled air which carried the aromas of over a dozen different types of flowers. 'And it certainly smells nice.'

Khara smiled at him and pulled Wind Blade from its scabbard.

'Let's begin then,' said Falk and immediately went on the attack.

They practised intensively and the middle of the day flew by without incident – apart from the servants who happened to be passing and retreated in terror when they heard the sound of fighting. The old man was surprised that he had to delve so far back through his centuries of experience in order to surprise the young woman, and none of his tricks fooled her more than once. He was quite exhausted and gasping for air when Jelninolan appeared at an archway with a satisfied grin on her face. He looked at the elf in gratitude. He could now break off the session before he completely ran out of ideas, and much more importantly, he would at last get some information about Ahren.

'She's mastered the Elfish foot-techniques better than you have, old man', scolded the elf.

Khara bowed ceremoniously in gratitude to her mistress's words of praise, and Falk simply ignored the jibe. 'What do you know about Ahren?' he asked.

The priestess smiled and raised her hand in a calming gesture. 'He's sleeping at the moment. He has a bump on the back of his head and he's somewhat hungry. Otherwise, he feels relatively safe. I only got the slightest hint of fear, more than an echo than anything else, probably as a result of his having been captured. I'm convinced he's with Bergen.'

'Did you see that in his dreams?' Falk inquired further, still not fully convinced of Ahren's safety, although not as uneasy as he had been.

Jelninolan hesitated and her eyes darted over to Khara, who was still standing there with her head bowed. 'He was dreaming about...other things. It's more of a sensation. He doesn't seem to be looking for Bergen anymore, so I presume he's found him.'

Khara straightened up and was surprised at the look on the others' faces because they were both giving her cheeky smiles. Then Falk went over to Jelninolan and gave her a firm hug.

'Thank you,' he said, and the elf patted his back.

'We're all very fond of him – each in their own way,' she said in a friendly voice and released herself from him. 'We should continue working on the Triumvirate. The threat of Thousand Halls becoming embroiled in the conflict makes absolutely no sense. We really need to pursue that.'

Falk furrowed his brows as he considered the matter. 'I thought the same thing myself.' He looked wistfully around the courtyard and gestured Khara towards him.

'The break is over. Now we have to surrender to the three-headed dragon,' he said grimly.

Khara giggled and Jelninolan gave him a scolding look for his lack of respect. Then they went up to their lodgings and prepared for another round of negotiations.

***

Ahren had no idea what time it was when he awoke. Wherever they were now, there were no air vents and no windows, just cracks in the leaky timbers of the wooden walls, through which the rays of sun peeked, bathing the inside in a gloomy light. He was sweating; there were too many people in this confined space, which made the air warm and sticky.

The apprentice stood up and saw that Bergen was no more than two paces away from him, sitting in a corner and eying him keenly. The man had taken off his armour and was wearing his blue linens, which revealed that he too was sweating.

'Uncomfortable, isn't it?' asked the captain, looking around scornfully. 'We've you to thank for that. We had a very nice set-up in the warehouse, but this place is a little less hospitable.' He shrugged his shoulders fatalistically. 'Anyway, we won't be hiding here much longer if the catapults down on the Plains are anything to go by.'

Ahren shook his head and made a quick mental calculation. 'Two days. Then Justinian is going to attack', he said hoarsely. His mouth was dry, and Bergen tossed over a field flask to him from which the apprentice drank greedily.

'And how exactly are you supposed to know that?' asked the captain sarcastically. 'The Emperor is hardly going to divulge his tactics to a young upstart like yourself.'

'I was there when he dictated the peace conditions with the Brazen City to Uldini. We were given a week and almost five days have passed. After that, he's going to attack and capture the city in order to save face.' Ahren had figured out a rough plan for bringing the pig-headed Paladin to his senses, and the first part of it involved laying out the facts in front of him. 'Uldini, Falk and Jelninolan are trying to persuade the Triumvirate to reach a peaceful solution – one that is attractive enough for the Sunplains for the Sun Emperor to spare you.'

'Jelninolan is here as well?' asked Bergen in surprise. 'Considering you've named all those names, and that you claim to tell the truth, you're either a pathetic Paladin that lets himself be captured far too easily, or you're a remarkably well-informed spy.'

Ahren frowned in irritation and waved his hand dismissively. 'I don't have as much experience as the rest of you. So what? At least I'm not trying to evade my responsibility by hiding myself in ridiculous conflicts.' He had hardly finished speaking when Bergen leaped to his feet and was standing over him. An enormous, calloused hand gripped the apprentice around the throat and pinned him to the floor. The enraged face of the captain was now looming over him.

'Don't you dare talk to me about responsibility!' he roared. 'My responsibility cost me everyone that was dear to me! Dorian had one daughter, I had four! Elmsi was four months old during the Night of Blood! The pressure on Ahren's throat was increasing and he struggled in vain to loosen the captain's grip. Ahren would somehow have to sweep aside the other Paladin's emotions or drown within them.

'Then help to save the Brazen City! There are too many sons and daughters living here that will have to pay for your pride,' he gasped.

The pressure increased as Bergen leaned downwards. 'This has nothing to do with pride. These men and women are my new family, and I won't hand them over like a bucket of slop to a backstabbing ruler who hasn't an ounce of honour in his body. I just want to protect them!'

Ahren's vision was becoming blurred and his heart was hammering in his chest. He had to persuade this man and quickly!

'You want to protect your people, and I understand that,' he wheezed painfully. 'But I do too. Both the citizens of the Brazen City and the legion that is approaching. The Dark Days are coming, and we have to stick together because *I want to save them all.*' He uttered the final words with all the strength he could muster, and with all the willpower and persuasiveness he could squeeze out.

Bergen's hand loosened immediately, and he jolted backwards – it seemed almost as if Ahren had stabbed him. 'You *are* a Paladin,' he whispered hoarsely. He was clearly in shock. 'Only young and green and uncorrupted, and I'd forgotten what that feeling is.' He stood up and lifted Ahren so easily that he felt as if he were a little child. Ahren could see the conflict raging within the powerful man. His blue eyes looked conflicted and his fists clenched and opened repeatedly.

'Blindfold him!' he finally commanded loudly. 'He will take a message to the Triumvirate. The Blue Cohorts will be on the marketplace tomorrow at noon for negotiations.' There was the sound of murmuring in the room and Bergen whispered into Ahren's ear. 'This is your chance. Ensure that my people come away scot free, and I will comply with any conditions. Fail and you can fight the oncoming war on your own.'

Ahren nodded in a daze, and heavy material was pulled roughly down over his eyes. Before he knew it, strong hands grabbed him and bundled him out through a door. He could smell the fire coming from a forge and felt the cool wind on his skin as he was led hither and thither and spun around repeatedly so that he lost all sense of direction.

Suddenly the hands were gone and Ahren gingerly removed the blindfold. He was standing on a small crossing and the passers-by were eying him suspiciously. Everywhere were boarded-up doors and damaged house fronts. There must have been a lot of looting the previous night and any sign of welcome had vanished from the faces of the citizens. Ahren tried to get his bearings and ran as quickly as he could towards the centre of the city. He was running to his friends and hopefully towards a solution. The sands of time were running out for all of them.

***

'Well, that was joyless,' said Uldini drily, as they left the meeting hall. The Triumvirate had banished them from the room and forbidden any further negotiations until such time as Ahren was presented to them or until they admitted to fabricating the whole story of the Thirteenth Paladin.

Uldini floated up the stairs in front of the others, who looked shell-shocked. 'Let's see if the magic net can help us any further,' he said half-heartedly. They didn't expect results until the following morning and so Uldini was stunned when he sensed the magic tension in the room, which suggested a positive signal. 'I have something!' he cried out, flabbergasted, and everyone froze in anticipation as the Arch Wizard closed his eyes. 'He's...outside the door... *downstairs?*'

Everyone stared in shock and Falk quickly woke Culhen, who was having a snooze. The wolf opened his eyes wide and then stormed past them, and down the steps.

Falk stared angrily at Uldini. 'Sometimes you're absolutely useless,' he scolded as he ran down after the wolf.

'I am a Paladin and I urgently need to speak to the delegation from the Sun Emperor!' They could hear Ahren's frustrated voice trying in vain to persuade the guards at the door to give him entry. The two men sprang aside in amazement as a large wolf raced past them out of the vestibule before leaping up onto the young man, who collapsed in relief under the yelping animal's weight. The overwrought guards were about to reach for their weapons when the Sun Emperor's emissaries also scrambled out and landed in an unceremonious heap on top of the brown-haired boy, embracing him and shedding tears of joy and laughter as he cried out again and again; 'I've found him! I've found him!'

The afternoon went quickly for the re-united companions. Ahren had to describe his experiences with the Blue Cohorts in great detail, and he for his part, asked them a great many questions about what had happened in his absence, and what the current state of play was in the negotiations. With the exchange of information complete, their thoughts turned to what should happen next.

'When this is all over, I'm going to beat Bergen black and blue!' grumbled Falk and pointed at the bruises around Ahren's neck. Even Jelninolan scowled, and Ahren was surprised when it was Uldini who jumped to the captain's defence.

'Just remember how angry you were when I first visited you in Deepstone. You nearly went for me then, and we'd already known each other for several centuries. Bergen learned that the war against HIM, WHO FORCES was going to start again from Ahren, the war that you Paladins have been in fear of for so long, and that he was to offer himself up to the mercy of the Sun Emperor' The Arch Wizard flashed a friendly look at Ahren. 'Your apprentice made a very good fist of it, all things considered.'

Ahren gave Uldini a thankful nod and the Ancient continued: 'The ultimatum expires tomorrow evening and we have to go back to the Sun Emperor, which means we have today and tomorrow to persuade everyone within the city walls to support a peace agreement. Bergen has already said that he wants to see the Blue Cohorts spared, and the Emperor will only consider that if the Triumvirate accede as much as possible to his demands. So, we need to get Windita and the others to sing from the same hymn-sheet.'

'Now that we can present Ahren, this part of the proceedings should be easier,' prophesied Falk as he placed a proprietorial hand on his apprentice's shoulder.

'But before that he needs to wash himself thoroughly,' interrupted Khara, scrunching her nose. 'He's looking a little worse for wear, and he smells...well...pungent.'

Falk mockingly sniffed the air in Ahren's direction, then took his hand away and wiped it dramatically on his jerkin. 'Maybe you're right,' he said mischievously. Ahren decided to play along and folded his arms in mock annoyance. There was much merriment and laughter, and relief that they were all re-united again as they set about preparing for their final negotiations with the Triumvirate.

Ahren had a queasy feeling in his stomach as he spruced himself up. A lot would be hanging on his words and the impression he would make on the representatives of the Brazen City. He would have loved to have taken a breather after his talk with Bergen, but the strong midday sun was moving relentlessly westwards and reminding him that the fifth day was coming to its inevitable close. Finally, everyone was ready, and Ahren put aside the brush he was using to comb Culhen's fur. The vain wolf had been watching him and had announced that he too needed some pampering. Ahren had given in with a laugh and had spoiled his four-pawed friend until everybody was ready. The animal's fur glistened and was as smooth as silk and the wolf was admiring himself in the full-length mirror in the corner of the guest room.

We can do that every day from now on, he said, fully satisfied with himself.

Ahren slapped him on the head. *Forget it. We have more important things to be doing than making sure you look good,* he scolded.

The apprentice checked that he himself looked presentable and when the ladies came out of the bathroom, they were all ready to go down the stairs. They had all decided on as martial a presentation as possible, and so anyone that possessed armour had polished it until it was spick and span and was now wearing it. Ahren and Jelninolan were wearing their ribbon armour, Trogadon was dressed in the chainmail of his Ancestry Name, while Falk looked splendid in the armour of the Paladins. Only Uldini was unarmed as always. This was the first time anybody had seen Khara in her new armour, which she had made for her by the blacksmiths in the city. Ahren could see a thin chainmail which protected her torso and with thin metal plates protecting her vital places. Her arms and legs were protected by metal bands which allowed her great flexibility and freedom of movement. The apprentice recognised the bluish shimmer of Dwarf Steel and raised his eyebrows in surprise.

Uldini noticed his reaction and nodded while furrowing his brows. 'Khara spared neither money nor effort,' he said looking at Khara accusingly. 'It was my money she didn't spare, let me add.'

Jelninolan twisted the childlike figure's ear and leaned into him. 'The poor thing had to face all sorts of dangers over the last few moons without any protection, and you're giving out because of a few measly gold coins?' she asked indignantly.

Uldini grimaced but stood his ground. 'You should have paid the bill then...' he began, but the elf twisted the ear a little more and Uldini raised his hands in surrender. 'Alright, alright, you're spot on.'

'If you'd exhibited those diplomatic skills when you were dealing with the Triumvirate,' interjected Trogadon with a laugh, 'then we might all be on our way back to the Sun Emperor whistling happily.'

The priestess let go of Uldini and took a challenging step towards the dwarf, who grinned at her broadly. 'No need for that, dearest. And anyway, I have something for your protégé too' he said, after looking at Khara's new outfit critically. He picked up an oily cloth bundle which he had brought back from the forge where he had been working earlier that day, and he approached the young woman.

'If you drown her in oil now...' warned Jelninolan, and the dwarf stopped abruptly.

'You're spoiling the surprise,' he growled good-naturedly, before obediently unfolding the cloth to reveal a thin, lightly curved blade the length of a fore-arm, which he presented to Khara as he bowed slightly.

Her eyes opened wide in amazement and she jumped forward with a cry of joy, grasping Whisper Blade and performing a few flowing movements with it. 'It's perfectly balanced and it's exactly the right length,' she said in surprise.

Trogadon nodded and grinned, baring his teeth in the process. 'I measured your forearm when you were asleep,' he said proudly.

Khara embraced him forcefully, and Ahren thought to himself with amusement that he didn't know any other woman who would be so overjoyed at receiving an instrument of murder.

Trogadon reciprocated the hug and looked over her shoulder at Ahren. 'You'd be better off thanking Ahren. I offered to forge a dagger for him, but he insisted that I make Whisper Blade for you instead.' He gave Ahren a knowing wink.

Khara released the dwarf from her embrace and looked at Ahren in surprise, who promptly blushed a deep red.

'You talked about it so affectionately, and I didn't know what I was going to do with a dagger so...' he stammered, but the swordfighter was already embracing him. Ahrens heart was racing, and the scent in her hair was making him dizzy as he awkwardly patted her back. 'You're welcome,' he mumbled. It was then that Uldini's voice cut through the room: 'We can only be glad that HE, WHO FORCES isn't a pretty young woman. Otherwise we'd all be lost.'

Loud laughter filled the room and Khara let him go and examined his face carefully. Ahren turned away, fearful of what she could read there, and walked quickly to the door.

'In case you've forgotten,' he said, imitating Uldini's normal sarcastic tone, 'we have a city to save.'

Another wave of enthusiasm swept through the group, and Ahren fled down the stairs, happier to face the Triumvirate than the young woman who was following him.

Chapter 20

Ahren looked nervously at the heavy double-doors which would be opening very shortly. Uldini had insisted on following official protocol for the day's negotiations, and so there were four honour guards standing to attention left and right of the doors, and a liveried servant awaited the Arch Wizard's signal that they were ready.

Ahren could feel Khara's eyes on the back of his neck, but he kept his eyes fixed forward and tried to concentrate on the mission in hand. Culhen was certainly not helping matters.

She's a bit skinny for a good she-wolf, was the commentary he was hearing. *And the Alpha-male in the pack needs to be able to fight better than the others in the pack. But she beats you nearly every time,* opined the Culhen, quoting the laws of the wolves.

I swear by the THREE if you don't shut up, I'm going to shear your fur off later, threatened the young Paladin. At which point Culhen looked at him accusingly but stopped communicating.

Uldini gestured to the servant. The doors swung open, revealing the meeting room. Ahren saw the three representatives, who had already been described to him in great detail. They were standing in anticipation at the other side of the conference table, craning their necks to catch sight of him. Uldini, ever the intriguer, had ensured that the young man would be right behind Falk's broad back, so that he would remain for the most part hidden during their entrance. They reached the table, and Uldini bowed gallantly in front of Windita and her fellows.

'Honoured representatives of the Brazen City, allow me to present to you Ahren, the Thirteenth Paladin.'

With that Falk took a step to the side, revealing his apprentice, who was standing bolt upright. Ahren really hoped that the three figures facing him would ignore the thin layer of sweat on his forehead. He suppressed the urge to fidget nervously but bowed slightly instead. 'I heard you wanted to meet me personally to confirm my existence,' he said with as much self-confidence as he could muster. 'And so, I have broken off my negotiations with Bergen, so that I could be here with you.' He had worked on that last sentence during the afternoon. He knew he was hamming it up and even fibbing ever so slightly, but he hoped his casual mention of the mercenary captain would have the desired effect.

Although Falk frowned and Uldini threw him a mischievous grin, the Triumvirate seemed indeed impressed. The two ladies bowed their heads politely and the dwarf seemed to be eying him a little less suspiciously than he had only a moment earlier. He was stroking his beard thoughtfully, in a futile attempt to tame it.

'There's not much flesh and bones on the lad. Could be anybody. I don't see any armour, nor are there any weapons made from Deep Steel,' he grumbled as he thought aloud.

Ahren couldn't stop himself from rolling his eyes as he heard the same old argument again. Not for the first time did he wish he had a giveaway birthmark, which would prove that he was a Paladin, just like in the old heroic sagas he had loved as a child. But at least he was used to the scepticism.

'I'm sure I'll grow into my role,' he said drily, causing Trogadon to chortle appreciatively. 'But my Naming only took place last winter, and in the most difficult of circumstances when there was no time to receive the gifts from HIM, WHO IS.'

The mention of the god of the dwarves caused Xobutumbur to make a gesture of humility, and Ahren waited for a heartbeat before continuing.

369

'I have two Paladins and two Ancients who can vouch for me, as well as Trogadon, Bearer of the Ancestry Name. And if that doesn't work, perhaps a little presentation might persuade you.' He gestured Culhen, who had been waiting in the background, to come forward. The wolf approached, puffed up full in the knowledge of his own importance. 'This is Culhen, my companion animal, selected by the goddess of the elves to look after me and to stand by my side.' Ahren pointed at Xobutumbur, who was staring at Trogadon, as if he was only now seeing him properly for the first time. 'Please tell me, Culhen, what the distinguished Clan Elder had for his lunch.'

Culhen approached the sceptical dwarf, while the two Triumvirate ladies observed the little drama with amusement. Ahren was sure that they had already been persuaded, but he wanted to make his position clear in no uncertain terms, and so he continued with his little drama.

The wolf sniffed at the flinching dwarf, sneezed, whined once, and trotted back to Ahren, who listened to the wolf's remarks. 'You had strong-smelling fermented fish. Together with three tankards of beer, or perhaps four,' he announced self-confidently.

'You said you wanted to abstain from alcohol before the negotiations, my esteemed Xobutumbur,' scolded Palustra softly, and the dwarf coughed in embarrassment, before looking at Ahren grumpily.

'Spies could have told you that,' he grunted irritably.

Windita reacted even before Ahren and tapped the table with her finger. 'Tut, tut, my old friend. Now you're simply being stubborn. I think the Triumvirate can now accept Ahren's claim to being the Thirteenth Paladin of the gods.' She looked left and right, and Palustra nodded and smiled at the apprentice. Trogadon was speaking insistently in the rumbling Dwarfish tongue to Xobutumbur, before the Elder bowed his head slightly, first to the warrior, and then to Ahren.

'Well at last we're making progress,' said Uldini loudly, and made a hand gesture which caused a chair to slide into position, which he promptly sat down on, the others following suit.

'What did you say to the Clan Elder?' whispered Ahren to Trogadon while the chairs were being moved into position.

'Just that I'll vouch for you, and if he wasn't happy with that, we could have a good old-fashioned ritual fist-fight. He rather likes his teeth, which is why he agreed with the others, I think,' he murmured with a grin.

Ahren pressed the dwarf's powerful upper arm in thanks and then turned his attention to the negotiations that were about to begin.

It was late at night and everyone was dog-tired. The Triumvirate had slowly but surely acceded to most of Uldini's demands, which involved returning to the status quo before the siege. However, there was one sticking point preventing final agreement. Windita and the others insisted on their right to sell weapons and arms in other markets, and they argued that it would be an advantage in the preparations for the war against the Adversary if more weapons made from Dwarf Steel found their way into the hands of the Jorath peoples. Uldini blocked this move however, knowing full well that Justinian would never agree to it for fear of the Eternal Empire gaining access to these weapons. This would result in the Sunplains losing an important advantage they had in their war against Quin-Wa.

Ahren and Khara sat there in silence, unable to contribute anything to the detailed discussions while the others sought a way out of the impasse. Ahren tried very hard to follow the proceedings, but his lack of involvement eventually led to him losing concentration and focussing instead on keeping his eyes open.

Suddenly he felt Khara's elbow digging into his ribs as she tried to ensure he stayed awake. She glared at him. 'You're a Paladin here, so behave like one,' she hissed severely.

'I've no idea what I'm supposed to say. And to be honest I'm on their side. It makes perfect sense to me to arm as many people as possible with Dwarf Steel weapons,' he whispered back quietly.

'Then find a way of implementing it,' whispered the swordswoman casually. 'Maybe there's a less obvious way.'

Ahren could see in her eyes that she had no idea of how he was to put this into effect either, but in contrast to him, it wasn't her responsibility. She looked at him quizzically and he racked his overtired brain in search of a solution.

Ahren stood up with an apologetic bow towards the Triumvirate and did some stretches in a corner of the room, trying to re-energise his body and to clear his mind. Unfortunately, he still wasn't able to achieve the Void, so he had to manage without the spiritual clarity of the trance-like state. It was his mental connection with the wolf that was still preventing him from experiencing the condition again, even when Culhen was fast asleep, as he was now. Ahren did a few more stretches, and then decided to imitate Falk, who had hung his weapon and shield on the arms of his chair to make sitting more comfortable. Slowly and carefully he took off his bow and quiver, and then Wind Blade. He was about to hang the weapon up when Windita interrupted Uldini in mid-flow, as the Arch Wizard was making another long-winded attempt at persuading them of his point of view.

'Apologies, worthy Paladin, but may I look at your weapon for a moment?' she asked excitedly.

It took Ahren a moment to realise in his weariness that it was *him* she was addressing so politely, and not Falk. Part of him was delighted at the respect Windita had shown him. He passed Wind Blade across the table to her.

'I'm not sure this is the opportune moment for something like this...' began Uldini, who was piqued by the interruption, but Jelninolan stopped him from continuing, when she noticed the expression on the blond woman's face as she bent over Wind Blade's handle to examine it.

'Where did you get this weapon?' she asked Ahren excitedly.

'From an armourer in Three Rivers,' he replied vaguely, and looked helplessly over at Falk, who simply shrugged his shoulders.

'Do you know what that is?' demanded the blond woman, who was wearing the leather apron of the blacksmiths' guild, as she tapped on the design on top of the handle.

Ahren shook his head in reply and hoped that Windita would carry on speaking and he would find out what was so special about it.

'This is the insignia of the House of Regelsten,' she said, her eyes fixed firmly on Ahren. 'How did you get this weapon if you didn't purchase it here?'

'I got it from Falagarda Regelsten. She gave it to me as a gift when I was travelling through Three Rivers, and she taught me the basic techniques.' His voice resonated with warmth as he remembered back to that time, for he owed a lot to the friendship and assistance she had given him.

'Falagarda is in *Three Rivers*?' repeated Windita in disbelief, and she blinked. This information was clearly new to her, and Ahren wasn't sure at first if the blond woman took it to be good or bad news. The other two members of the Triumvirate looked similarly shocked, and it was impossible to figure out what they were thinking either.

Windita pressed the blade to her breast and only now became aware of the visitors' questioning looks. 'Falagarda is a cousin of mine,' she said hoarsely. 'We grew up together and were very close until an accident occurred.' Her voice became quieter. 'A man died and Falagarda was blamed for it although she couldn't have prevented it. We had to banish her in order to maintain peace. I didn't know until now that she was still alive.' She looked at Ahren warmly. 'You say she is a blacksmith in Three Rivers?'

Ahren nodded, relieved that he hadn't somehow caused a scandal, and he began to speak candidly. 'She seems to be doing very well and she was very friendly towards me. I was able to repay the favour in the autumn of last year when I suggested she might be a trading partner to the dwarves of the Silver Cliff.' He laughed nervously as he added: 'Well at least one Regelsten will be able to continue selling weapons made from Dwarf Steel.'

The room went deathly silent, and Ahren broke into a sweat as he thought in a panic that he must have put his foot in it. Windita and Uldini were staring at each other across the table and seemed to be involved in some kind of mental duel. The apprentice held his breath and noticed that Windita was gripping the weapon so hard her knuckles were completely white. It suddenly struck the young Forest Guardian that he was practically unarmed, and he looked over pleadingly to Khara, who gave him the tiniest of nods and slowly began to loosen Wind Blade.

Then Xobutumbur leaped up and ran from the room cursing furiously in Dwarfish while Palustra started speaking agitatedly to Windita in the language of the Sunplains. The blond woman gave an almost imperceptible nod while Falk whispered urgently to Jelninolan and Trogadon.

'What's going on?' asked Ahren quietly, but everyone ignored him. He moved closer to Khara, and for the moment it didn't bother him if everybody thought he was looking for her protection by hiding behind the young woman. 'Do you know what's going on here?' he whispered to her, keeping an eye on everyone at the same time. It looked at least as if nobody was angry with him anymore, but he wasn't sure if his tired joke hadn't provoked something dangerous.

Khara shrugged her shoulders but said nothing, her hand gripping her weapon and her body ready for action.

Then Xobutumbur came back, and in his powerful hands was an old leather scroll, whose musty smell permeated the room. The dwarf rolled it out very carefully on the table and everybody leaned over it. Ahren and Khara would also have liked to see what was being looked at, but the wall of bodies prevented them.

Suddenly Palustra let out a cry of triumph, causing Ahren to flinch backwards, and she pointed at a passage in the document. A heartbeat later and cries of joy came from the conference table. Ahren felt an invisible power grasping him by the shoulders and pulling him forward. It was Uldini who had magically drawn the apprentice towards him, and in a completely untypical gesture the Arch Wizard planted two smackers on his cheeks. 'May you be twice blessed, you numbskull!' he cried out. 'Maybe not your head, but certainly your heart!' He pulled the flabbergasted youth towards him, while the others gave him congratulatory slaps on the back. Ahren suddenly remembered back to the similar reaction he had encountered when he had quite inadvertently saved the Voice of the Forest – and he was just as baffled now as he had been then.

Jelninolan finally took pity on him and read from the document lying on the table. 'Henceforth let it be known that any member of the Regelsten family possesses the right to sell the steel of the dwarves in their place of residence, provided that they be in possession of the relevent trade contracts,' she quoted, at which point the others cheered.

Ahren gave a puzzled look, as did Khara, and so Uldini decided to clarify the situation for them. 'Whenever we sign a peace treaty, the original text from the old agreement is kept intact as much as possible, also the passage that guaranteed that dwarf weapons could only be sold in the Brazen City as per the contracts of the time between Thousand Halls and the resident Regelstens. But now that we are about to seal a new contract, the trade agreements between the dwarves and the Regelsten family which existed before the completion of the contract, and which are written in the passage, are still valid. Or, to put it more clearly: the agreement between the dwarves of the Silver Cliff and Falagarda Regelsten of Three Rivers.' The dwarf hugged the baffled young man again before continuing. 'Don't you understand? Falagarda has an agreement with the dwarves, she's a Regelsten and she lives in Three Rivers. If my Emperor signs this, the Brazen City will be well within its rights to do business with the rest of the world through Falagarda of Three Rivers.'

Falk smiled wickedly. 'He won't be very happy about that, but having already broken one agreement through treachery, he's hardly going to try to undermine the new agreement. And Three Rivers will become the most powerful trading city in the north.'

Ahren's face slowly broke into a smile as he began to understand how this chain of events, beginning with his innocent visit to the good armourer's shop, would result in two cities flourishing. Even if he didn't understand all the details, the others seemed convinced that they would finally reach an agreement which would be beneficial to all parties and would guarantee the Blue Cohorts' freedom.

Despite the joyful atmosphere in the room however, Ahren couldn't help thinking of Bergen's fate. The Paladin, as decreed by the will of the Sun Emperor, would spend his days in prison until the onset of the Dark

Days, and this seemed to the young man to be an outrageous miscarriage of justice. But he had to admit to himself that he couldn't see any way of righting the wrong. Justinian seemed to possess such overwhelming authority that he couldn't see any way he would be able to change the Emperor's mind.

'Stop moping, lad!' cried Trogadon and slapped him hard on the back. 'Today we've reached a peace deal without shedding one drop of blood. That's something you can be proud of.'

Ahren sighed and turned to look at the dwarf. 'You've forgotten the dead from the last few days and nights. How many people were ambushed? How many have starved to death?'

Falk looked at Ahren in annoyance. 'You're working yourself up too much. Everything you've described was already happening before we arrived. But we've put an end to it. The last reserves of corn will already be handed out tonight so that nobody else need starve, and as soon as Bergen has signed the contract tomorrow at noon, we'll ride to the Emperor and this nightmare will finally be over.'

Everyone nodded, and even Xobutumbur seemed satisfied. Ahren thought it best to leave it at that and suppressed a yawn. Suddenly, now that he was no longer being carried along on the wings of all this feverish excitement, he felt terribly tired. He leaned heavily on the back of the chair, and Falk looked at him understandingly.

'Will you all be alright on your own?' the old Forest Guardian asked Uldini and indicated towards Ahren. The Arch Wizard gave an understanding nod. Falk invited the young Paladin to follow him. 'Anyone who has no good ideas to offer is better off coming with me and getting some sleep. Tomorrow is going to be another long day and we don't want to have you snoring during the treaty signing.'

Ahren, Khara and Trogadon were all happy to take up his offer, and they headed back up the stairs to their sleeping quarters. Culhen followed them a moment later, and when they arrived at the room, everybody was too tired to speak. Ahren was asleep as soon as his head hit the pillow, dreaming of massive spiders' webs, which interweaved the past, the present and the future. He had to travel along the webs, keeping his balance as he was chased by a dark, misshapen shadow. And he knew that one false move on his part would change the fate of whole empires forever.

Ahren's eyelids were stuck closed when he heard the furious hammering on the door. 'Wake up, lad!' shouted his master, and the apprentice finally managed to open his eyes. He could just about make Falk out, struggling into his armour, while Trogadon was opening the door and telling the distraught servant that they would be down very shortly.

Ahren was able to manage no more than a questioning grunt as he sat up. A quick look out the open window suggested that it was at least another two hourglasses until dawn.

'There's trouble,' said Falk curtly, and Ahren gave a resigned nod. He stood up slowly and promised himself that he would sleep for a week as soon as this crisis was over. Luckily, he had been too tired to undress, and so he simply strapped on his weapon and then went to the window to breathe in the cool night breeze and wake up fully from the land of dreams.

Khara came out of the neighbouring room, armed and ready. She was fully alert and fixing her hair with her blade brooch. Ahren couldn't believe she was so ready for battle already.

He cleared his throat and breathed in more of the cold mountain air. 'What's up?' he asked.

Falk shrugged his shoulders. 'Uldini has asked us to go downstairs, and in full military gear. Which means there must be complications.'

Trogadon had turned to face them in the meantime and was making smacking noises with his lips and grotesque facial gestures in an effort to limber up his face. 'He's hardly created trouble with the Triumvirate, has he?' he finally asked in a concerned voice.

Falk thought for a moment before shaking his head. 'Jelninolan is with him. She would have stopped him.'

'Then it has to be something else,' said Ahren queasily.

'Maybe pillagers, who haven't heard about the peace agreement?' suggested Khara.

'Guessing will get us nowhere,' said Falk with a groan as he put on his shoulder pieces. The leather straps were still hanging loosely on him as he hadn't fastened the armour plates tightly yet, which were making clattering sounds on his body. 'Follow me! We'll know more soon enough.' Ahren trotted behind Falk and the others, one hand on Culhen, who was yawning beside him.

At the foot of the stairs, the door to the meeting room was open and Ahren could hear concerned voices discussing something in low tones. The group increased their speed and a dark premonition chased the tiredness out of their bones.

They entered the room and saw Windita and Palustra, who were sitting together with Uldini and Jelninolan. There was no sign of Xobutumbur.

Uldini pointed to the dwarf's empty chair. 'He's late,' he said bluntly. 'A dwarf messenger came a while ago with an urgent message and then Xobutumbur stormed out of the room. He shouted that he'd be back soon and just had to arrest a few idiots, but there's been no sign of him since.'

'We are forbidden from entering the halls of the Brazen Clan so we can't find out what's going on and the guards keep fobbing us off by telling us it's an internal Clan matter,' explained Palustra sadly.

'We thought you might be able to look', said Windita, turning to Trogadon. 'You should be able to get past the guards, and as the bearer of an Ancestry Name, they ought to allow you to bring your friends with you.'

The warrior nodded calmly. 'One Clan Elder coming up!' he said jokingly, but then became serious. 'Why should we all go down there?' he probed.

'Because there's a Doppler in the Clan Vaults,' said Jelninolan darkly. 'I've been wanting to keep an eye on him since we've all been together, and I spun a charm net. He's beneath us in the Hall of the Dwarves.' She frowned sadly. 'Unfortunately, he's sensed me. He knows that I know where he is.'

Uldini pointed to a long, vellum roll, freshly written on, lying on the table. 'The two ladies and I will continue working on the peace treaty. You lot and Jelninolan bring Xobutumbur here and neutralise the Doppelganger if possible.' He looked at them intensely. 'He's made a mistake and is sitting in a trap now. If Jelninolan seals the door behind you, he will not be able to escape.'

Ahren and Khara finished tightening the last few straps on Falk's armour, and he nodded grimly. 'It will be a good day if we manage to catch one of those dirty swine.'

Trogadon was already standing at the door, hopping from one foot to the other. 'We'd better hurry. My folk don't understand treachery. If he's slipped in disguised as a dwarf, everyone is going to take him at this word.'

Ahren swallowed hard. 'Did you not talk yesterday of a messenger from Thousand Halls?'

Falk cursed and strode towards the door. 'Who told them they had the support of the Dwarfish kingdom. That must have been the Doppler bringing false news to rile up the dwarves of the Brazen Clan'

'Hurry!' cried Uldini after them. 'Who knows what other damage he's causing!'

They ran out into the night and towards the broad stairs that lay there in the darkness of the marketplace, and that led down to the enormous gate to the Clan Halls, looking like a portal leading into the underworld. Quickly but carefully they descended the steps, Trogadon in front, who was saying something in the rumbling tongue of the little folk to the suspicious looking guards. He received a grumpy answer in reply, after which he pulled his large hammer from behind his back and slammed it thunderously down on the ground. Ahren almost expected mortar to crumble and rain down from the archway, but the only reaction was a rumbling laugh from the guards. They opened the heavy gate a little, and Trogadon and the others slipped through the gap. Hardly were they inside the dimly lit reception hall when Jelninolan spun around and quickly cast a spell on the portal.

'Nobody will get in or out now without my permission,' she said firmly.

Ahren couldn't help feeling that she had just locked them in with an extremely dangerous creature, but he decided to keep that thought to himself.

Chapter 21

They were standing in a circular hall, which was illuminated by the flame coming from a small Deep Fire in a bowl hanging from the ceiling, which lent the room the characteristic red light that this hot and eternal molten metal gave off. They saw no dwarves and only three passageways leading in the cardinal directions.

Trogadon clicked his tongue dismissively. 'The classical building style. Not very original, but useful for our purposes.' He pointed east. 'Over there are the sleeping quarters, where most of the dwarves are at this time. As far as I know, the Brazen Clan have adapted to the human life-rhythms.' His hand pointed to the western corridor. 'In that direction are the mines. A confusing labyrinth, given the position and mining of the ore.' Then he pointed north. 'That way you'll find rooms like the kitchen, the chamber of the Clan Elders and the common room. I think we should start there.' The others agreed and he went to the front. 'It's better that any dwarves we meet see one of their own first. Partly because you're only here on account of my having threatened the guards,' he explained.

'What did you say?' asked Ahren curiously.

'That I'd open the gate one way or the other. Either with their help or with my hammer. They thought I was joking,' said the warrior drily.

Ahren had experienced how he could operate the venerable weapon and had no doubt that he would have got it open. But it would have been loud and wearisome, and he was glad that the gate had remained attached to its hinges.

'Culhen is bound to be able to get the scent of the Doppelganger,' said Ahren, and he gave the wolf a quick command. Culhen stretched his nose into the air.

He's here, but the air smells funny. Too many people in too small a space. Culhen gave his master a pained look. *And they don't wash very often, and they eat too much fermented fish.*

'Culhen has confirmed that he is here, but the air is too full of different smells. It might take him some time,' he said, translating the essentials to the others.

'Yes, even I can smell the fish,' said Trogadon, shaking his head. 'It's actually a traditional dish of the Ice Landers. The Brazen Clan adopted it and they have it specially carted here from a harbour four leagues away.'

'Less talking and more scouting,' said Khara curtly, her hand on Wind Blade. Ahren noticed that Whisper Blade was tied behind her back, out of the way. She saw his reaction and whispered: 'I need to practise before using it in an emergency.'

Ahren gave a nod of approval. He remembered the problems he'd had with his bow the previous year, after its string had been replaced with Selsena's hair. It had taken him considerable time to master the changes and his fighting ability had temporarily suffered. It made perfect sense to him that she wanted to master her new weapon first.

'Can you cast another Charm Net?' he asked Jelninolan, but she shook her head.

'Then the Doppelganger will know exactly where we are, and I don't want us to fall into a trap,' she replied in a low voice.

Ahren groaned and he too placed his hand on his weapon. 'We need to find Xobutumbur first,' he whispered, and Trogadon pointed along the corridor they had just entered, and moved forwards. Oil was burning in two gullies along the walls, casting a consistent, warm light onto the ceiling and enabling them to see further down the tunnel. The air was warm and sticky, the scent from the burning oil combining with the musty smell you would find in a poorly ventilated room. The ceiling was only high enough for them to stand upright, and Falk's helmet kept scratching the ceiling. Luckily, it didn't take them long to reach the common room, which only barely reminded Ahren of the hall they had seen that time in the Silver Cliff. The ceiling of the room was considerably lower than the other one; there were ten small fire-pits instead of one big one; and the benches were decidedly narrower and lower. There were also no upper tiers and doorways that Ahren had seen by the dozen in the Trading Hall. Everything seemed much more private here, and also more isolated. Ahren felt the vaults to be more threatening than in the Silver Cliff.

Two very young dwarves were tending the fires, and they looked terrified when they saw the intruders. Ahren noticed that to their credit, they didn't take to their heels, but grasped their pokers instead and slowly approached the group.

One of the dwarves, blond-haired and with only the beginnings of a beard, called out to them hastily, and Trogadon answered severely. The two had a brief discussion, during which time the young dwarf kept glancing over at the non-dwarf visitors. Finally, Trogadon dismissed him with an imperious wave of his hand, and the two young dwarves returned to their work, nervously glancing over at the strangers.

'They say that Xobutumbur went into his chamber some time ago and hasn't come out since. Hulrigum, the Lord of the Arsenal is the only person who has been with him,' said Trogadon, summarising the conversation.

'Did they tell you where his chamber is?' asked Falk, on edge.

Trogadon pointed at one of the few doors that led out of the room. 'Just behind that.'

'Quick, then!' ordered Jelninolan.

They approached the dark-grey stone door with its insignia of a hammer lying on top of a flattened mountain-top. The Brazen Clan coat-of-arms, thought Ahren, having seen a similar sign outside on the entrance door. It was closed, and when Trogadon knocked, nobody answered.

Trogadon gave the others a worried look, and Falk signalled to him to enter. They each pulled a weapon, and Trogadon was just placing his hand on the stone handle when Culhen caught a whiff of something.

The man with the many faces was here, he said nervously, and the wolf's head turned, searching from left to right.

'Be careful, the shape-changer could be nearby,' warned Ahren. A wave of tension rippled through the little group, and when Trogadon shouldered the door violently open, everybody was poised for action. Ahren tried to take in every detail of what he could see, and his eyes were immediately drawn to the pool of blood on the floor, at the far end of the modestly furnished room.

They all ran into the room, Trogadon in front, his face ashen-white. He gestured urgently to Jelninolan to join him. Whatever he had seen, Jelninolan started violently backwards as if she'd been hit. Then she stormed forward and disappeared behind the large stone writing desk which took up the far half of the room, and from under which, blood was oozing towards them. Ahren craned his neck, and then wished he hadn't, overcome by a feeling of nausea.

Xobutumbur's right arm and left leg were lying covered in blood in two corners of the room. The mutilated dwarf was literally swimming in his own blood, which was streaming from the gaping wounds and the cuts on his face. In a heartbeat Jelninolan's hands were glowing green as she cauterised the stumps with magic flames and then laid her healing hands over the face with its unkempt beard.

Ahren was astounded at how tough the dwarf was, who didn't even scream. The apprentice was furious at the sight of the poor maimed soul.

'I might be able to save him, but it will take time,' said the elf over her shoulder. 'You'd better find the Doppelganger before he causes any more damage.'

Xobutumbur gasped for breath and uttered forth two words: 'Hulrigum. Deep Fire.' His words echoed spine-chillingly in the over-full yet quiet room.

Trogadon and Falk looked at each other, and then ran cursing towards the common room. Khara and Ahren followed, along with Culhen, who was sniffing the ground.

'If he's taken on the figure of the Master of the Arsenal, then he'll have access to the complete weaponry of the Clan,' shouted Trogadon as he ran ahead.

I can follow him. Have his scent, now I know what his present shape smells like, said Culhen, his nose close to the floor.

'Culhen has his scent!' shouted Ahren, and the dwarf let the wolf take the lead.

He led them back to the reception hall and then into the western passage, where the mines were. Culhen determinedly led them through a maze of tunnels which had been formed for the sole purpose of reaching as many ore veins as possible as quickly as possible. The tunnels were only dimly lit, which proved lucky for them, because they spotted the torchlight in front of them in good time. They stood and then proceeded to creep quietly forward. They could hear a Dwarfish voice which seemed to be lecturing in the Dwarfish tongue.

'The speaker is talking about the perfidy of the Sun Emperor,' whispered Trogadon. The warrior continued to translate in hushed tones as they crept forward. 'It's time that the Brazen Clan took up arms. Dwarf honour demands it, and so on.' Then Trogadon's face drained of colour. 'He says, it's a nice irony that the Legion will be killed by the very heat they yearn for so much.' His eyes opened wide as he looked at the others. 'He wants to flood the side of the mountain where the switchback is with Deep Fire.'

Everyone looked shell-shocked. 'That will mean war between the Sunplainers and Thousand Halls,' whispered Falk hoarsely. 'Forwards!' he commanded urgently.

They stormed into a large storeroom, roughly twenty paces long and broad and with no other exit. Half a dozen dwarves were stacking barrels on top of each other near a small square hole on the opposite wall. A seventh dwarf with a golden chain, from which a stylised hammer was hanging, was preaching to them. None of the seven were armed, and Ahren could see on the faces of the workers that they were performing their duties half-heartedly.

Trogadon didn't waste a heartbeat. Before anybody had a chance to react, the warrior had already stormed into the room and without saying a word smashed his hammer into the side of the dwarf with the golden chain, sending him flying in a wide arc and smashing him into the wall, from where he slid to the ground as a lifeless heap. With his voice sounding like a bugle, Trogadon bellowed a single command, and the other dwarves fled out of the rom. Contented with his work, Trogadon shouldered his hammer and turned to face his friends. 'Well, that was easy', he said with a laugh as Ahren pointed behind him in horror. The shattered body of the dwarf seemed to smelt together and gradually produce strange-looking limbs, as well as gain weight.

Trogadon retreated at this peculiar performance back to his friends and Falk grimly drew his sword.

'He's taking on his war-shape. You need to damage his brain; every other organ and bone will heal within moments!' the old Paladin shouted. He stepped forward and ordered the others to form a semi-circle. 'Don't let him escape into the tunnel, or there will be a massacre among the dwarves.'

Ahren took his bow from his shoulder and went down on one knee. There were more than enough blades in the room, and if the brain was a weak point in the creature, then maybe an arrow at the right moment would end the battle. He placed Wind Blade on the ground in front of him, ready for defence purposes if needed. Then he placed an arrow in position and watched the others as they stepped closer to the Doppelganger, who was still transforming himself.

The apprentice felt nauseous as he saw four spidery legs breaking out of the tuberous body and straightening out in a flash. Four equally long, spindly and strange-looking limbs, ending in deadly points with sharp bone-blades grew out of the upper part of the being. To Ahren's horror, the figure in front of him didn't seem to have any distinguishable head, but rather a circle of eyes all around the whole body which was covered in bone plate. Ahren could make out neither throat nor mouth, just two tiny nostrils and two bulbous earlobes. The battle-creature seemed to combine maximum deadliness with maximum invulnerability. When it finally began to run forward on its blade-like legs, Ahren screamed in horror. Its movements were so jerky that Ahren could hardly follow them, and Trogadon was already bleeding from two slight cuts on his arms.

'It's too fast for me,' roared the dwarf as the bulbous creature easily and lithely evaded the warrior's hammer-blows. 'I'll pull back to the doorway,' he called as the Doppelganger began scrabbling up to the low ceiling in preparation for an attack from above. Khara's and Falk's weapons clanged loudly as they fought hard to parry the spinning forelegs of their enemy.

Trogadon stepped quickly behind Ahren and took up a wide-legged posture at the door. Speed was of no use to the creature there and the dwarf was at an advantage. If it wanted to flee, it would have to get past the dwarf and his hammer, while the others could sandwich it in from behind.

Ahren was amazed by the cool calculation of the warrior, who acknowledged his weakness in the face of his seemingly superior opponent but changed his strategy in the blink of an eye so that he could still be useful.

As opposed to me, thought Ahren, as Falk glanced over to him, looking for help. The strange-looking creature had turned him into a silent observer, while his friends were trying desperately to keep it in check. Khara had managed to connect a few times with the Doppelganger's stomach, but the bone-protected skin prevented the blade from penetrating through to the flesh, and any cuts she made, healed before her eyes.

Ahren shot a trial arrow, aiming at one of the creature's eyes, but his enemy jerked sideways, and the projectile ricocheted harmlessly off the bone-armour.

Culhen threw himself into the fray too, and Ahren's heart missed a beat as one of the spear-like forelegs came flashing towards the wolf. Culhen evaded the danger however, and the Paladin breathed a sigh of relief. He took another arrow from his quiver and considered his options. In the end he decided to aim for another eye but waited for the moment Khara was attacking the Doppelganger and with such violence that it was momentarily distracted. The arrow sank into the bulbous black eye of the creature with a soft squelching sound, and the Doppelganger jerked convulsively.

The apprentice let out a yell of joy, thinking he had had hit the battle-figure's brain, but then he watched in disbelief as the arrow was driven back out of the wound, which slowly but surely closed up.

'Where is his brain?' asked Ahren in frustration. The thing was hard enough to fight as it was, but the fact that it regenerated itself so quickly, made victory ultimately impossible. Falk's chest was already rising and falling under the strain of the relentless attacks, and it was only his Deep Steel armour and his shield that were protecting him from injury. Khara had three stab wounds on her left arm, where the tip of one of the creature's bone-arms had effortlessly sliced through the chainmail.

'No idea', panted Falk laboriously. 'It's in a different place every time', he gasped, before being set upon again by the creature.

Ahren feverishly thought for a moment and then decided to have another go. As Falk was beginning a counterattack, Ahren extended his bow to the maximum. His arms were burning, and the wood creaked in protest as the tension in the unicorn hair became incredible. Then he let the arrow fly, having angled the direction in such a way that the projectile flew upwards and plunged into one of the eyes in the torso.

The Doppelganger shuddered once again, but this time the shaft was sticking so deep in its body that it wasn't expelled as the wound closed together. Satisfied, Ahren drew another arrow out of his quiver. He would carry on shooting into the eyes of the creature, and from different angles until he finally connected with the brain. He was about to take aim again, when he realised that his enemy knew what was on his mind. Following a wild hail of blows that forced Khara to retreat, the creature spun to the left and stormed forwards on its circling forelegs towards Ahren, who threw himself sideways at the last moment, rolling over in the process. He felt sharp pains when one of the bone-blades stroked along the hands which were gripping his bow.

He's trying to destroy my weapon! shot through his head as he performed a diving roll behind Falk, who was giving him cover with his shield.

The Doppelganger seemed to hesitate, before trying to pass Trogadon, but the dwarf planted his hammer in the middle of the creature's body, causing it to crash into the nearest wall. New wounds decorated the dwarf's neck just above his chainmail, but that didn't seem to bother him in the slightest.

Ahren took advantage of the creature's temporary wooziness to shoot another arrow into its body, this time angling downwards, but that still didn't finish the Doppelganger off.

Falk, Khara and Culhen encircled the ugly deformity as it pulled itself together, and Ahren noticed that the two humans were imitating its tactics with their weapons while Culhen distracted it with a leaping attack. The four forelegs shot upwards, preparing to stab the flying wolf, as Falk and Khara stabbed their weapons deep into either end of their monstrous enemy's torso. It was only this action that saved the wolf's life, for the Doppler threw itself around, pulling its forelegs in, just as the animal was about to land with all its weight on the creature, which a fraction of a heartbeat earlier had its bone-spears ready to skewer the attacking wolf. Although that had been avoided, Ahren could see flecks of blood on the wolf's white fur, and a red mist descended on the apprentice.

He sprang up and began shooting arrow after arrow into his writhing enemy. Half of the missiles ricocheted harmlessly off the bone-plate; the other half dug deep into the flesh. Ahren was completely out of his mind with rage and he moved ever closer to the creature. He was standing no more than a pace away from the monster when he shot a single arrow with such force and at such close range that it pierced through the boneplate in the lower part of the body and penetrated with a satisfied squelch deep into the flesh. The blade-like forelegs shot towards him and Ahren noticed too late that he was within his enemy's range, but luckily Falk slammed his shield in a downward direction, thus saving his apprentice from injury.

Ahren was pulling out another arrow when he realised that the movements of the battle-creature were slowing. 'Aim below!' he screamed and Khara and Falk followed his order. They stabbed repeatedly into the area where Ahren's last arrow had penetrated, and the young Forest Guardian emptied his quiver as their enemy's resistance lessened.

When it was all over nobody could say who had delivered the fatal blow. Suddenly the bulbous creature was perfectly still, its legs had given way under its own weight and the forelegs had given up the fight. There was blood everywhere, and most of it was their own, as many of them had cuts and stab-wounds.

Falk thrust his sword one last time into the lifeless creature, before sitting with the others, who were leaning against the wall and gasping for breath. Culhen's nose was on Ahren's lap, and the wolf gazed up at him with pain-filled eyes, complaining to his master of his suffering. Ahren took that to be a good sign – the wolf's wounds couldn't be as serious as they looked. In the distance they could hear cries of alarm and the tramping of boots. Falk gave a tired smile.

'Why do the reinforcements always come after the battle is over?' he asked hoarsely. 'Tell them what we did here,' he said, turning to Trogadon. 'We're in a pretty bad way and it's a long way to Uldini. I don't think Jelninolan will have any strength left to help us, and I really don't want us to have to fight our way through a few angry dwarves.'

When the first guards stormed into the room, they were startled to find the companions laughing in relief at the fact that they were all still alive.

When they finally stepped out of the Clan Halls, the sun was just rising over the city walls, casting the marketplace, milling with people, in a warm light. Everywhere was the sound of laughter and chatter, and the smell of fried corn-biscuits wafting from out of dozens of windows and over the crowd before dispersing into the surrounding streets.

They climbed the steps, their wounds temporarily dressed, holding onto each other for support and they saw the Brazen City awakening to new, and hopeful life – the citizens' hunger was being sated and their fear was vanishing.

They pushed themselves through the laughing people, who shrank back at the sight of the groups' shattered bodies but continued to nibble on the flat biscuits which were being passed around.

'The news of the peace treaty must have quickly done the rounds and the food supplies in the warehouses have been released,' said Falk quietly.

Ahren breathed in the aroma of the food and saw a little child taking an enormous bite from a corn-biscuit. The nutritious golden food was being handed out through the windows of all the surrounding houses, and inside, volunteer cooks were kneading and baking and serving the citizens. The sight of all these people, standing around peacefully and enjoying their food and water together, almost moved Ahren to tears.

Falk put a hand on his shoulder and whispered quietly: 'Enjoy this moment. This is what we're fighting for. They'll never know what a close shave it was earlier.'

They pushed their way forward towards the entrance to the main building, and Ahren experienced a feeling of pure joy. Then he shuddered as he realised the truth of what Falk had said. After Trogadon had explained to the alarmed guards what had happened, and their wounds had been tended to, they had inspected the barrels of Deep Fire and the hole, by which they had been stacked. One of the guards had explained to Trogadon that it was an old ventilation shaft which led directly to the mountain slope where the switchback wound its way up. If the Doppelganger's plan had succeeded, a whole legion of soldiers would have been burned to death in a most horrific manner, and the Sunplains would have immediately declared war on the dwarves of Thousand Halls. The Brazen City would have been pounded into dust by Justinian's catapults and HE, WHO FORCES would have made mincemeat out of the fighting empires, which in turn would have made the Paladins' task of annihilating him almost impossible.

A tumultuous cry brought the apprentice back to reality. Somebody was pointing excitedly at Falk and was triggering off all his neighbours. 'Look – there's the Paladin! There's Baron Falkenstein!' The citizens of the Brazen City began crying out in jubilation and cheering in gratitude. Luckily, the travellers were already at the entrance of the main building and they stumbled inside, except for Falk, who waved at the crowd outside and gave an embarrassed smile. Normally Ahren would have been miffed at being so completely ignored, but at that moment he was far too tired, hungry, wounded and dirty to give it a second thought. He just wanted to get to Uldini, have a bath and collapse into bed.

Two of his wishes had been realised. Ahren gave a sigh of contentment as he enjoyed the comfortably warm water that had been prepared for him in a solid wooden bathtub situated in his own room. On account of the group's size, they had all been offered individual accommodation, and now that the crisis was over and the Doppler exterminated, he had his own private space at last.

He playfully splashed a little water on Culhen's muzzle. The wolf grunted in response and curled himself up even more so that only his furry white back could be seen. Ahren giggled and then winced when a freshly healed wound came in contact with the edge of the tub.

Uldini had healed everyone, but the number of wounds, and the fact that Jelninolan had been out of commission, meant that he had really only managed to do a patchwork job. The freshly knitted skin was very sensitive, and so Ahren decided to leave the wolf alone and stretch out in the bath in order to really relax.

He ran through the present situation in his head again and allowed himself a little smile. Jelninolan had sent a message that she would be able to save Xobutumbur's life, but not his limbs. The dwarf would, nevertheless, be able to sign the peace document along with the rest of the Triumvirate at noon, which Ahren and his companions would then deliver to the Sun Emperor. His ultimatum would expire on the following evening, by which time they would have long since reached him. They had saved the city with minimum loss of blood, and the sounds of the citizens celebrating wafted in through the window.

There was still some time until the treaty signing, and Ahren was determined to take forty winks in the meantime. He was just climbing out of the bath when there was a knock at the door.

'Are you awake, boy?' It was Falk, speaking in a low voice.

'One moment!' replied Ahren quietly, and he quickly threw on his linen garment before opening the door to his master.

Falk looked at him with raised eyebrows as he pushed his way into the room.

'I was just about to take a short nap,' said Ahren, hoping the old Forest Guardian would take the hint and leave him in peace.

Falk nodded and looked him up and down. 'You're still growing, aren't you?' he asked out of the blue, and Ahren shrugged his shoulders. So many things had happened that he really hadn't been taking any notice. He was still several fingerbreadths shorter than Falk, but the young man was certain that even if he were to tower over his master someday, he would still be looking up to him.

'I just wanted to make sure you understand the procedure at midday,' said Falk coming to the heart of the matter. 'We are going to be arresting Bergen as a matter of formality, and then we'll have to deliver him to the Sun Emperor. That's what the agreement he'll be signing states, and that's the only way we'll get everything we require.'

Ahren frowned. That's the way the wind's blowing, he thought. Falk wanted to make sure that his apprentice wouldn't create a scene later, and would stick to the agreement that had been negotiated. 'I don't like the fact that we're locking up a man who loyally stood by the people of this city and who stopped an act of treachery. If I had my way, I'd lock up the Sun Emperor.'

Falk guffawed cheerfully. 'That's a picture I'd love to see too.' Then he became serious. 'I'm sure that Uldini can ensure that Bergen will serve out his time on a nice, spacious estate, and he won't be rotting away in a hole in the ground. At the end of the day, he's going to have to be capable of fighting, and although the Sun Emperor might be stubborn and sometimes unfair, he's certainly not stupid.'

'Is that allowed?' asked Ahren in disbelief. He had always associated imprisonment with dungeons, and when Falk nodded in confirmation, the young Paladin was completely confused.

Falk placed a calloused hand on the apprentice's neck and gave him a quick hug. 'Oh, Ahren, you still have to learn so much about politics, but never let it darken your heart.' Then he let him go and looked into his eyes. 'Now that you know what's awaiting Bergen, can I count on you?'

Ahren thought he wouldn't mind spending a few years himself relaxing in peace and quiet on a distant estate without fear of Dark Ones or other dangers, and then nodded firmly.

'Good', said Falk. 'Then I'll leave you to your beauty sleep.' His voice was dripping with sarcasm. I'm going out into the courtyard to do a little training myself.'

Ahren sighed bitterly and rolled his eyes as his master went toward the door. 'Wait for me, I'll go with you,' he said, giving in, and finished getting dressed.

'Good lad,' said his master. Ahren didn't need to look at Falk to know there was a self-satisfied grin on his face.

Chapter 22

They were standing in the middle of the sun-soaked inner courtyard of the main building and were just practising a series of attack and parry moves when Jelninolan came through the archway, settled down on a stone bench beside a large tree, smiled and breathed in its aromas with her eyes closed. Ahren saw immediately that having performed an excess of healing magic she had slipped into a passive, almost apathetic state, which would last for a while longer.

They stopped their training and went over to the elf, who totally ignored them.

'How are you?' asked Falk in a soft tone, and gently shook her shoulder until she opened her eyes.

She smiled up at them, and the dark rings under her eyes gave her a ghostly appearance. 'Exhausted. Run-down. But contented. Xobutumbur is alive and is already back in the meeting room.' The emotional depth was missing from her voice, and Ahren looked over at Falk with concern, but the old man played down the issue.

'She'll be alright,' he said. 'The healing magic for the dwarf was terribly draining, and the first few hours afterwards are the worst. She had to heal Xobutumbur's wounds on her own yesterday and she needs some time.' Then he turned to Jelninolan again. 'Did you come here for a particular reason?' he asked gently.

The priestess had closed her eyes again and was lost in the smells coming from the flowers. After some heartbeats, she blinked, and a look of intense concentration came over her face. 'I'm supposed to tell you that it will be time soon,' she said in a flat voice, and turned her attention back to the flowers.

Falk groaned. 'Uldini really should have been more considerate and not sent Jelninolan to us as a messenger in her condition.' He gently reached his hand out towards her. 'Come, we'll bring you with us.' Ahren followed suit, and they both led the stupefied priestess back to the meeting room. Everyone had already gathered there, and Ahren was flabbergasted to see that Xobutumbur was standing up. He had a patch over his right eye, and his right arm was missing completely. He was struggling to support himself with a crutch under his left armpit which compensated for his missing left leg. He was discussing something earnestly with Windita, and Ahren couldn't believe how self-composed the Clan Elder appeared.

'A stubborn old chap,' said Trogadon as he approached Ahren. 'Never gives up.' He looked up at Ahren. 'Do you know what he said earlier when he came in and everybody wanted to send him back to bed? "As long as I have my head and my voice, I'm going to serve the Brazen Clan". Damn it, but even I would be willing to follow a Clan Elder like him.'

This was the first time Ahren had heard Trogadon say anything praiseworthy towards another dwarf. It seemed that with the passage of time and the distance from the Silver Cliff, his indestructible friend's bitterness towards his own folk was beginning to fade.

Uldini spotted them and gestured them towards him. 'The sun is almost at its zenith. We should go out now and hope that Bergen will be punctual.'

Everyone got themselves ready and even Ahren fiddled with his armour and tried tidying his hair with his hand. Falk had been careful in the courtyard that they wouldn't scuff their armour too much while they practised, but a little sprucing up wouldn't do any harm. Then he suddenly felt a small hand at his neck, straightening his collar, and when he turned around, there was Khara, looking him up and down with a critical eye. 'We need to get something more suitable for you when it comes to official engagements', she said, and clicked her tongue disapprovingly.

'At best you look like a bodyguard, and at worst like a common-or-garden spy who's lost his way.' And she started picking at his armour and shaking her head in disapproval. 'When was the last time you had a haircut?'

Ahren shrugged his shoulders. 'Sometime in the spring. That's the last time Falk cut the long bits off with his knife.' Ahren himself cut the bits that fell in front of his eyes and didn't care about the rest.

Khara rolled her eyes and produced a silver hair band, which reminded Ahren a little of the colour of Falk's armour. Then she grasped his hair at the back of his neck and tied it up. She tilted her head from side to side, before eventually finishing the surprise inspection with a wink. 'That will do at a pinch. Let's just hope the people of the Brazen City don't look too carefully, and that the Thirteenth Paladin manages to pass muster.'

Ahren was hot and cold at the same time. He had completely forgotten that the signing of the peace treaty would be his first public engagement! He still hadn't been named When they'd been on King's Island, so this was his first official appearance as a genuine Paladin. He immediately wished that Khara had warned him about it a lot earlier or hadn't told him at all. The dignitaries and his friends left the room one by one, as he grew increasingly nervous, his self-confidence shrinking in contrast. With his hands dripping in sweat and his heart pounding, he followed the others out into the sunshine and towards the tumultuous cheering of the multitude.

So far, so good. Everything was running smoothly, and Ahren was happy with his anonymous position in the third row of dignitaries, standing with the others on the platform that had been erected on the marketplace, directly in front of the main building. The wooden structure, eight paces by eight, was clearly regularly used for official occasions as it looked somewhat the worse for wear. At the front of the platform, which was roughly a good pace high, stood a pedestal, upon which lay the peace treaty ready to be signed, along with a large white quill and a little glass inkwell. Windita had turned towards the cheering crowd and announced that an end to their deprivations was at hand.

Ahren could see that the marketplace was full to overflowing with people filling the side-streets, determined to experience this historic event. He noticed that many of the younger and more agile citizens had climbed onto the flat roofs for a better vantage point. Falk was looking around nervously, and Uldini too seemed troubled, exchanging concerned glances with the others. Windita was punctuating her speech with ever-longer pauses and gradually the young Forest Guardian understood what was going on. The blond Ice Lander was playing for time while all the dignitaries waited for the arrival of Bergen and his Blue Cohorts. She finally looked over at the Arch Wizard helplessly, but he just shrugged his shoulders.

'But that's enough talk,' announced Windita. 'The time has come for us to renew the peace between the Brazen City and the Sunplains.' The noise was deafening as hats were thrown in the air, tankards were clanked together, and people shouted out their joy at the end of the conflict that had threatened their city for so long. One by one the members of the Triumvirate stepped forward and signed the document. Then Uldini, tongues of blue light flashing from his body, floated forward and magically cast his name onto the parchment. The Arch Wizard was playing the Almighty Ancient once again and a murmur of awe and admiration rose from the multitude.

Falk glanced around the crowd and nodded, satisfied. 'Good, no troublemakers,' he said quietly.

Ahren looked at him quizzically, and his master bent over and whispered into his apprentice's ear: 'There was a lot of bad blood. We were afraid somebody might want to seek revenge on Uldini because of the last few months. That's why he's putting on this magic show. Attacking a messenger is one thing, but a flame-throwing Ancient is quite another,' he explained quietly.

Ahren nodded and looked around the crowd with an uneasy feeling in his stomach, but the only thing he could see was relieved faces, joy and the odd look of amazement at Uldini's tricks.

The Arch Wizard finished and there was another roar of approval, while those on the podium looked around with concern. Of course, the contract was now valid, Ahren understood that much, but it was doomed to failure unless Bergen signed it and allowed himself to be arrested, otherwise Justinian would never recognise it.

The long hiatus in the ceremonies did not go unnoticed, and the unrest among the crowd was beginning to manifest itself, as questioning voices grew louder.

'This is not good,' warned Falk, pushing himself in front of Jelninolan, who was still stupefied.

'Am I too late?' shouted a powerful voice from a side street at the edge of the marketplace, and Ahren came marching onto the square accompanied by his Blue Cohorts, causing people to move aside willingly or be swept aside by the muscular man and his entourage. Ahren recognised the faces of his captors again, but there was no sign of the tattered and stoical attitudes they had previously.

Each one of them appeared in deep blue, smoothly polished armour as they marched in perfect unison, following their leader to the podium. They gave the impression of a perfectly drilled military unit, and Ahren could see why so many tales of their derring-do had developed over time. They had planned their appearance perfectly, and within a few paces, they were surrounded by a jubilant throng that offered them safe passage to the platform by opening up in front of them, as if they were walking through a field of corn.

'That bastard always knew how to turn it on for the crowd,' muttered Falk grumpily, and it struck Ahren that his master was jealous of the love the people felt for the captain who was getting closer by the heartbeat. Then the old man's demeanour changed, and he put his hand before his face in shock. 'Oh, Bergen, what *have* you done?!' he uttered, and Uldini and Jelninolan too looked at the man in disbelief. Ahren craned his neck to get a better look at the mercenary, who was now no more than four paces away, but he couldn't make out anything unusual. His distinctive face with its fine wrinkles of a man in his late forties was relaxed and smiling, and he looked at them in an almost fatherly manner as he finally reached the platform. His Paladin armour, lighter and wilder than Falk's, shimmered in the sunlight, as did his brutal-looking axe.

Falk and Bergen looked deeply into one another's eyes, and Ahren found it impossible to guess what messages they were conveying to each other after so many hundreds of years. Then Bergen raised his hand upward in a request for help, and after less than a heartbeat's hesitation,

Falk grasped his counterpart's arm in a warrior's greeting, and pulled him onto the podium with a quiet groan.

For a moment, time seemed to stand still. Ahren wasn't sure they weren't going to fight with each other because of the way they were standing – each clasping the other's forearm, their bodies tense like two aggressive predatory animals. An almost shy smile began to light up Bergen's face, giving him an impish look, at which point they burst out laughing, embraced and slapped each other on the back. The Cohorts had in the meantime, taken position around the podium, protecting their leader from over-enthusiastic citizens who were still cheering wildly. Then the enormous man released himself from Falk, who looked unusually small in comparison, and turned to face the young Forest Guardian. 'I hear you were all busy last night?' he whispered to him.

Ahren nodded a little too keenly. He quickly tried to appear calm, before responding: 'There was a Doppelganger roaming among the dwarves and we defeated him.'

Bergen smirked at the exaggerated coolness of the apprentice, which he saw through immediately, and punched the young man's arm playfully. 'Good work, brother.' Then he turned and walked to the front of the podium, where he dramatically raised the quill and dunked it in the inkwell.

A deathly silence descended on the crowd, and Ahren's whispered question could almost be heard echoing throughout the square. 'Why did he call me brother?' he stuttered. As an only child, he found this expression particularly strange.

'This is the address we Paladins use among ourselves. It means that he's recognised you as part of the family.' Ahren grinned from ear to ear, and Falk instinctively frowned. 'Don't be getting any ideas. So long as I

404

am your master, I may call you whatever I want. Mostly blockhead, but sometimes lazybones,' he grumbled, albeit good-naturedly.

Ahren was hardly listening though – revelling instead in the pleasant feeling of at last being part of the Paladin community. He'd found his first brother, and out there were ten more siblings waiting for him. Suddenly, he couldn't wait to meet them all.

'The Blue Cohorts hereby accept the conditions as laid down in this peace treaty,' announced Bergen, and signed the parchment with a dramatic flourish.

'His signature takes up as much space as the rest of them put together,' commented Falk testily, and Ahren looked at his master in dismay.

'Do you like him or not?' he asked, coming straight to the point.

'I love him as a brother, which is why his affections drive me to distraction. He is my mirror-image as only a direct *opposite* can be,' said Falk. Ahren chewed the inside of his cheek, trying to follow the old man's obscure logic.

There was a roar of jubilation as Uldini and Bergen shook hands dramatically, and then the Arch Wizard gestured Falk and Ahren forward, at which point the young Paladin's knees turned to jelly. He swallowed hard and positioned himself beside Falk and Bergen, and Uldini began to speak in a magically enhanced voice.

'Good citizens of the Brazen City – peace has been sealed!' he uttered, beginning his speech, and the earth rumbled under the acclamation of the throng. 'Today is a great day, because today it is our honour to reveal something new to you.' The earth trembled again, but this time Ahren realised that it had nothing to do with the crowd.

'The Thirteenth Paladin has been named and is standing here before you. He is ready, along with his brothers and sisters, to face the threat of the Adversary, and to...' continued Uldini, as the earth shook for a third time.

'Master, something is very wrong here!' gasped Ahren fearfully, as a dark, circular object flew with breath-taking speed over their heads, before disappearing over the western city wall.

'Was that a rock?' asked Ahren in disbelief, and the first cries of horror could be heard coming from the crowd. The earth shook again, and this time Ahren could see a pall of smoke rising from part of the city wall.

Uldini's eyes seemed to be spewing molten energy as he growled under his breath: 'What in the name of all the Dark Ones does my Emperor think he's playing at? He's bombarding the city!'

'But the deadline hasn't expired!' cried Ahren helplessly.

'The Doppler!' shouted Falk over the noise of the crowd. 'Who knows what he was up to or where he was *before* yesterday. I'd bet my life on it that he was down below with the legions, spreading unrest.'

'Like, for example, encouraging them to move the attack to a day earlier', said Khara darkly. Another rock flew over her but fell to earth on the other side of the mountain.

'We have to get to the gate. Maybe I can stop the attack from there!' shouted Uldini.

Bergen gave a determined nod. 'Blue Cohorts!' he shouted. 'Wedge formation! Proceed to the palace gate!' he bellowed, and as if by magic the mercenaries moved into position.

'Fly ahead and hold them up!' urged Falk to Uldini as another rock hit the city wall. 'They're still fine-tuning the catapults and only one in every ten missiles is hitting the wall, but it won't be long before their vanguard is storming into the city centre.'

'Which is exactly why I'm staying with you,' snarled Uldini defiantly. 'If a rock hits you, that's three Paladins gone in one blow, I can deflect one or two of the damn things, but Jelninolan is hopeless for now.' He gestured over to the stupefied elf.

Falk bit his tongue and stayed silent and they pressed their way, assisted by the mercenaries, through the panic-stricken people, who were screaming and running helter-skelter. Ahren took Jelninolan by one arm and pushed her forwards, while Khara took her by the other, and unceremoniously shoved anybody out of the way who got too near the elf.

Another boulder whizzed past over their heads towards the far wall, only to drop at the last moment on top of a warehouse, smashing it into a cloud of stones and dust.

Ahren could already see the city gate; there were less than five-hundred paces separating them from the mighty doors, but progress was almost impossible due to the terrified men, women and children chaotically running and stumbling. Ahren felt his throat tighten as a feeling of helplessness and utter despair spread through his body. He realised that they were making no progress now, and his efforts had all been in vain.

'We need to get the people to safety!' he screamed at the top of his voice. 'Then we'll be able to move forward!'

'Good idea!' shouted Uldini in response. 'You wouldn't happen to have a second city up your sleeve where we could store them?' The Arch Wizard's tone was cutting, but suddenly Ahren burst out laughing.

Culhen, play the big bad wolf, and pave a path for me to the podium, he ordered the wolf, who had been staying loyally by his side.

The wolf gave him a quizzical look, but then obeyed. With hackles raised and teeth bared, the wolf growled and yelped and howled until a path opened before them.

'What are you doing?' shouted Falk, trying to stop his apprentice, who was already beginning to squeeze his way through the narrow gap.

'I'm sorting out a second city for us!' cried Ahren. Then he fixed his eyes on the dwarf Xobutumbur, who was still standing on the podium with the other Triumvirate members, trying to deal with the panic. Ahren waved his arms wildly, until finally the injured dwarf spotted him. A ring of city guards had replaced the Cohorts and were guarding the podium, holding Ahren back, and the dwarf had to laboriously lean down in order to be able to hear the apprentice, who was shouting at him.

'Open the Clan Halls! Let the people in down there!' he screamed with all his might, but Xobutumbur's face hardened and he stubbornly shook his head.

'We have to get to the city gate, and then we can stop this madness! But we can't do it if the streets are full of people. They're going to die out here!' he pleaded. The dwarf's face revealed the inner conflict that was raging between his loyalty to the laws of his folk, and his pity for the people surrounding him.

'Do you want to be the hero who saved the Brazen City or the dwarf who tore it asunder?' shouted Ahren in utter frustration, as he was being pulled away by the throng. Another building was hit by a boulder causing a wave of people to move from left to right, dragging Ahren along in a mass of terrified bodies. The young Forest Guardian tried in vain to resist, and saw the Blue Cohorts fighting their way towards him, presumably at Bergen's behest, who was pointing in his direction.

Suddenly a horn, which Xobutumbur had pressed to his lips, split the air with a loud, short blast. Then there were two more blasts echoing above the cacophony of terrified citizens. With tears of joy Ahren heard the enormous gates to the Clan Halls creaking open, and he bowed his head thankfully towards the one-eyed dwarf, who pressed the horn to his chest and solemnly looked back at the apprentice.

Cries of relief could be heard everywhere, and the movement of the masses changed direction, as the welcoming caves offered sanctuary to the panicked mob. Less than ten heartbeats later Ahren was carried by the throng as far as the mercenaries, who grasped him firmly and pulled him into the safety of their troop.

'Well done, boy!' shouted Falk above the noise, and Trogadon gave him a congratulatory slap on the shoulder. 'You really must have pestered old Xobutumbur. Not even I would have been able to persuade him to open gates. The word of a Clan Elder is law during war.'

Ahren was about to answer but was horrified to see a boulder heading straight for the marketplace. It was going to land slap-bang in the middle of the throng and kill dozens of people. 'Uldini!' he screamed and pointed at the falling missile.

The Arch Wizard reacted immediately by making a pushing gesture with his hands, causing the projectile to deviate course and land on one of the empty houses on the edge of the marketplace.

Bergen shook his head disapprovingly, and Uldini puffed himself up to his fullest extent. 'What's wrong with you?' he shouted indignantly. 'Have you seen the size of those things?'

'You're losing your touch', said the captain sarcastically. 'I've seen you sweep dragons from the sky that were twice the size of that pebble.'

'I'm using my strength economically, thank you very much,' snorted Uldini, as they continued moving towards the city gate. 'Who knows how many more of these boulders I'm still going to have to deal with.'

Now that the crowd had created a gap they could slip through, their progress was much quicker. One hundred heartbeats and two further diverted missiles later, and they arrived at the city gate, which a terrified contingent of city guards was trying to keep closed.

'OUT OF MY WAY!' roared Uldini, casting an almighty spell past the soldiers who were desperately leaping out of the way. The powerful magic smashed into the gate and lifted it straight out of its hinges.

'Now *there's* the old Uldini!' said Bergen admiringly.

'Shut your gob!' snarled Falk and Ahren simultaneously, both knowing how dangerous it was to antagonise a wizard that was under the influence of fighting magic.

'A chip off the old block,' chuckled Bergen.

Uldini, in the meantime, had floated forward. His body was emitting flashes of lightning in all directions, and his voice sounded like distant thunder as he stepped towards the flabbergasted soldiers of the 17th Legion. They had just ducked out of the way of the exploded city gate when they heard his command. 'CEASE FIRE!' Uldini's thunderous voice shook the ground and rolled down the mountainside. 'We have a damned peace accord in the bag, and if one more rock comes flying up the side of this mountain, I'm going to send it straight back onto the head of your screwball commander. And now, WITHDRAW YOUR FORCES!'

Ahren wasn't sure if the future scribes of history would see things exactly the same way, but he couldn't help thinking of a litter of terrified rabbits as he watched the solders of the 17th Legion cast aside their weapons and run helter-skelter back down the switchback while the retreat bugle sounded again and again. Culhen was licking his chops, and Ahren held onto him just in case he decided to bite the panic-stricken soldiers in the backside.

Chapter 23

Their descent off the mountain resembled a force of nature, or at least it must have appeared so to the soldiers on the Plains. Uldini's rage discharged itself in the form of lightning flashes that exploded rocks, caused the earth to sink, and sent thunderclaps into the valley. Falk and the others kept a safe distance away, not being certain that they themselves would be spared the Wizard's magic.

'He's very close to an Unleashing. We'd best not annoy him. With a bit of luck, he will have expended his energy by the time we get to the foot of the mountain,' whispered Falk. They all kept their heads down and spoke as little as possible.

Another two attempts at bombarding the city were attempted by foolhardy catapult crews, but Uldini made good his threat on each occasion by ensuring the boulders dropped back down on the engines of war, smashing them to pieces. Soon all the crews had fled, leaving the remaining catapults as grotesque warnings on the Plains.

The nearer they reached the valley, the less power Uldini emitted, and when they rounded the last bend in the switchback, the Arch Wizard had almost returned to himself.

'To be honest with you all, I don't think *I'm* going to be the main target of the Sun Emperor's rage when we're standing in front of him,' said Bergen smugly, and when Ahren spotted Falk's grimace, he realised that what the mercenary had said might not be that far from the truth.

'Now that we're no longer in danger of being roasted alive or crushed by boulders, maybe you can tell me what you've been up to with your Blessing of the Gods,' asked Falk in a biting tone.

'What are you talking about?' interjected Ahren, confused. The Blessing of the Gods was the most valuable thing a Paladin possessed, it made him or her a warrior of the gods, and enabled the Thirteen to fight against HIM, WHO FORCES. Ahren had spent the whole of the previous year protecting his Blessing from the dark god's attacks, and the very idea that the Blessing of another Paladin might somehow be damaged frightened him.

Falk pointed to Bergen. 'When he was a Paladin, he was no more than twenty-five summers old.'

Ahren stared at the gigantic Paladin's strands of grey hair in disbelief. The Paladin looked back at him and grinned. 'Time hasn't been so kind to me as it has to you, big brother,' he replied sarcastically.

'Stop telling fairy tales,' commanded Falk. 'You know that Blessings don't wear away. Otherwise, the First would be ancient by now.'

'The First submits to no rules, but you're right of course. I cheated a little,' admitted Bergen. He gestured to the mercenaries in their blue armour, who were securing the area around them. 'Whenever I accept someone into the Blue Cohorts, they receive a little tincture of my Blessing. Enough to make them stronger and faster, and it enables them to live until they're two hundred years old, provided they haven't suffered a violent death in the meantime. It ages me one or two moons, but it's worth it,'

The Paladin's obvious fondness for his people that his words revealed, moved Ahren deeply, but Bergen's open confession shocked him nonetheless. 'You give away some of your Blessing?' he asked in disbelief, and Falk's pale face spoke volumes.

'Why not?' said Bergen calmly. 'It's my Blessing, and if I want to share it with others, nobody is going to stop me. Apart from the gods of course, and they haven't said anything yet.'

Falk's eyes were threatening to pop out of his head as he struggled for words. Ahren intervened before things had a chance to get nasty. 'Luckily, there hasn't been any serious damage,' he said, glancing reassuringly over at Falk. 'The Dark Days will be upon us in a few summers, and it will make no difference if you're twenty or forty years old. My master is living proof that a Paladin of advanced years loses none of their fighting strength'.

Khara gasped, and only then did Ahren realise what he had just said. Terrified, he looked over at Falk, who fixed him with narrowed eyes. 'Interesting,' he said quietly. 'Would you like to elaborate?'

Ahren shook his head, panic-stricken, and looked to the ground, barely daring to breathe.

You should never antagonise the Alpha, warned Culhen in his mind. *Who's going to feed me if he kills you?*

The young Forest Guardian might well have dug an even greater hole for himself were it not for the intervention of the sound of loud clip-clopping. Selsena came galloping down the switchback, her mane flying and her hooves sparkling. Falk's expression suddenly looked for all the world like that of a godsday student whose trousers had ripped.

'Oh, damn,' was all he said, and Ahren understood why. The Elfish warhorse was sending out a wave of anger and scorn, and the only one not affected was Trogadon, who looked around with interest, while the others winced under the Titejunanwa's emotional onslaught.

'Whatever it is she's telling you, I'm delighted not to be on the receiving end,' he said cheerfully, while the others looked daggers at him.

Falk stopped and spread out his arms apologetically and tried to explain to the Titejunanwa why he had left the city without her. He stammered out bits of words, only to be interrupted every time.

'Please understand...but I just wanted to...we had no choice...' And so it went on for a considerable time before he gave up, and with shoulders slumped, he finally said: 'Yes...you're right.'

Having watched the drama unfold before him, Bergen finally stepped forward to Selsena. 'Good to see that you haven't lost it over the years, my queen.' He placed his hand between her nostrils and her anger abated like a gentle summer breeze.

'See what I mean?' said Falk sulkily. 'He can even control Selsena better than I can.'

Ahren suppressed a smile and thought to himself that the Paladins were indeed a big family – as was reflected by the tensions that were inevitably created by the family members' differing, and peculiar personalities.

A carriage like the one they had travelled on from Water Heart was awaiting them at the foot of the mountain. The sun had already sunk below the horizon and so the vehicle was a welcome sight to Ahren and his companions, as it meant they would not have to march through the night. The only difference this time was that it was accompanied by two hundred heavily armed soldiers who had surrounded it in double quick time, dampening Ahren's enthusiasm for the carriage considerably.

A commander bedecked with military medals on his chest saluted Uldini briskly. 'The Sun Emperor conveys greetings to you, Advisor Getobo. He congratulates you on the delivery of the traitors known as the Blue Cohorts, and their leader, Bergen Olgitram.' Then an evil smirk appeared on his face. 'Oh yes, he also wishes to speak to you immediately concerning your attack on his soldiers and catapults.'

At the man's words, the Blue Cohorts went into a defensive position, but Bergen called a halt with a raise of his hand. 'Steady on there, all of you. We have signed a peace agreement and we are all going to keep to it. I am sure the Emperor has no intention of breaking two agreements in the one year,' he said, loudly and emphatically.

The Blue Cohorts lowered their weapons and the commander looked distinctly less confident than he had before.

'I love this chap,' said Trogadon with a satisfied chuckle, and stretched up to clap Bergen on his upper arm. 'If you were half the size, I'd make you an honorary dwarf.'

Bergen grinned down at him and the commander cleared his throat in an attempt to win back the upper hand. 'If you would like to climb aboard. The Sun Emperor awaits you.'

It was clear to everyone that this was no request, and so they all clambered aboard, the Blue Cohorts around them as protection, and they, in turn, surrounded by soldiers of the Sunplains.

As Ahren climbed in he thought, not for the first time, about how they should all be allies against the Adversary, and wondered why the gods made it so difficult for the free peoples not to bash each others' heads in.

The carriage rumbled its way through the night and the companions sat inside, musing. Bergen had fished out a couple of dice from his pocket and was sitting with Trogadon. Depending on who was lucky or unlucky, the other would groan or laugh. Jelninolan had fallen into a deep sleep, which Uldini took to be a good sign.

'When she wakes up again, she'll be back to her old self. She surrendered herself completely to the side-effects of the healing magic to recover more quickly, although we really could have done with her help today.'

Ahren was sitting with Falk and grooming Culhen, something which the wolf was clearly enjoying. 'Why does she find it so difficult to find a middle way,' he asked cautiously. 'She must have centuries of experience at this stage.'

Uldini raised his eyebrows and looked critically at him. 'The two of us have cast more powerful spells in the last two years than in the two hundred years before. Believe it or not, we had very restful lives before you went and touched the gods' Stone.' He bit his lower lip and lowered his voice. 'Don't tell him this, but I think Bergen might be right – we really have become somewhat rusty.' He tensed up, as if his admission were painful to him, then floated over towards Jelninolan, slamming the bedroom door behind him.

Ahren wanted to discuss the matter with Falk, but when the young man turned, he saw the old man looking over resentfully at Bergen, who was having a whale of a time with Trogadon.

'I knew they'd get on with each other, but that's pathetic,' he grumbled sulkily. His jealousy was almost tangible as he saw how well the two were bonding.

'Trogadon gets on well with everybody who laughs and drinks, you know that,' said Ahren, trying to appease his master. The apprentice was amazed at the power of Falk's emotions - no matter what Bergen did, he always seemed to touch a nerve as far as the old man was concerned.

'Why did he call you big brother?' asked Ahren, hoping to distract his master, and at the same time find out a little more about the complicated relationship between Bergen and the old Forest Guardian.

'That's the nickname the other Paladins gave me because I always looked after them and alerted them when things got too dangerous. Just like a big brother does,' he answered absently, his eyes still fixed on the dicers.

Ahren thought there were considerably worse nicknames his master might have been called, and he began to suspect that Bergen didn't have a problem with Falk, but that it was his master who was the sole cause of their relationship being so complicated. The apprentice simply couldn't see what the issue was. He decided to play for time and took advantage of the Forest Guardian's temporary loquacity. 'Who is "the First" that you referred to earlier? It sounded almost like a title,' he asked casually.

'It's something like a nickname. The First Paladin that the gods created is still alive. He's so old that nobody knows his name, because none of the Ancients who were alive that time were there at his creation, and he himself won't tell anybody. He's a cold and calculating strategist, and luckily, we have no idea as to his whereabouts. But one thing is certain though: as soon as war breaks out, he will find us more quickly than we would like.'

Ahren started. 'Is there any Paladin you *don't* have a problem with?'

Ahren regretted the harshness of his question as soon as it was out of his mouth, but it didn't seem to affect Falk, who simply shook his head. 'That's something different to me and Bergen. The rest of us never referred to the First as a brother, and it would never have struck him either. There was always a chasm between him and us which none of us ever succeeding in bridging.' Falk finally looked away from the two gamblers and looked Ahren fixedly in the eyes. 'The gods gave us the option of passing on our gift to our children once we tired of the fight. But the First, as one of the earliest of the original Paladins, never took advantage of this opportunity. Think about it: What kind of a man decides in favour of millennia of fighting?'

Ahren shivered when he heard these words, and he felt queasy at the realisation that one day he would have to fight alongside such a person against a god. The Thirteen would have to be singing from the same hymn sheet as soon as Ahren had found all the Paladins, and he was beginning to realise that this would be no easy task.

When Falk turned away to take up his sulking watch again, Ahren exploded in anger. 'I just don't believe this!' he hissed furiously. 'You're behaving just like a godsday youngster who refuses to play with the other children because nobody asked him to! Just go over and throw a few dice with them. In the name of the THREE, you deserve a break!'

Falk glared at him, and Ahren knew he was going to pay a price for his disrespectful words towards his master, but he maintained his stare until the old man finally nodded. He stood up jerkily, as if every movement was difficult, and went over to the two merrymakers, who greeted him cheerfully and invited him to sit down. Trogadon pressed one of the wine bottles he'd found on a small shelf on the wall into the old man's hand and Bergen slapped him cheerfully on the back. Before ten heartbeats had passed the trio were laughing and cursing over their bets.

Satisfied, Ahren continued grooming Culhen and was surprised when the wolf spoke. *That was good work, Ahren. The pack survives through the cooperation of its members* echoed in his head. There was something stately and worthy about the wolf's voice, and Ahren marvelled, not for the first time, at how multi-facetted Culhen's personality had become.

Any chance of a bit of rabbit? asked Culhen hopefully, looking up at his master with amber eyes, and licking his chops. Ahren noticed immediately how quickly the young, playful version of the wolf had returned.

The apprentice chuckled and tickled him between the ears. 'I'll look and see if there's anything left over.'

Ahren was tired but couldn't fall asleep. Impressions from outside constantly disturbed him and kept him awake as he lay there; sleep kept slipping through his grasp like a nimble weasel, that twisted at the last moment as he tried to catch it. He heard the snoring of Trogadon and creaking of the carriage, felt its rocking movement, and smelled the stale air of the overfull cabin. He threw off his blanket in frustration and stood up.

He went quietly to the door that led outside, opened it carefully and pulled himself gracefully up onto the roof. The Plains were only silhouettes in the night sky, and even the torches of the military escort on either side, hardly cast any light up where Ahren was. So long as he remained quiet, he would not be discovered, and he would have some peace and quiet at last.

Slowly and with great concentration he went through *The Twelve Greetings to the Sun* in an attempt to subdue his restlessness. The movements helped him to come to terms with the events of the day, and to finally dispel the feeling of helplessness that had overcome him for a few terrible paralysing moments on the marketplace. A feeling of contentment began to spread within him when he realised that he had managed to save so many people. Not he, he corrected himself, as he recognised how many times he might have failed or even been killed without the help of the others. The very thought made him dizzy. He felt a deep gratitude towards every single one of them, and promised himself never to forget this feeling, no matter what awaited them in the future.

Suddenly he heard a noise behind him, and he spun around into a low defensive position, his hands ready in front of him to parry any oncoming blows.

'Not bad.' It was Khara's low voice in the darkness. 'The arms just a little higher or your head is unprotected.' The young woman stepped towards him, and Ahren instinctively retreated a pace. The confusion he felt any time he was alone with her hadn't abated since they had shared the sunrise on the tavern roof, and he tried to avoid the swordswoman if at all possible.

Khara noticed his reaction but said nothing, looking with sad eyes out into the night instead.

'We seem to be right night owls,' said Ahren in an attempt at a joke, but it had no effect on Khara. 'Is everything alright?' he finally asked.

Khara gestured to the carriage below. 'Jelninolan released me from my servitude today. I'm free to go wherever I want to.' Her voice had taken on a tone of great fragility, and Ahren had to resist the impulse to hug her.

'She isn't herself at the moment,' said Ahren, trying to explain the situation, Khara shook her head.

'You're wrong,' she said, contradicting him. 'She's saying very little, but what she is saying comes from her heart. I am no longer her servant, and I have to decide what I want to do next.'

A cold, moist hand gripped Ahren's heart, squeezing it slowly but relentlessly as the realisation dawned on him that the young woman could leave her companions in the morning, and he would in all probability never see her again. 'Have you any idea of what you want to do?' he asked quietly, completely caught in the grip of his fear.

Khara shrugged her shoulders. 'This has hit me completely unexpectedly. For many years my life has been determined by others. Strictly speaking, I have no reason to stay with all of you, but on the other hand there is no place I currently want to return to,' she said helplessly.

'That's all nonsense,' said Ahren, suddenly agitated. 'We all like you, and you're a great help to us.' He was delighted to be able to hide behind the group as he continued his argument. 'We need you.' He had almost said 'I need you,' but stopped speaking for fear of revealing himself.

Khara examined him intently, her face sceptical.

Ahren decided to appeal to her honour, knowing that this was the be-all and end-all of her very existence. 'Besides, you really don't want to hear that the Thirteenth Paladin was defeated in a fight with a bandit, whom you could have defeated with your hands behind your back,' he said conspiratorially and with an ironic smile.

Khara looked at him in shock, before her astonished reaction gave way slowly to a smile. 'Well, if you put it like that, I suppose I'll just have to stay,' she responded mischievously. Then she suddenly became serious. 'Thank you. If the others see things the same way, then I will gladly continue to help you all.'

'Why don't we celebrate with a swordfight?' asked Ahren roguishly, and secretly more relieved than he was willing to admit to himself.

Khara jumped at the idea and soon the amazed guards heard the clinking of swords and the sound of quiet laughter coming from the roof of the carriage and echoing into the night air.

Khara announced her intention of staying the next morning, and the reactions ranged from sheer joy to mild surprise that her continued help had ever been in doubt.

Jelninolan was coming back to her old self slowly but was unable to give her view on the matter. The rest of the party, however, welcomed the swordsgirl into the group once more as a free woman.

They were sitting together at breakfast, devouring the sweet, sticky pastries that had been handed to them by a servant. They would shortly be arriving at the tented encampment of the Sun Emperor, and an uneasy silence hung over the group.

Then Jelninolan appeared at the door to her sleeping quarters and blinked at the others in confusion. 'What are we doing here?' she mumbled. 'We need to defend the city.'

Uldini rose up, laughing. 'You must have missed something, Auntie. We're just delivering the peace treaty, and we were able to prevent the Doppelganger's second act of subterfuge by stopping the 17th Legion's assault on the city,' he announced with satisfaction.

'*You* must have missed something,' said the elf, now totally awake, with considerable vehemence. 'I'm talking about his third plan. What about the Dark Ones that are moving towards the Brazen City? I warned you about them yesterday morning when my charm net sounded alarm bells.'

A shocked silence filled the room as everyone stared in disbelief at the priestess.

'Tell me you're joking,' gasped Falk, but the elf shook her head firmly.

Uldini closed his eyes and Ahren inferred from the tone in the Arch Wizard's voice that he was finding it hard to maintain his composure. 'After your healing of Xobutumbur, you were completely away with the fairies and your babbling made hardly any sense at all. I'm certain I would have picked up on a well-articulated warning concerning the imminent attack of a large horde of Dark Ones.'

Jelninolan frowned. 'Oh dear,' she said uncertainly, 'maybe I only dreamed the whole thing.'

Uldini wiped his brow and let out a protracted sigh. 'Alright,' he said resignedly. 'How much time do we have?'

'They'll reach the city by nightfall,' prophesied the priestess. 'I'm going to cast a new net now and see if I can get an overview of the situation. But we need to turn around immediately.'

'Out of the question,' interjected Falk. 'It's true that we're not prisoners, but guests of the Emperor against our wills, if you see what I mean.'

'And anyway, we're going to need his help,' said Uldini quickly. He floated to the door, pulled it open and screamed: 'Chop, chop, chop! There's an emergency, and we need to get to the Emperor as quickly as possible!'

Despite his reputational damage, his order was acceded to immediately, and the enormous carriage gathered speed while the soldiers proceeded to quick march.

Ahren sat there in a state of shock, scarcely able to believe what he had just heard. All their efforts to protect the Brazen City from harm were once more in danger of coming to nought. Now he understood why the others became extremely anxious whenever Doppelgangers crossed their paths. Their reputations as master strategists were well deserved. The Doppler's attempt to delude the dwarves into using Deep Fire had seemed diabolic to Ahren, and then there was the parallel acceleration of the assault by the Plainers as an ingenious back-up plan. But the massed attack by Dark Ones was surely the high point of the Doppelganger, and Ahren had to grudgingly admire his perfidious audacity. If everything had gone according to the Doppler's plans, then the Brazen City and the Sunplainers would have torn each other to shreds before the Dark Ones would have attacked the survivors from both armies. But although Ahren and his comrades had succeeded in foiling one part of the Doppelganger's scheme, the Dark Ones could still overrun the city, because the city guards were unprepared. The city walls had been damaged by catapults, and Uldini himself had blown up the city gate the previous day.

Ahren slumped down, feeling utterly miserable, but then he felt his master's hand on his shoulder.

'Are you alright?' asked Falk quietly.

'We've only just saved them. Twice, in fact. Is that not enough?' groaned Ahren in frustration.

Falk grinned and then looked in resignation at Ahren. 'Welcome to our world,' he said. 'Uldini alone saved King's Island nine times during the Dark Days.'

'Ten times,' corrected the Ancient, grinding his teeth. 'You've forgotten the pestilence the dastardly necromancer tried to unleash.'

'You know what I mean,' said Falk, turning to Ahren.

Ahren gave a tired nod, and Falk took away his hand.

'Good,' he said. 'Then it will all end when HE, WHO FORCES has been conquered. And we're far from achieving that yet.'

'I'll stay in the carriage and cast a strong magic net,' said Jelninolan decisively. 'You persuade the Sun Emperor to help us, and then we'll ride like the wind – or tomorrow morning we might be looking at a few smoking ruins, where once a city stood.'

'Out of the question!' shouted Justinian furiously. 'I'm supposed to herd my exhausted legion up the mountain to defend a city that has defied them all these moons, and release a pack of traitors to boot?' The ruler jabbed a finger towards Bergen, who was casually leaning against a side table, throwing a grape into his mouth. 'The senate will skin me alive for that!'

'It's the only way we can save the Brazen City, my Emperor!' pleaded Uldini forcefully.

They had been brought before the monarch immediately on their arrival. Uldini had presented the peace treaty to him and related the news of the imminent attack, at which point the present argument had flared into life.

'Maybe I don't want to save it,' said Justinian excitedly. 'Maybe I won't sign anything. Maybe I'll wait until the Dark Ones have overpowered the resistance and then march in myself!'

Uldini became ashen-faced and Ahren gasped when he heard the Sun Emperor's cold-blooded plan. The man had outlined in a few short sentences a tactic that would make him ruler of the Brazen City, and with minimum force. The loss of life and the destruction he was willing to consider made him appear inhuman.

'You're going to lose many of the blacksmiths,' implored Falk, and Ahren saw the ruler hesitate for a moment.

'Right then, I'll think about it. But I'm not going to let *him,* and his people fight alongside us only to have them escape at the first opportunity.' Once again, he jabbed his finger towards Bergen, who grinned back, thus enraging the irate man even further.

Ahren was relieved that the mercenary said nothing, but he sensed that they were not making any progress. Justinian was simply too accustomed to getting his own way, and Uldini had been his advisor for too long to recognise what really needed to be done. A plan formed in the young Forest Guardian's head, and he was determined to try it out. Everyone kept telling him he was a Paladin, and maybe it was time he behaved accordingly.

'That's enough!' he cried out in a loud voice, and Justinian, Emperor of the Sunplains, not to mention Uldini, Supreme Commander of the Ancients, looked aghast at the apprentice who had so rudely interrupted them.

'You're behaving like a spoilt child that refuses to let go of its toy, even if it means breaking it, I mean, come on! But the Paladins will *not* help you!' Ahren folded his arms, and the ruler's eyes almost popped out of his head in amazement, while Ahren's friends looked uneasily at the young Forest Guardian.

'Lad...' began Falk, but Ahren was already speaking again.

'And I mean not only now in this battle, but never again!' he shouted. 'The Dark Days are coming and not a single Paladin will enter your empire to come to your defence, and I'm pretty sure the Ancients will follow our example!' He pointed a scolding finger at Justinian, who was speechless at being lectured to in this manner. 'You are willing to sacrifice a city to buttress your position? Then we Paladins will simply sacrifice your empire. As soon as the Dark Ones realise that you're sitting ducks, without magic or protection, their hordes will overrun you and wipe the Sunplains off the map. The other rulers will think twice then before putting their own interests before the interests of this entire creation.' Ahren waved his hand dismissively. 'I congratulate you, Justinian, the Third of that Name, your attitude is going to be a useful example of selfish dereliction of duty.' Ahren gestured the others towards him and turned towards the exit. 'Come on,' he said derogatively, 'I'm sure we're needed somewhere else.'

The sweat was rolling in streams down his back as he walked towards the archway which marked the way out. If the others didn't follow him now, he was nothing more than a petulant yob, who had lost any right to participate in any future significant decisions. With an iron will, he forced his legs to take step after step, but could hear no movement behind him. It was costing him a terrible effort not to turn around and look pleadingly at his friends, and his hope had almost evaporated by the time he was three paces from the exit.

Then he heard the echoing of footsteps and Falk was beside him and giving him an encouraging wink. Suddenly Khara was to his left, and she nodded at him in approval. Now Ahren heard several more steps as they strode towards the door, and as he was passing over the threshold, he heard Justinian's urgent outcry.

'Stay still or I'll have you all thrown into the dungeon!' screamed the flabbergasted monarch in a strangled voice.

Relieved, Ahren spun around and fixed the thin figure with a penetrating stare. 'If you try that, then we'll fight our way out of here,' threatened the apprentice. 'We are a collection of Paladins and Wizards. Either we massacre half a legion on our way out of here or your troops tear us to pieces, and you lose the support of the rest of the Ancients and Paladins when they hear about this bloodbath, not to mention your bringing about the fall of the entire creation!'

Ahren knew that he couldn't maintain his bluff for much longer. His hands were trembling so much that he was hiding them behind his back, and he sincerely hope that the Sun Emperor was interpreting his shaking body as an indication of suppressed rage. Ahren knew that his plan would fall apart the instant Justinian ordered an attack on them, because he had no intention of sacrificing innocent people or putting his friends into mortal danger.

What followed was a staring duel between the apprentice and the Emperor that lasted for several heartbeats. The others pointedly stood close to Ahren, their hands on their weapons.

Finally, just as Ahren felt he could last no longer, the figure in the white tunic slumped dramatically. 'Very well,' said the Emperor flatly, 'come back in. You win.'

Ahren didn't take in much of the discussion that followed. His body was trembling so much that he was sure his armour was rattling. Trogadon took him good-naturedly aside and gave him copious amounts of wine, while Falk stood in front of him, so that Justinian could see no sign of the apprentice's weakness.

'Some day you're going to be the death of me,' growled his master in a low voice. 'That was a risky, not to mention arrogant strategy of yours to speak for us all. If Justinian didn't already have such a dangerous enemy in Quin-Wa, who is both an Ancient and a Paladin, he would never have fallen for it.'

Ahren nodded absently, as he had been doing since Falk had begun lecturing him. The old Paladin seemed to realise that his protégé was incapable of absorbing information for the time being, and so saved his rebuke for later.

'Good, so let's get going,' announced Uldini finally, and Falk and Trogadon dragged Ahren unceremoniously out of the room. They went down the corridors of the temporary palace and then along the rows of the tents outside without saying a word.

They finally reached the stables where Selsena was being housed, and Uldini said loudly: 'We need to pick out horses and head off immediately. Khara, be so good as to fetch Jelninolan, so she can tell us what's awaiting us tonight. I'll fly on ahead and warn the Brazen City because under the current circumstances they're hardly likely to believe a messenger who's going to ask them to admit an entire legion.' Then his voice sank to a hoarse whisper while Khara ran off to fetch the elf. 'And we two will have a little chat until the others arrive,' he growled to Ahren between clenched teeth and blue flashes played around his fingers.

Uldini pulled no punches as he told the apprentice what he thought of Ahren's actions, and he really let fly. Some of his more colourful language even caused Trogadon to raise an eyebrow, but the contrite young man simply let the tirade flow over him. In his own way Uldini was just as unused to being ordered around the place as the Sun Emperor. The young Paladin had put the Arch Wizard into an impossible position, forcing him to choose between Ahren and Justinian, and the predicament had been torture. Now he was letting it all out, and electrical discharges were darting out of the fingers and eyes of the childlike figure, forcing Falk and the dwarf hither and thither as they stamped or slapped out little fires in the smouldering straw and wood.

Finally, it all got too much for Falk. 'I know you're irate but we're standing in a wooden stable in an enormous tented city. If you keep igniting little fires, you're going to burn everything down, and I'm pretty sure that if you incinerate the Emperor's temporary accommodation, he won't forgive you today or tomorrow,' he said with gritted teeth, tightly holding his singed palm under his armpit.

Uldini looked away from Ahren for the first time. There was smoke everywhere and Trogadon was just throwing a pail of water over a smouldering fire. The Arch Wizard closed his mouth, gave Ahren a last murderous look, then turned around and floated in a defiant sulk out of the stable.

Ahren dared to move at last, and quickly stamped out a small fire that had been burning for some time in the straw beside his foot.

'You do understand that your little bluff could have led to a war that might have torn Jorath asunder?' asked Falk in a surprisingly calm voice.

Ahren nodded first, but then shook his head. 'Justinian likes power, I understand that much. A war with the Paladins would have been of no benefit to him, and the Dark Days are at hand. He needs us and he knows it.'

Falk looked at him in astonishment and Trogadon laughed uproariously. 'Your pup is beginning to know his own worth. It's going

429

to become much harder for you to penetrate his stubborn head with your lectures in the future' he bellowed.

Ahren wasn't certain if his calculations during the audience with the Sun Emperor had been completely correct, but during Uldini's tirade he had gone through the situation again and again in his head, and the apprentice simply didn't know what else he could have done. He suddenly felt a wave of pride coming from Selsena, and a smile appeared on his face. He looked over gratefully at the Titejunanwa, who had followed the whole episode from her box.

'Thanks for your support, dear,' grumbled Falk, who had of course also picked up on her message. Then he went over to open the gate so that she could step out. 'Go and get yourselves a few reliable horses. We need to ride up the switchback as quickly as possible if we want to get there before the Dark Ones.'

A short time later they stood with their saddled horses outside the stables and spotted Khara and Jelninolan running towards them.

'What did you see?' demanded Uldini as soon as they were within earshot, and the priestess frowned as she reached them and mounted one of the horses gracefully. 'The Swarm Claws from Geraton are on their way, and the Glower Bear who has been on our tracks the whole time. There are also roughly three hundred Low Fangs, not to mention at least four High Fangs,' she reported anxiously.

Uldini grimaced. 'That's more than I'd anticipated,' he said darkly.

While the others mounted their horses, Jelninolan continued. 'The swarm is coming from the east. They must have wintered over the sea after I had blown them out there with my storm that time. The call of the Doppler reached them as they were returning to Geraton. The Fangs are coming from the south. I'm sure they're going to climb the face of the mountain and swarm over the walls. The Glower Bear is coming through the Plains, so he's going to have to take the switchback.'

Uldini nodded intently. 'I'll grab every crossbow man and woman I can find in the legion, and I'll handle the Swarm Claws at the northern wall. The city foot-soldiers can deal with the Low Fangs, and you, Jelninolan, stop the High Fangs and prevent the pack from coordinating their movements. Bergen and the Blue Cohorts are our trump card. They will assist wherever the walls are threatened. The rest of you join up with the Pike Carriers of the 17th legion and confront the Glower Bear.'

Ahren was amazed at the speed with which the Arch Wizard divided them up but remembered then that half of his companions had fought battles such as this a dozen times.

'Should we not intercept the bear before he reaches the city?' asked Ahren uncertainly. Why should they climb up to the city if they know the Dark One will be starting his ascent from the foot of the mountain?

Falk scratched his beard and thought for a moment. 'No,' he said finally. 'Glower Bears may not be the best climbers, but if he's decided on a different route for the first hundred paces of his ascent, then suddenly we'll have him at our backs, and we'll have to fight him from below. This way we can expect him, and with a bit of luck, we'll be able to knock him backwards down the mountain with the pikes. That won't kill him, but hopefully it will make him withdraw temporarily at least.'

'You must be joking, master!' cried Ahren, and Khara too looked sceptically at the old Forest Guardian. How could a creature possibly survive a fall down the mountainside?

'Those animals are extraordinarily tough,' explained Falk. 'They have a thick layer of fat lying over their muscular layer. He might break a few ribs, but nothing more than that.'

Ahren's shoulders slumped and he looked despondently down at Culhen, who was staying close beside him. *You stay well back from that bear, do you hear me now?* the apprentice instructed his friend, and Culhen gave no indication that he disagreed.

'Then it's decided,' said Uldini firmly and floated up into the air. 'I'll coordinate the defence and see you above. Then he flew away in a straight line towards the city skyline, which soared above them in the glittering morning sunshine, blissfully unaware of what threatened to befall it.

The ascent was gruelling even on horseback. They constantly had to avoid columns of soldiers marching laboriously in step up the mountain – the very same soldiers that only the night before had scampered down the mountain at Uldini's command.

'They'll be exhausted by the time they get to the top,' whispered Trogadon to Falk, so quietly that even Ahren could hardly make out what he had said.

'I know,' said Falk in agreement. 'But we have no choice. Every armed soldier will help, no matter how tired they are.'

'There will be a lot of casualties,' prophesied the dwarf darkly, and Falk nodded silently.

Ahren looked with concern down at the faces of the men and women they were riding past and asked himself how many of them would live to see the next morning. No matter how great his wish was, he knew that he could only protect these people to a limited degree. These brave souls were dragging themselves up the mountain to protect other people's lives and to take a stand against the Darkness, whose insidious grasping for the free peoples was to be felt for the first time in the upcoming battle. The most he could do was to stand by them bravely and do his bit in their quest for victory.

Around midday they overtook Bergen and the Blue Cohorts. The Paladin had set off that morning directly after his release by the Sun Emperor with the intention of getting to the Brazen City as quickly as possible, and Ahren was amazed to see how fresh the mercenaries looked, in spite of having been on their feet for almost two days in a row.

Falk had noticed this too as they passed by the troop dressed in blue with a friendly wave. 'Bergen's Blessing must give them amazing stamina,' he said thoughtfully. 'No wonder they're so famous everywhere. They are far greater than normal humans, even if they only have a tincture of the Blessing of the gods within them.'

Ahren sensed that Falk was torn between admiration and disgust. He felt the same conflict too. His experience with HIM, WHO FORCES the previous year, when the dark god had tried to tear the Blessing of the gods out of the young Paladin still affected him deeply.

'Would you do it?' asked Ahren quietly. 'Share your Blessing I mean?'

Falk raised his eyebrows immediately and shook his head vehemently. 'Absolutely not. The Blessing was not designed for normal mortals. The gods picked us out, and for a reason, hard though it may be to recognise. And anyway, I wouldn't know how. I asked both Uldini and Jelninolan, and neither of them has any idea of how he managed it. And they also consider it to be as dangerous as I do.' He glanced back over his shoulder at Bergen, who was now two hundred paces away. 'When we're confronting the Adversary, we're going to need the power of the Thirteen Paladins to defeat him. If every Paladin starts handing out their Blessing, then who knows if there will be enough power left to finish the matter once and for all.'

Lost in thought, they continued riding, and for a brief moment the upcoming battle was forgotten.

Darkness came over the Brazen City more quickly than Ahren would have liked. He was standing on the archway that up to the previous day had boasted the city gate. Now the remains of the gate had been swept aside, and a phalanx of two hundred pike bearers, twenty men and women wide and ten rows deep effectively blocked entrance into the city. The carriers' broad-headed pikes pointed down the mountainside, the ends of their weapons anchored three fingers deep into the ground. Falk, Trogadon and Khara were with them, while Ahren stood atop the archway with twenty carefully selected crossbow men and women. Their job was to stop any Swarm Claw outliers from diving on the those fighting at the gate, while Uldini with his fire magic, and a contingent of crossbow men and women attempted to keep the bulk of the bloodthirsty birds at bay. Ahren also hoped he might have a lucky shot and hit the Glower Bear, but he kept that thought to himself. Culhen ran here and there along the city walls in their vicinity, ready to warn of any lurking Low Fangs.

Falk looked up at Ahren, his expression serious, and nodded once. The old Paladin was the living image of a hero from the sagas, sitting on Salena's back, bedecked in full armour and carrying shield and sword.

Ahren nodded back and tried in vain to calm his nerves. Once this was over, he was going to practise achieving the Void as hard as he could. He closed his eyes and felt the strong wind blowing into his face and through his hair.

They had arrived in the early afternoon and the Brazen City had resembled a hornets' nest as the citizens sought out safety and more and more of the soldiers of the 17th Legion arrived, dividing themselves up into the different streets and setting up barricades to secure various parts of the city. Even Ahren could see that the narrow alleyways and tightly packed flat roofs made a defence more difficult, as the Low Fangs would be able to scale the walls with ease and avoid the obstructions below. This would make things more difficult for the crossbow men and women on the rooftops, having to deal not only with the Swarm Claws in the air, but also the Low Fangs on the roofs. Each of the crossbow soldiers had a spear carrier for protection, and Ahren felt nauseous when he realised how chaotic everything would become as soon as the fighting broke out in the inner city. At least the civilian population was safe. The Brazen Clan had once again opened up their halls to the people, and fifty determined warrior dwarves, armed with heavy axes and broad shields, were protecting the heavy gate from attacks by Dark Ones.

Torches were lit as the evening drew in and visibility worsened. Rillans like blue-white moons flew through the dusk air. Jelninolan was sending these magical messengers as missives were sent from one commander of the defence forces to the next. The elf was responsible for smooth communications during the battle now that Uldini's normal tactic of having an overview from above was impossible to implement due to the imminent arrival of the flying Swarm Claws. And so, the magical lights delivered the elf's commands as she sat in the middle of her powerful Charm Net, ready to pick up on the enemies' movements.

Ahren looked doubtfully up at the heavens and thanked the gods that at least the sky was clear on top of the mountain and the moon was shining brightly. He and the crossbow soldiers would have no chance against the Swarm Claws if it were totally dark.

A heavy silence fell over the streets as the defence forces waited on edge for the arrival of the servants of the dark god. Ahren kept catching himself out, looking with concern over at Khara, and he scolded himself for not staying fully concentrated. The young woman was in good hands, with Trogadon and Falk on either side, and she was well capable of looking after herself – or so Ahren told himself again and again.

The first cry of alarm echoed from the other side of the city, and even before the first Rilllan whizzed in their direction, Ahren knew that the battle for the Brazen City had just begun.

Chapter 24

It was sheer torture for Ahren to remain at his post and listen helplessly to the sounds of fighting and screaming coming from the southern side of the city. The young Forest Guardian knew he had to stay put and support his friends – that there was no point in running around like a headless chicken. But that made things no easier when it came to listening to other people fighting and dying.

He sighed almost in relief when at last he saw a dark cloud of black birds with leather wings rising above the shelter of the northern mountain ridges, a manifestation of blood and claws swarming towards the city with the mission of destroying its defenders. He drew an arrow from his quiver and deftly shot a Swarm Claw that had come too close, and watched it tumble to the ground. The crossbow men and women left and right did the same, and a part of Ahren's brain took great satisfaction at the admiring glances he was earning as he systematically shot one Swarm Claw after the other out of the night skies.

Tragically, however, for every one of the murderous birds he killed, another three made it safely to the narrow city streets, where they were far enough away to be safe from the arrows and bolts, and from where there could be heard the screams of pain, as the razor-sharp beaks and claws of the Swarm Claws ripped into the soldiers fighting at ground level.

His face the picture of concentration, Ahren redoubled his efforts and emptied his first quiver in double quick time. As he was placing the second quiver against the battlement, he saw in the distance, the first squat figures of the Low Fangs springing over the roofs, every one of these misshapen creatures deformed by the Dark god into its own unique form. They were still far enough away for Ahren to continue concentrating on the Swarm Claws, but once he had emptied the second quiver, he noticed that the centre of the city had been transformed into a witches cauldron, with the defenders caught up in a maelstrom of claws, beaks and spurting blood, trying desperately to distinguish friend from foe.

Ahren began a new quiver and sought out his targets among the intensive single combats that were playing out on the surrounding rooftops. Wherever he thought he could help, an arrow shot into a Low Fang or a Swarm Claw. Few of these shots proved fatal, but most tipped the balance in a heartbeat. And yet on three occasions he saw soldiers he was trying to assist tumbling to their deaths under the claws of the Low Fangs, and every time it tore at his heart.

Enraged, he was just peppering one of the creatures with three arrows dispatched at lightning speed when he heard a hoarse cry of terror behind him Ahren spun around and saw what had horrified one of the pike men so much. The massive figure of the Glower Bear was pushing his way up the mountain, a smoke and muscle force of nature, his contours barely visible through the bubbling black smoke that constantly rose up from him. Several of the crossbow men and women shot instinctively at the shadowy beast who promised death in smoke and darkness.

'Cease fire!' barked Ahren in a commanding voice, and to his surprise the soldiers followed his order. 'The bolts are simply ricocheting off him. You're wasting your ammunition while your comrades are being torn to pieces by the Swam Claws. Direct your projectiles to the heavens and put your faith in Baron Falkenstein.'

There were low cheers all around him as the archers gained renewed courage, and they recommenced their targeting of the birdlike Dark Ones.

Falk looked up towards Ahren and saluted him, and his eyes were glowing with pride. Then the old Paladin turned back and barked out an order of his own. The Pike Carriers raised their weapons and now there was a forest of steel pike-heads in position facing the Glower Bear, who was forty paces away and sniffing the air. His glowing red eyes looked curiously at the soldiers ranged against him. Then he stood up on his hind paws and let forth an earth-splitting roar, which shook Ahren to the very core. The sound echoed powerfully over the soldiers who crouched down.

'Stand your ground!' roared Falk and drew his sword. 'If the Speer Wall doesn't hold, the beast will cause carnage in the city!'

The figure, almost five paces high, went back down on his four paws again and began trotting towards them awkwardly. Meanwhile the Pike Bearers resumed their upright position and resumed their formation, while Ahren could see Khara and Trogadon taking up their positions on the flanks. Selsena scraped the ground with her hooves and lowered her horn as the Glower Bear picked up speed.

Ahren was so caught up in the action that he forgot his own advice, and it was only Culhen's warning that saved him from a plummet attack of a Swarm Claw.

Watch out! roared the wolf, and the apprentice instinctively ducked his head, and escaped with just a few bloody scratches on his scalp as a Dark One brushed past him.

Ahren raised his bow and shot the creature out of the sky, but suddenly there were two dozen more Swarm Claws heading directly towards him and the crossbow soldiers. Ahren's fingers flew into action as arrow after arrow raced from the bowstring, cutting a swathe through the small swarm. His comrades defended themselves bravely, but in a single heartbeat he saw two of them fall victim to the natural weapons of the murderous birds. With his bow in his right hand, Ahren drew Wind

Blade with his left, and swung it above and below in a defence parry so that he was standing in a glittering copula of razor-sharp steel, which injured three Swarm Claws before they could get through to him.

He was about to help one of his fellows when he heard an almighty crash behind him, so loud that he almost fell off the wall. The young Forest Guardian recovered his balance in a crouching position, and Wind Blade continued with its complicated patterns above his head, while he risked a look downwards which took his breath away.

The Glower Bear had crashed his way into the phalanx, snapping the thick spears as if they were straws and not pikes as fat as a forearm. Here and there was a spearhead sticking into the smoking bear skin, but to his horror, the only thing Ahren could see that slowed down the creature was the bodies of the soldiers hopelessly wedged together, which the Glower Bear rampaged into with swipes of his paws, every one of which tore off limbs or sundered bodies apart.

Ahren turned away with a feeling of nausea, still fighting off the oncoming Swarm Claws, when a Rillan came whizzing past and Jelninolan's ghostly voice sounded above the city gate: 'Keep your eyes peeled – a High Fang is diverting a swarm towards you!'

The young Forest Guardian hurriedly looked around him until he finally spotted a pale figure watching both him and the crossbow men and women. Ahren could see three eyes in a white-hued face that looked quite human, and it dawned on him that this was the High Fang in question. The unearthly creature cowered one hundred paces away on a flat roof and coordinated through commanding arm movements the focused Swarm Claw attack on their positions.

Breathing heavily, Ahren tried his best to ignore everything around him: the screams of the dying pike bearers and archers, the bloody chaos in the streets of the Brazen City, and the increasing panic within his own heart that he couldn't slay them all at once. The young man sensed that he needed to act, or he would be trapped in this deadly paralysis.

Give me cover! he transmitted to Culhen and leaped from the wall onto one of the nearby flat roofs, where he rolled up onto his feet with a gasp. The wolf leaped after him, simultaneously plucking a Swarm Claw out of the sky with his mouth and preventing it from slicing Ahren's neck with its beak. *Tastes like rotten rabbit,* complained the wolf before spitting out the cadaver in disgust.

Ahren's manoeuvre meant he was no longer a focus of the swarm for a moment and he quickly used the opportunity to turn his bow towards the High Fang, who was still directing the birds on their bloodthirsty mission. A magic fireball was burning above the Brazen City – thrown undoubtedly by Uldini in the direction of the furious cloud of Swarm Claws, from which the winged Dark Ones launched attack after attack. Now that there were fewer crossbow men and women, the first of the animals were gliding down towards the defenders before the destroyed city gate, who were risking their lives in their attempt to push back the Glower Bear. There were screams from the wedged in pike bearers as they saw the harbingers of death approaching from above.

Ahren pulled an arrow from his quiver and banished the wolf, who was springing into the air again and catching another Swarm Claw, from his thoughts. For a fraction of a heartbeat, he attained the peace of the Void, and Ahren used this moment to let his arrow fly. The tip of the projectile flew in a low arc over the houses of the Brazen City before landing in the throat of the High Fang, who with a look of surprise toppled backwards off the building and smashed down onto the darkened street below.

Ahren suppressed a scream of delight and spun around to see if his action had brought about the desired effect, but there didn't seem to be much of a change. And so, he remained where he was, targeting the Dark Ones that were tormenting the crossbow soldiers that remained above the city gate.

At some point his quiver was empty, but so too was the sky above the fourteen remaining soldiers who ranged above the gate. They waved over at him in gratitude, then turned their attention towards saving the pike bearers from the onslaught of Swarm Claws. The death of the High Fang had clearly ensured no further attacks on the crossbow men and women, temporarily at least.

Ahren observed how Falk and Trogadon attacked the Glower Bear on either side of his flanks, who reacted furiously by swiping left and right, almost casually tossing another four pike bearers aside, where they lay on the ground, lifeless and bloody.

Trogadon smashed one mighty hammer blow after another on the raging Dark One, but if the beast felt anything, he certainly wasn't showing it. Falk, for his part, was thrusting his sword repeatedly at the creature's neck, while Selsena was using her horn to keep the bear at bay. The area before the gate was a mass of dead, wounded and terrified pike bearers, the latter nevertheless stabbing at the Glower Bear from every possible angle, trying to stop the smoking figure of fire and claws.

Ahren had no more arrows to intervene, and his way back to the wall was obstructed by individual close combat fights and corpses, the area now swarming with Low Fangs. And so Ahren drew his sword and pointed towards the city gate. *We should help the others,* he said to Culhen, and jumped off the roof, landing with an unintended crash and rolling forward. The drop was further than he had calculated, and Ahren realised that pride did indeed come before a fall, sometimes quite literally. Culhen landed gently beside him, and the wolf's eyes blazed defiantly out into the darkness, while he mercifully refrained from commenting on their contrasting landings.

Ahren used the animal to pull himself back onto his feet and together they forced their way to the gate, where a horrifying sight presented itself to them. Trogadon was down on his knees, his chainmail top of Deep Steel was still intact, but Ahren could tell by the dwarf's tell-tale slumped posture that he had several broken ribs. At least two dozen pike bearers were helping Falk to contain the Glower Bear, but with every swipe of the paw there were fewer, and Selsena's flanks had tell-tale signs of claw marks from which deep-red blood was seeping. Falk had lost his helmet, the sweat was rolling down his back, and Ahren could see that the thrusts and parries of his master no longer exhibited their familiar panache.

He saw all this with a troubled eye, but one realisation caused his heart to miss a beat. Khara was nowhere to be seen, and he hadn't seen her since the first of the Glower Bear attack. Terrible visions raged through his head as he raced towards the bear and the surrounding piles of bodies. What if Khara was one of the lifeless forms scattered about in the weak light of the torches? Or what if she had been tossed down the mountain like so many unfortunate souls that had been swept aside by the Glower Bear's paws?

With tears in his eyes, Ahren came to a halt beside Trogadon to take up his position at the flank of the smoking monster. 'Where's Khara?' he asked breathlessly as he evaded a swipe of the paw, which was almost the size of his torso.

Trogadon didn't answer, but only shook his head. Ahren could see that the dwarf's neck was shimmering a deep-blue colour, and so bruised that the squat figure was only still alive because of his incredible robustness.

With all the willpower he could muster, Ahren pushed aside his fears for the swordswoman's safety, and indicated to Trogadon that he should pull back. Then he stabbed wildly into the smoking skin of the bear in the hope of giving Falk a break as soon as the Dark One's head would spin around to the apprentice.

Ahren almost wet himself when his plan worked and he was looking into the bear's ferociously blazing red eyes, which loomed above his fangs, the length of a forearm. The mighty animal howled at him, his mouth wide open, and the sheer power of the noise almost knocked Ahren off his feet. This was followed by a quick bite, then a downward paw-strike intended to pin Ahren to the ground, and the young man seized his chance. He threw himself to the side – not to the safety on the right, but to the left, directly under the beast's chin and within reach of his fangs. He rolled into position and plunged Wind Blade with a triumphant grimace straight up into the animal's throat, intending to put an end to the destructive power of the monster for once and for all.

The steel slipped through the skin and muscles deep into the flesh of the neck...and snapped when the Glower Bear shook his head, tossing Ahren away.

Completely dumbstruck, Ahren was thrown against the city wall, just at that moment when he expected to be the victorious hero. His right foot broke under the force of the collision, and his vision was blurred even before he hit the ground. Dazed, he tried to make out Wind Blade's broken handle, which he was still holding in his left hand, and he felt a sharp pain in his chest as he tried to come to terms with what had just occurred. None of his daring deeds had ever misfired so badly before, and as Falk frantically stabbed at the Glower Bear, the massive creature trundled ever closer to the young Paladin, who tried in vain to pull himself up. Culhen threw himself into the beast's path with an almighty howl, but was flung casually aside into Selsena's flank, the horse tumbling to the ground with a whinny and landing on top of Falk in the process.

The last remaining pike bearers dropped their weapons and fled back into the city as the Glower Bear loomed over Ahren.

The feeling of having been betrayed by the gods overwhelmed Ahren as he looked death in the face and prepared to breathe his last. The only glimmer of hope for the future without Ahren was that he could sense Culhen was still alive. Then something happened behind the Glower Bear. One of the soldier corpses was pushed aside, and an arm peeked forth from under it. With lightning speed and unerring accuracy, it swung Wind Blade and sliced the Glower Bear's right Achilles tendon.

The young Paladin was certain he heard a snapping sound as the tendon was sliced in two, and then the Bear roared and began to sway.

Khara pulled herself up out of the hiding place she had been lurking in for a considerable time and sliced at the other leg, causing the massive figure to fall directly forward.

Ignoring the scraping feel in the bones of his foot, Ahren threw himself sideways with all his might to escape the collapsing colossus, which would have crushed him to smithereens otherwise. Dust and earth were thrown into the air as the Glower Bear crashed into the city wall, and Ahren crawled painfully away from the monster, who could only shake his head in bemusement. Khara leaped gracefully onto the creature's back and with two quick movements she was at the Glower Bear's neck, before he had a chance to find his bearings. She grasped Wind Blade with both hands and drove it with all her might in between his cervical vertebra. A grinding sound could be heard, and the gigantic creature shuddered. Then the Glower Bear rose up to his full height once more, and Khara leaped off in a graceful arc only to land unceremoniously on a heap of bodies which broke her fall. The enormous Dark One on the other hand, completely stunned, fell with a thundering crash onto his side, trying desperately to soften the fall with his claws.

Ahren saw to his horror how the creature tried once again to get up, only for Trogadon to drag himself over in great pain and smash his hammer with an almighty blow and a grimace on his face onto Wind Blade, which was driven to its hilt deep into the monster's neck.

Like a puppet whose strings have been cut, the bear collapsed onto the ground and from one heartbeat to the next, it was all over.

Trogadon looked regretfully at Wind Blade, a twisted mess in the animal's neck, and he turned to the gasping swordswoman. 'Really sorry about your weapon,' he panted through his squashed throat. 'I'll make you a new one, I promise.'

Ahren didn't hear if the young woman replied because above him the last remaining crossbow men and women were cheering lustily, who just like Ahren, could barely believe their luck at still being alive.

They gathered at the archway to the city, Falk supporting Trogadon, and Khara helping Ahren and his broken foot by placing his arm around her shoulder. Selsena and Culhen, both badly bruised, trotted behind and seemed to be sympathising with each other in a way only known to companion animals. Then they entered the Brazen City with a few soldiers surrounding them and went in search of one of the Ancients.

'You really have to stop coming to my rescue all the time,' teased Ahren in a manner that suggested he was truly grateful to her.

Khara nodded with an almost shy smile. 'If you stop behaving like a Susekan,' she answered sarcastically. This nickname for a poor swordsman in the language of the Empire meant something like 'milksop' and it was a word he hadn't heard in a while – and certainly didn't miss.

'How was I supposed to know that the blade would snap?' he asked obstreperously. Falk, hearing this, gave him a clip on the ear.

'The forty spearheads stuck in his body might have given you a hint, you dunderhead.' He shook his head wearily. 'A strategy that doesn't consider the possibility of failure is a game of pure chance.' He undoubtedly would have continued talking were it not for the hand to hand combat they saw before them, involving at least thirty pairs of Low Fangs and Blue Cohorts.

It was an unequal fight if ever there were one. The Low Fangs' strategy was bloodily chaotic, while the mercenaries followed a focussed plan. Every parry, every manoeuvre, every feint was carefully coordinated, and there was a contingency plan for every eventuality. If a thrust didn't hit home, then the nearest Cohort finished the job. It was a lesson in coordinated fighting that impressed Ahren no end.

He looked over at Falk, who recognised that his apprentice now understood what he'd said. The old man nodded grimly but remained silent. Ahren now realised that he would have to study tactics and strategy from now on, and he sighed, wondering if his lessons would ever come to an end.

Epilogue

The new day was dawning but still Ahren had found no sleep. He was sitting with the others on top of a more secluded part of the walls, looking down over the Sunplains, whose golden and green fields were lying there in the soft morning sunshine, blissfully unaware of the previous night's battle. Uldini and Jelninolan had healed them to some extent, but as there were so many wounded in need of treatment, they had refused a complete recovery, which meant that Ahren was still limping and Trogadon could barely speak.

At least you're alright, Culhen, thought Ahren and he pressed the wolf towards him, who thanked him with a slobbery lick on his cheek. Jelninolan was still healing the wounded and Khara was assisting her.

'More than eight hundred dead Legionnaires, almost five hundred of whom died at the gate, and another hundred that the Glower Bear surprised on his way up. The rest were killed by Swarm Claws and Low Fangs', Uldini was reporting, having just got an overview of the battle's outcome. 'It would have been tight without the assistance of Bergen and the mercenaries, and I've impressed on the survivors the importance of reporting that back to the Emperor.'

'Are you not going to tell him yourself?' asked Falk in surprise.

Uldini shook his head sadly. 'I received a dispatch from a courier at daybreak. The Emperor congratulates me, and on account of my services to the Empire he is releasing me from my duties.' He looked glum. 'We bit off a bit more than we could chew in relation to him. Do you know that I had my own tower in the Sun Palace?' He sighed bitterly. 'I'm really going to miss that.'

'You wouldn't have visited it until all this was over anyway, so stop carrying on', scolded Falk.

'But it was still nice to know that I *could* have visited it,' sulked the Ancient. Then he became serious again. 'Bergen and his people have been pardoned, and believe it or not, they've even been given a new contract. This time given to them directly by the Brazen City. So, they can take up their positions as city guards without fear of treachery.'

'We should get out of here while we can,' warned Falk. 'If Justinian finds out he's signed a peace treaty that contains a loophole he didn't spot, whereby the Dwarfish weapons can be sent to Hjalgar, we won't be welcome in his empire for some time to come.'

Uldini frowned again. 'Oh god, I'd forgotten about that. Alright, one, two moons and then we're gone. First we have to find a clue as to where we can find the next Paladin.'

'Maybe Bergen can help us there. The evening we were playing with dice he mentioned a clue that sounded promising,' said Falk, placating the Arch Wizard.

Ahren's ears pricked up. 'What did he say?' he interjected and felt his foot.

'Don't touch it or it won't heal properly,' snapped Falk before replying. 'There's a tribe in the Southern Jungles who pray to a goddess called "the Sleeping Mother." Apparently, they're referring to a woman who doesn't grow old, and who has pale skin that refuses to tan.' He looked over meaningfully at Uldini, who immediately danced for joy.

'That has to be Sunju,' he said, delightedly, 'but why has she never made contact and what's she doing there? She can't be angry with us; she was always the most cheerful of your lot.'

Falk scratched his beard and ruminated. 'You know how she felt after Starlight died. That shook her to the core, and she was never the same after that.'

There was a silence and Ahren nearly burst with curiosity. 'Who are those two?' he finally asked impatiently.

'Sunju is a Paladin. She was always a great friend and goodness personified. When her companion died, something died within her too. It's true that she didn't lose anyone in the Night of Blood, but she had been broken before then.' Falk looked out onto the Plains. 'We knew she'd wanted to go south, but then we never heard about her again.'

Ahren gave Culhen a hug. Life without his wolf would be a fate worse than death, he thought.

I'll remind you of that thought the next time you chase me away because you're annoyed, said Culhen snippily, but pressed in against the apprentice nonetheless and nuzzled against him.

'Did Bergen lose his companion animal too? I didn't see any around him', said Ahren cautiously. If such a thing had happened to Sunju, then Bergen could have suffered a similar loss. It was only the previous night that Ahren had seen how quickly fatal mistakes could occur when fighting a deadly enemy.

Falk grinned and pointed his finger upward. 'No, you've just been looking in the wrong places.'

Ahren followed the direction and tilted his head back. High above him he could see a black dot, doing gentle circles in the warm thermals. 'Is that a falcon?' he asked, irritated.

'Not any old falcon. It's Karkas, Bergen's companion,' responded his master mischievously. 'The two are very close. He rarely shows Karkas, and they generally meet when there's nobody around. The bird is his eyes and ears on the battlefield. Another reason why he's such a good commander. The falcon always tells him who's where during the conflict. Those two have perfected their connection.'

Ahren pinched Culhen's ear playfully, and the wolf nipped the apprentice's hand in revenge. 'We'll find our own way too,' said Ahren quietly to his friend.

'You two are making a very good fist of it,' said Falk reassuringly, and Ahren was delighted to hear it, as Falk praised him so sparingly. 'My biggest worry is that you have so much less time than we had to learn. Which is why we're all taking such pains to drum the essentials into that stubborn head of yours,' he said emphatically. Ahren nodded absently as he looked down onto the city.

'Have we done the right thing?' he asked the group, looking down at a pile of bodies that were awaiting collection on the street below.

Trogadon still had difficulty speaking so he simply laid a hand on the apprentice's shoulder and nodded enthusiastically. But Falk replied in a determined voice. 'We've saved the Brazen City, cemented its relationship with the Sunplains, and prevented Bergen and his people from being condemned as traitors. All in all, not a bad day's work.' He shook Ahren by the arm until the apprentice looked away from the corpses. 'We're waging war. And unfortunately, wars always involve loss of life. You've protected those who couldn't fight. Those who can, must protect themselves or we'll all be lost.'

Ahren gave a cautious nod and then stood when he realised they were about to receive honoured guests. Windita and Palustra climbed the stone staircase of the wall, followed by Bergen, who was wearing a tabard bearing the symbol of the Brazen City, and looking very satisfied with himself.

'A good morning to you all,' said Palustra politely. 'We are here to express our gratitude to you once again for everything you have done for our city,' she said, with genuine warmth.

'Without you the city would most likely have been reduced to rubble,' said Windita darkly and the blond woman shivered at the thought. 'Please be our guests for however long you please.'

'I'm afraid you'll have to put up with us for a little while longer,' joked Falk, gesturing towards Ahren's and Trogadon's injuries. 'Where is Xobutumbur? Did he survive the night?' asked the old Forest Guardian fearfully.

Palustra smiled and raised a reassuring hand. The Clan Elder is doing well. He's avoiding stairs for the time being as a result of his injuries.'

Falk nodded sympathetically and Windita spoke again. 'If there is anything we can do for you, please let us know,' she said in a ceremonious tone, and Falk was about to decline her offer when Ahren interjected.

'There is one little thing,' he said in a firm voice. He had hoped that the Triumvirate would offer them assistance and was determined to accept. Only a few moons previously and he would have been horrified at the thought of taking advantage of somebody's gratitude in this way, but now he knew they had to make use of any chance that was available.

'We are going to need a delivery of one thousand swords, shields and coats of mail within the next three summers,' he said loudly.

The reaction was as he had predicted. The ladies gasped, Falk glared at him, and both Trogadon and Bergen grinned encouragingly.

'Seven hundred of each are to be delivered to the Falkenstein barony in the Knight Marshes, and the other three hundred to the village of Deepstone in Hjalgar,' continued Ahren. Not being interrupted, he carried on. 'We are going to need a well-equipped army everywhere, and even if

Three Rivers sells these arms in the next while, I doubt that they will get as far as Deepstone.' Windita was about to interject, but Ahren raised his arm imperiously. 'We have helped to save your homeland. These weapons will help to save our homeland. I think my request is more than reasonable.' He folded his arms and looked the two dignitaries in the eye. Much to his surprise, he was neither sweating nor trembling. He had stood in front of a Glower Bear and defied an Emperor. He was expressing a point that came from his heart, which gave him the security he needed to remain calm.

Culhen gave a triumphant howl in the apprentice's head when the two representatives of the Brazen City glanced at each other before nodding their assent. They gave Ahren their hands, which he firmly shook, then he took Windita's again and spoke again. 'And one more thing. Bergen and the Blue Cohorts will be free to go when we call for them. The Dark Days will be coming, and then we will need the infamous commander and his notorious mercenaries.' At those last words he winked at Bergen, who looked back innocently as if butter wouldn't melt in his mouth.

'Agreed', said Windita, and Ahren leaned back, relieved. The two ladies nodded and Palustra murmured: 'We shall retire now before your demands prove even more costly, young Paladin.' Ahren winced mentally at the jibe, but then he remembered what he had sworn to himself in the Eastern Forest, when he had led Sven into exile. They didn't all have to like him. He would still be their Paladin and protector.

It was sometime later, and they were all in high spirits. Bergen remained with them, and had passed a skin of strong wine around, from which everybody had drunk in silence. Now the three veterans were exchanging stories of past battles and Ahren was listening intently. He was interested less in the historical timeline or the heroic nature of the tales, but rather in the tactical lessons he could glean from them. He was determined to learn, and he was taking advantage of every opportunity.

Finally, Khara came up to them and Bergen sprang lightly to his feet before bowing elegantly before her. 'Here we have the heroine of the battle. Compliments, my dear, on your killing of the Glower Bear. If only I were eight hundred years younger,' he cried out and breathed a kiss on the back of her hand, looking at her with exaggerated soulfulness before grinning mischievously.

Khara laughed and gave a mock curtsey in return, while Ahren leaned in towards Falk. 'You were absolutely right, master,' he whispered. 'He really is annoying.'

The swordswoman grabbed the wineskin, took a deep draught and then tossed it to Trogadon. 'I'm no heroine without my sword. That man has transformed mine into a better class of horseshoe,' she said teasingly.

It took Trogadon two attempts before he finally managed to get the words through his throat, purple with bruises. 'I have spoken to Xobutumbur,' he croaked. 'I'm allowed to use the Heart Forge of the Clans and will forge Wind Blades for the two of you. They shouldn't break so easily.'

In the next heartbeat the dwarf hat two skittish young people hanging off his sore neck, embracing him and thanking him noisily. The warrior winced in pain, his damaged ribs protesting loudly, before he finally embraced them anyway. Then he looked at Ahren and shrugged his shoulders apologetically. 'We'll still have to go to Thousand Halls for your Paladin armour sometime. There simply isn't enough Deep Steel available anywhere else.'

'We're going to make a proper Paladin out of you yet,' said Bergen good-naturedly. Then he stood up and gave Ahren a bear hug. 'If we're going to get all soppy, I might as well get it over with now.' He released the apprentice, held him by the shoulders and fixed him with his pale-blue eyes. 'You said you wanted to save everybody, and you've done that. And so, I will follow you whenever you call.' He clapped Ahren on the back again, then turned around. 'I'd better check on my lads and lassies. They tend to get carried away when they celebrate. We don't want to lose our jobs the very first evening.' Then he stormed down the stairs, and Ahren blinked owlishly after him. The man really was an emotional hurricane, who stormed over you for a moment before disappearing, leaving a trail of chaos in his wake.

Ahren was gathering himself together and contemplating the journey to the Southern Jungles that awaited them when he heard an urgent voice in his head.

That's all well and good, grumbled the wolf, *but am I going to get anything to eat at all today?*

***

He could neither stand nor look straight, but he really didn't care. Even if he had tried to remember, he wouldn't be able to say in which godforsaken one-horse town he was holed up in. The only thing important to him was the fact that the wine and lodgings were cheap, and one gold coin a week would more than suffice for both. His supplies were slowly running out, but that bothered him just as little, in his stupefaction, as his not having taken a bath for several weeks. If his brain somehow managed to think clearly enough for him to realise all this, he probably still wouldn't change a thing. He lived in a world of rage and self-pity.

He was just grasping the half-full jug of wine on the dirt-encrusted corner-table he'd been sitting at for weeks when he noticed that a woman was standing in front of him and eyeing him up and down.

'I haven't finished my wine, come back later,' he grunted harshly, before taking a deep swig from the jug. Some liquid poured down his chin and added another stain to his already filthy shirt.

'I'm no barmaid,' laughed a delightful sounding voice, and the person sat down at his table.

He tried to see clearly and rubbed his knuckles over his good eye. His eye began to focus, and with great concentration he could make out a kind, smiling, blond woman of no more than thirty winters looking back at him confidently. Even that was unusual, as he had experienced often enough lately. His tattered appearance usually provoked sarcasm, disgust, scolding and the odd expulsion from one village or other, and he was looked at in no other way than suspiciously, or with unhidden loathing.

He returned the favour by staring back at the beauty just as intensely, stretching himself so that she could enjoy every one of his deformities. Her eyes were unusually brown and seemed almost too big for her face. He also saw a finely shaped nose, high cheek bones and little dimples as she smiled at him. She was wearing a plain white robe and had something on her lap that he couldn't make out.

'What do you want?' he snorted and drank some more wine. If he finished it quickly enough, he might be able to persuade this strange woman to buy him another jug.

She laughed her bright laugh again and shook her head gently. 'The question isn't what do *I* want, but rather, what do *you* want,' she said, correcting him. There was something in her question that reawakened pictures in his head, which he would prefer buried, and he threw his jug to the floor, causing it to smash. 'I want more wine!' he shouted at her, but the strange creature seemed completely unruffled by his behaviour, her smile permanently chiselled, like a mask that would never leave her, no matter what the bearer was doing.

'I mean, what do you *really* want?' she whispered urgently into his ear, and he doubled over gasping as the images overwhelmed him, the ones he had drowned so carefully in alcohol over all those months.

'Revenge,' growled Sven and stared at her, his face contorted with rage, his nose and left eye both festering ruins. 'I want revenge.'

The woman laid her hand on his forearm and leaned her face with its frozen smile in towards him. She took a golden book from her lap and placed it on the table before him.

'Then let me tell you about the Illuminated Path.' She began to speak, and he listened.

See how Ahren's adventures continue:

The Thirteenth Paladin, volume IV "The Sleeping Mother"

Available in August 2020

Dear Reader:

If you enjoyed this book, please leave a short rating in the shop, where you bought it. As I am an independent author with no backing of a publisher, every positive comment helps to convince others, to read my novels.

Sam Feuerbach:
The Gravedigger's Son and the Waif Girl

The first volume in Sam Feuerbach's best-selling saga, winner of the German Fantasy Prize 2018 for best Audio Book.
More than 14.000 enthusiastic reviews (Amazon/Audible)
High Fantasy Middle Ages Series in four volumes

Farin, the gravedigger's son, lives in the medieval village of Heap. The eighteen-year-old is an outsider, bullied and ostracised by the villagers. His father has succumbed to a life of drinking, and so the young man has no option but to take over the job of gravedigger. Farin's life takes a dramatic twist when the village witch dies, and he prepares her for burial. He finds an amulet hanging around the deceased preparer of poisons neck, and he can't resist trying the trinket on...

Printed by Amazon Italia Logistica S.r.l.
Torrazza Piemonte (TO), Italy